PENGUIN CLASSICS

THE COUNTRY OF THE POINTED FIRS

SARAH ORNE JEWETT was born in 1849 into a financially independent, middle-class family in South Berwick, Maine. She went intermittently to a local school, but was mostly self-educated and read voraciously. Inspired by Harriet Beecher Stowe's novel set in Maine, *The Pearl of Orr's Island*, she began to write about her native region of New England. Her first story appeared in 1868 in the *Atlantic Monthly*, which continued to publish her work. Friendships were of fundamental importance to her, particularly, though not exclusively, with women. She became part of Boston's cultural elite, and was good friends with her publisher James T. Fields and his wife Annie. After his death in 1881 she moved in with Annie, spending half the year with her around Boston and the other half in the family house in Maine. Her novels include *Deephaven* (1877) and *The Country of the Pointed Firs* (1896), both of which reveal a sense of community and place, and *A Country Doctor* (1884), written in memory of her father, a local doctor. She also published nine volumes of short stories between 1879 and 1899. Sarah Orne Jewett incurred serious injuries in 1902 after being thrown from a carriage. This prevented any further writing. She died in 1909.

ALISON EASTON was educated at Edinburgh and Sussex, and is Senior Lecturer in English at Lancaster University, where she teaches American literature before 1900 and women's writing. She was Co-Director of the Centre for Women's Studies at Lancaster between 1991 and 1994. She is the author of *The Making of the Hawthorne Subject* (1995).

SARAH ORNE JEWETT

THE COUNTRY
OF THE POINTED FIRS
AND OTHER STORIES

Edited with an introduction by
ALISON EASTON

PENGUIN BOOKS

PENGUIN BOOKS

Published by the Penguin Group
Penguin Books Ltd, 80 Strand, London, WC2R 0RL, England
Penguin Books USA Inc., 375 Hudson Street, New York, New York 10014, USA
Penguin Books Australia Ltd, Ringwood, Victoria, Australia
Penguin Books Canada Ltd, 10 Alcorn Avenue, Toronto, Ontario, Canada M4V 3B2
Penguin Books (NZ) Ltd, 182–190 Wairau Road, Auckland 10, New Zealand

Penguin Books Ltd, Registered Offices: 80 Strand, London, WC2R 0RL, England

This edition first published 1995
9 10 8

Filmset by Datix International Limited, Bungay, Suffolk
Printed and bound in Great Britain by Antony Rowe Ltd.,
Chippenham, Wiltshire
Set in 9.25/11.75 pt Monophoto Bembo

CONTENTS

THE COUNTRY OF THE POINTED FIRS

CONTENTS

INTRODUCTION
The Country of the Pointed Firs: History and Utopia

It is evening in Jewett's small fictional town of Dunnet Landing and three women sit talking. The stories they are telling, though new to their younger friend, a city visitor, are familiar to both older women, raised there though separated from one another in their married lives. Long stretches of the past converge on this one small spot: '"There, it does seem so pleasant to talk with an old acquaintance that knows what you know ... Conversation's got to have some root in the past"'. A neighbour at the door requesting medicine for a sick child is a temporary interruption, yet it serves as another reminder of a web of connections linking so many in this isolated community of a few streets, scattered farmsteads and small island homes among the fishing grounds. Even the subject of their longest story, a jilted and despairing woman in self-exile on a tiny, remote island, cannot break the threads of connection which extend backwards in time and outwards in space, since Joanna Todd's fiercely defended island solitude had elicited sympathy and tactful attention as well as vulgar curiosity, and the bay had filled with boats on the day of her funeral.

As the women proceed with Joanna's story, their shared narration ceases to be mere repetition and becomes for each woman a rethinking of what could have been merely a stereotypical love story. Theirs is a process of coming to a more open and compassionate understanding. The point of telling Joanna's story is not her failed romance, but the older women's remembrance as an act of community. This community is as capable of narrow-mindedness, unkindness and feuding as any other, but it cares as best it can about those who do not share its sense of relatedness and responsibility. The unnamed young visitor, who hears Joanna's story and is the novel's narrator, comes to participate in this. With a neighbour's help she repeats Joanna's journey to that island and, standing at the grave, senses Joanna's feelings during her long hermitage. At the novel's end one of the older women, Mrs Todd, gives the narrator Joanna's coral pin and thereby quietly brings her into a network, the links of which are shared griefs, families, neighbours and friendships. The brooch, bought by her husband Nathan Todd for his cousin Joanna and passed by her to Mrs Todd, connects all their very different emotional histories, their loves, disappointments, despairs, recuperations and deaths, the stories of which we are told briefly in the course of the novel.

This is the fiction of community (the term is Susan Zagarell's) – not just a novel about a particular community and the narratives it continually creates to sustain itself, but also a novel which explores what in general 'community' might possibly be and mean. It recognizes in its members' stories (and Joanna's is only one of many) not only the 'place remote and islanded' in each of us but also, most vitally, the connections still maintained between this and all the other inhabited islands, sea-roads and mainland of collective living. The novel does not have a single plot. Instead a number of people's stories are told, interweaving in the narrator's and readers' minds. Whereas earlier in nineteenth-century literature Melville's suicidal Ishmael goes on an heroic whaling voyage and Twain's lone Huck lights out for the 'territory' west of settled America, Jewett's Mrs Todd rejects a journey 'out west' as an alternative to Joanna's eight-mile boat ride to a life on Shell-heap Island ('dreadful small place' though it is 'to make a world of'). Although at the margins of the community, Joanna is still part of it, and her story is one of many which the narrator gets to hear in the course of her stay.

When *The Country of the Pointed Firs* was published in 1896, its setting would have seemed startlingly different from the world many Americans saw themselves inhabiting. Much of America by then thought of itself as a continental nation (Jewett ironically reverses this in calling the best of her small offshore islands a 'complete and tiny continent'). Railroads had recently opened up great tracts of the West to large-scale farming, and giant corporations and factories dominated manufacturing, making America the world's leading industrial power. New cities had mushroomed within a few decades, housing a rapidly growing population, and mass immigration was altering a hitherto predominantly Anglo-Saxon culture in the North and Mid-West. The status of some women was slowly but definitely changing, though that of African-Americans was mostly ignored by white America. Of course, not all of the country was thus affected, but this new industrial and urban world, rather than that of rural New England, had become the dominant image of American culture. The scale of the changes and their speed – a mere half-century – left many Americans dislocated and bewildered.

Contemporary novels by Dreiser, Norris and Crane, such as *Sister Carrie*, *The Octopus* and *Maggie*, address these disturbing new conditions directly. Yet the best work of Jewett, pushed until fairly recently into a backwater reserved for nineteenth-century women writers and stigmatized as 'local color literature', also speaks to and for her times and challenges their vision of modernity with stories which seek to connect past with the present and a continuing, though different future. *The Country of the Pointed Firs* is neither a quaint literary survival of an earlier New England culture nostalgically re-created as some lost domain, nor is it testimony of a moribund and marginalized world. Jewett wants to relate New England to the rest of America, not simply set them in opposition. In subtle ways she takes up and challenges the view prevailing among the new urban middle-class who believed New England to be in irrecoverable decline, and who as a result cultivated highly romanticized collective memories of an old-fashioned participatory democracy and a lost world of neighbourly small townships amid farming country.

Historical studies now confirm something of Jewett's sense of the region's unimpaired vitality. Dunnet Landing does not belong to the past. Certainly there had been changes with the run-down of the shipping industry (mentioned in Jewett's novel), and marginal farms had been abandoned (see the story 'The Queen's Twin'). But, although no longer a pre-industrial 'island' community, this world still thrived. The novel only hints at its commercial links with the outside world (the fishing industry and the wholesale egg merchant) and prefers instead to stress how a sense of community is bound up with certain continuities which had been lost to many Americans – continuities both between economic existence and one's natural surroundings and between the individual and modes of production. Though middle-aged and old people dominate *The Country of the Pointed Firs*, they establish a line of connection, and there are children at the huge Bowden family reunion to suggest a continuing future. Symptomatically the person who touts a view of the town's decline, Captain Littlepage, tells his superannuated tales in what is an only temporarily empty schoolroom.

Jewett, born in 1849 and raised in the small town of South Berwick in Maine, had a different perspective on rural New England than the urban bourgeoisie. She wasn't simply a middle-class summer tourist. As a doctor's daughter she had been frequently taken on her father's rounds in the 1850s and 1860s, and she continued to spend at least part of most years there as an adult. Although she wasn't of the same class as the farming and fishing people of many of her stories and the child's and adolescent's point of view had its limitations as well as its privileges, none the less she was able to ground her fiction on her particular experience of how this region, still deeply traditional in her childhood, had evolved in the closing years of the century.

Jewett, however, also lived in Boston as a member of its literary and intellectual establishment, and she could never have been insulated from its collective sense of massive social change taking place outside rural New England. So her stance is a double one – insider and outsider – a position which she welcomed as an artist and urged on her protégée Willa Cather. She praised Cather's use of her own Nebraskan and Virginian childhoods but commented that the younger writer did not yet see this 'quite enough from the outside'. In making the narrator of *The Country of the Pointed Firs* a professional writer, Jewett is able to assess this double perspective, recognize the possible loss of rootedness and celebrate the artistic possibilities.

So Jewett belonged to two worlds, Maine and Boston, and it made her response to the new America distinct in certain ways from her contemporaries who either rejoiced in what she had once called 'the destroying left hand of progress', or were involved in various reform movements, or resorted to mere nostalgia to blank out modernity. Her early work certainly shows a distaste for newly industrialized America. It is rarely the immediate subject of her writing (just the occasional story featuring railroad, factory, city visit, businessman or immigrants). But it has instead an implied existence outside the fictional scene and, as we shall see, helps to constitute the novel's overall meaning.

Jewett was neither reactionary nor conventionally progressive (in the ways her contemporaries would have understood these terms). *The Country of the Pointed Firs* is a constructive response to a changing America rather than a retreat from it. It is important to realize that the novel is set in the 1890s, not in some timeless traditional world. It is a 'remedy' (to use an important word in the novel) – not necessarily a cure but something like those unpretentious, unofficial, efficacious herbs provided for her sick neighbours by Mrs Todd, remedies with their origins in past generations yet concocted for present ailments. Jewett's remedy is a fiction of community, offered at a time when the whole notion of community was at bay. She responds to the rootlessness, fragmentation, anomies and powerlessness of Americans beginning to experience the effects of this newly urbanized, industrialized and increasingly bureaucratized society.

Fictions of community are not dominated by a hero's or heroine's story; their narratives are not shaped by the romance or quest plot of certain special individualized lives (note how weddings are played down in most Jewett stories). If we try to read *The Country of the Pointed Firs* as a conventional realistic novel, say as the story of Mrs Todd, our expectations will be frustrated: hints are not followed through and narratives are dropped.

Instead, the novel is full of people familiarly mentioned even if we never meet them. The setting of a long street looking out to the islands and fishing grounds gives both villagers and readers a panoramic sense of the life going on around them – whether it's the whole village at a funeral, or a boat coming in, or why a hired chaise is going past on a particular day, or why a visitor can move from one household only at a certain time. Mrs Todd's door is open to her neighbours rather than shut against the outside world to protect a family within. Dunnet Landing inhabitants are still private people who share their feelings shyly and with dignified brevity only with a chosen few in this scattered and busy community, but they have a common past (even though memories of that past are individual). As this essay began by showing, conversation and storytelling are central to the novel's action. In this kind of fiction, as Sandra Zagarell observes, 'everyday' objects and activities are 'saturated with meanings in which the personal and the communal unite'. Jewett's stories are dominated by the grander rituals of watching the dead and dying, funerals, a family reunion and visits, but ordinary activities are also made into little rituals which retain a certain freshness and delight – potato-digging, herb-gathering, picking fruit, cooking chowder, feeding the birds, choosing a haddock off the lines, laying the table.

Such fictions of community are rare in nineteenth-century American literature. Earlier writings by men focus on a lone hero's quest for autonomy and truth in a difficult negotiation with a mass democratic society, and these goals are often achieved only when alone (or nearly alone) in a natural, unspoiled wilderness. But in *The Country of the Pointed Firs* Captain Littlepage gets to tell his story only to the novel's gently indulgent narrator, whose neighbourly willingness to listen to this redundant voyager not only briefly relieves his loneliness, but also restores her sense of connection with the village after momentarily feeling detached from it. Littlepage's tale is not like the conversations of the women, but is presented as a near monologue barely responding to its present surroundings. His metaphysical search for knowledge in the tradition of Melville and Poe takes place elsewhere amid shipwreck, ice and abandonment, and the hostile baffling vision, delivered to him only secondhand, is presented as at odds with a scientific America which has now charted his *terra incognita* on the schoolroom map. He draws on

Milton's epic poem *Paradise Lost* to try to express events, but is only a 'little page' in literature to Jewett. Bewildered and lost in his delusions and without the comforts of home or family, he later sits alone as three women, traditionally stay-at-home figures, drive past on their way to the great family reunion which is the book's guarantee of continuity.

Thus, despite the fact that many of Jewett's contemporaries were fascinated by Arctic exploration, *The Country of the Pointed Firs* marginalizes the fiction of her literary fathers. But even the fiction of her literary mothers needed revision, closer though it was to her interests. Most novels written by women in the mid nineteenth century are domestic, like Jewett's, but with a more conventional focus: a young heroine grows up, struggles for livelihood and love in a hostile social world, and comes to accept positively the necessity of submission to God's and (good) men's will. These novels' moral and spiritual centre is a feminized Christianity – a combination of passionate religious belief and prevailing notions of femininity, brought to bear on some of the social issues of the day (Harriet Beecher Stowe's *Uncle Tom's Cabin* is the most celebrated example).

In many ways Jewett puts behind her that mid-century, middle-class ideology of femininity as pious, submissive, domestic, asexual motherhood (a notion to be found more in the literature of the day than in fact). We have only to compare *The Country of the Pointed Firs* with Stowe's 1862 *The Pearl of Orr's Island* (also set on the Maine Coast and Jewett's childhood inspiration) to see how Jewett has shifted the focus away from childhood, parenting, young romance and early death. She also excises both the sentimentality (sincerely felt, yet disparaged by Jewett) and the profoundly Christian vision of heaven which so engages Stowe's imagination. For example, the effect of pre Civil War religious beliefs are directly attacked in the story of Joanna Todd, and Mrs Todd even knocks the minister over when his incompetence as a sailor nearly capsizes the boat.

Furthermore, the older women who occasionally took over a chapter of Stowe's narrative become the centre of Jewett's attention, and the scattered township ceases to be a backdrop to the main plot. Romance (in the sense of a heterosexual love plot) is not the key story of women's lives. Mrs Todd's account of the man she had loved and lost in her youth is told only briefly, unsentimentally and with a fine sense of the complexity of these memories and the mixture of emotions involved. But, unlike her contemporary Kate Chopin, Jewett does not write fictions attacking marriage and children as an impediment to self-realization. While Jewett's fiction does reflect the 1870s–1880s image of Eastern America as an 'epoch of single women' (Susan B.

Anthony) with more white middle-class women working for their living, owning property and not marrying, she sidesteps the public debate about this by making Mrs Todd a widow of a brief marriage and, unlike her other contemporary Alice Terry Cooke, Jewett largely avoids the spectacle of overworked farmers' wives oppressed by their husbands' greed and insensitivity. Many of Jewett's women still keep house contentedly.

None the less, she is rejecting the two central tenets of nineteenth-century gender relations – the separation of women's and men's lives, and the place of women within the private sphere of the home and their exclusion from the public realm of politics and business. Her characters mostly do not exist in that separate sphere of urban bourgeois femininity. By focusing mainly on the agricultural class, she shows women's working lives and their involvement in the community. Mrs Todd owns her house, makes her living as a herbalist and is seen outside the house as often as inside, working her garden, walking the streets and country fields, managing a boat or a horse. Jewett's women characters, uncowed by patriarchal expectations (witness Mrs Todd shrugging off the man's criticism of her boat handling), arguably reflect something of that opening up of the lives of a generation of middle-class women. She does this without subscribing to the more individualistic goal of self-realization against a hostile male world which women writers were increasingly confronting.

Jewett, however, does retain one key aspect of women's lives in the nineteenth century – what Caroll Smith-Rosenberg calls the 'female world of love and ritual'. In the nineteenth century, in an era when middle-class women and men were expected to lead very separate lives, emotionally charged friendships between women (including married women) flourished openly and were socially accepted by both women and men as a quite ordinary form of female affection. Although by the end of the century these networks of friendships were being attacked medically and educationally, Jewett's fiction still confidently occupies this female world.

This female world of love and ritual had a special importance for Jewett personally. From childhood she expressed a complete lack of interest in marriage. Her primary relationships were with women, including Annie Fields, with whom she lived for thirty years until Jewett's death in 1909. Fields's and Jewett's relationship was recognized and respected – what was called at that time a 'Boston marriage'. This kind of household was not regarded as being in radical opposition to heterosexual institutions; it was simply seen an important part of the spectrum of relationships for women, and Jewett's fiction reflects this.

'There is something transfiguring in the best of friendship,' wrote Jewett to a friend. The parallel with the New Testament story of the Transfiguration which she then went on to make – the subsequent effects after the descent from the mountain to 'the fret of everyday life' – suggests that she thought such friendships were profoundly transformative within a wider world. Instead of portraying that world of female friendship within the enclosed middle-class home, Jewett makes it the emotional centre of a whole community and the model for social relationships with men as well as women. Twentieth-century readers unschooled in nineteenth-century female relationships may fail to understand the profound and potentially transformative nature of the relationship which is indicated by this term, which the narrator uses to describe, at the outset of the novel, her relationship not with a woman (that follows in the novel's second chapter) but with a place and a community, Dunnet Landing: 'The process of falling in love at first sight is as final as it is swift in such a case, but the growth of true friendship may be a lifelong affair.'

The basic pattern of this 'friendship' in *The Country of the Pointed Firs*, as Sarah Way Sherman and Marjorie Pryce both suggest, is to be found in certain mother/daughter relationships – Mrs Todd and her mother Mrs Blackett, and in certain ways Mrs Todd and the narrator (there is a negative version in the story of Joanna Todd). Green Island is the physical embodiment of what this mother/child relationship can mean at its best, and the visit there is the heart of the book. We are first shown Green Island immediately after the encounter with Littlepage's phantasmagorical vision of a land beyond Greenland: ' "That's where mother lives," said Mrs Todd. "Can't we see it plain?" ' Though an 'outer island' to the township (and to her readers' urban America), the island becomes the centre when the narrator and her guide, Mrs Todd's brother William, climb to the island's highest point and are given 'a sense of liberty in space and time'. The visit there combines high ceremony with familial ordinariness, the best room and the kitchen, much as Mrs Todd's plans for this visit had been accompanied with a special drink which quite simply gave them a 'quiet evening'. Earlier nineteenth-century fiction expressed its religion of the home idealistically and emotionally, but here the mother's home retains a basis in the very ordinary even while taking on a quality of sacredness. The strong feeling of rootedness and centredness here is a symbol, as Kathryn Allen Rabuzzi suggests, of being at home with oneself.

Furthermore, during the visit to Green Island Mrs Todd, as a gesture of friendship, takes the narrator to 'where the pennyroyal grew', her 'sainted place' previously shown only to her mother. It is the site of a complex grief involving loving, loss, hope and death, where her favourite healing herb flourishes. *Mentha pulegium* eases depressed states of mind and was used to sweeten casks of stale drinking water after long periods at sea, but it also regulates menstrual flow and hence is an abortifacient. These powers over conception, life and death made this herb in classical times the mint of Demeter, Earth goddess and mother of Persephone, whose marriage to the God of the Underworld and subsequent return to her mother changed the earth's seasons. The seasons are central in the life of this herbalist. She has her time of summer gathering and of winter syrups and cordials: '"I ain't had such a season in years,"' she tells the narrator, whom she trusts because, daughter-like, she has learnt some of her skills. She also links the seasons in a positive way with the permanent human patterns of love and grief: '"Them feelin's come back when you think you've done with 'em, as sure as spring comes with the year."'

Sherman's study of Jewett shows most interestingly the enthusiasm among some nineteenth-century American women writers for this mythology of the mother goddess (for example, Jewett's partner Annie Fields wrote a version of the Persephone myth in which the virgin becomes the mature woman through sexuality and death). Other nineteenth-century thinkers believed that those still living in regions of agriculture and husbandry continued to be moved by the archaic powers expressed in classical myths – a European model of historical continuity which Jewett subscribes to, hence some of the parallels in *The Country of the Pointed Firs* between ancient Greek literature and Mrs Todd in her power and wisdom.

The nineteenth century saw this myth of Persephone in terms of both the transformation of the dangerous male into a loving husband and the woman's return to her mother. This pattern of return is found not only in the central episode of the visit to the appropriately named Green Island but also in the opening chapter (see its surprising title for a first-time visit) which brings the narrator to live with Mrs Todd. It is also probably the source of the narrator's strange sense of remembrance conjured up by Mrs Todd's potions.

But in the relationship between 'mother' and 'daughter' Jewett is not announcing the end of the mother and daughter's separation and their merging into some undifferentiated oneness (as some critics have suggested). Instead she offers us a model of the ways in which people (men as well as women) can continue to connect and take pleasure in the recognition of each other as distinct, independent but interrelated beings. These are suggested in the novel's praise of 'courtesies' in opposition to the 'anxious civility' which conventionally masks animosities. These courtesies are a conscious expression of community. A highly individualistic culture such as mainstream America is caught up in a dualistic notion of self and other, and so tends to emphasize a need to achieve autonomy and focus on problems of separateness, domination and submission. In Jewett's narrative of community where people 'know' each other, the issue is instead about relationship and the contented mutual recognition of difference, such as has been proposed by the psychoanalytic critic Jessica Benjamin. This is a lifelong process, active, empowering and a source of delight, interest and attunement.

Seen within this model of relationship, the visit to Green Island becomes more than simply the 'return to the mother'. Mrs Todd visits, but then goes home to what her mother takes pleasure in calling 'a good house where she really belonged'. She recognizes that her daughter 'wanted more scope . . . an' to live in a large place where more things grew'. Yet mother and daughter separated by the sea and physically so different, watch each other's homes across the bay, beam with enjoyment at one another's faces when they meet, cook together, laugh, enjoy music, talk freely and share the place which holds Mrs Todd's most intimate memories. The quality of self-forgetfulness which the narrator identifies in Mrs Blackett is not loss of self but a sympathetic knowing of the other freely offered by an unthreatened ego. The narrator realizes that Mrs Blackett's gift of doing this has a social importance beyond the family, creating balance and cohesiveness. It is very different from Joanna's disastrous total giving over of herself to her faithless lover 'that got what he wanted out of folks' and her reactive pursuit of aloneness. The obverse side of individualism can be complete self-obliteration, but this is avoided. This society tolerates idiosyncrasy to a degree which surprises the narrator. Not everyone is emotionally strong, but many are protected and their capacities nurtured (see the mother/son relationship of Mrs Blackett and William).

Furthermore, women here are never only either a mother or a child. While 'you never get over bein' a child long's you have a mother to go to', Mrs Todd also says that at times she 'felt good sight the oldest', and her mother's childlike quality is mentioned several times with delight. Mrs Todd, in carefully showing the narrator the daguerreotype of the flowerlike face of Mrs Blackett as a young woman, ensures that we see the latter in other roles than that of old mother. Mrs Todd and Joanna, friends of the same age, alternate mother and child roles in her crisis.

'I looked up,' says the narrator of Mrs Blackett, 'and we understood each other without speaking,' This power of self-surrender and sympathy is described by the narrator as 'tact': 'Tact is after all a kind of mindreading, and my hostess held the golden gift.' Mrs Todd has the same gift – her invitations to the narrator to go on excursions are a conversational dance of indirection designed to leave her lodger increasingly skilled in perceiving her friend's wishes yet uncoerced by them. Her approach is the opposite of the minister's ('very numb in his feelin's'), who resorts to his 'authority' in an attempt to bring Joanna back into his church.

We are also asked to imagine that the book's very existence is dependent on the narrator-writer learning that 'tact' herself, since it gives her access to the town's inner stories and the power to tell them with an eloquent brevity and a kind of subliminal symbolism that suggests the emotional complexity of their lives. The narrator begins her education in community by setting aside her writing to learn to prescribe herbs (thus freeing Mrs Todd to gather herbs for the town's future well-being). When she reasserts her own vocation as a writer by hiring the schoolroom, Mrs Todd very happily acknowledges this act of self-assertion as part of a maturing relationship between equals, and it leads therefore not to antagonism or separation but to a deeper intimacy with the older woman.

The sense of recognition and connection is further embodied in the construction of the narrative itself – the frequent use of conversation to tell the stories, the way the stories are folded into other stories, the various voices with their different perspectives, the continual sense of audience and shared discussion, the way the action constantly circles back on itself.

It is this interplay (not opposition) between self-assertion and mutual recognition which makes possible Jewett's optimistic vision in her fiction. Throughout her career she tended to seek upbeat endings to her fiction, but optimism was not easy to achieve and in her earlier work she sometimes reaches for a facile conclusion within the conventions of mid-century domestic fiction. Patriarchy and class power-structures could not be ignored. *The Country of the Pointed Firs*, in common with most nineteenth-century women's writing, does acknowledge the existence of patriarchy and the need to respond to it assertively and even humorously: the ministers, the doctor, the seamen who assume they know best about boats, the military in the form of the innocuous grotesqueries of Sant Bowden, the little girl eventually stopped from wearing boy's clothes on shipboard, the gender divisions of work which mean that few Bowden men die at home. So, when Mrs Todd determines to skipper the boat herself because 'we don't want to carry no men folks havin' to be considered every minute an' takin' up all our time', she acknowledges the continuing social power of nineteenth-century gender relations shaping the different ways in which men and women respond.

However, some of the effect of those power-structures in society is lessened by the sense of connection and recognition with which Jewett invests this community. Writing at a time when the American women's movement had lost momentum and was restricting its efforts to gaining the suffrage, Jewett must have seen that she could not alter patriarchy, but she could, however, imagine a society in which people with particular qualities are a promise of different kinds of gender roles. In Dunnet Landing Mrs Todd and the doctor are allies at a time when the conventional medical establishment was actually virulently opposed to alternative practitioners (and indeed accused them of abortion – the pennyroyal can be taken as a benign rewriting of this). Mrs Todd teases the man who criticizes her in the boat. Sant Bowden's attempts to make his family reunion a military exercise are rendered innocent (remarkably, given the still vivid holocaust of the Civil War). Her brother William Blackett resembles his mother, and Elijah Tilley in his domesticated bereavement comes to understand his wife's existence. The town's select men hardly feature. Admittedly, a certain tension does still remain between the ideal of community seen from this predominately female perspective and another underdeveloped account of society which acknowledges continuing inequalities and antagonisms. None the less, though the power-structures cannot be entirely dismantled, something of the ways of relating exemplified in the mother/child relationship are carried over to some extent into the wider community.

The redemptive notion of the community is realized most explicitly with the Bowden reunion, and Jewett tries not to present a falsely idealized picture. In these chapters the image of the visit to family widens to include most of the district while retaining Mrs Blackett at its centre. The house is likened to a 'motherly' hen, and the celebration draws on the 'instincts of a far forgotten childhood'. With an awareness of these families' customary isolation in the winter-marooned farms and islands, there is also a sense of a countrywide network of connections spanning generations: for example, Mrs Blackett looking across to her dead sister's farm with pleasure. The focus until now has been largely on women. Here we see the intersection of women's and men's lives (though still from a female perspective). The narrator, coming presumably from the city, begins to use a rather inflated language to communicate her excitement at this ritual of rural community, but this is checked by the readers' awareness of non-Bowdens' exclusion and by Mrs Todd's surprisingly trenchant dislikes at this love feast. Unlike the narrator, she can hear – and laugh at – the out-of-tune voice among the singers.

It is important to see the fictional Dunnet Landing as part of late nineteenth-century America. This world is not in a simple sense 'traditional', but an imagined world based on both Jewett's knowledge of contemporary Maine and her enhanced and adapted sense of its possibilities. Its crucial relation to the rest of 1890s America is made clear in the final chapter when Dunnet Landing is seen from a distance and, most importantly, from a mental perspective beyond Maine. At this point the narrator depressingly feels Dunnet Landing and the world outside Maine are opposed ('the gifts of peace are not for those who live in the thick of battle'). Yet the narrator sees that, despite the township's apparently crumbled appearance and disabled schooners, a force for good also resides there – Mrs Todd, viewed now from a distance, reveals a personal power and unhusbanded self-possession.

Taken as a whole, the novel confronts the premises of American modernity. Jewett dismisses the dominant cultural philosophy of her times, Social Darwinism, which socially and economically powerful elites endorsed as progressive and natural. This was a cut-throat vision of life where progress is linked with the survival of the fittest and the fall of the weak. In *The Country of the Pointed Firs* there is, instead, regret that certain people's talents have been frustrated. She quotes Darwin on the personal supremacy of sea captains, only to mock this idea with her portrait of the superannuated Littlepage. As the narrator leaves Dunnet Landing, a more Darwinian sense of nature nearly reasserts itself in the picture of the gulls swooping on the fish and old Elijah's struggle through the seas. But the narrator is now wise enough to place this and the rest of her time in Dunnet Landing into a different context than that of Darwinism – that of cyclical seasonal change. She neither dwells on the struggle, nor consoles herself with summery pictures. She knows that the green on the islands merely gives the illusion of continuing summer; she also knows the sheep are now well prepared to stand the cold. Symbolically as well as literally Mrs Todd's cordials are also ready for the coming winter.

The Country of the Pointed Firs is utopian, not in the common sense of illusion and false hope, but in the sense of trying to imagine a better mode of social relationships. By often oblique references it acknowledges contemporary social, economic and political realities but always in an attempt to transform them into positive forms. It is no accident that key issues of Jewett's day are taken up here, and we need to be sensitive to these subtle references.

The issues Jewett addresses thus obliquely are strikingly numerous. Firstly there are medical controversies, in particular the debates about women doctors (subject of Jewett's second novel, *The Country Doctor*) and the attempt to outlaw alternative medical therapies (homoeopathy and herbalism). There was current debate about the role of childless and single women, and worry about the strained relationships in the middle class between mothers and daughters who from the 1870s were following different life paths for the first time that century. Increasing class conflict, generated by economic differences and too often obscured by America's ideology of equality, is rendered surprisingly inoperative through the novel's central friendship between landlady and upper-class paying guest – in a sense a daughter for the childless Mrs Todd who had indeed lost her first real love to class prejudice. We are reminded of big business in the narrator's humorous references to her 'industries' and to Mrs Todd as her 'business partner', and there is of course always an implicit contrast being made with the frightening new cities which lacked this village's intimate, useful and respectful contact with the wild (the sea, fields, woods) – a contrast made explicit in her story 'The White Heron'. The narrator's fear, as she stands on the departing steamer, of becoming a 'foreigner' in the world beyond Dunnet Landing evokes images of those thousands of immigrants who yearly came by ship to America at that time and poured into its cities (Jewett's later tale, 'The Foreigner', hints at a less benign fate for those immigrants even in Dunnet Landing). The opening up of the American West is in contrast to the 'gold-digging' of potatoes on that island on the far eastern seaboard, and America's current fear of 'sectional differences' within what was now a continental nation is transcended in Jewett's celebration of the local.

Another clue to what Jewett is creating in *The Country of the Pointed Firs* may lie in the two quotations by Flaubert (one was abbreviated) she had displayed on her desk, which can be translated thus: 'Write about life in the way you write history' and 'It [Art] is not a matter of getting people to laugh or cry, or of making them furious, but of acting on them as nature does, that is to say, making them dream'. 'Dream' here means a complex wonderment at the nature of things as they are. Jewett weds her utopianism to realism. Like her literary contemporaries she is profoundly dedicated to realism in fiction and committed to the depiction of ordinary scenes and objects of daily living. But this commonplace world reveals a power to sustain and transform, like the 'humble compounds brewed at intervals with molasses or vinegar or spirits in a small caldron on Mrs Todd's kitchen stove'. Jewett's utopia is the stronger for explicitly rejecting the idea that absolute perfection is possible. The 'brave new world' of the island in Shakespeare's *The Tempest* (a mythic image re-created in this novel's forerunner, *Pearl of Orr's Island*) is now just a 'weather-beaten lobster smack' called *Miranda*. Dunnet Landing has its suffering and losses: emblematically Mrs Tilley's best china service, supposedly intact, includes a hidden broken cup.

The vision which *The Country of the Pointed Firs* offers is not present in Jewett's earlier work – the novel is unique in this respect. It was something which she had to work towards. Once achieved, she was clearly happy to return to Dunnet Landing in some of her subsequent fiction, though 'The Foreigner' is a darker version of the mother/daughter relationship, 'The Queen's Twin' more a grotesque aristocratic obsession rather than an assertion of democratic equality, and 'William's Wedding' was still unfinished at Jewett's death. The reader will discover in the earlier tales included in this Penguin collection rather sombre pictures of small rural communities which are barely offset by comedy in the narration or by moralistic conclusions. Relations between women and men are uneasy, and involve conscious and unconscious game-playing ('Marsh Rosemary', 'Miss Peck's Promotion', 'The Guests of Mrs Timms'); class differences disturbingly skew the love between a maid servant and her mistress's niece ('Martha's Lady'); and a child's rapport with nature is preserved by rejecting modernity rather than transfiguring it ('A White Heron'). 'The King of Folly Island' contrasts bleakly with *The Country of the Pointed Firs*. This is a hostile community, with a daughter without her mother and cough drops for tuberculosis. The tale's strong parallels between the city businessman and the 'pioneer' islander bode ill for contemporary America. In the best of this early work Jewett preserves certain moral ambiguities and resists conventional narrative structures; in others (not reprinted here) she resorts to the stereotyped moralities and storylines of earlier popular women's fiction.

The narrator of *The Country of the Pointed Firs* dreamt of Dunnet Landing before she came, with its 'mixture of remoteness, and childish certainty of being the centre of civilization'. Jewett attempts to show that in some important sense this dream place is indeed 'central' to her contemporary America. Like Green Island the reader can 'see it plain', and like the pennyroyal growing there it purports to be the 'right pattern', the true form. The sun on Green Island 'made it seem like a sudden revelation of the world beyond this which some believe to be so near'. We don't usually expect to find utopias amid the ordinary, but this novel suggests that this better world may exist not 'beyond this' but within the present and the 'commonplace'.

Many thanks to David Easton, Tony Pinkney and Jenny Phillips for comments on the introduction, John Phillips and Jenny Phillips for help with nautical footnotes, Claire MacDonald for information on responses to Arctic explorations, David Carroll, Julia Briggs and Nancy S. Reinhardt, Curator of Special Collections, Miller Library, Colby College, for a copy of 'William's Wedding' from the 1910 edition of *The Country of the Pointed Firs*. This edition is in celebration of my mother, Margaret Grieve Easton, who was so pleased with the Penguin commission, greatly enjoyed the novel and died, at Mrs Blackett's age, in August 1994 just as I was finishing the project.

A NOTE ON THE TEXT

The Country of the Pointed Firs was originally published in four issues of the *Atlantic Monthly* magazine in 1896. When publishing it as a book later in the same year, Jewett added two chapters to the original ending at the Bowden reunion, 'Along the Shore' and 'A Backward Glance', and made one extended chapter, 'The Bowden Reunion', out of two. It was in this form that it was reprinted until her death in 1909; there are no variants in these editions. The manuscript has not survived.

Jewett, however, wrote four more tales set in Dunnet Landing, told by the same narrator and featuring Mrs Todd, her family and other villagers: 'The Queen's Twin', 'A Dunnet Shepherdess', 'The Foreigner' and (still unfinished at her death) 'William's Wedding'. After her death her publisher Houghton Mifflin added first 'A Dunnet Shepherdess' and 'William's Wedding' (in 1910) and then 'The Queen's Twin' (in 1919) to subsequent editions of the novel, so for the next fifty or so years the novel was usually read in this unauthorized form.

I have chosen to reprint Jewett's original 1896 book-form text for two reasons. First, Jewett seems never to have taken any steps to incorporate the later tales, despite suggestions that she might do so (see discussion by Marco A. Portales). Second, I believe that the expanded version spoils the integrity of her text, making it increasingly a more conventional novel in form and thus losing the delicate suggestiveness and web-like effect of the sketch structure. The 1910 text creates something of an ongoing plot round William's courtship.

However, read separately these additional Dunnet Landing stories are very good, so I have reprinted three of them here, but placed them in the chronological order of her short fiction's composition. Anyone wishing to test my opinion about the right copy-text for this edition can find the posthumous, extended version of the novel in *Four Stories by American Women*, edited by Cynthia Griffin Woolf (London: Penguin, 1990).

Selecting additional stories to accompany the novel has not been easy. I realize that a fully representative sample would have to include work which is more conventional in either form or social values than *The Country of the Pointed Firs* might lead one to expect, but I have decided to favour more distinctive pieces.

Sources and dates of stories are as follows: 'A White Heron' and 'Marsh Rosemary' from *A White Heron and Other Stories* (1886); 'The King of Folly Island', 'The Courting of Sister Wisby' and 'Miss Peck's Promotion' from *The King of Folly Island and Other People* (1888); 'The Guests of Mrs Timms' from *The Life of Nancy* (1895); 'The Queen's Twin' and 'Martha's Lady' from *The Queen's Twin and Other Stories* (1899); 'The Foreigner' from *Atlantic Monthly* vol. 86, August 1900; and 'William's Wedding' from *The Country of the Pointed Firs* (1910). The texts are printed as they appear in their first editions, with the following exceptions: the spacing of contractions has been adjusted slightly throughout (for example, 'did n't' becomes 'didn't' and 'T was' becomes ''Twas'); boat names and book titles have been placed in italics; the full-stop after 'Mr', 'Mrs' and chapter titles has been omitted; single quotation marks are used instead of double (and vice versa); and Arabic instead of Roman numerals used for chapter numbers.

FURTHER READING

Elizabeth Ammons, *Conflicting Stories: American Writers at the Turn into the Twentieth Century* (New York: Oxford University Press, 1991).

Josephine Donovan, *New England Local Color Literature: A Women's Tradition* (New York: Frederick Ungar, 1983).

Marilyn Sanders Mobley, *Folk Roots and Mythic Wings in Sarah Orne Jewett and Toni Morrison: The Cultural Function of Narrative* (Baton Rouge: Louisiana State University Press, 1991).

Gwen L. Nagel, *Critical Essays on Sarah Orne Jewett* (Boston: G. K. Hall, 1984).

Marco A. Portales, 'History of a Text: Jewett's *The Country of the Pointed Firs*', *New England Quarterly* 55 (1982), pp. 586–92.

Marjorie Pryse, Introduction in *The Country of the Pointed Firs and Other Stories* (New York: Norton, 1981).

Sarah Way Sherman, *Sarah Orne Jewett, an American Persephone* (Hanover: University Press of New England, 1989).

Sandra A. Zagarell, 'Narratives of Community: The Identification of a Genre', *Signs* 13 (1988), pp. 498–527.

OTHER WORKS CITED IN THE INTRODUCTION

Jessica Benjamin, *The Bonds of Love: Psychoanalysis, Feminism, and the Problem of Domination* (New York: Pantheon, 1988).

Kathryn Allen Rabuzzi, *The Sacred and the Feminine: Toward a Theology of Housework* (New York: Seabury Press, 1982).

Carroll Smith-Rosenberg, *Disorderly Conduct: Visions of Gender in Victorian America* (New York: Knopf, 1985).

THE COUNTRY OF THE
POINTED FIRS

To Alice Greenwood Howe

I

THE RETURN

There was something about the coast town of Dunnet which made it seem more attractive than other maritime villages of eastern Maine. Perhaps it was the simple fact of acquaintance with that neighborhood which made it so attaching, and gave such interest to the rocky shore and dark woods, and the few houses which seemed to be securely wedged and tree-nailed in among the ledges by the Landing. These houses made the most of the seaward view, and there was a gayety and determined floweriness in their bits of garden ground; the small-paned high windows in the peaks of their steep gables were like knowing eyes that watched the harbor and the far sea-line beyond, or looked northward all along the shore and its background of spruces and balsam firs.[1] When one really knows a village like this and its surroundings, it is like becoming acquainted with a single person. The process of falling in love at first sight is as final as it is swift in such a case, but the growth of true friendship may be a lifelong affair.

After a first brief visit made two or three summers before in the course of a yachting cruise, a lover of Dunnet Landing returned to find the unchanged shores of the pointed firs, the same quaintness of the village with its elaborate conventionalities; all that mixture of remoteness, and childish certainty of being the centre of civilization of which her affectionate dreams had told. One evening in June, a single passenger landed upon the steamboat wharf. The tide was high, there was a fine crowd of spectators, and the younger portion of the company followed her with subdued excitement up the narrow street of the salt-aired, white clapboarded little town.

MRS TODD

Later, there was only one fault to find with this choice of a summer lodging-place, and that was its complete lack of seclusion. At first the tiny house of Mrs Almira Todd, which stood with its end to the street, appeared to be retired and sheltered enough from the busy world, behind its busy bit of a green garden, in which all the blooming things, two or three gay hollyhocks and some London-pride, were pushed back against the gray-shingled wall. It was a queer little garden and puzzling to a stranger, the few flowers being put at a disadvantage by so much greenery; but the discovery was soon made that Mrs Todd was an ardent lover of herbs, both wild and tame, and the sea-breezes blew into the low end-window of the house laden with not only sweet-brier and sweet-mary, but balm and sage and borage and mint, wormwood and southernwood. If Mrs Todd had occasion to step into the far corner of her herb plot, she trod heavily upon thyme, and made its fragrant presence known with all the rest. Being a very large person, her full skirts brushed and bent almost every slender stalk that her feet missed. You could always tell when she was stepping about there, even when you were half awake in the morning, and learned to know, in the course of a few weeks' experience, in exactly which corner of the garden she might be.

At one side of this herb plot were other growths of a rustic pharmacopœia, great treasures and rarities among the commoner herbs. There were some strange and pungent odors that roused a dim sense and remembrance of something in the forgotten past. Some of these might once have belonged to sacred and mystic rites, and have had some occult knowledge handed with them down the centuries; but now they pertained only to humble compounds brewed at intervals with molasses or vinegar or spirits in a small caldron on Mrs Todd's kitchen stove. They were dispensed to suffering neighbors, who usually came at night as if by stealth, bringing their own ancient-looking vials to be filled. One nostrum was called the Indian remedy and its price was but fifteen cents; the whispered directions could be heard as customers passed the windows. With most remedies the purchaser was allowed to depart unadmonished from the kitchen, Mrs Todd being a wise saver of steps; but with certain vials she gave cautions, standing in the doorway, and there were other doses which had to be accompanied on their healing way as far as the gate, while she muttered long chapters of directions, and kept up an air of secrecy and importance to the last. It may not have been only the common ails of humanity with which she tried to cope; it seemed sometimes as if love and hate and jealousy and adverse winds at sea might also find their proper remedies among the curious wild-looking plants in Mrs Todd's garden.

The village doctor and this learned herbalist were upon the best of terms. The good man may have counted upon the unfavorable effect of certain potions which he should find his opportunity in counteracting; at any rate, he now and then stopped and exchanged greetings with Mrs Todd over the picket fence. The conversation became at once professional after the briefest preliminaries, and he would stand twirling a sweet-scented sprig in his fingers, and make suggestive jokes, perhaps about her faith in a too persistent course of thoroughwort elixir,[1] in which my landlady professed such firm belief as sometimes to endanger the life and usefulness of worthy neighbors.

To arrive at this quietest of seaside villages late in June, when the busy herb-gathering season was just beginning, was also to arrive in the early prime of Mrs Todd's activity in the brewing of old-fashioned spruce beer.[2] This cooling and refreshing drink had been brought to wonderful perfection through a long series of experiments; it had won immense local fame, and the supplies for its manufacture were always giving out and having to be replenished. For various reasons, the seclusion and uninterrupted days which had been looked forward to proved to be very rare in this otherwise delightful corner of the world. My hostess and I had made our shrewd business agreement on the basis of a simple cold luncheon at noon, and liberal restitution in the matter of hot suppers, to provide for which the lodger might sometimes be seen hurrying down the road, late in the day, with cunner[3] line in hand. It was soon found that this arrangement made large allowance for Mrs Todd's slow herb-gathering progresses through woods and pastures. The spruce-beer customers were pretty steady in hot weather and there were many demands for different soothing syrups and elixirs with which the unwise curiosity of my early residence had made me acquainted. Knowing Mrs Todd to be a widow, who had little beside this slender business and the income from one hungry lodger to maintain her, one's energies and even interest were quickly bestowed, until it became a matter of course that she should go afield every pleasant day, and that the lodger should answer all peremptory knocks at the side door.

In taking an occasional wisdom-giving stroll in Mrs Todd's company, and in acting as business partner during her frequent absences, I found the July days fly fast, and it was not until I felt myself confronted with too great pride and pleasure in the display, one night, of two dollars and twenty-seven cents which I had taken in during the day, that I remembered a long piece of writing, sadly belated now, which I was bound to do. To have been patted kindly on the shoulder and called 'darlin',' to have been offered a surprise of early mushrooms for supper, to have had all the glory of making two dollars and twenty-seven cents in a single day, and then to renounce it all and withdraw from these pleasant successes, needed much resolution. Literary employments are so vexed with uncertainties at best, and it was not until the voice of conscience sounded louder in my ears than the sea on the nearest pebble beach that I said unkind words of withdrawal to Mrs Todd. She only became more wistfully affectionate than ever in her expressions, and looked as disappointed as I expected when I frankly told her that I could no longer enjoy the pleasure of what we called 'seein' folks.' I felt that I was cruel to a whole neighborhood in curtailing her liberty in this most important season for harvesting the different wild herbs that were so much counted upon to ease their winter ails.

'Well, dear,' she said sorrowfully, 'I've took great advantage o' your bein' here. I ain't had such a season for years, but I have never had nobody I could so trust. All you lack is a few qualities, but with time you'd gain judgment an' experience, an' be very able in the business. I'd stand right here an' say it to anybody.'

Mrs Todd and I were not separated or estranged by the change in our business relations; on the contrary, a deeper intimacy seemed to begin. I do not know what herb of the night[4] it was that used sometimes to send out a penetrating odor late in the evening, after the dew had fallen, and the moon was high, and the cool air came up from the sea. Then Mrs Todd would feel that she must talk to somebody, and I was only too glad to listen. We both fell under the spell, and she either stood outside the window, or made an errand to my sitting-room, and told, it might be very commonplace news of the day, or, as happened one misty summer night, all that lay deepest in her heart. It was in this way that I came to know that she had loved one who was far above her.

'No, dear, him I speak of could never think of me,' she said. 'When we was young together his mother didn't favor the match, an' done everything she could to part us; and folks thought we both married well, but 'twa'n't what either one of us wanted most; an' now we're left alone again an' might have had each other all the time. He was above bein' a seafarin' man, an' prospered more than most; he come of a high family, an' my lot was plain an' hard-workin'. I ain't seen him for some years; he's forgot our youthful feelin's, I expect, but a woman's heart is different; them feelin's comes back when you think you've done with 'em, as sure as spring comes with the year. An' I've always had ways of hearin' about him.'

She stood in the centre of a braided rug, and its rings of black and gray seemed to circle about her feet in the dim light. Her height and massiveness in the low room gave her the look of a huge sibyl,[5] while the strange fragrance of the mysterious herb blew in from the little garden.

THE SCHOOLHOUSE

For some days after this, Mrs Todd's customers came and went past my windows, and, haying-time being nearly over, strangers began to arrive from the inland country, such was her widespread reputation. Sometimes I saw a pale young creature like a white windflower[1] left over into midsummer, upon whose face consumption had set its bright and wistful mark; but oftener two stout, hard-worked women from the farms came together, and detailed their symptoms to Mrs Todd in loud and cheerful voices, combining the satisfactions of a friendly gossip with the medical opportunity. They seemed to give much from their own store of therapeutic learning. I became aware of the school in which my landlady had strengthened her natural gift; but hers was always the governing mind, and the final command, 'Take of hy'sop one handful' (or whatever herb it was), was received in respectful silence. One afternoon, when I had listened, – it was impossible not to listen, with cottonless ears,[2] – and then laughed and listened again, with an idle pen in my hand, during a particularly spirited and personal conversation, I reached for my hat, and, taking blotting book and all under my arm, I resolutely fled further temptation, and walked out past the fragrant green garden and up the dusty road. The way went straight uphill, and presently I stopped and turned to look back.

The tide was in, the wide harbor was surrounded by its dark woods, and the small wooden houses stood as near as they could get to the landing. Mrs Todd's was the last house on the way inland. The gray ledges of the rocky shore were well covered with sod in most places, and the pasture bayberry[3] and wild roses grew thick among them. I could see the higher inland country and the scattered farms. On the brink of the hill stood a little white schoolhouse, much wind-blown and weather-beaten, which was a landmark to seagoing folk; from its door there was a most beautiful view of sea and shore. The summer vacation now prevailed, and after finding the door unfastened, and taking a long look through one of the seaward windows, and reflecting afterward for some time in a shady place near by among the bayberry bushes, I returned to the chief place of business in the village, and to the amusement of two of the selectmen,[4] brothers and autocrats of Dunnet Landing, I hired the schoolhouse for the rest of the vacation for fifty cents a week.

Selfish as it may appear, the retired situation seemed to possess great advantages, and I spent many days there quite undisturbed, with the sea-breeze blowing through the small, high windows and swaying the heavy outside shutters to and fro. I hung my hat and luncheon-basket on an entry nail as if I were a small scholar, but I sat at the teacher's desk as if I were that great authority, with all the timid empty benches in rows before me. Now and then an idle sheep came and stood for a long time looking in at the door. At sundown I went back, feeling most businesslike, down toward the village again, and usually met the flavor, not of the herb garden, but of Mrs Todd's hot supper, halfway up the hill. On the nights when there were evening meetings or other public exercises that demanded her presence we had tea very early, and I was welcomed back as if from a long absence.

Once or twice I feigned excuses for staying at home, while Mrs Todd made distant excursions, and came home late, with both hands full and a heavily laden apron. This was in pennyroyal[5] time, and when the rare lobelia was in its prime and the elecampane was coming on. One day she appeared at the schoolhouse itself, partly out of amused curiosity about my industries; but she explained that there was no tansy in the neighborhood with such snap to it as some that grew about the schoolhouse lot. Being scuffed down all the spring made it grow so much the better, like some folks that had it hard in their youth, and were bound to make the most of themselves before they died.

4

AT THE SCHOOLHOUSE WINDOW

One day I reached the schoolhouse very late, owing to attendance upon the funeral of an acquaintance and neighbor, with whose sad decline in health I had been familiar, and whose last days both the doctor and Mrs Todd had tried in vain to ease. The services had taken place at one o'clock, and now, at quarter past two, I stood at the schoolhouse window, looking down at the procession as it went along the lower road close to the shore. It was a walking funeral, and even at that distance I could recognize most of the mourners as they went their solemn way. Mrs Begg had been very much respected, and there was a large company of friends following to her grave. She had been brought up on one of the neighboring farms, and each of the few times that I had seen her she professed great dissatisfaction with town life. The people lived too close together for her liking, at the Landing, and she could not get used to the constant sound of the sea. She had lived to lament three seafaring husbands, and her house was decorated with West Indian curiosities, specimens of conch shells and fine coral which they had brought home from their voyages in lumber-laden ships.[1] Mrs Todd had told me all our neighbor's history. They had been girls together, and, to use her own phrase, had 'both seen trouble till they knew the best and worst on 't.' I could see the sorrowful, large figure of Mrs Todd as I stood at the window. She made a break in the procession by walking slowly and keeping the after-part of it back. She held a handkerchief to her eyes, and I knew, with a pang of sympathy, that hers was not affected grief.

Beside her, after much difficulty, I recognized the one strange and unrelated person in all the company, an old man who had always been mysterious to me. I could see his thin, bending figure. He wore a narrow, long-tailed coat and walked with a stick, and had the same 'cant to leeward'[2] as the wind-bent trees on the height above.

This was Captain Littlepage, whom I had seen only once or twice before, sitting pale and old behind a closed window; never out of doors until now.

Mrs Todd always shook her head gravely when I asked a question, and said that he wasn't what he had been once, and seemed to class him with her other secrets. He might have belonged with a simple which grew in a certain slug-haunted corner of the garden, whose use she could never be betrayed into telling me, though I saw her cutting the tops by moonlight once, as if it were a charm, and not a medicine, like the great fading bloodroot leaves.

I could see that she was trying to keep pace with the old captain's lighter steps. He looked like an aged grasshopper of some strange human variety. Behind this pair was a short, impatient, little person, who kept the captain's house and gave it what Mrs Todd and others believed to be no proper sort of care. She was usually called 'that Mari' Harris' in a subdued conversation between intimates, but they treated her with anxious civility when they met her face to face.

The bay-sheltered islands and the great sea beyond stretched away to the far horizon southward and eastward; the little procession in the foreground looked futile and helpless on the edge of the rocky shore. It was a glorious day early in July, with a clear, high sky; there were no clouds, there was no noise of the sea. The song sparrows sang and sang, as if with joyous knowledge of immortality, and contempt for those who could so pettily concern themselves with death. I stood watching until the funeral procession had crept round a shoulder of the slope below and disappeared from the great landscape as if it had gone into a cave.

An hour later I was busy at my work. Now and then a bee blundered in and took me for an enemy; but there was a useful stick upon the teacher's desk, and I rapped to call the bees to order as if they were unruly scholars, or waved them away from their riots over the ink, which I had bought at the Landing store, and discovered too late to be scented with bergamot,[3] as if to refresh the labors of anxious scribes. One anxious scribe felt very dull that day; a sheep-bell tinkled near by, and called her wandering wits after it. The sentences failed to catch these lovely summer cadences. For the first time I began to wish for a companion and for news from the outer world, which had been, half unconsciously, forgotten. Watching the funeral gave one a sort of pain. I began to wonder if I ought not to have walked with the rest, instead of hurrying away at the end of the services. Perhaps the Sunday gown I had put on for the occasion was making this disastrous change of feeling, but I had now made myself and my friends remember that I did not really belong to Dunnet Landing.

I sighed, and turned to the half-written page again.

5

CAPTAIN LITTLEPAGE

It was a long time after this; an hour was very long in that coast town where nothing stole away the shortest minute. I had lost myself completely in work, when I heard footsteps outside. There was a steep footpath between the upper and the lower road, which I climbed to shorten the way, as the children had taught me, but I believed that Mrs Todd would find it inaccessible, unless she had occasion to see me in great haste. I wrote on, feeling like a besieged miser of time, while the footsteps came nearer, and the sheep-bell tinkled away in haste as if someone had shaken a stick in its wearer's face. Then I looked, and saw Captain Littlepage passing the nearest window; the next moment he tapped politely at the door.

'Come in, sir,' I said, rising to meet him; and he entered, bowing with much courtesy. I stepped down from the desk and offered him a chair by the window, where he seated himself at once, being sadly spent by his climb. I returned to my fixed seat behind the teacher's desk, which gave him the lower place of a scholar.

'You ought to have the place of honor, Captain Littlepage,' I said.

'A happy, rural seat of various views,'[1]

he quoted, as he gazed out into the sunshine and up the long wooded shore. Then he glanced at me, and looked all about him as pleased as a child.

'My quotation was from *Paradise Lost*: the greatest of poems, I suppose you know?' and I nodded. 'There's nothing that ranks, to my mind, with *Paradise Lost*; it's all lofty, all lofty,' he continued. 'Shakespeare was a great poet; he copied life, but you have to put up with a great deal of low talk.'

I now remembered that Mrs Todd had told me one day that Captain Littlepage had overset his mind with too much reading; she had also made dark reference to his having 'spells' of some unexplainable nature. I could not help wondering what errand had brought him out in search of me. There was something quite charming in his appearance: it was a face thin and delicate with refinement, but worn into appealing lines, as if he had suffered from loneliness and misapprehension. He looked, with his careful precision of dress, as if he were the object of cherishing care on the part of elderly unmarried sisters, but I knew Mari' Harris to be a very common-place, inelegant person, who would have no such standards; it was plain that the captain was his own attentive valet. He sat looking at me expect-antly. I could not help thinking that, with his queer head and length of thinness, he was made to hop along the road of life rather than to walk. The captain was very grave indeed, and I bade my inward spirit keep close to discretion.

'Poor Mrs Begg has gone,' I ventured to say. I still wore my Sunday gown by way of showing respect.

'She has gone,' said the captain, – 'very easy at the last, I was informed; she slipped away as if she were glad of the opportunity.'

I thought of the Countess of Carberry,[2] and felt that history repeated itself.

'She was one of the old stock,' continued Captain Littlepage, with touching sincerity. 'She was very much looked up to in this town, and will be missed.'

I wondered, as I looked at him, if he had sprung from a line of ministers; he had the refinement of look and air of command which are the heritage of the old ecclesiastical families of New England. But as Darwin[3] says in his autobiography, 'there is no such king as a sea-captain; he is greater even than a king or a schoolmaster!'

Captain Littlepage moved his chair out of the wake of the sunshine, and still sat looking at me. I began to be very eager to know upon what errand he had come.

'It may be found out some o' these days,' he said earnestly. 'We may know it all, the next step; where Mrs Begg is now, for instance. Certainty, not conjecture, is what we all desire.'

'I suppose we shall know it all some day,' said I.

'We shall know it while yet below,' insisted the captain, with a flush of impatience on his thin cheeks. 'We have not looked for truth in the right direction. I know what I speak of; those who have laughed at me little know how much reason my ideas are based upon.' He waved his hand toward the village below. 'In that handful of houses they fancy that they comprehend the universe.'

I smiled, and waited for him to go on.

'I am an old man, as you can see,' he continued, 'and I have been a shipmaster the greater part of my life, – forty-three years in all. You may not think it, but I am above eighty years of age.'

He did not look so old, and I hastened to say so.

'You must have left the sea a good many years ago, then, Captain Littlepage?' I said.

'I should have been serviceable at least five or six years more,' he answered. 'My acquaintance with certain – my experience upon a certain occasion, I might say, gave rise to prejudice. I do not mind telling you that I chanced to learn of one of the greatest discoveries that man has ever made.'

Now we were approaching dangerous ground, but a sudden sense of his sufferings at the hands of the ignorant came to my help, and I asked to hear more with all the deference I really felt. A swallow flew into the schoolhouse at this moment as if a kingbird[4] were after it, and beat itself against the walls for a minute, and escaped again to the open air; but Captain Littlepage took no notice whatever of the flurry.

'I had a valuable cargo of general merchandise from the London docks to Fort Churchill, a station of the old company on Hudson's Bay,' said the captain earnestly. 'We were delayed in lading, and baffled by head winds and a heavy tumbling sea all the way north-about and across. Then the fog kept us off the coast; and when I made port at last, it was too late to delay in those northern waters with such a vessel and such a crew as I had. They cared for nothing, and idled me into a fit of sickness; but my first mate was a good, excellent man, with no more idea of being frozen in there until spring than I had, so we made what speed we could to get clear of Hudson's Bay and off the coast. I owned an eighth of the vessel, and he owned a sixteenth of her. She was a full-rigged ship, called the *Minerva*,[5] but she was getting old and leaky. I meant it should be my last v'y'ge in her, and so it proved. She had been an excellent vessel in her day. Of the cowards aboard her I can't say so much.'

'Then you were wrecked?' I asked, as he made a long pause.

'I wa'n't caught astern o' the lighter[6] by any fault of mine,' said the captain gloomily. 'We left Fort Churchill and run out into the Bay with a light pair o' heels;[7] but I had been vexed to death with their red-tape rigging at the company's office, and chilled with stayin' on deck an' tryin' to hurry up things, and when we were well out o' sight o' land, headin' for Hudson's Straits, I had a bad turn o' some sort o' fever, and had to stay below. The days were getting short, and we made good runs, all well on board but me, and the crew done their work by dint of hard driving.'

I began to find this unexpected narrative a little dull. Captain Littlepage spoke with a kind of slow correctness that lacked the longshore high flavor to which I had grown used; but I listened respectfully while he explained the winds having become contrary, and talked on in a dreary sort of way about his voyage, the bad weather, and the disadvantages he was under in the lightness of his ship, which bounced about like a chip in a bucket,[8] and would not answer the rudder or properly respond to the most careful setting of sails.

'So there we were blowin' along anyways,' he complained; but looking at me at this moment, and seeing that my thoughts were unkindly wandering, he ceased to speak.

'It was a hard life at sea in those days, I am sure,' said I, with redoubled interest.

'It was a dog's life,' said the poor old gentleman, quite reassured, 'but it made men of those who followed it. I see a change for the worse even in our own town here; full of loafers now, small and poor as 't is, who once would have followed the sea, every lazy soul of 'em. There is no occupation so fit for just that class o' men who never get beyond the fo'cas'le.[9] I view it, in addition, that a community narrows down and grows dreadful ignorant when it is shut up to its own affairs, and gets no knowledge of the outside world except from a cheap, unprincipled newspaper.[10] In the old days, a good part o' the best men here knew a hundred ports and something of the way folks lived in them. They saw the world for themselves, and like's not their wives and children saw it with them. They may not have had the best of knowledge to carry with 'em sight-seein', but they were some acquainted with foreign lands an' their laws, an' could see outside the battle for town clerk here in Dunnet; they got some sense o' proportion. Yes, they lived more dignified, and their houses were better within an' without. Shipping's a terrible loss to this part o' New England from a social point o' view, ma'am.'

'I have thought of that myself,' I returned, with my interest quite awakened. 'It accounts for the change in a great many things, – the sad disappearance of sea-captains, – doesn't it?'

'A shipmaster was apt to get the habit of reading,' said my companion, brightening still more, and taking on a most touching air of unreserve. 'A captain is not expected to be familiar with his crew, and for company's sake in dull days and nights he turns to his book. Most of us old shipmasters came to know 'most everything about something; one would take to readin' on farming topics, and some were great on medicine, – but Lord help their poor crews! – or some were all for history, and now and then there'd be one like me that gave his time to the poets. I was well acquainted with a shipmaster that was all for bees an' bee-keepin'; and if you met him in port and went aboard, he'd sit and talk a terrible while about their havin' so much information, and the money that could be made out of keepin' 'em. He was one of the smartest captains that ever sailed the seas, but they used to call the *Newcastle*, a great bark he commanded for many years, Tuttle's beehive. There was old Cap'n Jameson: he had notions of Solomon's Temple,[11] and made a very handsome little model of the same, right from the Scripture measurements, same's other sailors make little ships and design new tricks of rigging and all that. No, there's nothing to take the place of shipping in a place like ours. These bicycles offend me dreadfully; they don't afford no real opportunities of experience such as a man gained on a voyage. No: when folks left home in the old days they left it to some purpose, and when they got home they stayed there and had some pride in it. There's no large-minded way of thinking now: the worst have got to be best and rule everything; we're all turned upside down and going back year by year.'

'Oh no, Captain Littlepage, I hope not,' said I, trying to soothe his feelings.

There was a silence in the schoolhouse, but we could hear the noise of the water on a beach below. It sounded like the strange warning wave that gives notice of the turn of the tide. A late golden robin,[12] with the most joyful and eager of voices, was singing close by in a thicket of wild roses.

THE WAITING PLACE

'How did you manage with the rest of that rough voyage on the *Minerva*?' I asked.

'I shall be glad to explain to you,' said Captain Littlepage, forgetting his grievances for the moment. 'If I had a map at hand I could explain better. We were driven to and fro 'way up toward what we used to call Parry's Discoveries,[1] and lost our bearings. It was thick and foggy, and at last I lost my ship; she drove on a rock, and we managed to get ashore on what I took to be a barren island, the few of us that were left alive. When she first struck, the sea was somewhat calmer than it had been, and most of the crew, against orders, manned the long-boat and put off in a hurry, and were never heard of more. Our own boat upset, but the carpenter kept himself and me above water, and we drifted in. I had no strength to call upon after my recent fever, and laid down to die; but he found the tracks of a man and dog the second day, and got along the shore to one of those far missionary stations that the Moravians[2] support. They were very poor themselves, and in distress; 'twas a useless place. There were but few Esquimaux left in that region. There we remained for some time, and I became acquainted with strange events.'

The captain lifted his head and gave me a questioning glance. I could not help noticing that the dulled look in his eyes had gone, and there was instead a clear intentness that made them seem dark and piercing.

'There was a supply ship expected, and the pastor, an excellent Christian man, made no doubt that we should get passage in her. He was hoping that orders would come to break up the station; but everything was uncertain, and we got on the best we could for a while. We fished, and helped the people in other ways; there was no other way of paying our debts. I was taken to the pastor's house until I got better; but they were crowded, and I felt myself in the way, and made excuse to join with an old seaman, a Scotchman, who had built him a warm cabin, and had room in it for another. He was looked upon with regard, and had stood by the pastor in some troubles with the people. He had been on one of those English exploring parties[3] that found one end of the road to the north pole, but never could find the other. We lived like dogs in a kennel, or so you'd thought if you had seen the hut from the outside; but the main thing was to keep warm; there were piles of birdskins to lie on, and he'd made him a good bunk, and there was another for me. 'Twas dreadful dreary waitin' there; we begun to think the supply steamer was lost, and my poor ship broke up and strewed herself all along the shore. We got to watching on the headlands; my men and me knew the people were short of supplies and had to pinch themselves. It ought to read in the Bible, "Man cannot live by fish alone,"[4] if they'd told the truth of things; 't ain't bread that wears the worst on you! First part of the time, old Gaffett, that I lived with, seemed speechless, and I didn't know what to make of him, nor he of me, I dare say; but as we got acquainted, I found he'd been through more disasters than I had, and had troubles that wa'n't going to let him live a great while. It used to ease his mind to talk to an understanding person, so we used to sit and talk together all day, if it rained or blew so that we couldn't get out. I'd got a bad blow on the back of my head at the time we came ashore, and it pained me at times, and my strength was broken, anyway; I've never been so able since.'

Captain Littlepage fell into a reverie.

'Then I had the good of my reading,' he explained presently. 'I had no books; the pastor spoke but little English, and all his books were foreign; but I used to say over all I could remember. The old poets little knew what comfort they could be to a man. I was well acquainted with the works of Milton, but up there it did seem to me as if Shakespeare was the king; he has his sea terms very accurate, and some beautiful passages were calming to the mind. I could say them over until I shed tears; there was nothing beautiful to me in that place but the stars above and those passages of verse.

'Gaffett was always brooding and brooding, and talking to himself; he was afraid he should never get away, and it preyed upon his mind. He thought when I got home I could interest the scientific men in his discovery: but they're all taken up with their own notions; some didn't even take pains to answer the letters I wrote. You observe that I said this crippled man Gaffett had been shipped on a voyage of discovery. I now tell you that the ship was lost on its return, and only Gaffett and two officers were saved off the Greenland coast, and he had knowledge later that those men never got back to England; the brig they shipped on was run down in the night. So no other living soul had the facts, and he gave them to me. There is a strange sort of a country 'way up north beyond the ice, and strange folks living in it. Gaffett believed it was the next world to this.'

'What do you mean, Captain Littlepage?' I exclaimed. The old man was bending forward and whispering; he looked over his shoulder before he spoke the last sentence.

'To hear old Gaffett tell about it was something awful,' he said, going on with his story quite steadily after the moment of excitement had passed. ''Twas first a tale of dogs and sledges, and cold and wind and snow. Then they begun to find the ice grow rotten; they had been frozen in, and got into a current flowing north, far up beyond Fox Channel,[5] and they took to their boats when the ship got crushed, and this warm current took them out of sight of the ice, and into a great open sea; and they still followed it due north, just the very way they had planned to go. Then they struck a coast that wasn't laid down or charted, but the cliffs were such that no boat could land until they found a bay and struck across under sail to the other side where the shore looked lower; they were scant of provisions and out of water, but they got sight of something that looked like a great town. "For God's sake, Gaffett!" said I, the first time he told me. "You don't mean a town two degrees farther north than ships had ever been?" for he'd got their course marked on an old chart that he'd pieced out at the top; but he insisted upon it, and told it over and over again, to be sure I had it straight to carry to those who would be interested. There was no snow and ice, he said, after they had sailed some days with that warm current, which seemed to come right from under the ice that they'd been pinched up in and had been crossing on foot for weeks.'

'But what about the town?' I asked. 'Did they get to the town?'

'They did,' said the captain, 'and found inhabitants; 'twas an awful condition of things. It appeared, as near as Gaffett could express it, like a place where there was neither living nor dead. They could see the place when they were approaching it by sea pretty near like any town, and thick with habitations; but all at once they lost sight of it altogether, and when they got close inshore they could see the shapes of folks, but they never could get near them, – all blowing gray figures that would pass along alone, or sometimes gathered in companies as if they were watching. The men were frightened at first, but the shapes never came near them, – it was as if they blew back; and at last they all got bold and went ashore, and found birds' eggs and sea fowl, like any wild northern spot where creatures were tame and folks had never been and there was good water. Gaffett said that he and another man came near one o' the fog-shaped men that was going along slow with the look of a pack on his back, among the rocks, an' they chased him; but, Lord! he flittered away out o' sight like a leaf the wind takes with it, or a piece of cobweb. They would make as if they talked together, but there was no sound of voices, and "they acted as if they didn't see us, but only felt us coming towards them," says Gaffett one day, trying to tell the particulars. They couldn't see the town when they were ashore. One day the captain and the doctor were gone till night up across the high land where the town had seemed to be, and they came back at night beat out and white as ashes, and wrote and wrote all next day in their notebooks, and whispered together full of excitement, and they were sharp-spoken with the men when they offered to ask any questions.

'Then there came a day,' said Captain Littlepage, leaning toward me with a strange look in his eyes, and whispering quickly. 'The men all swore they wouldn't stay any longer; the man on watch early in the morning gave the alarm, and they all put off in the boat and got a little way out to sea. Those folks, or whatever they were, come about 'em like bats; all at once they raised incessant armies, and come as if to drive 'em back to sea. They stood thick at the edge o' the water like the ridges o' grim war; no thought o' flight, none of retreat. Sometimes a standing fight, then soaring on main wing tormented all the air.[6] And when they'd got the boat out o' reach o' danger, Gaffett said they looked back, and there was the town again, standing up just as they'd seen it first, comin' on the coast. Say what you might, they all believed 'twas a kind of waiting-place between this world an' the next.'

The captain had sprung to his feet in his excitement, and made excited gestures, but he still whispered huskily.

'Sit down, sir,' I said as quietly as I could, and he sank into his chair quite spent.

'Gaffett thought the officers were hurrying home to report and to fit out a new expedition when they were all lost. At the time, the men got orders not to talk over what they had seen,' the old man explained presently in a more natural tone.

'Weren't they all starving, and wasn't it a mirage or something of that sort?' I ventured to ask. But he looked at me blankly.

'Gaffett had got so that his mind ran on nothing else,' he went on. 'The ship's surgeon let fall an opinion to the captain, one day, that t'was some condition o' the light and the magnetic currents that let them see those folks. 'Twa'n't a right-feeling part of the world, anyway; they had to battle with the compass to make it serve, an' everything seemed to go wrong. Gaffett had worked it out in his own mind that they was all common ghosts, but the conditions were unusual favorable for seeing them. He was always talking about the Ge'graphical Society, but he never took proper steps, as I view it now, and stayed right there at the mission. He was a good deal crippled, and thought they'd confine him in some jail of a hospital. He said he was waiting to find the right men to tell, somebody bound north. Once in a while they stopped there to leave a mail or something. He was set in his notions, and let two or three proper explorin' expeditions go by him because he didn't like their looks; but when I was there he had got restless, fearin' he might be taken away or something. He had all his directions written out straight as a string to give the right ones. I wanted him to trust 'em to me, so I might have something to show, but he wouldn't. I suppose he is dead now. I wrote to him, an' I done all I could. 'Twill be a great exploit some o' these days.'

I assented absent-mindedly, thinking more just then of my companion's alert, determined look and the seafaring, ready aspect that had come to his face; but at this moment there fell a sudden change, and the old, pathetic, scholarly look returned. Behind me hung a map of North America,[7] and I saw, as I turned a little, that his eyes were fixed upon the northernmost regions and their careful recent outlines with a look of bewilderment.

7

THE OUTER ISLAND

Gaffett with his good bunk and the bird-skins, the story of the wreck of the *Minerva*, the human-shaped creatures of fog and cobweb, the great words of Milton with which he described their onslaught upon the crew, all this moving tale had such an air of truth that I could not argue with Captain Littlepage. The old man looked away from the map as if it had vaguely troubled him, and regarded me appealingly.

'We were just speaking of' – and he stopped. I saw that he had suddenly forgotten his subject.

'There were a great many persons at the funeral,' I hastened to say.

'Oh yes,' the captain answered, with satisfaction. 'All showed respect who could. The sad circumstances had for a moment slipped my mind. Yes, Mrs Begg will be very much missed. She was a capital manager for her husband when he was at sea. Oh yes, shipping is a very great loss.' And he sighed heavily. 'There was hardly a man of any standing who didn't interest himself in some way in navigation. It always gave credit to a town. I call it low-water mark now here in Dunnet.'

He rose with dignity to take leave, and asked me to stop at his house some day, when he would show me some outlandish things that he had brought home from sea. I was familiar with the subject of the decadence of shipping interests in all its affecting branches, having been already some time in Dunnet, and I felt sure that Captain Littlepage's mind had now returned to a safe level.

As we came down the hill toward the village our ways divided, and when I had seen the old captain well started on a smooth piece of sidewalk which would lead him to his own door, we parted, the best of friends. 'Step in some afternoon,' he said, as affectionately as if I were a fellow-shipmaster wrecked on the lee shore of age like himself. I turned toward home, and presently met Mrs Todd coming toward me with an anxious expression.

'I see you sleevin'¹ the old gentleman down the hill,' she suggested.

'Yes. I've had a very interesting afternoon with him,' I answered; and her face brightened.

'Oh, then he's all right. I was afraid 'twas one o' his flighty spells, an' Mari' Harris wouldn't' –

'Yes,' I returned, smiling, 'he has been telling me some old stories, but we talked about Mrs Begg and the funeral beside, and *Paradise Lost*.'

'I expect he got tellin' of you some o' his great narratives,' she answered, looking at me shrewdly. 'Funerals always sets him goin'. Some o' them tales hangs together toler'ble well,' she added, with a sharper look than before. 'An' he's been a great reader all his seafarin' days. Some thinks he overdid, and affected his head, but for a man o' his years he's amazin' now when he's at his best. Oh, he used to be a beautiful man!'

We were standing where there was a fine view of the harbor and its long stretches of shore all covered by the great army of the pointed firs, darkly cloaked and standing as if they waited to embark. As we looked far seaward among the outer islands, the trees seemed to march seaward still, going steadily over the heights and down to the water's edge.

It had been growing gray and cloudy, like the first evening of autumn, and a shadow had fallen on the darkening shore. Suddenly, as we looked, a gleam of golden sunshine struck the outer islands, and one of them shone out clear in the light, and revealed itself in a compelling way to our eyes. Mrs Todd was looking off across the bay with a face full of affection and interest. The sunburst upon that outermost island made it seem like a sudden revelation of the world beyond this which some believe to be so near.

'That's where mother lives,' said Mrs Todd. 'Can't we see it plain? I was brought up out there on Green Island. I know every rock an' bush on it.'

'Your mother!' I exclaimed, with great interest.

'Yes, dear, cert'in; I've got her yet, old's I be. She's one of them spry, light-footed little women; always was, an' light-hearted, too,' answered Mrs Todd, with satisfaction. 'She's seen all the trouble folks can see, without it's her last sickness; an' she's got a word of courage for everybody. Life ain't spoilt her a mite. She's eighty-six an' I'm sixty-seven, and I've seen the time I've felt a good sight the oldest. "Land sakes alive!" says she, last time I was out to see her. "How you do lurch about steppin' into a bo't!" I laughed so I liked to have gone right over into the water; an' we pushed off an' left her laughin' there on the shore.'

The light had faded as we watched. Mrs Todd had mounted a gray rock, and stood there grand and architectural, like a *caryatide*.[2] Presently she stepped down, and we continued our way homeward.

'You an' me, we'll take a bo't an' go out someday and see mother,' she promised me. ''Twould please her very much, an' there's one or two sca'ce herbs grows better on the island than anywheres else. I ain't seen their like nowheres here on the main.

'Now I'm goin' right down to get us each a mug o' my beer,' she announced as we entered the house, 'an' I believe I'll sneak in a little mite o' camomile.[3] Goin' to the funeral an' all, I feel to have had a very wearin' afternoon.'

I heard her going down into the cool little cellar, and then there was considerable delay. When she returned, mug in hand, I noticed the taste of camomile, in spite of my protest; but its flavor was disguised by some other herb that I did not know, and she stood over me until I drank it all and said that I liked it.

'I don't give that to everybody,' said Mrs Todd kindly; and I felt for a moment as it if were part of a spell and incantation, and as if my enchantress would now begin to look like the cobweb shapes of the arctic town. Nothing happened but a quiet evening and some delightful plans that we made about going to Green Island, and on the morrow there was the clear sunshine and blue sky of another day.

8

GREEN ISLAND

One morning, very early, I heard Mrs Todd in the garden outside my window. By the unusual loudness of her remarks to a passer-by, and the notes of a familiar hymn which she sang as she worked among the herbs, and which came as if directed purposely to the sleepy ears of my consciousness, I knew that she wished I would wake up and come and speak to her.

In a few minutes she responded to a morning voice from behind the blinds. 'I expect you're goin' up to your schoolhouse to pass all this pleasant day; yes, I expect you're goin' to be dreadful busy,' she said despairingly.

'Perhaps not,' said I. 'Why, what's going to be the matter with you, Mrs Todd?' For I supposed that she was tempted by the fine weather to take one of her favorite expeditions along the shore pastures to gather herbs and simples, and would like to have me keep the house.

'No, I don't want to go nowhere by land,' she answered gayly, – 'no, not by land; but I don't know's we shall have a better day all the rest of the summer to go out to Green Island an' see mother. I waked up early thinkin' of her. The wind's light northeast, – 'twill take us right straight out; an' this time o' year it's liable to change round southwest an' fetch us home pretty, 'long late in the afternoon. Yes, it's goin' to be a good day.'

'Speak to the captain and the Bowden boy, if you see anybody going by toward the landing,' said I. 'We'll take the big boat.'

'Oh, my sakes! now you let me do things my way,' said Mrs Todd scornfully. 'No, dear, we won't take no big bo't. I'll just git a handy dory,[1] an' Johnny Bowden an' me, we'll man her ourselves. I don't want no abler bo't than a good dory, an' a nice light breeze ain't goin' to make no sea; an' Johnny's my cousin's son, – mother'll like to have him come; an' he'll be down to the herrin' weirs all the time we're there, anyway; we don't want to carry no men folks havin' to be considered every minute an' takin' up all our time. No, you let me do; we'll just slip out an' see mother by ourselves. I guess what breakfast you'll want's about ready now.'

I had become well acquainted with Mrs Todd as landlady, herb-gatherer, and rustic philosopher; we had been discreet fellow-passengers once or twice when I had sailed up the coast to a larger town than Dunnet Landing to do some shopping; but I was yet to become acquainted with her as a mariner. An hour later we pushed off from the landing in the desired dory. The tide was just on the turn, beginning to fall, and several friends and acquaintances stood along the side of the dilapidated wharf and cheered us by their words and evident interest. Johnny Bowden and I were both rowing in haste to get out where we could catch the breeze and put up the small sail which lay clumsily furled along the gunwale. Mrs Todd sat aft, a stern and unbending law-giver.

'You better let her drift; we'll get there 'bout as quick; the tide'll take her right out from under these old buildin's; there's plenty wind outside.'

'Your bo't ain't trimmed proper, Mis' Todd!' exclaimed a voice from shore. 'You're lo'ded so the bo't'll drag; you can't git her before the wind, ma'am. You set 'midships, Mis' Todd, an' let the boy hold the sheet 'n' steer after he gits the sail up; you won't never git out to Green Island that way. She's lo'ded bad, your bo't is, – she's heavy behind's she is now!'

Mrs Todd turned with some difficulty and regarded the anxious adviser, my right oar flew out of water, and we seemed about to capsize. 'That you, Asa? Good-mornin',' she said politely. 'I al'ays liked the starn seat best. When'd you git back from up country?'

This allusion to Asa's origin was not lost upon the rest of the company. We were some little distance from shore, but we could hear a chuckle of laughter, and Asa, a person who was too ready with his criticism and advice on every possible subject, turned and walked indignantly away.

When we caught the wind we were soon on our seaward course, and only stopped to underrun a trawl,[2] for the floats of which Mrs Todd looked earnestly, explaining that her mother might not be prepared for three extra to dinner; it was her brother's trawl, and she meant to just run her eye along for the right sort of a little haddock. I leaned over the boat's side with great interest and excitement, while she skillfully handled the long line of hooks, and made scornful remarks upon worthless, bait-consuming creatures of the sea as she reviewed them and left them on the trawl or shook them off into the waves. At last we came to what she pronounced a proper haddock, and having taken him on board and ended his life resolutely, we went our way.

As we sailed along I listened to an increasingly delightful commentary upon the islands, some of them barren rocks, or at best giving sparse pasturage for sheep in the early summer. On one of these an eager little flock ran to the water's edge and bleated at us so affectingly that I would willingly have stopped; but Mrs Todd steered away from the rocks, and scolded at the sheep's mean owner, an acquaintance of hers, who grudged the little salt and still less care which the patient creatures needed. The hot midsummer sun makes prisons of these small islands that are a paradise in early June, with their cool springs and short thick-growing grass. On a larger island, farther out to sea, my entertaining companion showed me with glee the small houses of two farmers who shared the island between them, and declared that for three generations the people had not spoken to each other even in times of sickness or death or birth. 'When the news come that the war[3] was over, one of 'em knew it a week, and never stepped across his wall to tell the others,' she said. 'There, they enjoy it: they've got to have somethin' to interest 'em in such a place; 'tis a good deal more tryin' to be tied to folks you don't like than 'tis to be alone. Each of 'em tells the neighbors their wrongs; plenty likes to hear and tell again; them as fetch a bone'll carry one, an' so they keep the fight a-goin'. I must say I like variety myself; some folks washes Monday an' irons Tuesday the whole year round even if the circus is goin' by!'

A long time before we landed at Green Island we could see the small white house, standing high like a beacon, where Mrs Todd was born and where her mother lived, on a green slope above the water, with dark spruce woods still higher. There were crops in the fields, which we presently distinguished from one another. Mrs Todd examined them while we were still far at sea. 'Mother's late potatoes looks backward; ain't had rain enough so far,' she pronounced her opinion. 'They look weedier than what they call Front Street down to Cowper Centre. I expect brother William is so occupied with his herrin' weirs[4] an' servin' out bait to the schooners[5] that he don't think once a day of the land.'

'What's the flag for, up above the spruces there behind the house?' I inquired, with eagerness.

'Oh, that's the sign for herrin',' she explained kindly, while Johnny Bowden regarded me with contemptuous surprise. 'When they get enough for schooners they raise that flag; an' when 'tis a poor catch in the weir pocket they just fly a little signal down by the shore, an' then the small bo'ts comes and get enough an' over for their trawls. There, look! there she is: mother sees us; she's wavin' somethin' out o' the fore door! She'll be to the landin'-place quick's we are.'

I looked, and could see a tiny flutter in the doorway, but a quicker signal had made its way from the heart on shore to the heart on the sea.

'How do you suppose she knows it's me?' said Mrs Todd, with a tender smile on her broad face. 'There, you never get over bein' a child long's you have a mother to go to. Look at the chimney, now; she's gone right in an' brightened up the fire. Well, there, I'm glad mother's well; you'll enjoy seein' her very much.'

Mrs Todd leaned back into her proper position, and the boat trimmed again. She took a firmer grasp of the sheet, and gave an impatient look up at the gaff and the leech of the little sail, and twitched the sheet[6] as if she urged the wind like a horse. There came at once a fresh gust, and we seemed to have doubled our speed. Soon we were near enough to see a tiny figure with handkerchiefed head come down across the field and stand waiting for us at the cove above a curve of pebble beach.

Presently the dory grated on the pebbles, and Johnny Bowden, who had been kept in abeyance during the voyage, sprang out and used manful exertions to haul us up with the next wave, so that Mrs Todd could make a dry landing.

'You done that very well,' she said, mounting to her feet, and coming ashore somewhat stiffly, but with great dignity, refusing our outstretched hands, and returning to possess herself of a bag which had lain at her feet.

'Well, mother, here I be!' she announced with indifference; but they stood and beamed in each other's faces.

'Lookin' pretty well for an old lady, ain't she?' said Mrs Todd's mother, turning away from her daughter to speak to me. She was a delightful little person herself, with bright eyes and an affectionate air of expectation like a child on a holiday. You felt as if Mrs Blackett were an old and dear friend before you let go her cordial hand. We all started together up the hill.

'Now don't you haste too fast, mother,' said Mrs Todd warningly; ''tis a far reach o' risin' ground to the fore door, and you won't set an' get your breath when you're once there, but go trotting about. Now don't you go a mite faster than we proceed with this bag an' basket. Johnny, there, 'll fetch up the haddock. I just made one stop to underrun William's trawl till I come to jes' such a fish's I thought you'd want to make one o' your nice chowders of. I've brought an onion with me that was layin' about on the window-sill at home.'

'That's just what I was wantin',' said the hostess. 'I give a sigh when you spoke o' chowder, knowin' my onions was out. William forgot to replenish us last time he was to the Landin'. Don't you haste so yourself, Almiry, up this risin' ground. I hear you commencin' to wheeze a'ready.'

This mild revenge seemed to afford great pleasure to both giver and receiver. They laughed a little, and looked at each other affectionately, and then at me. Mrs Todd considerately paused, and faced about to regard the wide sea view. I was glad to stop, being more out of breath than either of my companions, and I prolonged the halt by asking the names of the neighboring islands. There was a fine breeze blowing, which we felt more there on the high land than when we were running before it in the dory.

'Why, this ain't that kitten I saw when I was out last, the one that I said didn't appear likely?'[7] exclaimed Mrs Todd as we went our way.

'That's the one, Almiry,' said her mother. 'She always had a likely look to me, an' she's right after her business. I never see such a mouser for one of her age. If 'twan't for William, I never should have housed that other dronin' old thing so long; but he sets by her on account of her havin' a bob tail. I don't deem it advisable to maintain cats just on account of their havin' bob tails; they're like all other curiosities, good for them that wants to see 'em twice. This kitten catches mice for both, an' keeps me respectable as I ain't been for a year. She's a real understandin' little help, this kitten is. I picked her from among five Miss Augusta Pennell had over to Burnt Island,' said the old woman, trudging along with the kitten close at her skirts. 'Augusta, she says to me, "Why, Mis' Blackett, you've took the homeliest," an' says I, "I've got the smartest; I'm satisfied."'

'I'd trust nobody sooner'n you to pick out a kitten, mother,' said the daughter handsomely, and we went on in peace and harmony.

The house was just before us now, on a green level that looked as if a huge hand had scooped it out of the long green field we had been ascending. A little way above, the dark spruce woods began to climb the top of the hill and cover the seaward slopes of the island. There was just room for the small farm and the forest; we looked down at the fish-house and its rough sheds, and the weirs stretching far out into the water. As we looked upward, the tops of the firs came sharp against the blue sky. There was a great stretch of rough pasture-land round the shoulder of the island to the eastward, and here were all the thick-scattered gray rocks that kept their places, and the gray backs of many sheep that forever wandered and fed on the thin sweet pasturage that fringed the ledges and made soft hollows and strips of green turf like growing velvet. I could see the rich green of bayberry bushes here and there, where the rocks made room. The air was very sweet; one could not help wishing to be a citizen of such a complete and tiny continent and home of fisherfolk.

The house was broad and clean, with a roof that looked heavy on its low walls. It was one of the houses that seem firm-rooted in the ground, as if they were two thirds below the surface, like icebergs. The front door stood hospitably open in expectation of company and an orderly vine grew at each side; but our path led to the kitchen door at the house-end, and there grew a mass of gay flowers and greenery, as if they had been swept together by some diligent garden broom into a tangled heap: there were portulacas[8] all along under the lower step and straggling off into the grass, and clustering mallows[9] that crept as near as they dared, like poor relations. I saw the bright eyes and brainless little heads of two half-grown chickens who were snuggled down among the mallows as if they had been chased away from the door more than once, and expected to be again.

'It seems kind o' formal comin' in this way,' said Mrs Todd impulsively, as we passed the flowers and came to the front doorstep; but she was mindful of the proprieties, and walked before us into the best room on the left.

'Why, mother, if you haven't gone an' turned the carpet!' she exclaimed, with something in her voice that spoke of awe and admiration. 'When'd you get to it? I s'pose Mis' Addicks come over an' helped you from White Island Landing?'

'No, she didn't,' answered the old woman, standing proudly erect, and making the most of a great moment. 'I done it all myself with William's help. He had a spare day, an' took right holt with me; an' 'twas all well beat on the grass, an' turned, an' put down again afore we went to bed. I ripped an' sewed over two o' them long breadths. I ain't had such a good night's sleep for two years.'

'There, what do you think o' havin' such a mother as that for eighty-six year old?' said Mrs Todd, standing before us like a large figure of Victory.[10]

As for the mother, she took on a sudden look of youth; you felt as if she promised a great future, and was beginning, not ending, her summers and their happy toils.

'My, my!' exclaimed Mrs Todd. 'I couldn't ha' done it myself, I've got to own it.'

'I was much pleased to have it off my mind,' said Mrs Blackett, humbly; 'the more so because along at the first of the next week I wasn't very well. I suppose it may have been the change of weather.'

Mrs Todd could not resist a significant glance at me, but, with charming sympathy, she forbore to point the lesson or to connect this illness with its apparent cause. She loomed larger than ever in the little old-fashioned best room, with its few pieces of good furniture and pictures of national interest. The green paper curtains were stamped with conventional landscapes of a foreign order, – castles on inaccessible crags, and lovely lakes with steep wooded shores; under-foot the treasured carpet was covered thick with home-made rugs. There were empty glass lamps and crystallized bouquets of grass and some fine shells on the narrow mantelpiece.

'I was married in this room,' said Mrs Todd unexpectedly; and I heard her give a sigh after she had spoken, as if she could not help the touch of regret that would forever come with all her thoughts of happiness.

'We stood right there between the windows,' she added, 'and the minister stood here. William wouldn't come in. He was always odd about seein' folks, just's he is now. I run to meet 'em from a child, an' William, he'd take an' run away.'

'I've been the gainer,' said the old mother cheerfully. 'William has been son an' daughter both since you was married off the island. He's been 'most too satisfied to stop at home 'long o' his old mother, but I always tell 'em I'm the gainer.'

We were all moving toward the kitchen as if by common instinct. The best room was too suggestive of serious occasions, and the shades were all pulled down to shut out the summer light and air. It was indeed a tribute to Society to find a room set apart for her behests out there on so apparently neighborless and remote an island. Afternoon visits and evening festivals must be few in such a bleak situation at certain seasons of the year, but Mrs Blackett was of those who do not live to themselves, and who have long since passed the line that divides mere self-concern from a valued share in whatever Society can give and take. There were those of her neighbors who never had taken the trouble to furnish a best room, but Mrs Blackett was one who knew the uses of a parlor.

'Yes, do come right out into the old kitchen; I shan't make any stranger of you,' she invited us pleasantly, after we had been properly received in the room appointed to formality. 'I expect Almiry, here, 'll be driftin' out 'mongst the pasture-weeds quick's she can find a good excuse. 'Tis hot now. You'd better content yourselves till you get nice an' rested, an' 'long after dinner the sea-breeze'll spring up, an' then you can take your walks, an' go up an' see the prospect from the big ledge. Almiry'll want to show off everything there is. Then I'll get you a good cup o' tea before you start to go home. The days are plenty long now.'

While we were talking in the best room the selected fish had been mysteriously brought up from the shore, and lay all cleaned and ready in an earthen crock on the table.

'I think William might have just stopped an' said a word,' remarked Mrs

Todd, pouting with high affront as she caught sight of it. 'He's friendly enough when he comes ashore, an' was remarkable social the last time, for him.'

'He ain't disposed to be very social with the ladies,' explained William's mother, with a delightful glance at me, as if she counted upon my friendship and tolerance. 'He's very particular, and he's all in his old fishin'-clothes today. He'll want me to tell him everything you said and done, after you've gone. William has very deep affections. He'll want to see you, Almiry. Yes, I guess he'll be in by an' by.'

'I'll search for him by 'n' by, if he don't,' proclaimed Mrs Todd, with an air of unalterable resolution. 'I know all of his burrows down 'long the shore. I'll catch him by hand 'fore he knows it. I've got some business with William, anyway. I brought forty-two cents with me that was due him for them last lobsters he brought in.'

'You can leave it with me,' suggested the little old mother, who was already stepping about among her pots and pans in the pantry, and preparing to make the chowder.

I became possessed of a sudden unwonted curiosity in regard to William, and felt that half the pleasure of my visit would be lost if I could not make his interesting acquaintance.

9

WILLIAM

Mrs Todd had taken the onion out of her basket and laid it down upon the kitchen table. 'There's Johnny Bowden come with us, you know,' she reminded her mother. 'He'll be hungry enough to eat his size.'

'I've got new doughnuts, dear,' said the little old lady. 'You don't often catch William 'n' me out o' provisions. I expect you might have chose a somewhat larger fish, but I'll try an' make it do. I shall have to have a few extra potatoes, but there's a field full out there, an' the hoe's leanin' against the well-house, in 'mongst the climbin'-beans.' She smiled, and gave her daughter a commanding nod.

'Land sakes alive! Le' 's blow the horn for William,' insisted Mrs Todd, with some excitement. 'He needn't break his spirit so far's to come in. He'll know you need him for something particular, an' then we can call to him as he comes up the path. I won't put him to no pain.'

Mrs Blackett's old face, for the first time, wore a look of trouble, and I found it necessary to counteract the teasing spirit of Almira. It was too pleasant to stay indoors altogether, even in such rewarding companionship; besides, I might meet William; and, straying out presently, I found the hoe by the well-house and an old splint basket at the woodshed door, and also found my way down to the field where there was a great square patch of rough, weedy potato-tops and tall ragweed. One corner was already dug, and I chose a fat-looking hill where the tops were well withered. There is all the pleasure that one can have in gold-digging in finding one's hopes satisfied in the riches of a good hill of potatoes. I longed to go on; but it did not seem frugal to dig any longer after my basket was full, and at last I took my hoe by the middle and lifted the basket to go back up the hill. I was sure that Mrs Blackett must be waiting impatiently to slice the potatoes into the chowder, layer after layer, with the fish.

'You let me take holt o' that basket, ma'am,' said a pleasant, anxious voice behind me.

I turned, startled in the silence of the wide field, and saw an elderly man, bent in the shoulders as fishermen often are, gray-headed and clean-shaven, and with a timid air. It was William. He looked just like his mother, and I had been imagining that he was large and stout like his sister, Almira Todd; and, strange to say, my fancy had led me to picture him not far from thirty and a little loutish. It was necessary instead to pay William the respect due to age.

I accustomed myself to plain facts on the instant, and we said good-morning like old friends. The basket was really heavy, and I put the hoe through its handle and offered him one end; then we moved easily toward the house together, speaking of the fine weather and of mackerel which were reported to be striking in all about the bay. William had been out since three o'clock, and had taken an extra fare of fish. I could feel that Mrs Todd's eyes were upon us as we approached the house, and although I fell behind in the narrow path, and let William take the basket alone and precede me at some little distance the rest of the way, I could plainly hear her greet him.

'Got round to comin' in, didn't you?' she inquired, with amusement. 'Well, now, that's clever. Didn't know's I should see you today, William, an' I wanted to settle an account.'

I felt somewhat disturbed and responsible, but when I joined them they were on most simple and friendly terms. It became evident that, with William, it was the first step that cost, and that, having once joined in social interests, he was able to pursue them with more or less pleasure. He was about sixty, and not young-looking for his years, yet so undying is the spirit of youth, and bashfulness has such a power of survival, that I felt all the time as if one must try to make the occasion easy for some one who was young and new to the affairs of social life. He asked politely if I would like to go up to the great ledge while dinner was getting ready; so, not without a deep sense of pleasure, and a delighted look of surprise from the two hostesses, we started, William and I, as if both of us felt much younger than we looked. Such was the innocence and simplicity of the moment that when I heard Mrs Todd laughing behind us in the kitchen I laughed too, but William did not even blush. I think he was a little deaf and he stepped along before me most businesslike and intent upon his errand.

We went from the upper edge of the field above the house into a smooth, brown path among the dark spruces. The hot sun brought out the fragrance of the pitchy bark, and the shade was pleasant as we climbed the hill. William stopped once or twice to show me a great wasps'-nest close by, or some fishhawks'-nests below in a bit of swamp. He picked a few sprigs of late-blooming linnæa[1] as we came out upon an open bit of pasture at the top of the island, and gave them to me without speaking, but he knew as well as I that one could not say half he wished about linnæa. Through this piece of rough pasture ran a huge shape of stone like the great backbone of an enormous creature. At the end, near the woods, we could climb up on it and walk along to the highest point; there above the circle of pointed firs we could look down over all the island, and could see the ocean that circled this and a hundred other bits of island-ground, the mainland shore and all the far horizons. It gave a sudden sense of space, for nothing stopped the eye or hedged one in, – that sense of liberty in space and time which great prospects always give.

'There ain't no such view in the world, I expect,' said William proudly, and I hastened to speak my heartfelt tribute of praise; it was impossible not to feel as if an untraveled boy had spoken, and yet one loved to have him value his native heath.

10

WHERE PENNYROYAL GREW

We were a little late to dinner, but Mrs Blackett and Mrs Todd were lenient, and we all took our places after William had paused to wash his hands, like a pious Brahmin, at the well, and put on a neat blue coat which he took from a peg behind the kitchen door. Then he resolutely asked a blessing in words that I could not hear, and we ate the chowder and were thankful. The kitten went round and round the table, quite erect, and, holding on by her fierce young claws, she stopped to mew with pathos at each elbow, or darted off to the open door when a song sparrow forgot himself and lit in the grass too near. William did not talk much, but his sister Todd occupied the time and told all the news there was to tell of Dunnet Landing and its coasts, while the old mother listened with delight. Her hospitality was something exquisite; she had the gift which so many women lack, of being able to make themselves and their houses belong entirely to a guest's pleasure, – that charming surrender for the moment of themselves and whatever belongs to them, so that they make a part of one's own life that can never be forgotten. Tact is after all a kind of mind-reading, and my hostess held the golden gift. Sympathy is of the mind as well as the heart, and Mrs Blackett's world and mine were one from the moment we met. Besides, she had that final, that highest gift of heaven, a perfect self-forgetfulness. Sometimes, as I watched her eager, sweet old face, I wondered why she had been set to shine on this lonely island of the northern coast. It must have been to keep the balance true, and make up to all her scattered and depending neighbors for other things which they may have lacked.

When we had finished clearing away the old blue plates, and the kitten had taken care of her share of the fresh haddock, just as we were putting back the kitchen chairs in their places, Mrs Todd said briskly that she must go up into the pasture now to gather the desired herbs.

'You can stop here an' rest, or you can accompany me,' she announced. 'Mother ought to have her nap, and when we come back she an' William'll sing for you. She admires music,' said Mrs Todd, turning to speak to her mother.

But Mrs Blackett tried to say that she couldn't sing as she used, and perhaps William wouldn't feel like it. She looked tired, the good old soul, or I should have liked to sit in the peaceful little house while she slept; I had had much pleasant experience of pastures already in her daughter's company. But it seemed best to go with Mrs Todd, and off we went.

Mrs Todd carried the gingham bag which she had brought from home, and a small heavy burden in the bottom made it hang straight and slender from her hand. The way was steep, and she soon grew breathless, so that we sat down to rest awhile on a convenient large stone among the bayberry.

'There, I wanted you to see this, – 'tis mother's picture,' said Mrs Todd; ''twas taken once when she was up to Portland, soon after she was married. That's me,' she added, opening another worn case, and displaying the full face of the cheerful child she looked like still in spite of being past sixty. 'And here's William an' father together. I take after father, large and heavy, an' William is like mother's folks, short an' thin. He ought to have made something o' himself, bein' a man an' so like mother; but though he's been very steady to work, an' kept up the farm, an' done his fishin' too right along, he never had mother's snap[1] an' power o' seein' things just as they be. He's got excellent judgment, too,' meditated William's sister, but she could not arrive at any satisfactory decision upon what she evidently thought his failure in life. 'I think it is well to see any one so happy an' makin' the most of life just as it falls to hand,' she said as she began to put the daguerreotypes[2] away again; but I reached out my hand to see her mother's once more, a most flowerlike face of a lovely young woman in quaint dress. There was in the eyes a look of anticipation and joy, a far-off look that sought the horizon; one often sees it in seafaring families, inherited by girls and boys alike from men who spend their lives at sea, and are always watching for distant sails or the first loom of the land.[3] At sea there is nothing to be seen close by, and this has its counterpart in a sailor's character, in the large and brave and patient traits that are developed, the hopeful pleasantness that one loves so in a seafarer.

When the family pictures were wrapped again in a big handkerchief, we set forward in a narrow footpath and made our way to a lonely place that faced northward, where there was more pasturage and fewer bushes, and we went down to the edge of short grass above some rocky cliffs where the deep sea broke with a great noise, though the wind was down and the water looked quiet a little way from shore. Among the grass grew such pennyroyal as the rest of the world could not provide. There was a fine fragrance in the air as we gathered it sprig by sprig and stepped along carefully, and Mrs Todd pressed her aromatic nosegay between her hands and offered it to me again and again.

'There's nothin' like it,' she said; 'oh no, there's no such pennyr'yal as this in the State of Maine. It's the right pattern of the plant, and all the rest I ever see is but an imitation.⁴ Don't it do you good?' And I answered with enthusiasm.

'There, dear, I never showed nobody else but mother where to find this place; 'tis kind of sainted to me. Nathan, my husband, an' I used to love this place when we was courtin', and' – she hesitated, and then spoke softly – 'when he was lost, 'twas just off shore tryin' to get in by the short channel out there between Squaw Islands, right in sight o' this headland where we'd set an' made our plans all summer long.'

I had never heard her speak of her husband before, but I felt that we were friends now since she had brought me to this place.

''Twas but a dream with us,' Mrs Todd said. 'I knew it when he was gone. I knew it' – and she whispered as if she were at confession – 'I knew it afore he started to go to sea. My heart was gone out o' my keepin' before I ever saw Nathan; but he loved me well, and he made me real happy, and he died before he ever knew what he'd had to know if we'd lived long together. 'Tis very strange about love. No, Nathan never found out, but my heart was troubled when I knew him first. There's more women likes to be loved than there is of those that loves. I spent some happy hours right here. I always liked Nathan, and he never knew. But this pennyr'yal always reminded me, as I'd sit and gather it and hear him talkin' – it always would remind me of – the other one.'

She looked away from me, and presently rose and went on by herself. There was something lonely and solitary about her great determined shape. She might have been Antigone alone on the Theban plain.⁵ It is not often given in a noisy world to come to the places of great grief and silence. An absolute, archaic grief possessed this countrywoman; she seemed like a renewal of some historic soul, with her sorrows and the remoteness of a daily life busied with rustic simplicities and the scents of primeval herbs.

I was not incompetent at herb-gathering, and after a while, when I had sat long enough waking myself to new thoughts, and reading a page of remembrance with new pleasure, I gathered some bunches, as I was bound to do, and at last we met again higher up the shore, in the plain everyday world we had left behind when we went down to the pennyroyal plot. As we walked together along the high edge of the field we saw a hundred sails about the bay and farther seaward; it was mid-afternoon or after, and the day was coming to an end.

'Yes, they're all makin' towards the shore, – the small craft an' the lobster smacks an' all,' said my companion. 'We must spend a little time with mother now, just to have our tea, an' then put for home.'

'No matter if we lose the wind at sundown; I can row in with Johnny,' said I; and Mrs Todd nodded reassuringly and kept to her steady plod, not quickening her gait even when we saw William come round the corner of the house as if to look for us, and wave his hand and disappear.

'Why, William's right on deck; I didn't know's we should see any more of him!' exclaimed Mrs Todd. 'Now mother'll put the kettle right on; she's got a good fire goin'.' I too could see the blue smoke thicken, and then we both walked a little faster, while Mrs Todd groped in her full bag of herbs to find the daguerreotypes and be ready to put them in their places.

THE OLD SINGERS

William was sitting on the side door step, and the old mother was busy making her tea; she gave into my hand an old flowered-glass tea-caddy.

'William thought you'd like to see this, when he was settin' the table. My father brought it to my mother from the island of Tobago; an' here's a pair of beautiful mugs that came with it.' She opened the glass door of a little cupboard beside the chimney. 'These I call my best things, dear,' she said. 'You'd laugh to see how we enjoy 'em Sunday nights in winter: we have a real company tea 'stead o' livin' right along just the same, an' I make somethin' good for a s'prise an' put on some o' my preserves, an' we get a-talkin' together an' have real pleasant times.'

Mrs Todd laughed indulgently, and looked to see what I thought of such childishness.

'I wish I could be here some Sunday evening,' said I.

'William an' me'll be talkin' about you an' thinkin' o' this nice day,' said Mrs Blackett affectionately, and she glanced at William, and he looked up bravely and nodded. I began to discover that he and his sister could not speak their deeper feelings before each other.

'Now I want you an' mother to sing,' said Mrs Todd abruptly, with an air of command, and I gave William much sympathy in his evident distress.

'After I've had my cup o' tea, dear,' answered the old hostess cheerfully; and so we sat down and took our cups and made merry while they lasted. It was impossible not to wish to stay on forever at Green Island, and I could not help saying so.

'I'm very happy here, both winter an' summer,' said old Mrs Blackett. 'William an' I never wish for any other home, do we, William? I'm glad you find it pleasant; I wish you'd come an' stay, dear, whenever you feel inclined. But here's Almiry; I always think Providence was kind to plot an' have her husband leave her a good house where she really belonged. She'd been very restless if she'd had to continue here on Green Island. You wanted more scope, didn't you, Almiry, an' to live in a large place where more things grew? Sometimes folks wonders that we don't live together; perhaps we shall some time,' and a shadow of sadness and apprehension flitted across her face. 'The time o' sickness an' failin' has got to come to all. But Almiry's got an herb that's good for everything.' She smiled as she spoke, and looked bright again.

'There's some herb that's good for everybody, except for them that thinks they're sick when they ain't,' announced Mrs Todd, with a truly professional air of finality. 'Come, William, let's have Sweet Home, an' then mother'll sing Cupid an' the Bee for us.'[1]

Then followed a most charming surprise. William mastered his timidity and began to sing. His voice was a little faint and frail, like the family daguerreotypes, but it was a tenor voice, and perfectly true and sweet. I have never heard Home, Sweet Home sung as touchingly and seriously as he sang it; he seemed to make it quite new; and when he paused for a moment at the end of the first line and began the next, the old mother joined him and they sang together, she missing only the higher notes, where he seemed to lend his voice to hers for the moment and carry on her very note and air. It was the silent man's real and only means of expression, and one could have listened forever, and have asked for more and more songs of old Scotch and English inheritance and the best that have lived from the ballad music of the war. Mrs Todd kept time visibly, and sometimes audibly, with her ample foot. I saw the tears in her eyes sometimes, when I could see beyond the tears in mine. But at last the songs ended and the time came to say good-by; it was the end of a great pleasure.

Mrs Blackett, the dear old lady, opened the door of her bedroom while Mrs Todd was tying up the herb bag, and William had gone down to get the boat ready and to blow the horn for Johnny Bowden, who had joined a roving boat party who were off the shore lobstering.

I went to the door of the bedroom, and thought how pleasant it looked, with its pink-and-white patchwork quilt and the brown unpainted paneling of its woodwork.

'Come right in, dear,' she said. 'I want you to set down in my old quilted rockin'-chair there by the window; you'll say it's the prettiest view in the house. I set there a good deal to rest me and when I want to read.'

There was a worn red Bible on the light-stand, and Mrs Blackett's heavy silver-bowed glasses; her thimble was on the narrow window-ledge, and folded carefully on the table was a thick striped-cotton shirt that she was making for her son. Those dear old fingers and their loving stitches, that heart which had made the most of everything that needed love! Here was the real home, the heart of the old house on Green Island! I sat in the rocking-chair, and felt that it was a place of peace, the little brown bedroom; and the quiet outlook upon field and sea and sky.

I looked up, and we understood each other without speaking. 'I shall like to think o' your settin' here today,' said Mrs Blackett. 'I want you to come again. It has been so pleasant for William.'

The wind served us all the way home, and did not fall or let the sail slacken until we were close to the shore. We had a generous freight of lobsters in the boat, and new potatoes which William had put aboard, and what Mrs Todd proudly called a full 'kag' of prime number one salted mackerel; and when we landed we had to make business arrangements to have these conveyed to her house in a wheelbarrow.

I never shall forget the day at Green Island. The town of Dunnet Landing seemed large and noisy and oppressive as we came ashore. Such is the power of contrast; for the village was so still that I could hear the shy whippoorwills singing that night as I lay awake in my downstairs bedroom, and the scent of Mrs Todd's herb garden under the window blew in again and again with every gentle rising of the sea-breeze.

12

A STRANGE SAIL

Except for a few stray guests, islanders or from the inland country, to whom Mrs Todd offered the hospitalities of a single meal, we were quite by ourselves all summer; and when there were signs of invasion, late in July, and a certain Mrs Fosdick appeared like a strange sail on the far horizon, I suffered much from apprehension. I had been living in the quaint little house with as much comfort and unconsciousness as if it were a larger body, or a double shell, in whose simple convolutions Mrs Todd and I had secreted ourselves, until some wandering hermit crab of a visitor marked the little spare room for her own. Perhaps now and then a castaway on a lonely desert island dreads the thought of being rescued. I heard of Mrs Fosdick for the first time with a selfish sense of objection; but after all, I was still vacation-tenant of the schoolhouse, where I could always be alone, and it was impossible not to sympathize with Mrs Todd, who, in spite of some preliminary grumbling, was really delighted with the prospect of entertaining an old friend.

For nearly a month we received occasional news of Mrs Fosdick, who seemed to be making a royal progress from house to house in the inland neighborhood, after the fashion of Queen Elizabeth. One Sunday after another came and went, disappointing Mrs Todd in the hope of seeing her guest at church and fixing the day for the great visit to begin; but Mrs Fosdick was not ready to commit herself to a date. As assurance of 'some time this week' was not sufficiently definite from a free-footed housekeeper's point of view, and Mrs Todd put aside all herb-gathering plans, and went through the various stages of expectation, provocation, and despair. At last she was ready to believe that Mrs Fosdick must have forgotten her promise and returned to her home, which was vaguely said to be over Thomaston way. But one evening, just as the supper-table was cleared and 'readied up,' and Mrs Todd had put her large apron over her head and stepped forth for an evening stroll in the garden, the unexpected happened. She heard the sound of wheels, and gave an excited cry to me, as I sat by the window, that Mrs Fosdick was coming right up the street.

'She may not be considerate, but she's dreadful good company,' said Mrs Todd hastily, coming back a few steps from the neighborhood of the gate. 'No, she ain't a mite considerate, but there's a small lobster left over from your tea; yes, it's a real mercy there's a lobster. Susan Fosdick might just as well have passed the compliment o' comin' an hour ago.'

'Perhaps she has had her supper,' I ventured to suggest, sharing the housekeeper's anxiety, and meekly conscious of an inconsiderate appetite for my own supper after a long expedition up the bay. There were so few emergencies of any sort at Dunnet Landing that this one appeared overwhelming.

'No, she's rode 'way over from Nahum Brayton's place. I expect they were busy on the farm, and couldn't spare the horse in proper season. You just sly out an' set the teakittle on again, dear, an' drop in a good han'ful o' chips; the fire's all alive. I'll take her right up to lay off her things, an' she'll be occupied with explanations an' gettin' her bunnit off, so you'll have plenty o' time. She's one I shouldn't like to have find me unprepared.'

Mrs Fosdick was already at the gate, and Mrs Todd now turned with an air of complete surprise and delight to welcome her.

'Why, Susan Fosdick,' I heard her exclaim in a fine unhindered voice, as if she were calling across a field, 'I come near giving of you up! I was afraid you'd gone an' 'portioned out my visit to somebody else. I s'pose you've been to supper?'

'Lor', no, I ain't, Almiry Todd,' said Mrs Fosdick cheerfully, as she turned, laden with bags and bundles, from making her adieux to the boy driver. 'I ain't had a mite o' supper, dear. I've been lottin'[1] all the way on a cup o' that best tea o' yourn, – some o' that Oolong[2] you keep in the little chist. I don't want none o' your useful herbs.'

'I keep that tea for ministers' folks,' gayly responded Mrs Todd. 'Come right along in, Susan Fosdick. I declare if you ain't the same old sixpence!'

As they came up the walk together, laughing like girls, I fled, full of cares, to the kitchen to brighten the fire and be sure that the lobster, sole dependence of a late supper, was well out of reach of the cat. There proved to be fine reserves of wild raspberries and bread and butter, so that I regained my composure, and waited impatiently for my own share of this illustrious visit to begin. There was an instant sense of high festivity in the evening air from the moment when our guest had so frankly demanded the Oolong tea.

The great moment arrived. I was formally presented at the stair-foot, and the two friends passed on to the kitchen, where I soon heard a hospitable clink of crockery and the brisk stirring of a teacup. I sat in my high-backed rocking-chair by the window in the front room with an unreasonable feeling of being left out, like the child who stood at the gate in Hans Andersen's story.³ Mrs Fosdick did not look, at first sight, like a person of great social gifts. She was a serious-looking little bit of an old woman, with a birdlike nod of the head. I had often been told that she was the 'best hand in the world to make a visit,' – as if to visit were the highest of vocations; that everybody wished for her, while few could get her; and I saw that Mrs Todd felt a comfortable sense of distinction in being favored with the company of this eminent person who 'knew just how'. It was certainly true that Mrs Fosdick gave both her hostess and me a warm feeling of enjoyment and expectation, as if she had the power of social suggestion to all neighboring minds.

The two friends did not reappear for at least an hour. I could hear their busy voices, loud and low by turns, as they ranged from public to confidential topics. At last Mrs Todd kindly remembered me and returned, giving my door a ceremonious knock before she stepped in, with the small visitor in her wake. She reached behind her and took Mrs Fosdick's hand as if she were young and bashful, and gave her a gentle pull forward.

'There, I don't know whether you're goin' to take to each other or not; no, nobody can't tell whether you'll suit each other, but I expect you'll get along some way, both having seen the world,' said our affectionate hostess. 'You can inform Mis' Fosdick how we found the folks out to Green Island the other day. She's always been well acquainted with mother. I'll slip out now an' put away the supper things an' set my bread to rise, if you'll both excuse me. You can come out an' keep me company when you get ready, either or both.' And Mrs Todd, large and amiable, disappeared and left us.

Being furnished not only with a subject of conversation, but with a safe refuge in the kitchen in case of incompatibility, Mrs Fosdick and I sat down, prepared to make the best of each other. I soon discovered that she, like many of the elder women of that coast, had spent a part of her life at sea, and was full of a good traveler's curiosity and enlightenment. By the time we thought it discreet to join our hostess we were already sincere friends.

You may speak of a visit's setting in as well as a tide's, and it was impossible, as Mrs Todd whispered to me, not to be pleased at the way this visit was setting in; a new impulse and refreshing of the social currents and seldom visited bays of memory appeared to have begun. Mrs Fosdick had been the mother of a large family of sons and daughters, – sailors and sailors' wives, – and most of them had died before her. I soon grew more or less acquainted with the histories of all their fortunes and misfortunes, and subjects of an intimate nature were no more withheld from my ears than if I had been a shell on the mantelpiece. Mrs Fosdick was not without a touch of dignity and elegance; she was fashionable in her dress but it was a curiously well-preserved provincial fashion of some years back. In a wider sphere one might have called her a woman of the world, with her unexpected bits of modern knowledge, but Mrs Todd's wisdom was an intimation of truth itself. She might belong to any age, like an idyl of Theocritus;[4] but while she always understood Mrs Fosdick, that entertaining pilgrim could not always understand Mrs Todd.

That very first evening my friends plunged into a borderless sea of reminiscences and personal news. Mrs Fosdick had been staying with a family who owned the farm where she was born, and she had visited every sunny knoll and shady field corner; but when she said that it might be for the last time, I detected in her tone something expectant of the contradiction which Mrs Todd promptly offered.

'Almiry,' said Mrs Fosdick, with sadness, 'you may say what you like, but I am one of nine brothers and sisters brought up on the old place, and we're all dead but me.'

'Your sister Dailey ain't gone, is she? Why, no, Louisa ain't gone!' exclaimed Mrs Todd, with surprise. 'Why, I never heard of that occurrence!'

'Yes'm; she passed away last October, in Lynn. She had made her distant home in Vermont State, but she was making a visit to her youngest daughter. Louisa was the only one of my family whose funeral I wasn't able to attend, but 'twas a mere accident. All the rest of us were settled right about home. I thought it was very slack of 'em in Lynn not to fetch her to the old place; but when I came to hear about it, I learned that they'd recently put up a very elegant monument, and my sister Dailey was always great for show. She'd just been out to see the monument the week before she was taken down, and admired it so much that they felt sure of her wishes.'

'So she's really gone, and the funeral was up to Lynn!' repeated Mrs Todd, as if to impress the sad fact upon her mind. 'She was some years younger than we be, too. I recollect the first day she ever came to school; 'twas that first year mother sent me inshore to stay with aunt Topham's folks and get my schooling. You fetched little Louisa to school one Monday mornin' in a pink dress an' her long curls, and she set between you an' me, and got cryin' after a while, so the teacher sent us home with her at recess.'

'She was scared of seeing so many children about her; there was only her and me and brother John at home then; the older boys were to sea with father, an' the rest of us wa'n't born,' explained Mrs Fosdick. 'That next fall we all went to sea together. Mother was uncertain till the last minute, as one may say. The ship was waiting orders, but the baby that then was, was born just in time, and there was a long spell of extra bad weather, so mother got about again before they had to sail, an' we all went. I remember my clothes were all left ashore in the east chamber in a basket where mother'd took them out o' my chist o' drawers an' left 'em ready to carry aboard. She didn't have nothing aboard, of her own, that she wanted to cut up for me, so when my dress wore out she just put me into a spare suit o' John's, jacket and trousers. I wasn't but eight years old an' he was most seven and large of his age. Quick as we made a port she went right ashore an' fitted me out pretty, but we was bound for the East Indies and didn't put in anywhere for a good while. So I had quite a spell o' freedom. Mother made my new skirt long because I was growing, and I poked about the deck after that, real discouraged, feeling the hem at my heels every minute, and as if youth was past and gone. I liked the trousers best; I used to climb the riggin' with 'em and frighten mother till she said an' vowed she'd never take me to sea again.'

I thought by the polite absent-minded smile on Mrs Todd's face this was no new story.

'Little Louisa was a beautiful child; yes, I always thought Louisa was very pretty,' Mrs Todd said. 'She was a dear little girl in those days. She favored your mother; the rest of you took after your father's folks.'

'We did certain,' agreed Mrs Fosdick, rocking steadily. 'There, it does seem so pleasant to talk with an old acquaintance that knows what you know. I see so many of these new folks nowadays, that seem to have neither past nor future. Conversation's got to have some root in the past, or else you've got to explain every remark you make, an' it wears a person out.'

Mrs Todd gave a funny little laugh. 'Yes'm, old friends is always best, 'less you can catch a new one that's fit to make an old one out of,' she said, and we gave an affectionate glance at each other which Mrs Fosdick could not have understood, being the latest comer to the house.

13

POOR JOANNA

One evening my ears caught a mysterious allusion which Mrs Todd made to Shell-heap Island. It was a chilly night of cold northeasterly rain, and I made a fire for the first time in the Franklin stove[1] in my room, and begged my two housemates to come in and keep me company. The weather had convinced Mrs Todd that it was time to make a supply of cough-drops, and she had been bringing forth herbs from dark and dry hiding-places, until now the pungent dust and odor of them had resolved themselves into one mighty flavor of spearmint that came from a simmering caldron of syrup in the kitchen. She called it done, and well done, and had ostentatiously left it to cool, and taken her knitting-work because Mrs Fosdick was busy with hers. They sat in the two rocking-chairs, the small woman and the large one, but now and then I could see that Mrs Todd's thoughts remained with the cough-drops. The time of gathering herbs was nearly over, but the time of syrups and cordials had begun.

The heat of the open fire made us a little drowsy, but something in the way Mrs Todd spoke of Shell-heap Island waked my interest. I waited to see if she would say any more, and then took a roundabout way back to the subject by saying what was first in my mind: that I wished the Green Island family were there to spend the evening with us, – Mrs Todd's mother and her brother William.

Mrs Todd smiled, and drummed on the arm of the rocking-chair. 'Might scare William to death,' she warned me; and Mrs Fosdick mentioned her intention of going out to Green Island to stay two or three days, if this wind didn't make too much sea.

'Where is Shell-heap Island?' I ventured to ask, seizing the opportunity.

'Bears nor'east somewheres about three miles from Green Island; right off-shore, I should call it about eight miles out,' said Mrs Todd. 'You never was there, dear; 'tis off the thoroughfares,[2] and a very bad place to land at best.'

'I should think 'twas,' agreed Mrs Fosdick, smoothing down her black silk apron. ''Tis a place worth visitin' when you once get there. Some o' the old folks was kind o' fearful about it. 'Twas 'counted a great place in old Indian times; you can pick up their stone tools 'most any time if you hunt about. There's a beautiful spring 'o water, too. Yes, I remember when they used to tell queer stories about Shell-heap Island. Some said 'twas a great bangeing-place³ for the Indians, and an old chief resided there once that ruled the winds; and others said they'd always heard that once the Indians come down from up country an' left a captive there without any bo't, an' 'twas too far to swim across to Black Island, so called, an' he lived there till he perished.'

'I've heard say he walked the island after that, and sharp-sighted folks could see him an' lose him like one o' them citizens Cap'n Littlepage was acquainted with up to the north pole,' announced Mrs Todd grimly. 'Anyway, there was Indians, – you can see their shell-heap that named the island; and I've heard myself that 'twas one o' their cannibal places, but I never could believe it. There never was no cannibals on the coast o' Maine. All the Indians o' these regions are tame-looking folks.'

'Sakes alive, yes!' exclaimed Mrs Fosdick. 'Ought to see them painted savages I've seen when I was young out in the South Sea Islands! That was the time for folks to travel, 'way back in the old whalin' days!'

'Whalin' must have been dull for a lady, hardly ever makin' a lively port, and not takin' in any mixed cargoes,' said Mrs Todd. 'I never desired to go a whalin' v'y'ge myself.'

'I used to return feelin' very slack an' behind the times, 'tis true,' explained Mrs Fosdick, 'but 'twas excitin', an' we always done extra well, and felt rich when we did get ashore. I liked the variety. There, how times have changed; how few seafarin' families there are left! What a lot o' queer folks there used to be about here, anyway, when we was young, Almiry. Everybody's just like everybody else, now; nobody to laugh about, and nobody to cry about.'

It seemed to me that there were peculiarities of character in the region of Dunnet Landing yet, but I did not like to interrupt.

'Yes,' said Mrs Todd after a moment of meditation, 'there was certain a good many curiosities of human natur' in this neighborhood years ago. There was more energy then, and in some the energy took a singular turn. In these days the young folks is all copy-cats, 'fraid to death they won't be all just alike; as for the old folks, they pray for the advantage o' bein' a little different.'

'I ain't heard of a copy-cat this great many years,' said Mrs Fosdick, laughing; ''twas a favorite term o' my grandmother's. No, I wa'n't thinking o' those things, but of them strange straying creatur's that used to rove the country. You don't see them now, or the ones that used to hive away in their own houses with some strange notion or other.'

I thought again of Captain Littlepage, but my companions were not reminded of his name; and there was brother William at Green Island, whom we all three knew.

'I was talking o' poor Joanna the other day. I hadn't thought of her for a great while,' said Mrs Fosdick abruptly. 'Mis' Brayton an' I recalled her as we sat together sewing. She was one o' your peculiar persons, wa'n't she? Speaking of such persons,' she turned to explain to me, 'there was a sort of a nun or hermit person lived out there for years all alone on Shell-heap Island. Miss Joanna Todd, her name was, – a cousin o' Almiry's late husband.'

I expressed my interest, but as I glanced at Mrs Todd I saw that she was confused by sudden affectionate feeling and unmistakable desire for reticence.

'I never want to hear Joanna laughed about,' she said anxiously.

'Nor I,' answered Mrs Fosdick reassuringly. 'She was crossed in love, – that was all the matter to begin with; but as I look back, I can see that Joanna was one doomed from the first to fall into a melancholy. She retired from the world for good an' all, though she was a well-off woman. All she wanted was to get away from folks; she thought she wasn't fit to live with anybody, and wanted to be free. Shell-heap Island come to her from her father, and first thing folks knew she'd gone off out there to live, and left word she didn't want no company. 'Twas a bad place to get to unless the wind an' tide were just right; 'twas hard work to make a landing.'

'What time of year was this?' I asked.

'Very late in the summer,' said Mrs Fosdick. 'No, I never could laugh at Joanna, as some did. She set everything by the young man an' they were going to marry in about a month, when he got bewitched with a girl 'way up the bay, and married her, and went off to Massachusetts. He wasn't well thought of, – there were those who thought Joanna's money was what had tempted him; but she'd given him her whole heart, an' she wa'n't so young as she had been. All her hopes were built on marryin', an' havin' a real home and somebody to look to; she acted just like a bird when its nest is spoilt. The day after she heard the news she was in dreadful woe, but the next she came to herself very quiet, and took the horse and wagon, and drove fourteen miles to the lawyer's, and signed a paper givin' her half of the farm to her brother. They never had got along very well together, but he didn't want to sign it, till she acted so distressed that he gave in. Edward Todd's wife was a good woman, who felt very bad indeed, and used every argument with Joanna; but Joanna took a poor old boat that had been her father's and lo'ded in a few things, and off she put all alone, with a good land breeze, right out to sea. Edward Todd ran down to the beach, an' stood there cryin' like a boy to see her go, but she was out o' hearin'. She never stepped foot on the mainland again long as she lived.'

'How large an island is it? How did she manage in winter?' I asked.

'Perhaps thirty acres, rocks and all,' answered Mrs Todd, taking up the story gravely. 'There can't be much of it that the salt spray don't fly over in storms. No, 'tis a dreadful small place to make a world of; it has a different look from any of the other islands, but there's a sheltered cove on the south side, with mud-flats across one end of it at low water where there's excellent clams, and the big shell-heap keeps some o' the wind off a little house her father took the trouble to build when he was a young man. They said there was an old house built o' logs there before that, with a kind of natural cellar in the rock under it. He used to stay out there days to a time, and anchor a little sloop⁴ he had, and dig clams to fill it, and sail up to Portland. They said the dealers always gave him an extra price, the clams were so noted. Joanna used to go out and stay with him. They were always great companions, so she knew just what 'twas out there. There was a few sheep that belonged to her brother an' her, but she bargained for him to come and get them on the edge o' cold weather. Yes, she desired him to come for the sheep; an' his wife thought perhaps Joanna'd return, but he said no, an' lo'ded the bo't with warm things an' what he thought she'd need through the winter. He come home with the sheep an' left the other things by the house, but she never so much as looked out o' the window. She done it for a penance. She must have wanted to see Edward by that time.'

Mrs Fosdick was fidgeting with eagerness to speak.

'Some thought the first cold snap would set her ashore, but she always remained,' concluded Mrs Todd soberly.

'Talk about the men not having any curiosity!' exclaimed Mrs Fosdick scornfully. 'Why, the waters round Shell-heap Island were white with sails all that fall. 'Twas never called no great of a fishin'-ground before. Many of 'em made excuse to go ashore to get water at the spring; but at last she spoke to a bo't-load, very dignified and calm, and said that she'd like it better if they'd make a practice of getting water to Black Island or somewheres else and leave her alone, except in case of accident or trouble. But there was one man who had always set everything by her from a boy. He'd have married her if the other hadn't come about an' spoilt his chance, and he used to get close to the island, before light, on his way out fishin', and throw a little bundle 'way up the green slope front o' the house. His sister told me she happened to see the first time what a pretty choice he made o' useful things that a woman would feel lost without. He stood off fishin', and could see them in the grass all day, though sometimes she'd come out and walk right by them. There was other bo'ts near, out after mackerel. But early next morning his present was gone. He didn't presume too much, but once he took her a nice firkin o' things he got up to Portland, and when spring come he landed her a hen and chickens in a nice little coop. There was a good many old friends had Joanna on their minds.'

'Yes,' said Mrs Todd, losing her sad reserve in the growing sympathy of these reminiscences. 'How everybody used to notice whether there was smoke out of the chimney. The Black Island folks could see her with their spy-glass, and if they'd ever missed getting some sign o' life they'd have sent notice to her folks. But after the first year or two Joanna was more and more forgotten as an every-day charge. Folks lived very simple in those days, you know,' she continued, as Mrs Fosdick's knitting was taking much thought at the moment. 'I expect there was always plenty of driftwood thrown up, and a poor failin' patch of spruces covered all the north side of the island, so she always had something to burn. She was very fond of workin' in the garden ashore, and that first summer she began to till the little field out there, and raised a nice parcel o' potatoes. She could fish, o' course, and there was all her clams an' lobsters. You can always live well in any wild place by the sea when you'd starve to death up country, except 'twas berry time. Joanna had berries out there, blackberries at least, and there was a few herbs in case she needed them. Mullein in great quantities and a plant o' wormwood I remember seeing once when I stayed there, long before she fled out to Shell-heap. Yes, I recall the wormwood, which is always a planted herb, so there must have been folks there before the Todd's day. A growin' bush makes the best gravestone; I expect that wormwood always stood for somebody's solemn monument. Catnip, too, is a very endurin' herb about an old place.'[5]

'But what I want to know is what she did for other things,' interrupted Mrs Fosdick. 'Almiry, what did she do for clothin' when she needed to replenish, or risin' for her bread, or the piece-bag[6] that no woman can live long without?'

'Or company,' suggested Mrs Todd. 'Joanna was one that loved her friends. There must have been a terrible sight o' long winter evenin's that first year.'

'There was her hens,' suggested Mrs Fosdick, after reviewing the melancholy situation. 'She never wanted the sheep after that first season. There wa'n't no proper pasture for sheep after the June grass was past, and she ascertained the fact and couldn't bear to see them suffer; but the chickens done well. I remember sailin' by one spring afternoon, an' seein' the coops out front o' the house in the sun. How long was it before you went out with the minister? You were the first ones that ever really got ashore to see Joanna.'

I had been reflecting upon a state of society which admitted such personal freedom and a voluntary hermitage. There was something mediæval in the behavior of poor Joanna Todd under a disappointment of the heart. The two women had drawn closer together, and were talking on, quite unconscious of a listener.

'Poor Joanna!' said Mrs Todd again, and sadly shook her head as if there were things one could not speak about.

'I called her a great fool,' declared Mrs Fosdick, with spirit, 'but I pitied her then, and I pity her far more now. Some other minister would have been a great help to her, – one that preached self-forgetfulness and doin' for others to cure our own ills; but Parson Dimmick was a vague person, well meanin', but very numb in his feelin's. I don't suppose at that troubled time Joanna could think of any way to mend her troubles except to run off and hide.'

'Mother used to say she didn't see how Joanna lived without having nobody to do for, getting her own meals and tending her own poor self day in an' day out,' said Mrs Todd sorrowfully.

'There was the hens,' repeated Mrs Fosdick kindly. 'I expect she soon came to makin' folks o' them. No, I never went to work to blame Joanna, as some did. She was full o' feeling, and her troubles hurt her more than she could bear. I see it all now as I couldn't when I was young.'

'I suppose in old times they had their shut-up convents for just such folks,' said Mrs Todd, as if she and her friend had disagreed about Joanna once, and were now in happy harmony. She seemed to speak with new openness and freedom. 'Oh yes, I was only too pleased when the Reverend Mr Dimmick invited me to go out with him. He hadn't been very long in the place when Joanna left home and friends. 'Twas one day that next summer after she went, and I had been married early in the spring. He felt that he ought to go out and visit her. She was a member of the church, and might wish to have him consider her spiritual state. I wa'n't so sure o' that, but I always liked Joanna, and I'd come to be her cousin by marriage. Nathan an' I had conversed about goin' out to pay her a visit, but he got his chance to sail sooner'n he expected. He always thought everything of her, and last time he come home, knowing nothing of her change, he brought her a beautiful coral pin from a port he'd touched at somewheres up the Mediterranean. So I wrapped the little box in a nice piece of paper and put it in my pocket, and picked her a bunch of fresh lemon balm,[7] and off we started.'

Mrs Fosdick laughed. 'I remember hearin' about your trials on the v'y'ge,' she said.

'Why, yes,' continued Mrs Todd in her company manner. 'I picked her the balm, an' we started. Why, yes, Susan, the minister liked to have cost me my life that day. He would fasten the sheet,[8] though I advised against it. He said the rope was rough an' cut his hand. There was a fresh breeze, an' he went on talking rather high flown, an' I felt some interested. All of a sudden there come up a gust, and he give a screech and stood right up and called for help, 'way out there to sea. I knocked him right over into the bottom o' the bo't, getting by to catch hold of the sheet an' untie it. He wasn't but a little man; I helped him right up after the squall passed, and made a handsome apology to him, but he did act kind o' offended.'

'I do think they ought not to settle them landlocked folks in parishes where they're liable to be on the water,' insisted Mrs Fosdick. 'Think of the families in our parish that was scattered all about the bay, and what a sight o' sails you used to see, in Mr Dimmick's day, standing across to the mainland on a pleasant Sunday morning, filled with church-going folks, all sure to want him some time or other! You couldn't find no doctor that would stand up in the boat and screech if a flaw struck her.'

'Old Dr Bennett had a beautiful sailboat, didn't he?' responded Mrs Todd. 'And how well he used to brave the weather! Mother always said that in time o' trouble that tall white sail used to look like an angel's wing comin' over the sea to them that was in pain. Well, there's a difference in gifts. Mr Dimmick was not without light.'

' 'Twas light o' the moon, then,' snapped Mrs Fosdick; 'he was pompous enough, but I never could remember a single word he said. There, go on, Mis' Todd; I forget a great deal about that day you went to see poor Joanna.'

'I felt she saw us coming, and knew us a great way off; yes, I seemed to feel it within me,' said our friend, laying down her knitting. 'I kept my seat, and took the bo't inshore without saying a word; there was a short channel that I was sure Mr Dimmick wasn't acquainted with, and the tide was very low. She never came out to warn us off nor anything, and I thought, as I hauled the bo't up on a wave and let the Reverend Mr Dimmick step out, that it was somethin' gained to be safe ashore. There was a little smoke out o' the chimney o' Joanna's house, and it did look sort of homelike and pleasant with wild mornin'-glory vines trained up; an' there was a plot o' flowers under the front window, portulacas and things. I believe she'd made a garden once, when she was stopping there with her father, and some things must have seeded in. It looked as if she might have gone over to the other side of the island. 'Twas neat and pretty all about the house, and a lovely day in July. We walked up from the beach together very sedate, and I felt for poor Nathan's little pin to see if 'twas safe in my dress pocket. All of a sudden Joanna come right to the fore door and stood there, not sayin' a word.'

14

THE HERMITAGE

My companions and I had been so intent upon the subject of the conversation that we had not heard anyone open the gate, but at this moment, above the noise of the rain, we heard a loud knocking. We were all startled as we sat by the fire, and Mrs Todd rose hastily and went to answer the call, leaving her rocking-chair in violent motion. Mrs Fosdick and I heard an anxious voice at the door speaking of a sick child, and Mrs Todd's kind, motherly voice inviting the messenger in: then we waited in silence. There was a sound of heavy dropping of rain from the eaves, and the distant roar and undertone of the sea. My thoughts flew back to the lonely woman on her outer island; what separation from humankind she must have felt, what terror and sadness, even in a summer storm like this!

'You send right after the doctor if she ain't better in half an hour,' said Mrs Todd to her worried customer as they parted; and I felt a warm sense of comfort in the evident resources of even so small a neighborhood, but for the poor hermit Joanna there was no neighbor on a winter night.

'How did she look?' demanded Mrs Fosdick, without preface, as our large hostess returned to the little room with a mist about her from standing long in the wet doorway, and the sudden draught of her coming beat out the smoke and flame from the Franklin stove. 'How did poor Joanna look?'

'She was the same as ever, except I thought she looked smaller,' answered Mrs Todd after thinking a moment; perhaps it was only a last considering thought about her patient. 'Yes, she was just the same, and looked very nice, Joanna did. I had been married since she left home, an' she treated me like her own folks. I expected she'd look strange, with her hair turned gray in a night or somethin', but she wore a pretty gingham dress I'd often seen her wear before she went away; she must have kept it nice for best in the afternoons. She always had beautiful, quiet manners. I remember she waited till we were close to her, and then kissed me real affectionate, and inquired for Nathan before she shook hands with the minister, and then she invited us both in. 'Twas the same little house her father had built him when he was a bachelor, with one livin'-room, and a little mite of a bedroom out of it where she slept, but 'twas neat as a ship's cabin. There was some old chairs, an' a seat made of a long box that might have held boat tackle an' things to lock up in his fishin' days, and a good enough stove so anybody could cook and keep warm in cold weather. I went over once from home and stayed 'most a week with Joanna when we was girls, and those young happy days rose up before me. Her father was busy all day fishin' or clammin'; he was one o' the pleasantest men in the world, but Joanna's mother had the grim streak, and never knew what 'twas to be happy. The first minute my eyes fell upon Joanna's face that day I saw how she had grown to look like Mis' Todd. 'Twas the mother right over again.'

'Oh dear me!' said Mrs Fosdick.

'Joanna had done one thing very pretty. There was a little piece o' swamp on the island where good rushes grew plenty, and she'd gathered 'em, and braided some beautiful mats for the floor and a thick cushion for the long bunk. She'd showed a good deal of invention; you see there was a nice chance to pick up pieces o' wood and boards that drove ashore, and she'd made good use o' what she found. There wasn't no clock, but she had a few dishes on a shelf, and flowers set about in shells fixed to the walls, so it did look sort of homelike, though so lonely and poor. I couldn't keep the tears out o' my eyes, I felt so sad. I said to myself, I must get mother to come over an' see Joanna; the love in mother's heart would warm her, an' she might be able to advise.'

'Oh no, Joanna was dreadful stern,' said Mrs Fosdick.

'We were all settin' down very proper, but Joanna would keep stealin' glances at me as if she was glad I come. She had but little to say; she was real polite an' gentle, and yet forbiddin'. The minister found it hard,' confessed Mrs Todd; 'he got embarrassed, an' when he put on his authority and asked her if she felt to enjoy religion in her present situation, an' she replied that she must be excused from answerin', I thought I should fly. She might have made it easier for him; after all, he was the minister and had taken some trouble to come out, though 'twas kind of cold an' unfeelin' the way he inquired. I thought he might have seen the little old Bible a-layin' on the shelf close by him, an' I wished he knew enough to just lay his hand on it an' read somethin' kind an' fatherly 'stead of accusin' her, an' then given poor Joanna his blessin' with the hope she might be led to comfort. He did offer prayer, but 'twas all about hearin' the voice o' God out o' the whirlwind; and I thought while he was goin' on that anybody that had spent the long cold winter all alone out on Shell-heap Island knew a good deal more about those things than he did. I got so provoked I opened my eyes and stared right at him.

'She didn't take no notice, she kep' a nice respectful manner towards him, and when there come a pause she asked if he had any interest about the old Indian remains, and took down some queer stone gouges and hammers off of one of her shelves and showed them to him same's if he was a boy. He remarked that he'd like to walk over an' see the shell-heap; so she went right to the door and pointed him the way. I see then that she'd made her some kind o' sandal-shoes out o' the fine rushes to wear on her feet; she stepped light an' nice in 'em as shoes.'

Mrs Fosdick leaned back in her rocking-chair and gave a heavy sigh.

'I didn't move at first, but I'd held out just as long as I could,' said Mrs Todd, whose voice trembled a little. 'When Joanna returned from the door, an' I could see that man's stupid back departin' among the wild rose bushes, I just ran to her an' caught her in my arms. I wasn't so big as I be now, and she was older than me, but I hugged her tight, just as if she was a child. "Oh, Joanna dear," I says, "won't you come ashore an' live 'long o' me at the Landin', or go over to Green Island to mother's when winter comes? Nobody shall trouble you, an' mother finds it hard bein' alone. I can't bear to leave you here" – and I burst right out crying. I'd had my own trials, young as I was, an' she knew it. Oh, I did entreat her; yes, I entreated Joanna.'

'What did she say then?' asked Mrs Fosdick, much moved.

'She looked the same way, sad an' remote through it all,' said Mrs Todd mournfully. 'She took hold of my hand, and we sat down close together; 'twas as if she turned round an' made a child of me. "I haven't got no right to live with folks no more," she said. "You must never ask me again, Almiry: I've done the only thing I could do, and I've made my choice. I feel a great comfort in your kindness, but I don't deserve it. I have committed the unpardonable sin;[1] you don't understand," says she humbly. "I was in great wrath and trouble, and my thoughts was so wicked towards God that I can't expect ever to be forgiven. I have come to know what it is to have patience, but I have lost my hope. You must tell those that ask how 'tis with me," she said, "an' tell them I want to be alone." I couldn't speak; no, there wa'n't anything I could say, she seemed so above everything common. I was a good deal younger then than I be now, and I got Nathan's little coral pin out o' my pocket and put in into her hand; and when she saw it and I told her where it come from, her face did really light up for a minute, sort of bright an' pleasant. "Nathan an' I was always good friends; I'm glad he don't think hard of me," says she. "I want you to have it, Almiry, an' wear it for love o' both o' us," and she handed it back to me. "You give my love to Nathan, – he's a dear good man," she said; "an' tell your mother, if I should be sick she mustn't wish I could get well, but I want her to be the one to come." Then she seemed to have said all she wanted to, as if she was done with the world, and we sat there for a few minutes longer together. It was real sweet and quiet except for a good many birds and the sea rollin' up on the beach; but at last she rose, an' I did too, and she kissed me and held my hand in hers a minute, as if to say good-by; then she turned and went right away out o' the door and disappeared.

'The minister come back pretty soon, and I told him I was all ready, and we started down to the bo't. He had picked up some round stones and things and was carrying them in his pocket-handkerchief; an' he sat down amidships without making any question, and let me take the rudder an' work the bo't, an' made no remarks for some time, until we sort of eased it off speaking of the weather, an' subjects that arose as we skirted Black Island, where two or three families lived belongin' to the parish. He preached next Sabbath as usual, somethin' high soundin' about the creation, and I couldn't help thinkin' he might never get no further; he seemed to know no remedies, but he had a great use of words.'

Mrs Fosdick sighed again. 'Hearin' you tell about Joanna brings the time right back as if 'twas yesterday,' she said. 'Yes, she was one o' them poor things that talked about the great sin; we don't seem to hear nothing about the unpardonable sin now, but you may say 'twas not uncommon then.'

'I expect that if it had been in these days, a person would be plagued to death with idle folks,' continued Mrs Todd, after a long pause. 'As it was, nobody trespassed on her; all the folks about the bay respected her an' her feelings; but as time wore on, after you left here, one after another ventured to make occasion to put somethin' ashore for her if they went that way. I know mother used to go see her sometimes, and send William over now and then with something fresh an' nice from the farm. There is a point on the sheltered side where you can lay a boat close to shore an' land anything safe on the turf out o' reach o' the water. There were one or two others, old folks, that she would see, and now an' then she'd hail a passin' boat an' ask for somethin'; and mother got her to promise that she would make some sign to the Black Island folks if she wanted help. I never saw her myself to speak to after that day.'

'I expect nowadays, if such a thing happened, she'd have gone out West to her uncle's folks or up to Massachusetts and had a change, an' come home good as new. The world's bigger an' freer than it used to be,' urged Mrs Fosdick.

'No,' said her friend. ''Tis like bad eyesight, the mind of such a person: if your eyes don't see right there may be a remedy, but there's no kind of glasses to remedy the mind. No, Joanna was Joanna, and there she lays on her island where she lived and did her poor penance. She told mother the day she was dyin' that she always used to want to be fetched inshore when it come to the last; but she'd thought it over, and desired to be laid on the island, if 'twas thought right. So the funeral was out there, a Saturday afternoon in September. 'Twas a pretty day, and there wa'n't hardly a boat on the coast within twenty miles that didn't head for Shell-heap cram-full o' folks, an' all real respectful, same's if she'd always stayed ashore and held her friends. Some went out o' mere curiosity, I don't doubt, – there's always such to every funeral; but most had real feelin', and went purpose to show it. She'd got most o' the wild sparrows[2] as tame as could be, livin' out there so long among 'em, and one flew right in and lit on the coffin an' begun to sing while Mr Dimmick was speakin'. He was put out by it, an' acted as if he didn't know whether to stop or go on. I may have been prejudiced, but I wa'n't the only one thought the poor little bird done the best of the two.'

'What became o' the man that treated her so, did you ever hear?' asked Mrs Fosdick. 'I know he lived up to Massachusetts for a while. Somebody who came from the same place told me that he was in trade there an' doin' very well, but that was years ago.'

'I never heard anything more than that; he went to the war in one o' the early rigiments. No, I never heard any more of him,' answered Mrs Todd. 'Joanna was another sort of person, and perhaps he showed good judgment in marryin' somebody else, if only he'd behaved straightforward and manly. He was a shifty-eyed, coaxin' sort of man, that got what he wanted out o' folks, an' only gave when he wanted to buy, made friends easy and lost 'em without knowin' the difference. She'd had a piece o' work tryin' to make him walk accordin' to her right ideas, but she'd have had too much variety ever to fall into a melancholy. Some is meant to be the Joannas in this world, an' 'twas her poor lot.'

15

ON SHELL-HEAP ISLAND

Some time after Mrs Fosdick's visit was over and we had returned to our
former quietness, I was out sailing alone with Captain Bowden in his large
boat. We were taking the crooked northeasterly channel seaward, and were
well out from shore while it was still early in the afternoon. I found myself
presently among some unfamiliar islands, and suddenly remembered the
story of poor Joanna. There is something in the fact of a hermitage that
cannot fail to touch the imagination; the recluses are a sad kindred, but they
are never commonplace. Mrs Todd had truly said that Joanna was like one
of the saints in the desert; the loneliness of sorrow will forever keep alive
their sad succession.

'Where is Shell-heap Island!' I asked eagerly.

'You see Shell-heap now, layin' 'way out beyond Black Island there,'
answered the captain, pointing with outstretched arm as he stood, and
holding the rudder with his knee.

'I should like very much to go there,' said I, and the captain, without
comment, changed his course a little more to the eastward and let the reef
out of his mainsail.[1]

'I don't know's we can make an easy landin' for ye,' he remarked
doubtfully. 'May get your feet wet; bad place to land. Trouble is I ought to
have brought a tag-boat;[2] but they clutch on to the water so, an' I do love to
sail free. This gre't boat gets easy bothered with anything trailin'. 'Tain't
breakin' much on the meetin'-house ledges; guess I can fetch[3] in to Shell-
heap.'

'How long is it since Miss Joanna Todd died?' I asked, partly by way of
explanation.

'Twenty-two years come September,' answered the captain, after reflection. 'She died the same year my oldest boy was born, an' the town house
was burnt over to the Port. I didn't know but you merely wanted to hunt
for some o' them Indian relics. Long's you want to see where Joanna lived –

No, 'tain't breaking over the ledges; we'll manage to fetch across the shoals somehow, 'tis such a distance to go 'way round, and tide's a-risin',' he ended hopefully, and we sailed steadily on, the captain speechless with intent watching of a difficult course, until the small island with its low whitish promontory lay in full view before us under the bright afternoon sun.

The month was August, and I had seen the color of the islands change from the fresh green of June to a sunburnt brown that made them look like stone, except where the dark green of the spruces and fir balsam kept the tint that even winter storms might deepen, but not fade. The few wind-bent trees on Shell-heap Island were mostly dead and gray, but there were some low-growing bushes, and a stripe of light green ran along just above the shore, which I knew to be wild morning-glories. As we came close I could see the high stone walls of a small square field though there were no sheep left to assail it; and below, there was a little harbor-like cove where Captain Bowden was boldly running the great boat in[4] to seek a landing-place. There was a crooked channel of deep water which led close up against the shore.

'There, you hold fast for'ard there,[5] an' wait for her to lift on the wave. You'll make a good landin' if you're smart; right on the port-hand side!' the captain called excitedly; and I, standing ready with high ambition, seized my chance and leaped over to the grassy bank.

'I'm beat if I ain't aground after all!' mourned the captain despondently.

But I could reach the bowsprit, and he pushed with the boat-hook, while the wind veered round a little as if on purpose and helped with the sail; so presently the boat was free and began to drift out from shore.

'Used to call this p'int Joanna's wharf privilege, but 't has worn away in the weather since her time. I thought one or two bumps wouldn't hurt us none, – paint's got to be renewed, anyway, – but I never thought she'd tetch. I figured on shyin' by,'[6] the captain apologized. 'She's too gre't a boat to handle well in here; but I used to sort of shy by in Joanna's day, an' cast a little somethin' ashore – some apples or a couple o' pears if I had 'em – on the grass, where she'd be sure to see.'

I stood watching while Captain Bowden cleverly found his way back to deeper water. 'You needn't make no haste,' he called to me; 'I'll keep within call. Joanna lays right up there in the far corner o' the field. There used to be a path led to the place. I always knew her well. I was out here to the funeral.'

I found the path; it was touching to discover that this lonely spot was not without its pilgrims. Later generations will know less and less of Joanna herself, but there are paths trodden to the shrines of solitude the world over, – the world cannot forget them, try as it may; the feet of the young find them out because of curiosity and dim foreboding, while the old bring hearts full of remembrance. This plain anchorite had been one of those whom sorrow made too lonely to brave the sight of men, too timid to front the simple world she knew, yet valiant enough to live alone with her poor insistent human nature and the calms and passions of the sea and sky.

The birds were flying all about the field; they fluttered up out of the grass at my feet as I walked along, so tame that I liked to think they kept some happy tradition from summer to summer of the safety of nests and good fellowship of mankind. Poor Joanna's house was gone except the stones of its foundations, and there was little trace of her flower garden except a single faded sprig of much-enduring French pinks, which a great bee and a yellow butterfly were befriending together. I drank at the spring, and thought that now and then someone would follow me from the busy, hard-worked, and simple-thoughted countryside of the mainland, which lay dim and dreamlike in the August haze, as Joanna must have watched it many a day. There was the world, and here was she with eternity well begun. In the life of each of us, I said to myself, there is a place remote and islanded, and given to endless regret or secret happiness; we are each the uncompanioned hermit and recluse of an hour or a day; we understand our fellows of the cell to whatever age of history they may belong.

But as I stood alone on the island, in the sea-breeze, suddenly there came a sound of distant voices; gay voices and laughter from a pleasure-boat that was going seaward full of boys and girls. I knew, as if she had told me, that poor Joanna must have heard the like on many and many a summer afternoon, and must have welcomed the good cheer in spite of hopelessness and winter weather, and all the sorrow and disappointment in the world.

16

THE GREAT EXPEDITION

Mrs Todd never by any chance gave warning overnight of her great projects and adventures by sea and land. She first came to an understanding with the primal forces of nature, and never trusted to any preliminary promise of good weather, but examined the day for herself in its infancy. Then, if the stars were propitious, and the wind blew from a quarter of good inheritance whence no surprises of sea-turns or southwest sultriness might be feared, long before I was fairly awake I used to hear a rustle and knocking like a great mouse in the walls, and an impatient tread on the steep garret stairs that led to Mrs Todd's chief place of storage. She went and came as if she had already started on her expedition with utmost haste and kept returning for something that was forgotten. When I appeared in quest of my breakfast, she would be absent-minded and sparing of speech, as if I had displeased her, and she was now, by main force of principle, holding herself back from altercation and strife of tongues.

These signs of a change became familiar to me in the course of time, and Mrs Todd hardly noticed some plain proofs of divination one August morning when I said, without preface, that I had just seen the Beggs' best chaise go by, and that we should have to take the grocery. Mrs Todd was alert in a moment.

'There! I might have known!' she exclaimed. 'It's the 15th of August, when he goes and gets his money. He heired an annuity from an uncle o' his on his mother's side. I understood the uncle said none o' Sam Begg's wife's folks should make free with it, so after Sam's gone it'll all be past an' spent, like last summer. That's what Sam prospers on now, if you can call it prosperin'. Yes, I might have known. 'Tis the 15th o' August with him, an' he gener'ly stops to dinner with a cousin's widow on the way home. Feb'uary an' August is the times. Takes him 'bout all day to go an' come.'

I heard this explanation with interest. The tone of Mrs Todd's voice was complaining at the last.

'I like the grocery just as well as the chaise,'[1] I hastened to say, referring to a long-bodied high wagon with a canopy-top, like an attenuated four-posted bedstead on wheels, in which we sometimes journeyed. 'We can put things in behind – roots and flowers and raspberries, or anything you are going after – much better than if we had the chaise.'

Mrs Todd looked stony and unwilling. 'I counted upon the chaise,' she said, turning her back to me, and roughly pushing back all the quiet tumblers on the cupboard shelf as if they had been impertinent. 'Yes, I desired the chaise for once. I ain't goin' berryin' nor to fetch home no more wilted vegetation this year. Season's about past, except for a poor few o' late things,' she added in a milder tone. 'I'm goin' up country. No, I ain't intendin' to go berryin'. I've been plottin' for it the past fortnight and hopin' for a good day.'

'Would you like to have me go too?' I asked frankly, but not without a humble fear that I might have mistaken the purpose of this latest plan.

'Oh certain, dear!' answered my friend affectionately. 'Oh no, I never thought o' anyone else for comp'ny, if it's convenient for you, long's poor mother ain't come I ain't nothin' like so handy with a conveyance as I be with a good bo't. Comes o' my early bringing-up. I expect we've got to make that great high wagon do. The tires want settin' and 'tis all loose-jointed, so I can hear it shackle the other side o' the ridge. We'll put the basket in front. I ain't goin' to have it bouncin' an' twirlin' all the way. Why, I've been makin' some nice hearts and 'rounds[2] to carry.'

These were signs of high festivity, and my interest deepened moment by moment.

'I'll go down to the Beggs' and get the horse just as soon as I finish my breakfast,' said I. 'Then we can start whenever you are ready.'

Mrs Todd looked cloudy again. 'I don't know but you look nice enough to go just as you be,' she suggested doubtfully. 'No, you wouldn't want to wear that pretty blue dress o' yourn 'way up country. 'Tain't dusty now, but it may be comin' home. No, I expect you'd rather not wear that and the other hat.'

'Oh yes. I shouldn't think of wearing these clothes,' said I, with sudden illumination. 'Why, if we're going up country and are likely to see some of your friends, I'll put on my blue dress, and you must wear your watch; I am not going at all if you mean to wear the big hat.'

'Now you're behavin' pretty,' responded Mrs Todd, with a gay toss of her head and a cheerful smile, as she came across the room, bringing a saucerful of wild raspberries, a pretty piece of salvage from supper-time. 'I was cast down when I see you come to breakfast. I didn't think 'twas just what you'd select to wear to the reunion, where you're goin' to meet everybody.'

'What reunion do you mean?' I asked, not without amazement. 'Not the Bowden Family's? I thought that was going to take place in September.'

'Today's the day. They sent word the middle o' the week. I thought you might have heard of it. Yes, they changed the day. I been thinkin' we'd talk it over, but you never can tell beforehand how it's goin' to be, and 'tain't worth while to wear a day all out before it comes.' Mrs Todd gave no place to the pleasures of anticipation, but she spoke like the oracle that she was. 'I wish my mother was here to go,' she continued sadly. 'I did look for her last night, and I couldn't keep back the tears when the dark really fell and she wa'n't here, she does so enjoy a great occasion. If William had a mite o' snap an' ambition, he'd take the lead at such a time. Mother likes variety, and there ain't but a few nice opportunities 'round here, an' them she has to miss 'less she contrives to get ashore to me. I do re'lly hate to go to the reunion without mother, an' 'tis a beautiful day; everybody'll be asking where she is. Once she'd have got here anyway. Poor mother's beginnin' to feel her age.'

'Why, there's your mother now!' I exclaimed with joy, I was so glad to see the dear old soul again. 'I hear her voice at the gate.' But Mrs Todd was out of the door before me.

There, sure enough, stood Mrs Blackett, who must have left Green Island before daylight. She had climbed the steep road from the water-side so eagerly that she was out of breath, and was standing by the garden fence to rest. She held an old-fashioned brown wicker cap-basket in her hand, as if visiting were a thing of every day, and looked up at us as pleased and triumphant as a child.

'Oh, what a poor, plain garden! Hardly a flower in it except your bush o' balm!' she said. 'But you do keep your garden neat, Almiry. Are you both well, an' goin' up country with me?' She came a step or two closer to meet us, with quaint politeness and quite as delightful as if she were at home. She dropped a quick little curtsey before Mrs Todd.

'There, mother, what a girl you be! I am so pleased! I was just bewailin' you,' said the daughter, with unwonted feeling. 'I was just bewailin' you, I was so disappointed, an' I kep' myself awake a good piece o' the night scoldin' poor William. I watched for the boat till I was ready to shed tears yesterday, and when 'twas comin' dark I kep' making errands out to the gate an' down the road to see if you wa'n't in the doldrums somewhere down the bay.'

'There was a head wind, as you know,' said Mrs Blackett, giving me the cap-basket, and holding my hand affectionately as we walked up the clean-swept path to the door. 'I was partly ready to come, but dear William said I should be all tired out and might get cold, havin' to beat all the way in. So we give it up, and set down and spent the evenin' together. It was a little rough and windy outside, and I guess 'twas better judgment; we went to bed very early and made a good start just at daylight. It's been a lovely mornin' on the water. William thought he'd better fetch across beyond Bird Rocks, rowin' the greater part o' the way; then we sailed from there right over to the Landin', makin' only one tack.[3] William'll be in again for me tomorrow, so I can come back here an' rest me over night, an' go to meetin' tomorrow, and have a nice, good visit.'

'She was just havin' her breakfast,' said Mrs Todd, who had listened eagerly to the long explanation without a word of disapproval, while her face shone more and more with joy. 'You just sit right down an' have a cup of tea and rest you while we make our preparations. Oh, I am so gratified to think you've come! Yes, she was just havin' her breakfast, and we were speakin' of you. Where's William?'

'He went right back; he said he expected some schooners in about noon after bait, but he'll come an' have his dinner with us tomorrow, unless it rains; then next day. I laid his best things out all ready,' explained Mrs Blackett, a little anxiously. 'This wind will serve him nice all the way home. Yes, I will take a cup of tea, dear, – a cup of tea is always good; and then I'll rest a minute and be all ready to start.'

'I do feel condemned for havin' such hard thoughts o' William,' openly confessed Mrs Todd. She stood before us so large and serious that we both laughed and could not find it in our hearts to convict so rueful a culprit. 'He shall have a good dinner tomorrow, if it can be got, and I shall be real glad to see William,' the confession ended handsomely, while Mrs Blackett smiled approval and made haste to praise the tea. Then I hurried away to make sure of the grocery wagon. Whatever might be the good of the reunion, I was going to have the pleasure and delight of a day in Mrs Blackett's company, not to speak of Mrs Todd's.

The early morning breeze was still blowing, and the warm, sunshiny air was of some ethereal northern sort, with a cool freshness as if it came over new-fallen snow. The world was filled with a fragrance of fir-balsam and the faintest flavor of seaweed from the ledges, bare and brown at low tide in the little harbor. It was so still and so early that the village was but half awake. I could hear no voices but those of the birds, small and great, – the constant song sparrows, the clink of a yellow-hammer over in the woods, and the far conversation of some deliberate crows. I saw William Blackett's escaping sail already far from land, and Captain Littlepage was sitting behind his closed window as I passed by, watching for some one who never came. I tried to speak to him, but he did not see me. There was a patient look on the old man's face, as if the world were a great mistake and he had nobody with whom to speak his own language or find companionship.

17

A COUNTRY ROAD

Whatever doubts and anxieties I may have had about the inconvenience of the Beggs' high wagon for a person of Mrs Blackett's age and shortness, they were happily overcome by the aid of a chair and her own valiant spirit. Mrs Todd bestowed great care upon seating us as if we were taking passage by boat, but she finally pronounced that we were properly trimmed. When we had gone only a little way up the hill she remembered that she had left the house door wide open, though the large key was safe in her pocket. I offered to run back, but my offer was met with lofty scorn, and we lightly dismissed the matter from our minds, until two or three miles further on we met the doctor, and Mrs Todd asked him to stop and ask her nearest neighbor to step over and close the door if the dust seemed to blow in the afternoon.

'She'll be there in her kitchen; she'll hear you the minute you call; 'twont give you no delay,' said Mrs Todd to the doctor. 'Yes, Mis' Dennett's right there, with the windows all open. It isn't as if my fore door opened right on the road, anyway.' At which proof of composure Mrs Blackett smiled wisely at me.

The doctor seemed delighted to see our guest; they were evidently the warmest friends, and I saw a look of affectionate confidence in their eyes. The good man left his carriage to speak to us, but as he took Mrs Blackett's hand he held it a moment, and, as if merely from force of habit, felt her pulse as they talked; then to my delight he gave the firm old wrist a commending pat.

'You're wearing well: good for another ten years at this rate,' he assured her cheerfully, and she smiled back. 'I like to keep a strict account of my old stand-bys,' and he turned to me. 'Don't you let Mrs Todd overdo today, – old folks like her are apt to be thoughtless;' and then we all laughed, and, parting, went our ways gayly.

'I suppose he puts up with your rivalry the same as ever?' asked Mrs

Blackett. 'You and he are as friendly as ever, I see, Almiry,' and Almira sagely nodded.

'He's got too many long routes now to stop to 'tend to all his door patients,' she said, 'especially them that takes pleasure in talkin' themselves over. The doctor and me have got to be kind of partners; he's gone a good deal, far an' wide. Looked tired, didn't he? I shall have to advise with him an' get him off for a good rest. He'll take the big boat from Rockland an' go off up to Boston an' mouse round among the other doctors, once in two or three years and come home fresh as a boy. I guess they think consider'ble of him up there.' Mrs Todd shook the reins and reached determinedly for the whip, as if she were compelling public opinion.

Whatever energy and spirit the white horse had to begin with were soon exhausted by the steep hills and his discernment of a long expedition ahead. We toiled slowly along. Mrs Blackett and I sat together, and Mrs Todd sat alone in front with much majesty and the large basket of provisions. Part of the way the road was shaded by thick woods, but we also passed one farmhouse after another on the high uplands, which we all three regarded with deep interest, the house itself and the barns and garden-spots and poultry all having to suffer an inspection of the shrewdest sort. This was a highway quite new to me; in fact, most of my journeys with Mrs Todd had been made afoot and between the roads, in open pasture-lands. My friend stopped several times for brief dooryard visits, and made so many promises of stopping again on the way home that I began to wonder how long the expedition would last. I had often noticed how warmly Mrs Todd was greeted by her friends, but it was hardly to be compared to the feeling now shown toward Mrs Blackett. A look of delight came to the faces of those who recognized the plain, dear old figure beside me; one revelation after another was made of the constant interest and intercourse that had linked the far island and these scattered farms into a golden chain of love and dependence.

'Now, we mustn't stop again if we can help it,' insisted Mrs Todd at last. 'You'll get tired, mother, and you'll think the less o' reunions. We can visit along here any day. There, if they ain't frying doughnuts in this next house, too! These are new folks, you know, from over St George way; they took this old Talcot farm last year. 'Tis the best water on the road, and the check-rein's[1] come undone – yes, we'd best delay a little and water the horse.'

We stopped, and seeing a party of pleasure-seekers in holiday attire, the thin, anxious mistress of the farmhouse came out with wistful sympathy to hear what news we might have to give. Mrs Blackett first spied her at the

half-closed door, and asked with such cheerful directness if we were trespass-
ing that, after a few words, she went back to her kitchen and reappeared
with a plateful of doughnuts.

'Entertainment for man and beast,' announced Mrs Todd with satisfaction.
'Why, we've perceived there was new doughnuts all along the road, but
you're the first that has treated us.'

Our new acquaintance flushed with pleasure, but said nothing.

'They're very nice; you've had good luck with 'em,' pronounced Mrs
Todd. 'Yes, we've observed there was doughnuts all the way along; if one
house is frying all the rest is; 'tis so with a great many things.'

'I don't suppose likely you're goin' up to the Bowden reunion?' asked the
hostess as the white horse lifted his head and we were saying goodbye.

'Why, yes,' said Mrs Blackett and Mrs Todd and I, all together.

'I am connected with the family. Yes, I expect to be there this afternoon.
I've been lookin' forward to it,' she told us eagerly.

'We shall see you there. Come and sit with us if it's convenient,' said dear
Mrs Blackett, and we drove away.

'I wonder who she was before she was married?' said Mrs Todd, who was
usually unerring in matters of genealogy. 'She must have been one of that
remote branch that lived down beyond Thomaston. We can find out this
afternoon. I expect that the families'll march together, or be sorted out some
way. I'm willing to own a relation that has such proper ideas of doughnuts.'

'I seem to see the family looks,' said Mrs Blackett. 'I wish we'd asked
her name. She's a stranger, and I want to help make it pleasant for all
such.'

'She resembles Cousin Pa'lina Bowden about the forehead,' said Mrs
Todd with decision.

We had just passed a piece of woodland that shaded the road, and come
out to some open fields beyond, when Mrs Todd suddenly reined in the
horse as if somebody had stood on the roadside and stopped her. She even
gave that quick reassuring nod of her head which was usually made to
answer for a bow, but I discovered that she was looking eagerly at a tall ash-
tree that grew just inside the field fence.

'I thought 'twas goin' to do well,' she said complacently as we went on
again. 'Last time I was up this way that tree was kind of drooping and
discouraged. Grown trees act that way sometimes, same's folks; then they'll
put right to it and strike their roots off into new ground and start all over
again with real good courage. Ash-trees is very likely to have poor spells;
they ain't got the resolution of other trees.'

I listened hopefully for more, it was this peculiar wisdom that made one value Mrs Todd's pleasant company.

'There's sometimes a good hearty tree growin' right out of the bare rock, out o' some crack that just holds the roots;' she went on to say, 'right on the pitch o' one o' them bare stony hills where you can't seem to see a wheel-barrowful o' good earth in a place, but that tree'll keep a green top in the driest summer. You lay your ear down to the ground an' you'll hear a little stream runnin'. Every such tree has got its own livin' spring; there's folks made to match 'em.'

I could not help turning to look at Mrs Blackett, close beside me. Her hands were clasped placidly in their thin black woolen gloves, and she was looking at the flowery wayside as we went slowly along, with a pleased, expectant smile. I do not think she had heard a word about the trees.

'I just saw a nice plant o' elecampane growin' back there,' she said presently to her daughter.

'I haven't got my mind on herbs today,' responded Mrs Todd, in the most matter-of-fact way. 'I'm bent on seeing folks,' and she shook the reins again.

I for one had no wish to hurry, it was so pleasant in the shady roads. The woods stood close to the road on the right; on the left were narrow fields and pastures where there were as many acres of spruces and pines as there were acres of bay and juniper and huckleberry, with a little turf between. When I thought we were in the heart of the inland country, we reached the top of a hill, and suddenly there lay spread out before us a wonderful great view of well-cleared fields that swept down to the wide water of a bay. Beyond this were distant shores like another country in the midday haze which half hid the hills beyond, and the far-away pale blue mountains on the northern horizon. There was a schooner with all sails set coming down the bay from a white village that was sprinkled on the shore, and there were many sailboats flitting about. It was a noble landscape, and my eyes, which had grown used to the narrow inspection of a shaded roadside, could hardly take it in.

'Why, it's the upper bay,' said Mrs Todd. 'You can see 'way over into the town of Fessenden. Those farms 'way over there are all in Fessenden. Mother used to have a sister that lived up that shore. If we started as early's we could on a summer mornin', we couldn't get to her place from Green Island till late afternoon, even with a fair, steady breeze, and you had to strike the time just right so as to fetch up 'long o' the tide and land near the flood.[2] 'Twas ticklish business, an' we didn't visit back an' forth as much as mother desired. You have to go 'way down the co'st to Cold Spring Light an' round that long point, – up here's what they call the Back Shore.'

'No, we were 'most always separated, my dear sister and me, after the first year she was married,' said Mrs Blackett. 'We had our little families an' plenty o' cares. We were always lookin' forward to the time we could see each other more. Now and then she'd get out to the island for a few days while her husband'd go fishin'; and once he stopped with her an' two children, and made him some flakes³ right there and cured all his fish for winter. We did have a beautiful time together, sister an' me; she used to look back to it long's she lived.

'I do love to look over there where she used to live,' Mrs Blackett went on as we began to go down the hill. 'It seems as if she must still be there, though she's long been gone. She loved their farm, – she didn't see how I got so used to our island; but somehow I was always happy from the first.'

'Yes, it's very dull to me up among those slow farms,' declared Mrs Todd. 'The snow troubles 'em in winter. They're all besieged by winter, as you may say; 'tis far better by the shore than up among such places. I never thought I should like to live up country.'

'Why, just see the carriages ahead of us on the next rise!' exclaimed Mrs Blackett. 'There's going to be a great gathering, don't you believe there is, Almiry? It hasn't seemed up to now as if anybody was going but us. An' 'tis such a beautiful day, with yesterday cool and pleasant to work an' get ready, I shouldn't wonder if everybody was there, even the slow ones like Phebe Ann Brock.'

Mrs Blackett's eyes were bright with excitement, and even Mrs Todd showed remarkable enthusiasm. She hurried the horse and caught up with the holiday-makers ahead. 'There's all the Dep'fords goin', six in the wagon,' she told us joyfully; 'an' Mis' Alva Tilley's folks are now risin' the hill in their new carryall.'

Mrs Blackett pulled at the neat bow of her black bonnet-strings, and tied them again with careful precision. 'I believe your bonnet's on a little bit sideways, dear,' she advised Mrs Todd as if she were a child; but Mrs Todd was too much occupied to pay proper heed. We began to feel a new sense of gayety and of taking part in the great occasion as we joined the little train.

18

THE BOWDEN REUNION

It is very rare in country life, where high days and holidays are few, that any occasion of general interest proves to be less than great. Such is the hidden fire of enthusiasm in the New England nature that, once given an outlet, it shines forth with almost volcanic light and heat. In quiet neighborhoods such inward force does not waste itself upon those petty excitements of every day that belongs to cities, but when, at long intervals, the altars to patriotism, to friendship, to the ties of kindred, are reared in our familiar fields, then the fires glow, the flames come up as if from the inexhaustible burning heart of the earth; the primal fires break through the granite dust in which our souls are set. Each heart is warm and every face shines with the ancient light. Such a day as this has transfiguring powers, and easily makes friends of those who have been cold-hearted, and gives to those who are dumb their chance to speak, and lends some beauty to the plainest face.

'Oh, I expect I shall meet friends today that I haven't seen in a long while,' said Mrs Blackett with deep satisfaction. 'Twill bring out a good many of the old folks, 'tis such a lovely day. I'm always glad not to have them disappointed.'

'I guess likely the best of 'em 'll be there,' answered Mrs Todd with gentle humor, stealing a glance at me. 'There's one thing certain: there's nothing takes in this whole neighborhood like anything related to the Bowdens. Yes, I do feel that when you call upon the Bowdens you may expect most families to rise up between the Landing and the far end of the Back Cove. Those that aren't kin by blood are kin by marriage.'

'There used to be an old story goin' about when I was a girl,' said Mrs Blackett, with much amusement. 'There was a great many more Bowdens then than there are now, and the folks was all setting in meeting a dreadful hot Sunday afternoon, and a scatter-witted little bound girl[1] came running to the meetin'-house door all out o' breath from somewheres in the neighborhood. "Mis' Bowden, Mis' Bowden!" says she. "Your baby's in a fit!" They used to tell that the whole congregation was up on its feet in a minute and right out into the aisles. All the Mis' Bowdens was setting right out for home; the minister stood there in the pulpit tryin' to keep sober, an' all at once he burst right out laughin'. He was a very nice man, they said, and he said he'd better give 'em the benediction, and they could hear the sermon next Sunday, so he kept it over. My mother was there, and she thought certain 'twas me.'

'None of our family was ever subject to fits,' interrupted Mrs Todd severely. 'No, we never had fits, none of us, and 'twas lucky we didn't 'way out there to Green Island. Now these folks right in front: dear sakes knows the bunches o' soothing catnip an' yarrow I've had to favor old Mis' Evins with dryin'! You can see it right in their expressions, all them Evins folks. There, just you look up to the crossroads, mother,' she suddenly exclaimed. 'See all the teams ahead of us. And oh, look down on the bay; yes, look down on the bay! See what a sight o' boats, all headin' for the Bowden place cove!'

'Oh, ain't it beautiful!' said Mrs Blackett, with all the delight of a girl. She stood up in the high wagon to see everything, and when she sat down again she took fast hold of my hand.

'Hadn't you better urge the horse a little, Almiry?' she asked. 'He's had it easy as we came along, and he can rest when we get there. The others are some little ways ahead, and I don't want to lose a minute.'

We watched the boats drop their sails one by one in the cove as we drove along the high land. The old Bowden house stood, low-storied and broad-roofed, in its green fields as if it were a motherly brown hen waiting for the flock that came straying toward it from every direction. The first Bowden settler had made his home there, and it was still the Bowden farm; five generations of sailors and farmers and soldiers had been its children. And presently Mrs Blackett showed me the stone-walled burying-ground that stood like a little fort on a knoll overlooking the bay, but, as she said, there were plenty of scattered Bowdens who were not laid there, – some lost at sea, and some out West, and some who died in the war; most of the home graves were those of women.

We could see now that there were different footpaths from along shore and across country. In all these there were straggling processions walking in single file, like old illustrations of the *Pilgrim's Progress*. There was a crowd about the house as if huge bees were swarming in the lilac bushes. Beyond the fields and cove a higher point of land ran out into the bay, covered with woods which must have kept away much of the northwest wind in winter.

Now there was a pleasant look of shade and shelter there for the great family meeting.

We hurried on our way, beginning to feel as if we were very late, and it was a great satisfaction at last to turn out of the stony highroad into a green lane shaded with old apple-trees. Mrs Todd encouraged the horse until he fairly pranced with gayety as we drove round to the front of the house on the soft turf. There was an instant cry of rejoicing, and two or three persons ran toward us from the busy group.

'Why, dear Mis' Blackett! – here's Mis' Blackett!' I heard them say, as if it were pleasure enough for one day to have a sight of her. Mrs Todd turned to me with a lovely look of triumph and self-forgetfulness. An elderly man who wore the look of a prosperous sea-captain put up both arms and lifted Mrs Blackett down from the high wagon like a child, and kissed her with hearty affection. 'I was master afraid she wouldn't be here,' he said, looking at Mrs Todd with a face like a happy sunburnt schoolboy, while everybody crowded round to give their welcome.

'Mother's always the queen,' said Mrs Todd. 'Yes, they'll all make everything of mother; she'll have a lovely time today. I wouldn't have had her miss it, and there won't be a thing she'll ever regret, except to mourn because William wa'n't here.'

Mrs Blackett having been properly escorted to the house, Mrs Todd received her own full share of honor, and some of the men, with a simple kindness that was the soul of chivalry, waited upon us and our baskets and led away the white horse. I already knew some of Mrs Todd's friends and kindred, and felt like an adopted Bowden in this happy moment. It seemed to be enough for any one to have arrived by the same conveyance as Mrs Blackett, who presently had her court inside the house, while Mrs Todd, large, hospitable, and pre-eminent, was the centre of a rapidly increasing crowd about the lilac bushes. Small companies were continually coming up the long green slope from the water, and nearly all the boats had come to shore. I counted three or four that were baffled by the light breeze, but before long all the Bowdens, small and great, seemed to have assembled, and we started to go up to the grove across the field.

Out of the chattering crowd of noisy children, and large-waisted women whose best black dresses fell straight to the ground in generous folds, and sunburnt men who looked as serious as if it were town-meeting day, there suddenly came silence and order. I saw the straight, soldierly little figure of a man who bore a fine resemblance to Mrs Blackett, and who appeared to marshal us with perfect ease. He was imperative enough, but with a grand military sort of courtesy, and bore himself with solemn dignity of importance. We were sorted out according to some clear design of his own, and stood as speechless as a troop to await his orders. Even the children were ready to march together, a pretty flock, and at the last moment Mrs Blackett and a few distinguished companions, the ministers and those who were very old, came out of the house together and took their places. We ranked by fours, and even then we made a long procession.

There was a wide path mowed for us across the field, and, as we moved along, the birds flew up out of the thick second crop of clover, and the bees hummed as if it still were June. There was a flashing of white gulls over the water where the fleet of boats rode the low waves together in the cove, swaying their small masts as if they kept time to our steps. The plash of the water could be heard faintly, yet still be heard; we might have been a company of ancient Greeks going to celebrate a victory, or to worship the god of harvests in the grove above. It was strangely moving to see this and to make part of it. The sky, the sea, have watched poor humanity at its rites so long; we were no more a New England family celebrating its own existence and simple progress; we carried the tokens and inheritance of all such households from which this had descended, and were only the latest of our line. We possessed the instincts of a far, forgotten childhood; I found myself thinking that we ought to be carrying green branches and singing as we went. So we came to the thick shaded grove still silent, and were set in our places by the straight trees that swayed together and let sunshine through here and there like a single golden leaf that flickered down, vanishing in the cool shade.

The grove was so large that the great family looked far smaller than it had in the open field; there was a thick growth of dark pines and firs with an occasional maple or oak that gave a gleam of color like a bright window in the great roof. On three sides we could see the water, shining behind the tree-trunks, and feel the cool salt breeze that began to come up with the tide just as the day reached its highest point of heat. We could see the green sunlit field we had just crossed as if we looked out at it from a dark room, and the old house and its lilacs standing placidly in the sun, and the great barn with a stockade of carriages from which two or three care-taking men who had lingered were coming across the field together. Mrs Todd had taken off her warm gloves and looked the picture of content.

'There!' she exclaimed. 'I've always meant to have you see this place, but I never looked for such a beautiful opportunity – weather an' occasion both made to match. Yes, it suits me: I don't ask no more. I want to know if you saw mother walkin' at the head! It choked me right up to see mother at the head, walkin' with the ministers,' and Mrs Todd turned away to hide the feelings she could not instantly control.

'Who was the marshal?' I hastened to ask. 'Was he an old soldier?'

'Don't he do well?' answered Mrs Todd with satisfaction.

'He don't often have such a chance to show off his gifts,' said Mrs Caplin, a friend from the Landing who had joined us. 'That's Sant Bowden; he always takes the lead, such days. Good for nothing else most o' his time; trouble is, he' –

I turned with interest to hear the worst. Mrs Caplin's tone was both zealous and impressive.

'Stim'lates,' [2] she explained scornfully.

'No, Santin never was in the war,' said Mrs Todd with lofty indifference. 'It was a cause of real distress to him. He kep' enlistin', and traveled far an' wide about here, an' even took the bo't and went to Boston to volunteer; but he ain't a sound man, an' they wouldn't have him. They say he knows all their tactics, an' can tell all about the battle o' Waterloo well's he can Bunker Hill.[3] I told him once the country'd lost a great general, an' I meant it, too.'

'I expect you're near right,' said Mrs Caplin, a little crestfallen and apologetic.

'I be right,' insisted Mrs Todd with much amiability. ''Twas most too bad to cramp him down to his peaceful trade, but he's a most excellent shoemaker at his best, an' he always says it's a trade that gives him time to think an' plan his manœuvres. Over to the Port they always invite him to march Decoration Day,[4] same as the rest, an' he does look noble; he comes of soldier stock.'

I had been noticing with great interest the curiously French type of face which prevailed in this rustic company. I had said to myself before that Mrs Blackett was plainly of French descent, in both her appearance and her charming gifts, but this is not surprising when one has learned how large a proportion of the early settlers on this northern coast of New England were of Huguenot blood, and that it is the Norman Englishman, not the Saxon, who goes adventuring to a new world.

'They used to say in old times,' said Mrs Todd modestly, 'that our family came of very high folks in France, and one of 'em was a great general in some o' the old wars. I sometimes think that Santin's ability has come 'way down from then. 'Tain't nothin' he's ever acquired; 'twas born in him. I don't know's he ever saw a fine parade, or met with those that studied up such things. He's figured it all out an' got his papers so he knows how to aim a cannon right for William's fish-house five miles out on Green Island, or up there on Burnt Island where the signal is. He had it all over to me one day, an' I tried hard to appear interested. His life's all in it, but he will have those poor gloomy spells come over him now an' then, an' then he has to drink.'

Mrs Caplin gave a heavy sigh.

'There's a great many such strayaway folks, just as there is plants,' continued Mrs Todd, who was nothing if not botanical. 'I know of just one sprig of laurel[5] that grows over back here in a wild spot, an' I never could hear of no other on this coast. I had a large bunch brought me once from Massachusetts way, so I know it. This piece grows in an open spot where you'd think 'twould do well, but it's sort o' poor-lookin'. I've visited it time an' again, just to notice its poor blooms. 'Tis a real Sant Bowden, out of its own place.'

Mrs Caplin looked bewildered and blank. 'Well, all I know is, last year he worked out some kind of a plan so's to parade the county conference in platoons, and got 'em all flustered up tryin' to sense his ideas of a holler square,'[6] she burst forth, 'They was holler enough anyway after ridin' 'way down from up country into the salt air, and they'd been treated to a sermon on faith an' works from old Fayther Harlow that never knows when to cease. 'Twa'n't no time for tactics then, – they wa'n't a-thinkin' of the church military. Sant, he couldn't do nothin' with 'em. All he thinks of, when he sees a crowd, is how to march 'em. 'Tis all very well when he don't 'tempt too much. He never did act like other folks.'

'Ain't I just been maintainin' that he ain't like 'em?' urged Mrs Todd decidedly. 'Strange folks has got to have strange ways, for what I see.'

'Somebody observed once that you could pick out the likeness of 'most every sort of a foreigner when you looked about you in our parish,' said Sister Caplin, her face brightening with sudden illumination. 'I didn't see the bearin' of it then quite so plain. I always did think Mari' Harris resembled a Chinee.'

'Mari' Harris was pretty as a child, I remember,' said the pleasant voice of Mrs Blackett, who, after receiving the affectionate greetings of nearly the whole company, came to join us, – to see, as she insisted, that we were out of mischief.

'Yes, Mari' was one o' them pretty little lambs that make dreadful homely old sheep,' replied Mrs Todd with energy. 'Cap'n Littlepage never'd look so disconsolate if she was any sort of a proper person to direct things. She might divert him; yes, she might divert the old gentleman, an' let him think he had his own way, 'stead o' arguing everything down to the bare bone. 'Twouldn't hurt her to sit down an' hear his great stories once in a while.'

'The stories are very interesting,' I ventured to say.

'Yes, you always catch yourself a-thinkin' what if they was all true, and he had the right of it,' answered Mrs Todd. 'He's a good sight better company, though dreamy, than such sordid creatur's as Mari' Harris.'

'Live and let live,' said dear old Mrs Blackett gently. 'I haven't seen the captain for a good while, now that I ain't so constant to meetin',' she added wistfully. 'We always have known each other.'

'Why, if it is a good pleasant day tomorrow, I'll get William to call an' invite the capt'in to dinner. William'll be in early so's to pass up the street without meetin' anybody.'

'There, they're callin' out it's time to set the tables,' said Mrs Caplin, with great excitement.

'Here's Cousin Sarah Jane Blackett! Well, I am pleased, certain!' exclaimed Mrs Todd, with unaffected delight; and these kindred spirits met and parted with the promise of a good talk later on. After this there was no more time for conversation until we were seated in order at the long tables.

'I'm one that always dreads seeing some o' the folks that I don't like, at such a time as this,' announced Mrs Todd privately to me after a season of reflection. We were just waiting for the feast to begin. 'You wouldn't think such a great creatur' 's I be could feel all over pins an' needles. I remember, the day I promised to Nathan, how it come over me, just's I was feelin' happy's I could, that I'd got to have an own cousin o' his for my near relation all the rest o' my life, an' it seemed as if die I should. Poor Nathan saw somethin' had crossed me, – he had very nice feelings, – and when he asked me what 'twas, I told him. "I never could like her myself," said he. "You sha'n't be bothered, dear," he says; an' 'twas one o' the things that made me set a good deal by Nathan, he didn't make a habit of always opposin', like some men. "Yes," says I, "but think o' Thanksgivin' times an' funerals; she's our relation, an' we've got to own her." Young folks don't think o' those things. There she goes now, do let's pray her by,' said Mrs Todd with an alarming transition from general opinions to particular animosities. 'I hate her just the same as I always did; but she's got on a real pretty dress. I do try to remember that she's Nathan's cousin. Oh dear, well; she's gone by after all, an' ain't seen me. I expected she'd come pleasantin' round just to show off an' say afterwards she was acquainted.'

This was so different from Mrs Todd's usual largeness of mind that I had a moment's uneasiness; but the cloud passed quickly over her spirit, and was gone with the offender.

There never was a more generous out-of-door feast along the coast than the Bowden family set forth that day. To call it a picnic would make it seem trivial. The great tables were edged with pretty oak-leaf trimming, which the boys and girls made. We brought flowers from the fence-thickets of the great field; and out of the disorder of flowers and provisions suddenly appeared as orderly a scheme for the feast as the marshal had shaped for the procession. I began to respect the Bowdens for their inheritance of good taste and skill and a certain pleasing gift of formality. Something made them do all these things in a finer way than most country people would have done them. As I looked up and down the tables there was a good cheer, a grave soberness that shone with pleasure, a humble dignity of bearing. There were some who should have sat below the salt for lack of this good breeding; but they were not many. So, I said to myself, their ancestors may have sat in the great hall of some old French house[7] in the Middle Ages, when battles and sieges and processions and feasts were familiar things. The ministers and Mrs Blackett, with a few of their rank and age, were put in places of honor, and for once that I looked any other way I looked twice at Mrs Blackett's face, serene and mindful of privilege and responsibility, the mistress by simple fitness of this great day.

Mrs Todd looked up at the roof of green trees, and then carefully surveyed the company. 'I see 'em better now they're all settin' down,' she said with satisfaction. 'There's old Mr Gilbraith and his sister. I wish they were settin' with us; they're not among folks they can parley with, an' they look disappointed.'

As the feast went on, the spirits of my companion steadily rose. The excitement of an unexpectedly great occasion was a subtle stimulant to her disposition, and I could see that sometimes when Mrs Todd had seemed limited and heavily domestic, she had simply grown sluggish for lack of proper surroundings. She was not so much reminiscent now as expectant, and as alert and gay as a girl. We who were her neighbors were full of gayety, which was but the reflected light from her beaming countenance. It was not the first time that I was full of wonder at the waste of human ability in this world, as a botanist wonders at the wastefulness of nature, the thousand seeds that die, the unused provision of every sort. The reserve force of society grows more and more amazing to one's thought. More than one face among the Bowdens showed that only opportunity and stimulus were lacking, — a narrow set of circumstances had caged a fine able character and held it captive. One sees exactly the same types in a country gathering as in the most brilliant city company. You are safe to be understood if the spirit of your speech is the same for one neighbor as for the other.

19

THE FEAST'S END

The feast was a noble feast, as has already been said. There was an elegant ingenuity displayed in the form of pies which delighted my heart. Once acknowledge that an American pie is far to be preferred to its humble ancestor, the English tart, and it is joyful to be reassured at a Bowden reunion that invention has not yet failed. Beside a delightful variety of material, the decorations went beyond all my former experience; dates and names were wrought in lines of pastry and frosting on the tops. There was even more elaborate reading matter on an excellent early-apple pie which we began to share and eat, precept upon precept. Mrs Todd helped me generously to the whole word *Bowden,* and consumed *Reunion* herself, save an indecipherable fragment; but the most renowned essay in cookery on the tables was a model of the old Bowden house made of durable gingerbread, with all the windows and doors in the right places, and sprigs of genuine lilac set at the front. It must have been baked in sections, in one of the last of the great brick ovens, and fastened together on the morning of the day. There was a general sigh when this fell into ruin at the feast's end, and it was shared by a great part of the assembly, not without seriousness, and as if it were a pledge and token of loyalty. I met the maker of the gingerbread house, which had called up lively remembrances of a childish story. She had the gleaming eye of an enthusiast and a look of high ideals.

'I could just as well have made it all of frosted cake,' she said, 'but 'twouldn't have been the right shade; the old house, as you observe, was never painted, and I concluded that plain gingerbread would represent it best. It wasn't all I expected it would be,' she said sadly, as many an artist had said before her of his work.

There were speeches by the ministers; and there proved to be a historian among the Bowdens, who gave some fine anecdotes of the family history; and then appeared a poetess, whom Mrs Todd regarded with wistful compassion and indulgence, and when the long faded garland of verses came to an appealing end, she turned to me with words of praise.

'Sounded pretty,' said the generous listener. 'Yes, I thought she did very well. We went to school together, an' Mary Anna had a very hard time; trouble was, her mother thought she'd given birth to a genius, an' Mary Anna's come to believe it herself. There, I don't know what we should have done without her; there ain't nobody else that can write poetry between here and 'way up towards Rockland; it adds a great deal at such a time. When she speaks o' those that are gone, she feels it all, and so does everybody else, but she harps too much. I'd laid half of that away for next time, if I was Mary Anna. There comes mother to speak to her, an' old Mr Gilbraith's sister; now she'll be heartened right up. Mother'll say just the right thing.'

The leave-takings were as affecting as the meetings of these old friends had been. There were enough young persons at the reunion, but it is the old who really value such opportunities; as for the young, it is the habit of every day to meet their comrades, – the time of separation has not come. To see the joy with which these elder kinsfolk and acquaintances had looked in one another's faces, and the lingering touch of their friendly hands; to see these affectionate meetings and then the reluctant partings, gave one a new idea of the isolation in which it was possible to live in that after all thinly settled region. They did not expect to see one another again very soon; the steady, hard work on the farms, the difficulty of getting from place to place, especially in winter when boats were laid up, gave double value to any occasion which could bring a large number of families together. Even funerals in this country of the pointed firs were not without their social advantages and satisfactions. I heard the words 'next summer' repeated many times, though summer was still ours and all the leaves were green.

The boats began to put out from shore, and the wagons to drive away. Mrs Blackett took me into the old house when we came back from the grove: it was her father's birthplace and early home, and she had spent much of her own childhood there with her grandmother. She spoke of those days as if they had but lately passed; in fact, I could imagine that the house looked almost exactly the same to her. I could see the brown rafters of the unfinished roof as I looked up the steep staircase, though the best room was as handsome with its good wainscoting and touch of ornament on the cornice as any old room of its day in a town.

Some of the guests who came from a distance were still sitting in the best room when we went in to take leave of the master and mistress of the house. We all said eagerly what a pleasant day it had been, and how swiftly the time had passed. Perhaps it is the great national anniversaries which our country has lately kept, and the soldiers' meetings that take place everywhere, which have made reunions of every sort the fashion. This one, at least, had been very interesting. I fancied that old feuds had been overlooked, and the old saying that blood is thicker than water had again proved itself true, though from the variety of names one argued a certain adulteration of the Bowden traits and belongings. Clannishness is an instinct of the heart, – it is more than a birthright, or a custom; and lesser rights were forgotten in the claim to a common inheritance.

We were among the very last to return to our proper lives and lodgings. I came near to feeling like a true Bowden, and parted from certain new friends as if they were old friends; we were rich with the treasure of a new remembrance.

At last we were in the high wagon again; the old white horse had been well fed in the Bowden barn, and we drove away and soon began to climb the long hill toward the wooded ridge. The road was new to me, as roads always are, going back. Most of our companions had been full of anxious thoughts of home, – of the cows, or of young children likely to fall into disaster, – but we had no reasons for haste, and drove slowly along, talking and resting by the way. Mrs Todd said once that she really hoped her front door had been shut on account of the dust blowing in, but added that nothing made any weight on her mind except not to forget to turn a few late mullein leaves that were drying on a newspaper in the little loft. Mrs Blackett and I gave our word of honor that we would remind her of this heavy responsibility. The way seemed short, we had so much to talk about. We climbed hills where we could see the great bay and the islands, and then went down into shady valleys where the air began to feel like evening, cool and damp with a fragrance of wet ferns.[1] Mrs Todd alighted once or twice, refusing all assistance in securing some boughs of a rare shrub which she valued for its bark, though she proved incommunicative as to her reasons. We passed the house where we had been so kindly entertained with doughnuts earlier in the day, and found it closed and deserted, which was a disappointment.

'They must have stopped to tea somewheres and thought they'd finish up the day,' said Mrs Todd. 'Those that enjoyed it best'll want to get right home so's to think it over.'

'I didn't see the woman there after all, did you?' asked Mrs Blackett as the horse stopped to drink at the trough.

'Oh yes, I spoke with her,' answered Mrs Todd, with but scant interest or approval. 'She ain't a member o' our family.'

'I thought you said she resembled Cousin Pa'lina Bowden about the forehead,' suggested Mrs Blackett.

'Well, she don't,' answered Mrs Todd impatiently. 'I ain't one that's ord'narily mistaken about family likenesses, and she didn't seem to meet with friends, so I went square up to her. "I expect you're a Bowden by your looks," says I. "Yes, I take it you're one o' the Bowdens." "Lor', no," says she. "Dennett was my maiden name, but I married a Bowden for my first husband. I thought I'd come an' just see what was a-goin' on!"'

Mrs Blackett laughed heartily. 'I'm goin' to remember to tell William o' that,' she said. 'There, Almiry, the only thing that's troubled me all this day is to think how William would have enjoyed it. I do so wish William had been there.'

'I sort of wish he had, myself,' said Mrs Todd frankly.

'There wa'n't many old folks there, somehow,' said Mrs Blackett, with a touch of sadness in her voice. 'There ain't so many to come as there used to be, I'm aware, but I expected to see more.'

'I thought they turned out pretty well, when you come to think of it; why, everybody was sayin' so an' feelin' gratified,' answered Mrs Todd hastily with pleasing unconsciousness; then I saw the quick color flash into her cheek, and presently she made some excuse to turn and steal an anxious look at her mother. Mrs Blackett was smiling and thinking about her happy day, though she began to look a little tired. Neither of my companions was troubled by her burden of years. I hoped in my heart that I might be like them as I lived on into age, and then smiled to think that I too was no longer very young. So we always keep the same hearts, though our outer framework fails and shows the touch of time.

' 'Twas pretty when they sang the hymn wasn't it?' asked Mrs Blackett at supper-time, with real enthusiasm. 'There was such a plenty o' men's voices; where I sat it did sound beautiful. I had to stop and listen when they came to the last verse.'

I saw Mrs Todd's broad shoulders began to shake. 'There was good singers there; yes, there was excellent singers,' she agreed heartily, putting down her teacup, 'but I chanced to drift alongside Mis' Peter Bowden o' Great Bay, an' I couldn't help thinkin' if she was as far out o' town as she was out o' tune, she wouldn't get back in a day.'

20

ALONG SHORE

One day as I went along the shore beyond the old wharves and the newer, high-stepped fabric of the steamer landing, I saw that all the boats were beached, and the slack water period of the early afternoon prevailed. Nothing was going on, not even the most leisurely of occupations, like baiting trawls or mending nets, or repairing lobster pots; the very boats seemed to be taking an afternoon nap in the sun. I could hardly discover a distant sail as I looked seaward, except a weather-beaten lobster smack,[1] which seemed to have been taken for a plaything by the light airs that blew about the bay. It drifted and turned about so aimlessly in the wide reach off Burnt Island, that I suspected there was nobody at the wheel, or that she might have parted her rusty anchor chain while all the crew were asleep.

I watched her for a minute or two; she was the old *Miranda*, owned by some of the Caplins, and I knew her by an odd shaped patch of newish duck that was set into the peak of her dingy mainsail. Her vagaries offered such an exciting subject for conversation that my heart rejoiced at the sound of a hoarse voice behind me. At that moment, before I had time to answer, I saw something large and shapeless flung from the *Miranda*'s deck that splashed the water high against her black side, and my companion gave a satisfied chuckle. The old lobster smack's sail caught the breeze again at this moment, and she moved off down the bay. Turning, I found old Elijah Tilley, who had come softly out of his dark fishhouse, as if it were a burrow.

'Boy got kind o' drowsy steerin' of her; Monroe he hove him right overboard; 'wake now fast enough,' explained Mr Tilley, and we laughed together.

I was delighted, for my part, that the vicissitudes and dangers of the *Miranda*, in a rocky channel, should have given me this opportunity to make acquaintance with an old fisherman to whom I had never spoken. At first he had seemed to be one of those evasive and uncomfortable persons who are so suspicious of you that they make you almost suspicious of yourself. Mr

Elijah Tilley appeared to regard a stranger with scornful indifference. You might see him standing on the pebble beach or in a fishhouse doorway, but when you came nearer he was gone. He was one of the small company of elderly, gaunt-shaped great fishermen whom I used to like to see leading up a deep-laden boat by the head, as if it were a horse, from the water's edge to the steep slope of the pebble beach. There were four of these large old men at the Landing, who were the survivors of an earlier and more vigorous generation. There was an alliance and understanding between them, so close that it was apparently speechless. They gave much time to watching one another's boats go out or come in; they lent a ready hand at tending one another's lobster traps in rough weather; they helped to clean the fish, or to sliver porgies[2] for the trawls, as if they were in close partnership; and when a boat came in from deep-sea fishing they were never far out of the way, and hastened to help carry it ashore, two by two, splashing alongside, or holding its steady head, as if it were a willful sea-colt. As a matter of fact no boat could help being steady and way-wise[3] under their instant direction and companionship. Abel's boat and Jonathan Bowden's boat were as distinct and experienced personalities as the men themselves, and as inexpressive. Arguments and opinions were unknown to the conversation of these ancient friends; you would as soon have expected to hear small talk in a company of elephants as to hear old Mr Bowden or Elijah Tilley and their two mates waste breath upon any form of trivial gossip. They made brief statements to one another from time to time. As you came to know them you wondered more and more that they should talk at all. Speech seemed to be a light and elegant accomplishment, and their unexpected acquaintance with its arts made them of new value to the listener. You felt almost as if a landmark pine[4] should suddenly address you in regard to the weather, or a lofty-minded old camel make a remark as you stood respectfully near him under the circus tent.

I often wondered a great deal about the inner life and thought of these self-contained old fishermen; their minds seemed to be fixed upon nature and the elements rather than upon any contrivances of man, like politics or theology. My friend, Captain Bowden, who was the nephew of the eldest of this group, regarded them with deference; but he did not belong to their secret companionship, though he was neither young nor talkative.

'They've gone together ever since they were boys, they know most everything about the sea amon'st them,' he told me once. 'They was always just as you see 'em now since the memory of man.'

These ancient seafarers had houses and lands not outwardly different from other Dunnet Landing dwellings, and two of them were fathers of families, but their true dwelling places were the sea, and the stony beach that edged its familiar shore, and the fishhouses, where much salt brine from the mackerel kits[5] had soaked the very timbers into a state of brown permanence and petrifaction. It had also affected the old fishermen's hard complexions, until one fancied that when Death claimed them it could only be with the aid, not of any slender modern dart, but the good serviceable harpoon of a seventeenth century woodcut.

Elijah Tilley was such an evasive, discouraged-looking person, heavy-headed, and stooping so that one could never look him in the face, that even after his friendly exclamation about Monroe Pennell, the lobster smack's skipper, and the sleepy boy, I did not venture at once to speak again. Mr Tilley was carrying a small haddock in one hand, and presently shifted it to the other hand lest it might touch my skirt. I knew that my company was accepted, and we walked together a little way.

'You mean to have a good supper,' I ventured to say, by way of friendliness.

'Goin' to have this 'ere haddock an' some o' my good baked potatoes; must eat to live,' responded my companion with great pleasantness and open approval. I found that I had suddenly left the forbidding coast and come into a smooth little harbor of friendship.

'You ain't never been up to my place,' said the old man. 'Folks don't come now as they used to; no, 'tain't no use to ask folks now. My poor dear she was a great hand to draw young company.'

I remembered that Mrs Todd had once said that this old fisherman had been sore stricken and unconsoled at the death of his wife.

'I should like very much to come,' said I. 'Perhaps you are going to be at home later on?'

Mr Tilley agreed, by a sober nod, and went his way bent-shouldered and with a rolling gait. There was a new patch high on the shoulder of his old waistcoat, which corresponded to the renewing of the *Miranda*'s mainsail down the bay, and I wondered if his own fingers, clumsy with much deep-sea fishing, had set it in.

'Was there a good catch today?' I asked, stopping a moment. 'I didn't happen to be on the shore when the boats came in.'

'No; all come in pretty light,' answered Mr Tilley. 'Addicks an' Bowden they done the best; Abel an' me we had but a slim fare. We went out 'arly, but not so 'arly as sometimes; looked like a poor mornin'. I got nine haddick, all small, and seven fish; the rest on 'em got more fish[6] than haddick. Well, I don't expect they feel like bitin' every day; we l'arn to humor 'em a little an' let 'em have their way 'bout it. These plaguey dog-fish[7] kind of worry 'em.' Mr Tilley pronounced the last sentence with much sympathy, as if he looked upon himself as a true friend of all the haddock and codfish that lived on the fishing grounds, and so we parted.

Later in the afternoon I went along the beach again until I came to the foot of Mr Tilley's land, and found his rough track across the cobble-stones and rocks to the field edge, where there was a heavy piece of old wreck timber, like a ship's bone, full of treenails. From this a little footpath, narrow with one man's treading, led up across the small green field that made Mr Tilley's whole estate, except a straggling pasture that tilted on edge up the steep hillside beyond the house and road. I could hear the tinkle-tankle of a cow-bell somewhere among the spruces by which the pasture was being walked over and forested from every side; it was likely to be called the wood lot before long, but the field was unmolested. I could not see a bush or a brier anywhere within the walls, and hardly a stray pebble showed itself. This was most surprising in that country of firm ledges, and scattered stones which all the walls that industry could devise had hardly begun to clear away off the land. In the narrow field I noticed some stout stakes, apparently planted at random in the grass and among the hills of potatoes, but carefully painted yellow and white to match the house, a neat sharp-edged little dwelling, which looked strangely modern for its owner. I should have much sooner believed that the smart young wholesale egg merchant of the Landing was its occupant than Mr Tilley, since a man's house is really but his larger body, and expresses in a way his nature and character.

I went up the field, following the smooth little path to the side door. As for using the front door, that was a matter of great ceremony; the long grass grew close against the high stone step, and a snowberry bush leaned over it, top-heavy with the weight of a morning-glory vine that had managed to take what the fishermen might call a half hitch about the door-knob. Elijah Tilley came to the side door to receive me; he was knitting a blue yarn stocking without looking on, and was warmly dressed for the season in a thick blue flannel shirt with white crockery buttons, a faded waistcoat and trousers heavily patched at the knees. These were not his fishing clothes. There was something delightful in the grasp of his hand, warm and clean, as if it never touched anything but the comfortable woolen yarn, instead of cold sea water and slippery fish.

'What are the painted stakes for, down in the field?' I hastened to ask, and he came out a step or two along the path to see; and looked at the stakes as if his attention were called to them for the first time.

'Folks laughed at me when I first bought this place an' come here to live,' he explained. 'They said 'twa'n't no kind of a field privilege at all; no place to raise anything, all full o' stones. I was aware 'twas good land, an' I worked some on it – odd times when I didn't have nothin' else on hand – till I cleared them loose stones all out. You never see a prettier piece than 'tis now; now did ye? Well, as for them painted marks, them's my buoys. I struck on to some heavy rocks that didn't show none, but a plow'd be liable to ground on 'em, an' so I ketched holt an' buoyed 'em same's you see. They don't trouble me no more'n if they wa'n't there.'

'You haven't been to sea for nothing,' I said laughing.

'One trade helps another,' said Elijah with an amiable smile. 'Come right in an' set down. Come in an' rest ye,' he exclaimed, and led the way into his comfortable kitchen. The sunshine poured in at the two further windows, and a cat was curled up sound asleep on the table that stood between them. There was a new-looking light oilcloth of a tiled pattern on the floor, and a crockery teapot, large for a household of only one person, stood on the bright stove. I ventured to say that somebody must be a very good housekeeper.

'That's me,' acknowledged the old fisherman with frankness. 'There ain't nobody here but me. I try to keep things looking right, same's poor dear left 'em. You set down here in this chair, then you can look off an' see the water. None on 'em thought I was goin' to get along alone, no way, but I wa'n't goin' to have my house turned upsi' down an' all changed about; no, not to please nobody. I was the only one knew just how she liked to have things set, poor dear, an' I said I was goin' to make shift, and I have made shift. I'd rather tough it out alone.' And he sighed heavily, as if to sigh were his familiar consolation.

We were both silent for a minute; the old man looked out of the window, as if he had forgotten I was there.

'You must miss her very much?' I said at last.

'I do miss her,' he answered, and sighed again. 'Folks all kep' repeatin' that time would ease me, but I can't find it does. No, I miss her just the same every day.'

'How long is it since she died?' I asked.

'Eight year now, come the first of October. It don't seem near so long. I've got a sister that comes and stops 'long o' me a little spell, spring an' fall, an' odd times if I send after her. I ain't near so good a hand to sew as I be to

93

knit, and she's very quick to set everything to rights. She's a married woman with a family; her son's folks lives at home, an' I can't make no great claim on her time. But it makes me a kind o' good excuse, when I do send, to help her a little; she ain't none too well off. Poor dear always liked her, and we used to contrive our ways together. 'Tis full as easy to be alone. I set here an' think it all over, an' think considerable when the weather's bad to go outside. I get so some days it feels as if poor dear might step right back into this kitchen. I keep a watchin' them doors as if she might step in to ary one. Yes, ma'am, I keep a-lookin' off an' droppin' o' my stitches; that's just how it seems. I can't git over losin' of her no way nor no how. Yes, ma'am, that's just how it seems to me.'

I did not say anything, and he did not look up.

'I git feelin' so sometimes I have to lay everything by an' go out door. She was a sweet pretty creatur' long's she lived,' the old man added mournfully. 'There's that little rockin' chair o' her'n, I set an' notice it an' think how strange 'tis a creatur' like her should be gone an' that chair be here right in its old place.'

'I wish I had known her; Mrs Todd told me about your wife one day,' I said.

'You'd have liked to come and see her; all the folks did,' said poor Elijah. 'She'd been so pleased to hear everything and see somebody new that took such an int'rest. She had a kind o' gift to make it pleasant for folks. I guess likely Almiry Todd told you she was a pretty woman, especially in her young days; late years, too, she kep' her looks and come to be so pleasant lookin'. There, 'tain't so much matter, I shall be done afore a great while. No; I sha'n't trouble the fish a great sight more.'

The old widower sat with his head bowed over his knitting, as if he were hastily shortening the very thread of time. The minutes went slowly by. He stopped his work and clasped his hands firmly together. I saw he had forgotten his guest, and I kept the afternoon watch with him. At last he looked up as if but a moment had passed of his continual loneliness.

'Yes, ma'am, I'm one that has seen trouble,' he said, and began to knit again.

The visible tribute of his careful housekeeping, and the clean bright room which had once enshrined his wife, and now enshrined her memory, was very moving to me; he had no thought for anyone else or for any other place. I began to see her myself in her home, – a delicate-looking, faded little woman, who leaned upon his rough strength and affectionate heart, who was always watching for his boat out of this very window, and who always opened the door and welcomed him when he came home.

'I used to laugh at her, poor dear,' said Elijah, as if he read my thought. 'I used to make light of her timid notions. She used to be fearful when I was out in bad weather or baffled about gittin' ashore. She used to say the time seemed long to her, but I've found out all about it now. I used to be dreadful thoughtless when I was a young man and the fish was bitin' well. I'd stay out late some o' them days, an' I expect she'd watch an' watch an' lose heart a-waitin'. My heart alive! what a supper she'd git, an' be right there watchin' from the door, with somethin' over her head if 'twas cold, waitin' to hear all about it as I come up the field. Lord, how I think o' all them little things!

'This was what she called the best room; in this way,' he said presently, laying his knitting on the table, and leading the way across the front entry and unlocking a door, which he threw open with an air of pride. The best room seemed to me a much sadder and more empty place than the kitchen; its conventionalities lacked the simple perfection of the humbler room and failed on the side of poor ambition; it was only when one remembered what patient saving, and what high respect for society in the abstract go to such furnishing that the little parlor was interesting at all. I could imagine the great day of certain purchases, the bewildering shops of the next large town, the aspiring anxious woman, the clumsy sea-tanned man in his best clothes, so eager to be pleased, but at ease only when they were safe back in the sail-boat again, going down the bay with their precious freight, the hoarded money all spent and nothing to think of but tiller and sail. I looked at the unworn carpet, the glass vases on the mantelpiece with their prim bunches of bleached swamp grass and dusty marsh rosemary, and I could read the history of Mrs Tilley's best room from its very beginning.

'You see for yourself what beautiful rugs she could make; now I'm going to show you her best tea things she thought so much of,' said the master of the house, opening the door of a shallow cupboard. 'That's real chiny, all of it on those two shelves,' he told me proudly. 'I bought it all myself, when we was first married, in the port of Bordeaux. There never was one single piece of it broke until – Well, I used to say, long as she lived, there never was a piece broke, but long at the last I noticed she'd look kind o' distressed, an' I thought 'twas 'count o' me boastin'. When they asked if they should use it when the folks was here to supper, time o' her funeral, I knew she'd want to have everything nice, and I said "certain." Some o' the women they come runnin' to me an' called me, while they was takin' of the chiny down, an' showed me there was one o' the cups broke an' the pieces wropped in paper and pushed way back here, corner o' the shelf. They didn't want me to go an' think they done it. Poor dear! I had to put right out o' the house when I see that. I knowed in one minute how 'twas. We'd got so used to sayin' 'twas all there just's I fetched it home, an' so when she broke that cup somehow or 'nother she couldn't frame no words to come an' tell me. She couldn't think 'twould vex me, 'twas her own hurt pride. I guess there wa'n't no other secret ever lay between us.'

The French cups with their gay sprigs of pink and blue, the best tumblers, an old flowered bowl and tea caddy, and a japanned waiter[8] or two adorned the shelves. These, with a few daguerreotypes in a little square pile, had the closet to themselves, and I was conscious of much pleasure in seeing them. One is shown over many a house in these days where the interest may be more complex, but not more definite.

'Those were her best things, poor dear,' said Elijah as he locked the door again. 'She told me that last summer before she was taken away that she couldn't think o' anything more she wanted, there was everything in the house, an' all her rooms was furnished pretty. I was goin' over to the Port an' inquired for errands. I used to ask her to say what she wanted cost or no cost – she was a very reasonable woman, an' 'twas the place where she done all but her extra shopping. It kind o' chilled me up when she spoke so satisfied.'

'You don't go out fishing after Christmas?' I asked, as we came back to the bright kitchen.

'No; I take stiddy to my knitting after January sets in,' said the old seafarer. ''Tain't worth while, fish make off into deeper water an' you can't stand no such perishin' for the sake o' what you get. I leave out a few traps in sheltered coves an' do a little lobsterin' on fair days. The young fellows braves it out, some on 'em; but, for me, I lay in my winter's yarn an' set here where 'tis warm, an' knit an' take my comfort. Mother learnt me once when I was a lad; she was a beautiful knitter herself. I was laid up with a bad knee, an' she said 'twould take up my time an' help her; we was a large family. They'll buy all the folks can do down here to Addicks' store. They say our Dunnet stockin's is gettin' to be celebrated up to Boston, – good quality o' wool an' even knittin' or somethin'. I've always been called a pretty hand to do nettin', but seines is master cheap to what they used to be when they was all hand worked. I change off to nettin' long towards spring, and I piece up my trawls and lines and get my fishin' stuff to rights. Lobster pots they require attention, but I make 'em up in spring weather when it's warm there in the barn. No; I ain't one o' them that likes to set an' do nothin'.'

'You see the rugs, poor dear did them; she wa'n't very partial to knittin',' old Elijah went on, after he had counted his stitches. 'Our rugs is beginnin' to show wear, but I can't master none o' them womanish tricks. My sister, she tinkers 'em up. She said last time she was here that she guessed they'd last my time.'

'The old ones are always the prettiest,' I said.

'You ain't referrin' to the braided ones now?' answered Mr Tilley. 'You see ours is braided for the most part, an' their good looks is all in the beginnin'. Poor dear used to say they made an easier floor. I go shufflin' round the house same's if 'twas a bo't, and I always used to be stubbin' up the corners o' the hooked kind. Her an' me was always havin' our jokes together same's a boy an' girl. Outsiders never'd know nothin' about it to see us. She had nice manners with all, but to me there was nobody so entertainin'. She'd take off anybody's natural talk winter evenin's when we set here alone, so you'd think 'twas them a-speakin'. There, there!'

I saw that he had dropped a stitch again, and was snarling the blue yarn round his clumsy fingers. He handled it and threw it off at arm's length as if it were a cod line; and frowned impatiently, but I saw a tear shining on his cheek.

I said that I must be going, it was growing late, and asked if I might come again, and if he would take me out to the fishing grounds some day.

'Yes, come any time you want to,' said my host, ''tain't so pleasant as when poor dear was here. Oh, I didn't want to lose her an' she didn't want to go, but it had to be. Such things ain't for us to say; there's no yes an' no to it.

'You find Almiry Todd one o' the best o' women?' said Mr Tilley as we parted. He was standing in the doorway and I had started off down the narrow green field. 'No, there ain't a better hearted woman in the State o' Maine. I've know her from a girl. She's had the best o' mothers. You tell her I'm liable to fetch her up a couple or three nice good mackerel early tomorrow.' he said. 'Now don't let it slip your mind. Poor dear, she always thought a sight o' Almiry, and she used to remind me there was nobody to fish for her; but I don't rec'lect it as I ought to. I see you drop a line yourself very handy now an' then.'

We laughed together like the best of friends, and I spoke again about the fishing grounds, and confessed that I had no fancy for a southerly breeze and a ground swell.

'Nor me neither,' said the old fisherman. 'Nobody likes 'em, say what they may. Poor dear was disobliged by the mere sight of a bo't. Almiry's got the best o' mothers, I expect you know; Mis' Blackett out to Green Island; and we was always plannin' to go out when summer come; but there, I couldn't pick no day's weather that seemed to suit her just right. I never set out to worry her neither, 'twa'n't no kind o' use; she was so pleasant we couldn't have no fret nor trouble. 'Twas never "you dear an' you darlin'" afore folks, an' "you divil" behind the door!'

As I looked back from the lower end of the field I saw him still standing, a lonely figure in the doorway. 'Poor dear,' I repeated to myself half aloud; 'I wonder where she is and what she knows of the little world she left. I wonder what she has been doing these eight years!'

I gave the message about the mackerel to Mrs Todd.

'Been visitin' with 'Lijah?' she asked with interest. 'I expect you had kind of a dull session; he ain't the talkin' kind; dwellin' so much long o' fish seems to make 'em lose the gift o' speech.' But when I told her that Mr Tilley had been talking to me that day, she interrupted me quickly.

'Then 'twas all about his wife, an' he can't say nothin' too pleasant neither. She was modest with strangers, but there ain't one o' her old friends can ever make up her loss. For me, I don't want to go there no more. There's some folks you miss and some folks you don't, when they're gone, but there ain't hardly a day I don't think o' dear Sarah Tilley. She was always right there; yes, you knew just where to find her like a plain flower. 'Lijah's worthy enough; I do esteem 'Lijah, but he's a ploddin' man.'

21

THE BACKWARD VIEW

At last it was the time of late summer, when the house was cool and damp in the morning, and all the light seemed to come through green leaves; but at the first step out of doors the sunshine always laid a warm hand on my shoulder, and the clear, high sky seemed to lift quickly as I looked at it. There was no autumnal mist on the coast, nor any August fog; instead of these, the sea, the sky, all the long shore line and the inland hills, with every bush of bay and every fir-top, gained a deeper color and a sharper clearness. There was something shining in the air, and a kind of lustre on the water and the pasture grass, – a northern look that, except at this moment of the year, one must go far to seek. The sunshine of a northern summer was coming to its lovely end.

The days were few at Dunnet Landing, and I let each of them slip away unwillingly as a miser spends his coins. I wished to have one of my first weeks back again, with those long hours when nothing happened except the growth of herbs and the course of the sun. Once I had not even known where to go for a walk; now there were many delightful things to be done and done again, as if I were in London. I felt hurried and full of pleasant engagements, and the days flew by like a handful of flowers flung to the sea wind.

At last I had to say goodbye to all my Dunnet Landing friends, and my homelike place in the little house, and return to the world in which I feared to find myself a foreigner. There may be restrictions to such a summer's happiness, but the ease that belongs to simplicity is charming enough to make up for whatever a simple life may lack, and the gifts of peace are not for those who live in the thick of battle.

I was to take the small unpunctual steamer that went down the bay in the afternoon, and I sat for a while by my window looking out on the green herb garden, with regret for company. Mrs Todd had hardly spoken all day except in the briefest and most disapproving way; it was as if we were on the edge of a quarrel. It seemed impossible to take my departure with anything like composure. At last I heard a footstep, and looked up to find that Mrs Todd was standing at the door.

'I've seen to everything now,' she told me in an unusually loud and business-like voice. 'Your trunks are on the w'arf by this time. Cap'n Bowden he come and took 'em down himself, an' is going to see that they're safe aboard. Yes, I've seen to all your 'rangements,' she repeated in a gentler tone. 'These things I've left on the kitchen table you'll want to carry by hand; the basket needn't be returned. I guess I shall walk over towards the Port now an' inquire how old Mis' Edward Caplin is.'

I glanced at my friend's face, and saw a look that touched me to the heart. I had been sorry enough before to go away.

'I guess you'll excuse me if I ain't down there to stand round on the w'arf and see you go,' she said, still trying to be gruff. 'Yes, I ought to go over and inquire for Mis' Edward Caplin; it's her third shock, and if mother gets in on Sunday she'll want to know just how the old lady is.' With this last word Mrs Todd turned and left me as if with sudden thought of something she had forgotten, so that I felt sure she was coming back, but presently I heard her go out of the kitchen door and walk down the path toward the gate. I could not part so; I ran after her to say goodbye, but she shook her head and waved her hand without looking back when she heard my hurrying steps, and so went away down the street.

When I went in again the little house had suddenly grown lonely, and my room looked empty as it had the day I came. I and all my belongings had died out of it, and I knew how it would seem when Mrs Todd came back and found her lodger gone. So we die before our own eyes; so we see some chapters of our lives come to their natural end.

I found the little packages on the kitchen table. There was a quaint West Indian basket which I knew its owner had valued, and which I had once admired; there was an affecting provision laid beside it for my seafaring supper, with a neatly tied bunch of southernwood and a twig of bay,[1] and a little old leather box which held the coral pin that Nathan Todd brought home to give to poor Joanna.

There was still an hour to wait, and I went up to the hill just above the schoolhouse and sat there thinking of things, and looking off to sea, and watching for the boat to come in sight. I could see Green Island, small and darkly wooded at that distance; below me were the houses of the village with their apple-trees and bits of garden ground. Presently, as I looked at the pastures beyond, I caught a last glimpse of Mrs Todd herself, walking slowly in the footpath that led along, following the shore toward the Port. At such a distance one can feel the large, positive qualities that control a character. Close at hand, Mrs Todd seemed able and warm-hearted and quite absorbed in her bustling industries, but her distant figure looked mateless and appealing, with something about it that was strangely self-possessed and mysterious. Now and then she stooped to pick something, – it might have been her favorite pennyroyal, – and at last I lost sight of her as she slowly crossed an open space on one of the higher points of land, and disappeared again behind a dark clump of juniper and the pointed firs.

As I came away on the little coastwise steamer, there was an old sea running[2] which made the surf leap high on all the rocky shores. I stood on deck, looking back, and watched the busy gulls agree and turn, and sway together down the long slopes of air, then separate hastily and plunge into the waves. The tide was setting in, and plenty of small fish were coming with it, unconscious of the silver flashing of the great birds overhead and the quickness of their fierce beaks. The sea was full of life and spirit, the tops of the waves flew back as if they were winged like the gulls themselves, and like them had the freedom of the wind. Out in the main channel we passed a bent-shouldered old fisherman bound for the evening round among his lobster traps. He was toiling along with short oars, and the dory tossed and sank and tossed again with the steamer's waves. I saw that it was old Elijah Tilley, and though we had so long been strangers we had come to be warm friends, and I wished that he had waited for one of his mates, it was such hard work to row along shore through rough seas and tend the traps alone. As we passed I waved my hand and tried to call to him, and he looked up and answered my farewells by a solemn nod. The little town, with the tall masts of its disabled schooners in the inner bay, stood high above the flat sea for a few minutes, then it sank back into the uniformity of the coast, and became indistinguishable from the other towns that looked as if they were crumbled on the furzy-green stoniness of the shore.

The small outer islands of the bay were covered among the ledges with turf that looked as fresh as the early grass; there had been some days of rain the week before, and the darker green of the sweet-fern was scattered on all the pasture heights. It looked like the beginning of summer ashore, though the sheep, round and warm in their winter wool, betrayed the season of the year as they went feeding along the slopes in the low afternoon sunshine.

Presently the wind began to blow, and we struck out seaward to double the long sheltering headland of the cape, and when I looked back again, the islands and the headland had run together and Dunnet Landing and all its coasts were lost to sight.

A WHITE HERON

I

The woods were already filled with shadows one June evening, just before
eight o'clock, though a bright sunset still glimmered faintly among the
trunks of the trees. A little girl was driving home her cow, a plodding,
dilatory, provoking creature in her behavior, but a valued companion for all
that. They were going away from whatever light there was, and striking
deep into the woods, but their feet were familiar with the path, and it was
no matter whether their eyes could see it or not.

There was hardly a night the summer through when the old cow could be
found waiting at the pasture bars; on the contrary, it was her greatest
pleasure to hide herself away among the huckleberry bushes, and though she
wore a loud bell she had made the discovery that if one stood perfectly still
it would not ring. So Sylvia had to hunt for her until she found her, and call
Co'! Co'! with never an answering Moo, until her childish patience was
quite spent. If the creature had not given good milk and plenty of it, the case
would have seemed very different to her owners. Besides, Sylvia had all the
time there was, and very little use to make of it. Sometimes in pleasant
weather it was a consolation to look upon the cow's pranks as an intelligent
attempt to play hide and seek, and as the child had no playmates she lent
herself to this amusement with a good deal of zest. Though this chase had
been so long that the wary animal herself had given an unusual signal of her
whereabouts, Sylvia had only laughed when she came upon Mistress Moolly
at the swampside, and urged her affectionately homeward with a twig of
birch leaves. The old cow was not inclined to wander farther, she even
turned in the right direction for once as they left the pasture, and stepped
along the road at a good pace. She was quite ready to be milked now, and
seldom stopped to browse. Sylvia wondered what her grandmother would
say because they were so late. It was a great while since she had left home at
half-past five o'clock, but everybody knew the difficulty of making this
errand a short one. Mrs Tilley had chased the horned torment too many

summer evenings herself to blame anyone else for lingering, and was only thankful as she waited that she had Sylvia, nowadays, to give such valuable assistance. The good woman suspected that Sylvia loitered occasionally on her own account; there never was such a child for straying about out-of-doors since the world was made! Everybody said that it was a good change for a little maid who had tried to grow for eight years in a crowded manufacturing town, but, as for Sylvia herself, it seemed as if she never had been alive at all before she came to live at the farm. She thought often with wistful compassion of a wretched geranium that belonged to a town neighbor.

'"Afraid of folks,"' old Mrs Tilley said to herself, with a smile, after she had made the unlikely choice of Sylvia from her daughter's houseful of children, and was returning to the farm. '"Afraid of folks," they said! I guess she won't be troubled no great with 'em up to the old place!' When they reached the door of the lonely house and stopped to unlock it, and the cat came to purr loudly, and rub against them, a deserted pussy, indeed, but fat with young robins, Sylvia whispered that this was a beautiful place to live in, and she never should wish to go home.

The companions followed the shady wood-road, the cow taking slow steps and the child very fast ones. The cow stopped long at the brook to drink, as if the pasture were not half a swamp, and Sylvia stood still and waited, letting her bare feet cool themselves in the shoal water, while the great twilight moths struck softly against her. She waded on through the brook as the cow moved away, and listened to the thrushes with a heart that beat fast with pleasure. There was a stirring in the great boughs overhead. They were full of little birds and beasts that seemed to be wide awake, and going about their world, or else saying good-night to each other in sleepy twitters. Sylvia herself felt sleepy as she walked along. However, it was not much farther to the house, and the air was soft and sweet. She was not often in the woods so late as this, and it made her feel as if she were a part of the gray shadows and the moving leaves. She was just thinking how long it seemed since she first came to the farm a year ago, and wondering if everything went on in the noisy town just the same as when she was there; the thought of the great red-faced boy who used to chase and frighten her made her hurry along the path to escape from the shadow of the trees.

Suddenly this little woods-girl is horror-stricken to hear a clear whistle not very far away. Not a bird's-whistle, which would have a sort of friendliness, but a boy's whistle, determined, and somewhat aggressive.

'Oh no, they're stuffed and preserved, dozens and dozens of them,' said the ornithologist, 'and I have shot or snared every one myself. I caught a glimpse of a white heron a few miles from here on Saturday, and I have followed it in this direction. They have never been found in this district at all. The little white heron, it is,'[1] and he turned again to look at Sylvia with the hope of discovering that the rare bird was one of her acquaintances.

But Sylvia was watching a hop-toad in the narrow footpath.

'You would know the heron if you saw it,' the stranger continued eagerly. 'A queer tall white bird with soft feathers and long thin legs. And it would have a nest perhaps in the top of a high tree, made of sticks, something like a hawk's nest.'

Sylvia's heart gave a wild beat; she knew that strange white bird, and had once stolen softly near where it stood in some bright green swamp grass, away over at the other side of the woods. There was an open place where the sunshine always seemed strangely yellow and hot, where tall, nodding rushes grew, and her grandmother had warned her that she might sink in the soft black mud underneath and never be heard of more. Not far beyond were the salt marshes just this side the sea itself, which Sylvia wondered and dreamed much about, but never had seen, whose great voice could sometimes be heard above the noise of the woods on stormy nights.

'I can't think of anything I should like so much as to find that heron's nest,' the handsome stranger was saying. 'I would give ten dollars to anybody who could show it to me,' he added desperately, 'and I mean to spend my whole vacation hunting for it if need be. Perhaps it was only migrating, or had been chased out of its own region by some bird of prey.'

Mrs Tilley gave amazed attention to all this, but Sylvia still watched the toad, not divining, as she might have done at some calmer time, that the creature wished to get to its hole under the door-step, and was much hindered by the unusual spectators at that hour of the evening. No amount of thought, that night, could decide how many wished-for treasures the ten dollars, so lightly spoken of, would buy.

The next day the young sportsman hovered about the woods, and Sylvia kept him company, having lost her first fear of the friendly lad, who proved to be most kind and sympathetic. He told her many things about the birds and what they knew and where they lived and what they did with themselves. And he gave her a jack-knife, which she thought as great a treasure as if she were a desert-islander. All day long he did not once make her troubled or afraid except when he brought down some unsuspecting singing creature from its bough. Sylvia would have liked him vastly better without his gun; she could not understand why he killed the very birds he seemed to like so much. But as the day waned, Sylvia still watched the young man with loving admiration. She had never seen anybody so charming and delightful; the woman's heart, asleep in the child, was vaguely thrilled by a dream of love. Some premonition of that great power stirred and swayed these young creatures who traversed the solemn woodlands with soft-footed silent care. They stopped to listen to a bird's song; they pressed forward again eagerly, parting the branches – speaking to each other rarely and in whispers; the young man going first and Sylvia following, fascinated, a few steps behind, with her gray eyes dark with excitement.

She grieved because the longed-for white heron was elusive, but she did not lead the guest, she only followed, and there was no such thing as speaking first. The sound of her own unquestioned voice would have terrified her – it was hard enough to answer yes or no when there was need of that. At last evening began to fall; and they drove the cow home together, and Sylvia smiled with pleasure when they came to the place where she heard the whistle and was afraid only the night before.

II

Half a mile from home, at the farther edge of the woods, where the land was highest, a great pine-tree stood, the last of its generation. Whether it was left for a boundary mark, or for what reason, no one could say; the wood-choppers who had felled its mates were dead and gone long ago, and a whole forest of sturdy trees, pines and oaks and maples, had grown again. But the stately head of this old pine[2] towered above them all and made a landmark for sea and shore miles and miles away. Sylvia knew it well. She had always believed that whoever climbed to the top of it could see the ocean; and the little girl had often laid her hand on the great rough trunk and looked up wistfully at those dark boughs that the wind always stirred, no matter how hot and still the air might be below. Now she thought of the tree with a new excitement, for why, if one climbed it at break of day could not one see all the world, and easily discover from whence the white heron flew, and mark the place, and find the hidden nest?

What a spirit of adventure, what wild ambition! What fancied triumph and delight and glory for the later morning when she could make known the secret! It was almost too real and too great for the childish heart to bear.

All night the door of the little house stood open and the whippoorwills[3] came and sang upon the very step. The young sportsman and his old hostess were sound asleep, but Sylvia's great design kept her broad awake and watching. She forgot to think of sleep. The short summer night seemed as long as the winter darkness, and at last when the whippoorwills ceased, and she was afraid the morning would after all come too soon, she stole out of the house and followed the pasture path through the woods, hastening toward the open ground beyond, listening with a sense of comfort and companionship to the drowsy twitter of a half-awakened bird, whose perch she had jarred in passing. Alas, if the great wave of human interest which flooded for the first time this dull little life should sweep away the satisfactions of an existence heart to heart with nature and the dumb life of the forest!

There was the huge tree asleep yet in the paling moonlight, and small and silly Sylvia began with utmost bravery to mount to the top of it, with tingling, eager blood coursing the channels of her whole frame, with her bare feet and fingers, that pinched and held like bird's claws to the monstrous ladder reaching up, up, almost to the sky itself. First she must mount the white oak tree that grew alongside, where she was almost lost among the dark branches and the green leaves heavy and wet with dew; a bird fluttered off its nest, and a red squirrel ran to and fro and scolded pettishly at the harmless housebreaker. Sylvia felt her way easily. She had often climbed there, and knew that higher still one of the oak's upper branches chafed against the pine trunk, just where its lower boughs were set close together. There, when she made the dangerous pass from one tree to the other, the great enterprise would really begin.

She crept out along the swaying oak limb at last, and took the daring step across into the old pine-tree. The way was harder than she thought; she must reach far and hold fast, the sharp dry twigs caught and held her and scratched her like angry talons, the pitch made her thin little fingers clumsy and stiff as she went round and round the tree's great stem, higher and higher upward. The sparrows and robins in the woods below were beginning to wake and twitter to the dawn, yet it seemed much lighter there aloft in the pine-tree, and the child knew she must hurry if her project were to be of any use.

The tree seemed to lengthen itself out as she went up, and to reach farther and farther upward. It was like a great main-mast to the voyaging earth; it must truly have been amazed that morning through all its ponderous frame as it felt this determined spark of human spirit wending its way from higher branch to branch. Who knows how steadily the least twigs held themselves to advantage this light, weak creature on her way! The old pine must have loved this new dependent. More than all the hawks, and bats, and moths, and even the sweet voiced thrushes, was the brave, beating heart of the solitary gray-eyed child. And the tree stood still and frowned away the winds that June morning while the dawn grew bright in the east.

Sylvia's face was like a pale star, if one had seen it from the ground, when the last thorny bough was past, and she stood trembling and tired but wholly triumphant, high in the tree-top. Yes, there was the sea with the dawning sun making a golden dazzle over it, and toward that glorious east flew two hawks with slow-moving pinions. How low they looked in the air from that height when one had only seen them before far up, and dark against the blue sky. Their gray feathers were as soft as moths; they seemed only a little way from the tree, and Sylvia felt as if she too could go flying away among the clouds. Westward, the woodlands and farms reached miles and miles into the distance; here and there were church steeples, and white villages, truly it was a vast and awesome world!

The birds sang louder and louder. At last the sun came up bewilderingly bright. Sylvia could see the white sails of ships out at sea, and the clouds that were purple and rose-colored and yellow at first began to fade away. Where was the white heron's nest in the sea of green branches, and was this wonderful sight and pageant of the world the only reward for having climbed to such a giddy height? Now look down again, Sylvia, where the green marsh is set among the shining birches and dark hemlocks,[4] there where you saw the white heron once you will see him again; look, look! a white spot of him like a single floating feather comes up from the dead hemlock and grows larger, and rises, and comes close at last, and goes by the landmark pine with steady sweep of wing and outstretched slender neck and crested head. And wait! wait! do not move a foot or a finger, little girl, do not send an arrow of light and consciousness from your two eager eyes, for the heron has perched on a pine bough not far beyond yours, and cries back to his mate on the nest and plumes his feathers for the new day!

The child gives a long sigh a minute later when a company of shouting cat-birds[5] comes also to the tree, and vexed by their fluttering and lawlessness the solemn heron goes away. She knows his secret now, the wild, light, slender bird that floats and wavers, and goes back like an arrow presently to his home in the green world beneath. Then Sylvia, well satisfied, makes her perilous way down again, not daring to look far below the branch she stands on, ready to cry sometimes because her fingers ache and her lamed feet slip. Wondering over and over again what the stranger would say to her, and what he would think when she told him how to find his way straight to the heron's nest.

'Sylvy, Sylvy!' called the busy old grandmother again and again, but nobody answered, and the small husk bed was empty and Sylvia had disappeared.

The guest waked from a dream, and remembering his day's pleasure hurried to dress himself that might it sooner begin. He was sure from the way the shy little girl looked once or twice yesterday that she had at least seen the white heron, and now she must really be made to tell. Here she comes now, paler than ever, and her worn old frock is torn and tattered, and smeared with pine pitch. The grandmother and the sportsman stand in the door together and question her, and the splendid moment has come to speak of the dead hemlock-tree by the green marsh.

But Sylvia does not speak after all, though the old grandmother fretfully rebukes her, and the young man's kind, appealing eyes are looking straight in her own. He can make them rich with money; he has promised it, and they are poor now. He is so well worth making happy, and he waits to hear the story she can tell.

No, she must keep silence! What is it that suddenly forbids her and makes her dumb? Has she been nine years growing and now, when the great world for the first time puts out a hand to her, must she thrust it aside for a bird's sake? The murmur of the pine's green branches is in her ears, she remembers how the white heron came flying through the golden air and how they watched the sea and the morning together, and Sylvia cannot speak; she cannot tell the heron's secret and give its life away.

Dear loyalty, that suffered a sharp pang as the guest went away disappointed later in the day, that could have served and followed him and loved him as a dog loves! Many a night Sylvia heard the echo of his whistle haunting the pasture path as she came home with the loitering cow. She forgot even her sorrow at the sharp report of his gun and the sight of thrushes and sparrows dropping silent to the ground, their songs hushed and their pretty feathers stained and wet with blood. Were the birds better friends than their hunter might have been, – who can tell? Whatever treasures were lost to her, woodlands and summer-time, remember! Bring your gifts and graces and tell your secrets to this lonely country child!

MARSH ROSEMARY

I

One hot afternoon in August, a single moving figure might have been seen following a straight road that crossed the salt marshes of Walpole. Everybody else had either stayed at home or crept into such shade as could be found near at hand. The thermometer marked at least ninety degrees. There was hardly a fishing-boat to be seen on the glistening sea, only far away on the hazy horizon two or three coasting schooners looked like ghostly flying Dutchmen,[1] becalmed for once and motionless.

Ashore, the flaring light of the sun brought out the fine, clear colors of the level landscape. The marsh grasses were a more vivid green than usual, the brown tops of those that were beginning to go to seed looked almost red, and the soil at the edges of the tide inlets seemed to be melting into a black, pitchy substance like the dark pigments on a painter's palette. Where the land was higher the hot air flickered above it dizzily. This was not an afternoon that one would naturally choose for a long walk, yet Mr Jerry Lane stepped briskly forward, and appeared to have more than usual energy. His big boots trod down the soft carpet of pussy-clover[2] that bordered the dusty, whitish road. He struck at the stationary procession of thistles with a little stick as he went by. Flight after flight of yellow butterflies fluttered up as he passed, and then settled down again to their thistle flowers, while on the shiny cambric back of Jerry's Sunday waistcoat basked at least eight large green-headed flies in complete security.

It was difficult to decide why the Sunday waistcoat should have been put on that Saturday afternoon. Jerry had not thought it important to wear his best boots or best trousers, and had left his coat at home altogether. He smiled as he walked along, and once when he took off his hat, as a light breeze came that way, he waved it triumphantly before he put it on again. Evidently this was no common errand that led him due west, and made him forget the hot weather, and caused him to shade his eyes with his hand, as he looked eagerly at a clump of trees and the chimney of a small house a little way beyond the boundary of the marshes, where the higher ground began.

Miss Ann Floyd sat by her favorite window, sewing, twitching her thread less decidedly than usual, and casting a wistful glance now and then down the road or at the bees in her gay little garden outside. There was a grim expression overshadowing her firmly-set, angular face, and the frown that always appeared on her forehead when she sewed or read the newspaper was deeper and straighter than usual. She did not look as if she were conscious of the heat, though she had dressed herself in an old-fashioned skirt of sprigged lawn and a loose jacket of thin white dimity[3] with out-of-date flowing sleeves. Her sandy hair was smoothly brushed; one lock betrayed a slight crinkle at its edge, but it owed nothing to any encouragement of Nancy Floyd's. A hard, honest, kindly face this was, of a woman whom everybody trusted, who might be expected to give of whatever she had to give, good measure, pressed down and running over.[4] She was a lonely soul; she had no near relatives in the world. It seemed always as if nature had been mistaken in not planting her somewhere in a large and busy household.

The little square room, kitchen in winter, and sitting-room in summer, was as clean and bare and thrifty as one would expect the dwelling-place of such a woman to be. She sat in a straight-backed, splint-bottomed[5] kitchen chair, and always put back her spool with a click on the very same spot on the window-sill. You would think she had done with youth and with love affairs, yet you might as well expect the ancient cherry-tree in the corner of her yard to cease adventuring its white blossoms when the May sun shone! No woman in Walpole had more bravely and patiently borne the burden of loneliness and lack of love. Even now her outward behavior gave no hint of the new excitement and delight that filled her heart.

'Land sakes alive!' she says to herself presently, 'there comes Jerry Lane. I expect, if he sees me setting' to the winder, he'll come in an' dawdle round till supper time!' But good Nancy Floyd smooths her hair hastily as she rises and drops her work, and steps back toward the middle of the room, watching the gate anxiously all the time. Now, Jerry, with a crestfallen look at the vacant window, makes believe that he is going by, and takes a loitering step or two onward, and then stops short; with a somewhat sheepish smile he leans over the neat picket fence and examines the blue and white and pink larkspur that covers most of the space in the little garden. He takes off his hat again to cool his forehead, and replaces it, without a grand gesture this time, and looks again at the window hopefully.

There is a pause. The woman knows that the man is sure she is there; a little blush colors her thin cheeks as she comes boldly to the wide-open front door.

'What do you think of this kind of weather?' asks Jerry Lane, complacently, as he leans over the fence, and surrounds himself with an air of self-sacrifice.

'I call it hot,' responds the Juliet from her balcony, with deliberate assurance, 'but the corn needs sun, everybody says. I shouldn't have wanted to toil up from the shore under such a glare, if I had been you. Better come in and set a while, and cool off,' she added, without any apparent enthusiasm. Jerry was sure to come, any way. She would rather make the suggestion than have him.

Mr Lane sauntered in, and seated himself opposite his hostess, beside the other small window, and watched her admiringly as she took up her sewing and worked at it with great spirit and purpose. He clasped his hands together and leaned forward a little. The shaded kitchen was very comfortable, after the glaring light outside, and the clean orderliness of the few chairs and the braided rugs and the table under the clock, with some larkspur and asparagus in a china vase for decoration, seemed to please him unexpectedly. 'Now just see what ways you women folks have of fixing things up smart!' he ventured gallantly.

Nancy's countenance did not forbid further compliment; she looked at the flowers herself, quickly, and explained that she had gathered them a while ago to send to the minister's sister, who kept house for him. 'I saw him going by, and expected he'd be back this same road. Mis' Elton's be'n havin' another o' her dyin' spells this noon, and the deacon went by after him hot foot. I'd souse her well with stone-cold water. She never sent for me to set up with her; she knows better. Poor man, 'twas likely he was right into the middle of tomorrow's sermon. 'T'ain't considerate of the deacon, and when he knows he's got a fool for a wife, he needn't go round persuading other folks she's so suffering as she makes out. They ain't got no larkspur this year to the parsonage, and I was going to let the minister take this over to Amandy; but I see his wagon over on the other road, going towards the village, about an hour after he went by here.'

It seemed to be a relief to tell somebody all these things after such a season of forced repression, and Jerry listened with gratifying interest. 'How you do see through folks!' he exclaimed in a mild voice. Jerry could be very soft spoken if he thought best. 'Mis' Elton's a die-away lookin' creatur'. I heard of her saying last Sunday, comin' out o' meetin', that she made an effort to git there once more, but she expected 'twould be the last time. Looks as if she eat well, don't she?' he concluded, in a meditative tone.

'Eat!' exclaimed the hostess, with snapping eyes. 'There ain't no woman in town, sick or well, can lay aside the food that she does. 'Tain't to the table afore folks, but she goes seeking round in the cupboards half a dozen times a day. An' I've heard her remark 'twas the last time she ever expected to visit the sanctuary as much as a dozen times within five years.'

'Some places I've sailed to they'd have hit her over the head with a club long ago,' said Jerry, with an utter lack of sympathy that was startling. 'Well, I must be gettin' back again. Talkin' of eatin' makes us think o' supper time. Must be past five, ain't it? I thought I'd just step up to see if there wa'n't anything I could lend a hand about, this hot day.'

Sensible Ann Floyd folded her hands over her sewing, as it lay in her lap, and looked straight before her without seeing the pleading face of the guest. This moment was a great crisis in her life. She was conscious of it, and knew well enough that upon her next words would depend the course of future events. The man who waited to hear what she had to say was indeed many years younger than she, was shiftless and vacillating. He had drifted to Walpole from nobody knew where, and possessed many qualities which she had openly rebuked and despised in other men. True enough, he was good-looking, but that did not atone for the lacks of his character and reputation. Yet she knew herself to be the better man of the two, and since she had surmounted many obstacles already she was confident that, with a push here and a pull there to steady him, she could keep him in good trim.[6] The winters were so long and lonely; her life was in many ways hungry and desolate in spite of its thrift and conformity. She had laughed scornfully when he stopped, one day in the spring, and offered to help her weed her garden; she had even joked with one of the neighbors about it. Jerry had been growing more and more friendly and pleasant ever since. His ease-loving careless nature was like a comfortable cushion for hers, with its angles, its melancholy anticipations and self-questionings. But Jerry liked her, and if she liked him and married him, and took him home, it was nobody's business; and in that moment of surrender to Jerry's cause she arrayed herself at his right hand against the rest of the world, ready for warfare with any and all of its opinions.

She was suddenly aware of the sunburnt face and light, curling hair of her undeclared lover, at the other end of the painted table with its folded leaf.

She smiled at him vacantly across the larkspur; then she gave a little start, and was afraid that her thoughts had wandered longer than was seemly. The kitchen clock was ticking faster than usual, as if it were trying to attract attention.

'I guess I'll be getting home,' repeated the visitor ruefully, and rose from his chair, but hesitated again at an unfamiliar expression upon his companion's face.

'I don't know as I've got anything extra for supper, but you stop,' she said, 'an' take what there is. I wouldn't go back across them marshes right in this heat.'

Jerry Lane had a lively sense of humor, and a queer feeling of merriment stole over him now, as he watched the mistress of the house. She had risen, too; she looked so simple and so frankly sentimental, there was such an incongruous coyness added to her usually straightforward, angular appearance, that his instinctive laughter nearly got the better of him, and might have lost him the prize for which he had been waiting these many months. But Jerry behaved like a man: he stepped forward and kissed Ann Floyd; he held her fast with one arm as he stood beside her, and kissed her again and again. She was a dear good woman. She had a fresh young heart, in spite of the straight wrinkle in her forehead and her work-worn hands. She had waited all her days for this joy of having a lover.

II

Even Mrs Elton revived for a day or two under the tonic of such a piece of news. That was what Jerry Lane had hung round for all summer, everybody knew at last. Now he would strike work and live at his ease, the men grumbled to each other; but all the women of Walpole deplored most the weakness and foolishness of the elderly bride. Ann Floyd was comfortably off, and had something laid by for a rainy day; she would have done vastly better to deny herself such an expensive and utterly worthless luxury as the kind of husband Jerry Lane would make. He had idled away his life. He earned a little money now and then in seafaring pursuits, but was too lazy, in the shore parlance, to tend lobster-pots. What was energetic Ann Floyd going to do with him? She was always at work, always equal to emergencies, and entirely opposed to dullness and idleness and even placidity. She liked people who had some snap to them, she often avowed scornfully, and now she had chosen for a husband the laziest man in Walpole. 'Dear sakes,' one woman said to another, as they heard the news, 'there's no fool like an old fool!'

The days went quickly by, while Miss Ann made her plain wedding clothes. If people expected her to put on airs of youth they were disappointed. Her wedding bonnet was the same sort of bonnet she had worn for a dozen years, and one disappointed critic deplored the fact that she had spruced up so little, and kept on dressing old enough to look like Jerry Lane's mother. As her acquaintances met her they looked at her with close scrutiny, expecting to see some outward trace of such a silly, uncharacteristic departure from good sense and discretion. But Miss Floyd, while she was still Miss Floyd, displayed no silliness and behaved with dignity, while on the Sunday after a quiet marriage at the parsonage she and Jerry Lane walked up the side aisle to their pew, the picture of middle-aged sobriety and respectability. Their fellow parishoners, having recovered from their first astonishment and amusement, settled down to the belief that the newly married pair understood their own business best, and that if anybody could make the best of Jerry and get any work out of him, it was his capable wife.

'And if she undertakes to drive him too hard he can slip off to sea, and they'll be rid of each other,' commented one of Jerry's 'longshore companions, as if it were only reasonable that some refuge should be afforded to those who make mistakes in matrimony.

There did not seem to be any mistake at first, or for a good many months afterward. The husband liked the comfort that came from such good housekeeping, and enjoyed a deep sense of having made a good anchorage in a well-sheltered harbor, after many years of thriftless improvidence and drifting to and fro. There were some hindrances to perfect happiness: he had to forego long seasons of gossip with his particular friends, and the outdoor work which was expected of him, though by no means heavy for a person of his strength, fettered his freedom not a little. To chop wood, and take care of a cow, and bring a pail of water now and then, did not weary him so much as it made him practically understand the truth of weakly Sister Elton's remark that life was a constant chore. And when poor Jerry, for lack of other interest, fancied that his health was giving way mysteriously, and brought home a bottle of strong liquor to be used in case of sickness, and placed it conveniently in the shed, Mrs Lane locked it up in the small chimney cupboard where she kept her camphor bottle and her opodeldoc[7] and the other family medicines. She was not harsh with her husband. She cherished him tenderly, and worked diligently at her trade of tailoress, singing her hymns gayly in summer weather; for she never had been so happy as now, when there was somebody to please beside herself, to cook for and sew for, and to live with and love. But Jerry complained more and more in his inmost heart that his wife expected too much of him. Presently he resumed an old habit of resorting to the least respected of the two country stores of that neighborhood, and sat in the row of loafers on the outer steps. 'Sakes alive,' said a shrewd observer one day, 'the fools set there and talk and talk about what they went through when they follered the sea, till when the womenfolks comes tradin' they are obleeged to climb right over 'em.'

But things grew worse and worse, until one day Jerry Lane came home a little late to dinner, and found his wife unusually grim-faced and impatient. He took his seat with an amiable smile, and showed in every way his determination not to lose his temper because somebody else had. It was one of the days when he looked almost boyish and entirely irresponsible. His hair was handsome and curly from the dampness of the east wind, and his wife was forced to remember how, in the days of their courtship, she used to wish that she could pull one of the curling locks straight, for the pleasure of seeing it fly back. She felt old and tired, and was hurt in her very soul by the contrast between herself and her husband. 'No wonder I am aging, having to lug everything on my shoulders,' she thought. Jerry had forgotten to do whatever she had asked him for a day or two. He had started out that morning to go lobstering, but he had returned from the direction of the village.

'Nancy,' he said pleasantly, after he had begun his dinner, a silent and solitary meal, while his wife stitched busily by the window, and refused to look at him, – 'Nancy, I've been thinking a good deal about a project.'

'I hope it ain't going to cost so much and bring in so little as your other notions have, then,' she responded, quickly; though somehow a memory of the hot day when Jerry came and stood outside the fence, and kissed her when it was settled he should stay to supper, – a memory of that day would keep fading and brightening in her mind.

'Yes,' said Jerry, humbly, 'I ain't done right, Nancy. I ain't done my part for our livin'. I've let it sag right on to you, most ever since we was married. There was that spell when I was kind of weakly, and had a pain acrost me. I tell you what it is: I never was good for nothin' ashore, but now I've got my strength up I'm going to show ye what I can do. I'm promised to ship with Cap'n Low's brother, Skipper Nathan, that sails out o' Eastport in the coasting trade, lumber and so on. I shall get good wages, and you shall keep the whole on 't 'cept what I need for clothes.'

'You needn't be so plaintive,' said Ann, in a sharp voice. 'You can go if you want to. I have always been able to take care of myself, but when it comes to maintainin' two, 'tain't so easy. When be you goin'?'

'I expected you would be sorry,' mourned Jerry, his face falling at this outbreak. 'Nancy, you needn't be so quick. 'Tain't as if I hadn't always set everything by ye, if I be wuthless.'

Nancy's eyes flashed fire as she turned hastily away. Hardly knowing where she went, she passed through the open doorway, and crossed the clean green turf of the narrow side yard, and leaned over the garden fence. The young cabbages and cucumbers were nearly buried in weeds, and the currant bushes were fast being turned into skeletons by the ravaging worms. Jerry had forgotten to sprinkle them with hellebore, after all, though she had put the watering-pot into his very hand the evening before. She did not like to have the whole town laugh at her for hiring a man to do his work; she was busy from early morning until late night, but she could not do everything herself. She had been a fool to marry this man, she told herself at last, and a sullen discontent and rage that had been of slow but certain growth made her long to free herself from this unprofitable hindrance for a time, at any rate. Go to sea? Yes, that was the best thing that could happen. Perhaps when he had worked hard a while on schooner fare, he would come home and be good for something!

Jerry finished his dinner in the course of time, and then sought his wife. It was not like her to go away in this silent fashion. Of late her gift of speech had been proved sufficiently formidable, and yet she had never looked so resolutely angry as to-day.

'Nancy,' he began, – 'Nancy, girl! I ain't goin' off to leave you, if your heart's set against it. I'll spudge up[8] and take right holt.'

But the wife turned slowly from the fence and faced him. Her eyes looked as if she had been crying. 'You needn't stay on my account,' she said. 'I'll go right to work an fit ye out. I'm sick of your meechin'[9] talk, and I don't want to hear no more of it. Ef *I* was a man' –

Jerry Lane looked crestfallen for a minute or two; but when his stern partner in life had disappeared within the house, he slunk away among the apple-trees of the little orchard, and sat down on the grass in a shady spot. It was getting to be warm weather, but he would go round and hoe the old girl's garden stuff by and by. There would be something goin' on aboard the schooner, and with delicious anticipation of future pleasure this delinquent

Jerry struck his knee with his hand, as if he were clapping a crony on the shoulder. He also winked several times at the same fancied companion. Then, with a comfortable chuckle, he laid himself down, and pulled his old hat over his eyes, and went to sleep, while the weeds grew at their own sweet will, and the currant worms went looping and devouring from twig to twig.

III

Summer went by, and winter began, and Mr Jerry Lane did not reappear. He had promised to return in September, when he parted from his wife early in June, for Nancy had relented a little at the last, and sorrowed at the prospect of so long a separation. She had already learned the vacillations and uncertainties of her husband's character; but though she accepted the truth that her marriage had been in every way a piece of foolishness, she still clung affectionately to his assumed fondness for her. She could not believe that his marriage was only one of his makeshifts, and that as soon as he grew tired of the constraint he was ready to throw the benefits of respectable home life to the four winds. A little sentimental speech-making and a few kisses the morning he went away, and the gratitude he might well have shown for her generous care-taking and provision for his voyage won her soft heart back again, and made poor, elderly, simple-hearted Nancy watch him cross the marshes with tears and foreboding. If she could have called him back that day, she would have done so and been thankful. And all summer and winter, whenever the wind blew and thrashed the drooping elm boughs against the low roof over her head, she was as full of fears and anxieties as if Jerry were her only son and making his first voyage at sea. The neighbors pitied her for her disappointment. They liked Nancy; but they could not help saying, 'I told you so.' It would have been impossible not to respect the brave way in which she met the world's eye, and carried herself with innocent unconsciousness of having committed so laughable and unrewarding a folly. The loafers on the store steps had been unwontedly diverted one day, when Jerry, who was their chief wit and spokesman, rose slowly from his place, and said in pious tones, 'Boys, I must go this minute. Grandma will keep dinner waiting.' Mrs Ann Lane did not show in her aging face how young her heart was, and after the schooner *Susan Barnes* had departed she seemed to pass swiftly from middle life and an almost youthful vigor to early age and a look of spent strength and dissatisfaction. 'I suppose he did find it dull,' she assured herself, with wistful yearning for his rough words of praise, when she sat down alone to her dinner, or looked up sadly from her work, and missed the amusing though unedifying conversation he was wont to offer occasionally on stormy winter nights. How much of his adventuring was true she never cared to ask. He had come and gone, and she forgave him his shortcomings, and longed for his society with a heavy heart.

One spring day there was news in the Boston paper of the loss of the schooner *Susan Barnes* with all on board, and Nancy Lane's best friends shook their sage heads, and declared that as far as regarded Jerry Lane, that idle vagabond, it was all for the best. Nobody was interested in any other member of the crew, so the misfortune of the *Susan Barnes* seemed of but slight consequence in Walpole, she having passed out of her former owners' hands the autumn before. Jerry had stuck by the ship; at least, so he had sent word then to his wife by Skipper Nathan Low. The *Susan Barnes* was to sail regularly between Shediac[10] and Newfoundland, and Jerry sent five dollars to Nancy, and promised to pay her a visit soon. 'Tell her I'm layin' up somethin' handsome,' he told the skipper with a grin, 'and I've got some folks in Newfoundland I'll visit with on this voyage, and then I'll come ashore for good and farm it.'

Mrs Lane took the five dollars from the skipper as proudly as if Jerry had done the same thing so many times before that she hardly noticed it. The skipper gave the messages from Jerry, and felt that he had done the proper thing. When the news came long afterward that the schooner was lost, that was the next thing that Nancy knew about her wandering mate; and after the minister had come solemnly to inform her of her bereavement, and had gone away again, and she sat down and looked her widowhood in the face, there was not a sadder nor a lonelier woman in the town of Walpole.

All the neighbors came to condole with our heroine, and, though nobody was aware of it, from that time she was really happier and better satisfied with life than she had ever been before. Now she had an ideal Jerry Lane to mourn over and think about, to cherish and admire; she was day by day slowly forgetting the trouble he had been and the bitter shame of him, and exalting his memory to something near saintliness. 'He meant well,' she told herself again and again. She thought nobody could tell so good a story; she felt that with her own bustling, capable ways he had no chance to do much that he might have done. She had been too quick with him, and alas, alas! how much better she would know how to treat him if she only could see him again! A sense of relief at his absence made her continually assure herself of her great loss, and, false even to herself, she mourned her sometime lover diligently, and tried to think herself a broken-hearted woman. It was thought among those who knew Nancy Lane best that she would recover her spirits in time, but Jerry's wildest anticipations of a proper respect to his memory were more than realized in the first two years after the schooner *Susan Barnes* went to the bottom of the sea. She mourned for the man he ought to have been, not for the real Jerry, but she had loved him in the beginning enough to make her own love a precious possession for all time to come. It did not matter much, after all, what manner of man he was; she had found in him something on which to spend her hoarded affection.

IV

Nancy Lane was a peaceable woman and a good neighbor, but she never had been able to get on with one fellow townswoman, and that was Mrs Deacon Elton. They managed to keep each other provoked and teased from one year's end to the other, and each good soul felt herself under a moral microscope, and understood that she was judged by a not very lenient criticism and discussion. Mrs Lane clad herself in simple black after the news came of her husband's timely death, and Mrs Elton made one of her farewell pilgrimages to church to see the new-made widow walk up the aisle.

'She needn't tell me she lays that affliction so much to heart,' the deacon's wife sniffed faintly, after her exhaustion had been met by proper treatment of camphor and a glass of currant wine, at the parsonage, where she rested a while after service. 'Nancy Floyd knows she's well over with such a piece of nonsense. If I had had my health, I should have spoken with her and urged her not to take the step in the first place. She hasn't spoken six beholden words to me since that vagabond came to Walpole. I dare say she may have heard something I said at the time she married. I declare for 't, I never was so outdone as I was when the deacon came home and told me Nancy Floyd was going to be married. She let herself down too low to ever hold the place again that she used to have in folks' minds. And it's my opinion,' said the sharp-eyed little woman, 'she ain't got through with her pay yet.'

But Mrs Elton did not know with what unconscious prophecy her words were freighted.

★

The months passed by: summer and winter came and went, and even those few persons who were misled by Nancy Lane's stern visage and forbidding exterior into forgetting her kind heart were at last won over to friendliness by her renewed devotion to the sick and old people of the rural community. She was so tender to little children that they all loved her dearly. She was ready to go to any household that needed help, and in spite of her ceaseless industry with her needle she found many a chance to do good, and help her neighbors to lift and carry the burdens of their lives. She blossomed out suddenly into a lovely, painstaking eagerness to be of use; it seemed as if her affectionate heart, once made generous, must go on spending its wealth wherever it could find an excuse. Even Mrs Elton herself was touched by her old enemy's evident wish to be friends, and said nothing more about poor Nancy's looking as savage as a hawk. The only thing to admit was the truth that her affliction had proved a blessing to her. And it was in a truly kind and compassionate spirit that, after hearing an awful piece of news, the deacon's hysterical wife forbore to spread it far and wide through the town first, and went down to the Widow Lane's one September afternoon. Nancy was stitching busily upon the deacon's new coat, and looked up with a friendly smile as her guest came in, in spite of an instinctive shrug as she had seen her coming up the yard. The dislike of the poor souls for each other was deeper than their philosophy could reach.

Mrs Elton spent some minutes in the unnecessary endeavor to regain her breath, and to her surprise found she must make a real effort before she could tell her unwelcome news. She had been so full of it all the way from home that she had rehearsed the whole interview; now she hardly knew how to begin. Nancy looked serener than usual, but there was something wistful about her face as she glanced across the room, presently, as if to understand the reason of the long pause. The clock ticked loudly; the kitten clattered a spool against the table-leg, and had begun to snarl the thread around her busy paws, and Nancy looked down and saw her; then the instant consciousness of there being some unhappy reason for Mrs Elton's call made her forget the creature's mischief, and anxiously lay down her work to listen.

'Skipper Nathan Low was to our house to dinner,' the guest began. 'He's bargaining with the deacon about some hay. He's got a new schooner, Skipper Nathan has, and is going to build up a regular business of freighting hay to Boston by sea. There's no market to speak of about here, unless you haul it way over to Downer, and you can't make but one turn a day.'

' 'Twould be a good thing,' replied Nancy, trying to think that this was all, and perhaps the deacon wanted to hire her own field another year. He had underpaid her once, and they had not been on particularly good terms ever since. She would make her own bargains with Skipper Nathan, she thanked him and his wife!

'He's been down to the provinces these two or three years back, you know,' the whining voice went on, and straightforward Ann Lane felt the old animosity rising within her. 'At dinner time I wasn't able to eat much of anything, and so I was talking with Cap'n Nathan, and asking him some questions about the mercy 'twas his life should ha' been spared when that schooner, the *Susan Barnes*, was lost so quick after he sold out his part of her. And I put in a word, bein' 's we were neighbors, about how edifyin' your course had be'n under affliction. I noticed then he'd looked sort o' queer whilst I was talkin', but there was all the folks to the table, and you know he's a very cautious man, so he spoke of somethin' else. 'Twa'n't half an hour after dinner, I was comin' in with some plates and cups, tryin' to help what my stren'th would let me, and says he, "Step out a little ways into the piece[11] with me, Mis' Elton. I want to have a word with ye." I went, too, spite o' my neuralgy, for I saw he'd got somethin' on his mind. "Look here," says he, "I gathered from the way you spoke that Jerry Lane's wife expects he's dead." Certain, says I, his name was in the list o' the *Susan Barnes*'s crew, and we read it in the paper. "No," says he to me, "he ran away the day they sailed; he wasn't aboard, and he's livin' with another woman down to Shediac." Them was his very words.'

Nancy Lane sank back in her chair, and covered her horror-stricken eyes with her hands. ''Tain't pleasant news to have to tell,' Sister Elton went on mildly, yet with evident relish and full command of the occasion. 'He said he seen Jerry the morning he came away. I thought you ought to know it. I'll tell you one thing, Nancy: I told the skipper to keep still about it, and now I've told you, I won't spread it no further to set folks a-talking. I'll keep it secret till you say the word. There ain't much trafficking betwixt here and there, and he's dead to you, certain, as much as if he laid up here in the burying-ground.'

Nancy had bowed her head upon the table; the thin sandy hair was streaked with gray. She did not answer one word; this was the hardest blow of all.

'I'm much obliged to you for being so friendly,' she said after a few minutes, looking straight before her now in a dazed sort of way, and lifting the new coat from the floor, where it had fallen. 'Yes, he's dead to me, – worse than dead, a good deal,' and her lip quivered. 'I can't seem to bring my thoughts to bear. I've got so used to thinkin' – No, don't you say nothin' to the folks, yet. I'd do as much for you.' And Mrs Elton knew that the smitten fellow-creature before her spoke the truth, and forebore.

Two or three days came and went, and with every hour the quiet, simple-hearted women felt more grieved and unsteady in mind and body. Such a shattering thunderbolt of news rarely falls into a human life. She could not sleep; she wandered to and fro in the little house, and cried until she could cry no longer. Then a great rage spurred and excited her. She would go to Shediac, and call Jerry Lane to account. She would accuse him face to face; and the woman whom he was deceiving, as perhaps he had deceived her, should know the baseness and cowardice of this miserable man. So, dressed in her respectable Sunday clothes, in the gray bonnet and shawl that never had known any journeys except to meeting,[12] or to a country funeral or quiet holiday-making, Nancy Lane trusted herself for the first time to the bewildering railway, to the temptations and dangers of the wide world outside the bounds of Walpole.

Two or three days later still, the quaint, thin figure familiar in Walpole highways flitted down the street of a provincial town. In the most primitive region of China this woman could hardly have felt a greater sense of foreign life and strangeness. At another time her native good sense and shrewd observation would have delighted in the experiences of this first week of travel, but she was too sternly angry and aggrieved, too deeply plunged in a survey of her own calamity, to take much notice of what was going on about her. Later she condemned the unworthy folly of the whole errand, but in these days the impulse to seek the culprit and confront him was irresistible.

The innkeeper's wife, a kindly creature, had urged this puzzling guest to wait and rest and eat some supper, but Nancy refused, and without asking her way left the brightly lighted, flaring little public room, where curious eyes already offended her, and went out into the damp twilight. The voices of the street boys sounded outlandish, and she felt more and more lonely. She longed for Jerry to appear for protection's sake; she forgot why she sought him, and was eager to shelter herself behind the flimsy bulwark of his manhood. She rebuked herself presently with terrible bitterness for a woman-ish wonder whether he would say, 'Why, Nancy, girl!' and be glad to see her. Poor woman, it was a work-laden, serious girlhood that had been hers, at any rate. The power of giving her whole self in unselfish, enthusiastic, patient devotion had not belonged to her youth only; it had sprung fresh and blossoming in her heart as every new year came and went.

One might have seen her stealing through the shadows, skirting the edge of a lumber-yard, stepping among the refuse of the harbor side, asking a question timidly now and then of some passer-by. Yes, they knew Jerry Lane, – his house was only a little way off; and one curious and compassionate Scotchman, divining by some inner sense the exciting nature of the errand, turned back, and offered fruitlessly to go with the stranger. 'You know the man?' he asked. 'He is his own enemy, but doing better now that he is married. He minds his work, I know that well; but he's taken a good wife.' Nancy's heart beat faster with honest pride for a moment, until the shadow of the ugly truth and reality made it sink back to heaviness, and the fire of her smouldering rage was again kindled. She would speak to Jerry face to face before she slept, and a horrible contempt and scorn were ready for him, as with a glance either way along the road she entered the narrow yard, and went noiselessly toward the window of a low, poor-looking house, from whence a bright light was shining out into the night.

Yes, there was Jerry, and it seemed as if she must faint and fall at the sight of him. How young he looked still! The thought smote her like a blow. They never were mates for each other, Jerry and she. Her own life was waning; she was an old woman.

He never had been so thrifty and respectable before; the other woman ought to know the savage truth about him, for all that! But at that moment the other woman stooped beside the supper table, and lifted a baby from its cradle, and put the dear, live little thing into its father's arms. The baby was wide awake, and laughed at Jerry, who laughed back again, and it reached up to catch at a handful of the curly hair which had been poor Nancy's delight.

The other woman stood there looking at them, full of pride and love. She was young, and trig, and neat. She looked a brisk, efficient little creature. Perhaps Jerry would make something of himself now; he always had it in him. The tears were running down Nancy's cheeks; the rain, too, had begun to fall. She stood there watching the little household sit down to supper, and noticed with eager envy how well cooked the food was, and how hungrily the master of the house ate what was put before him. All thoughts of ending the new wife's sin and folly vanished away. She could not enter in and break another heart; hers was broken already, and it would not matter. And Nancy Lane, a widow indeed, crept away again, as silently as she had come, to think what was best to be done, to find alternate woe and comfort in the memory of the sight she had seen.

★

The little house at the edge of the Walpole marshes seemed full of blessed shelter and comfort the evening that its forsaken mistress came back to it. Her strength was spent; she felt much more desolate now that she had seen with her own eyes that Jerry Lane was alive than when he was counted among the dead. An uncharacteristic disregard of the laws of the land filled this good woman's mind. Jerry had his life to live, and she wished him no harm. She wondered often how the baby grew. She fancied sometimes the changes and conditions of the far-away household. Alas! she knew only too well the weakness of the man, and once, in a grim outburst of impatience, she exclaimed, 'I'd rather she should have to cope with him than me!'

But that evening, when she came back from Shediac, and sat in the dark for a long time, lest Mrs Elton should see the light and risk her life in the evening air to bring unwelcome sympathy, – that evening, I say, came the hardest moment of all, when the Ann Floyd, tailoress, of so many virtuous, self-respecting years, whose idol had turned to clay, who was shamed, disgraced, and wronged, sat down alone to supper in the little kitchen.

She had put one cup and saucer on the table; she looked at them through bitter tears. Somehow a consciousness of her solitary age, her uncompanioned future, rushed through her mind; this failure of her best earthly hope was enough to break a stronger woman's heart.

Who can laugh at my Marsh Rosemary,[13] or who can cry, for that matter? The gray primness of the plant is made up of a hundred colors, if you look close enough to find them. This same Marsh Rosemary stands in her own place, and holds her dry leaves and tiny blossoms steadily toward the same sun that the pink lotus blooms for, and the white rose.[14]

THE KING OF FOLLY ISLAND

I

The September afternoon was nearly spent, and the sun was already veiled in a thin cloud of haze that hinted at coming drought and dustiness rather than rain. Nobody could help feeling sure of just such another golden day on the morrow; this was as good weather as heart could wish. There on the Maine coast, where it was hard to distinguish the islands from the irregular outline of the main-land, where the summer greenness was just beginning to change into all manner of yellow and russet and scarlet tints, the year seemed to have done its work and begun its holidays.

Along one of the broad highways of the bay, in the John's Island postmaster's boat, came a stranger – a man of forty-two or forty-three years, not unprosperous but hardly satisfied, and ever on the quest for entertainment, though he called his pleasure by the hard name of work, and liked himself the better for such a wrong translation. Fate had made him a businessman of good success and reputation; inclination, at least so he thought, would have led him another way, but his business ventures pleased him more than the best of his holidays. Somehow life was more interesting if one took it by contraries; he persuaded himself that he had been looking forward to this solitary ramble for many months, but the truth remained that he had found it provokingly hard to break away from his city office, his clerks, and his accounts. He had grown much richer in this last twelve-month, and as he leaned back in the stern of the boat with his arm over the rudder, he was pondering with great perplexity the troublesome question what he ought to do with so much money, and why he should have had it put into his careless hands at all. The bulk of it must be only a sort of reservoir for the sake of a later need and ownership. He thought with scorn of some liberal gifts for which he had been aggravatingly thanked and praised, and made such an impatient gesture with his shoulder that the boat gave a surprised flounce out of its straight course, and the old skipper, who was carefully inspecting the meagre contents of the mail-bag, nearly lost his big silver spectacles overboard. It would have been a strange and awesome calamity. There were no new ones to be bought within seven miles.

'Did a flaw strike her?' asked Jabez Pennell, who looked curiously at the sky and sea and then at his passenger. 'I've known of a porpus h'isting a boat, or mought be you kind o' shifted the rudder?'

Whereupon they both laughed; the passenger with a brilliant smile and indescribably merry sound, and the old postmaster with a mechanical grimace of the face and a rusty chuckle; then he turned to his letters again, and adjusted the rescued spectacles to his weather-beaten nose. He thought the stranger, though a silent young man, was a friendly sort of chap, boiling over with fun, as it were; whereas he was really a little morose – so much for Jabez's knowledge of human nature. 'Feels kind o' strange, 'tis likely; that's better than one o' your forrard kind,' mused Jabez, who took the visitor for one of the rare specimens of commercial travelers who sometimes visited John's Island – to little purpose it must be confessed. The postmaster cunningly concealed the fact that he kept the only store on John's Island; he might as well get his pay for setting the stranger across the bay, and it was nobody's business to pry into what he wanted when he got there. So Jabez gave another chuckle, and could not help looking again at the canvas-covered gun case with its neat straps, and the well-packed portmanteau that lay alongside it in the bows.

'I suppose I can find some place to stay in overnight?' asked the stranger, presently.

'Do' know's you can, I'm sure,' replied Mr Pennell. 'There ain't no reg'lar boarding places onto John's Island. Folks keep to theirselves pretty much.'

'I suppose money is of some object?' gently inquired the passenger.

'Waal, yes,' answered Jabez, without much apparent certainty. 'Yes, John's Island folks ain't above nippin' an' squeezin' to get the best of a bargain. They're pretty much like the rest o' the human race, an' want money, whether they've got any use for it or not. Take it in cold weather, when you've got pork enough and potatoes and them things in your sullar, an' it blows an' freezes so 'tain't wuth while to go out, 'most all that money's good for is to set an' look at. Now I need to have more means than most on 'em,' continued the speaker, plaintively, as if to excuse himself for any rumor of his grasping ways which might have reached his companion. 'Keeping store as I do, I have to handle' – But here he stopped short, conscious of having taken a wrong step. However, they were more than half across now, and the mail was overdue; he would not be forced into going back when it was ascertained that he refused to even look at any samples.

But the passenger took no notice of the news that he was sailing with the chief and only merchant of John's Island, and even turned slowly to look back at the shore they had left far away now, and fast growing dim on the horizon. John's Island was, on the contrary, growing more distinct, and there were some smaller fragments of land near it; on one he could already distinguish a flock of sheep that moved slowly down a barren slope. It was amazing that they found food enough all summer in that narrow pasture. The suggestion of winter in this remote corner of the world gave Frankfort a feeling of deep pity for the sheep, as well as for all the other inhabitants. Yet it was worth a cheerless year to come occasionally to such weather as this; and he filled his lungs again and again with the delicious air blown to him from the inland country of bayberry and fir balsams across the sparkling salt-water. The fresh north-west wind carried them straight on their course, and the postmaster's passenger could not have told himself why he was going to John's Island, except that when he had apparently come to the end of everything on an outreaching point of the main-land, he had found that there was still a settlement beyond – John's Island, twelve miles distant, and communication would be that day afforded. 'Sheep farmers and fishermen – a real old-fashioned crowd,' he had been told. It was odd to go with the postmaster: perhaps he was addressed by fate to some human being who expected him. Yes, he would find out what could be done for the John's-Islanders; then a wave of defeat seemed to chill his desire. It was better to let them work toward what they needed and wanted; besides, 'the gift without the giver were dumb.' Though after all it would be a kind of satisfaction to take a poor little neighborhood under one's wing, and make it presents of books and various enlightenments. It wouldn't be a bad thing to send it a Punch and Judy show, or a panorama.

'May I ask your business?' interrupted Jabez Pennell, to whom the long silence was a little oppressive.

'I am a sportsman,' responded John Frankfort, the partner in a flourishing private bank, and the merchant-postmaster's face drooped with disappointment. No bargains, then, but perhaps a lucrative boarder for a week or two; and Jabez instantly resolved that for not a cent less than a dollar a day should this man share the privileges and advantages of his own food and lodging. Two dollars a week being the current rate among John's-Islanders, it will be easily seen that Mr Pennell was a man of far-seeing business enterprise.

II

On shore, public attention was beginning to centre upon the small white sail that was crossing the bay. At the landing there was at first no human being to be seen, unless one had sharp eyes enough to detect the sallow, unhappy countenance of the postmaster's wife. She sat at the front kitchen window of the low-storied farm-house that was perched nearly at the top of a long green slope. The store, of which the post-office department was a small fraction, stood nearer the water, at the head of the little harbor. It was a high, narrow, smartly painted little building, and looked as if it had strayed from some pretentious inland village, but the tumble-down shed near by had evidently been standing for many years, and was well acquainted with the fish business. The landing-place looked still more weather-beaten; its few timbers were barnacled and overgrown with sea-weeds below high-water mark, and the stone-work was rudely put together. There was a litter of drift-wood, of dilapidated boats and empty barrels and broken lobster-pots, and a little higher on the shore stood a tar kettle, and, more prominent still, a melancholy pair of high chaise wheels, with their thorough-braces drawn uncomfortably tight by exposure to many seasonings of relentless weather.

The tide was high, and on this sheltered side of the island the low waves broke with a quick, fresh sound, and moved the pebbles gently on the narrow beach. The sun looked more and more golden red, and all the shore was glowing with color. The faint reddening tinge of some small oaks among the hemlocks farther up the island shore, the pale green and primrose of a group of birches, were all glorified with the brilliant contrast of the sea and the shining of the autumn sky. Even the green pastures and browner fields looked as if their covering had been changed to some richer material, like velvet, so soft and splendid they looked. High on a barren pasture ridge that sheltered the landing on its seaward side the huckleberry bushes had been brightened with a touch of carmine. Coming toward John's Island one might be reminded of some dull old picture that had been cleansed and wet, all its colors were suddenly grown so clear and gay.

Almost at the same moment two men appeared from different quarters of the shore, and without apparently taking any notice of each other, even by way of greeting, they seated themselves side by side on a worm-eaten piece of ship timber near the tar pot. In a few minutes a third resident of the island joined them, coming over the high pasture slope, and looking for one moment giant-like against the sky.

'Jabez needn't grumble to-day on account of no head-wind,' said one of the first comers. 'I was mendin' a piece o' wall that was overset, an' I see him all of a sudden, most inshore. My woman has been expecting a letter from her brother's folks in Castine. I s'pose ye've heard? They was all down with the throat distemper last we knew about 'em, an' she was dreadful put about because she got no word by the last mail. Lor', now wa'n't it just like Jabe's contrairiness to go over in that fussin' old dory o' his with no sail to speak of?'

'Wouldn't have took him half the time in his cat-boat,'[1] grumbled the elder man of the three. 'Thinks he can do as he's a mind to, an' we've got to make the best on't. Ef I was postmaster I should look out, fust thing, for an abler boat nor any he's got. He's gittin nearer every year, Jabe is.'

''Tain't fa'r to the citizens,' said the first speaker. 'Don't git no mail but twice a week anyhow, an' then he l'iters round long's he's a mind to, dickerin' an' spoutin' politics over to the Foreside. Folks may be layin' dyin', an' there's all kinds o' urgent letters that ought to be in owners' hands direct. Jabe needn't think we mean to put up with him f'rever;' and the irate islander, who never had any letters at all from one years' end to another's looked at both his companions for their assent.

'Don't ye git riled so, Dan'el,' softly responded the last-comer, a grizzled little fisherman-farmer, who looked like a pirate, and was really the most amiable man on John's Island – 'don't ye git riled. I don' know as, come to the scratch, ary one of us would want to make two trips back an' forrard every week the year round for a hundred an' twenty dollars. Take it in them high December seas, now, an' 'long in Jenoary an' March. Course he accommodates himself, an' it comes in the way o' his business, an' he gits a passenger now an' then. Well, it all counts, up, I s'pose.'

'There's somebody or 'nother aboard now,' said the opponent. 'They may have sent over for our folks from Castine. They was headin' on to be dangerous, three o' the child'n and Wash'n'ton himself. I may have to go up tonight. Dare say they've sent a letter we ain't got. Darn that Jabe! I've heard before now of his looking over everything in the bag comin' over – sortin' he calls it, to save time – but 't wouldn't be no wonder ef a letter blowed out o' his fingers now an' again.'

'There's King George, a-layin' off, ain't he?' asked the peacemaker, who was whittling a piece of dry kelp stalk that he had picked up from the pebbles, and all three men took a long look at the gray sail beyond the moorings.

'What a curi's critter that is!' exclaimed one of the group. 'I suppose, now, nothin's going' to tempt him to set foot on John's Island long's he lives – do you?' but nobody answered.

'Don't know who he's spitin' but himself,' said the peace-maker. 'I was underrunning my trawl last week, an' he come by with his fare o' fish, an' hove to to see what I was gittin'. Me and King George's al'a's kind o' fellowshiped a little by spells. I was off to the Banks,[2] you know, that time he had the gran' flare up an' took himself off, an' so he ain't counted me one o' his enemies.'

'I always give my vote that he wa'n't in his right mind; 'twa'n't all ugliness, now. I went to school with him, an' he was a clever boy as there was,' said the elder man, who had hardly spoken before. 'I never more'n half blamed him, however 'twas, an' it kind o' rankled me that he should ha' been drove off an' outlawed hisself this way. 'Twas Jabe Pennell; he thought George was stan'in' in his light 'bout the postmastership, an' he worked folks up, an' set 'em again him. George's mother's folks did have a kind of a punky[3] spot somewhere in their heads, but he never give no sign o' anything till Jabe Pennell begun to hunt him an' dare him.'

'Well, he's done a good thing sence he bought Folly Island. I hear say King George is gittin' rich,' said the peaceful pirate. ''Twas a hard thing for his folks, his wife an' girl. I think he's been more scattery[4] sence his wife died, anyway. Darn! how lonesome they must be in winter! I should think they'd be afeared a sea would break right over 'em. Pol'tics be hanged, I say, that'll drive a man to do such things as them – never step foot on any land but his own again! I tell ye we've each on us got rights.'

This was unusual eloquence and excitement on the speaker's part, and his neighbors stole a furtive look at him and then at each other. He was an own cousin to King George Quint, the recluse owner of Folly Island – an isolated bit of land several miles farther seaward – and one of the listeners reflected that this relationship must be the cause of his bravery.

The post-boat was nearly in now, and the three men rose and went down to the water's edge. The sail was furled, and the old dory slipped about uneasily on the low waves. The postmaster was greeted by friendly shouts from his late maligners, but he was unnecessarily busy with his sail and with his packages amidships, and took his time, as at least one spectator grumbled, about coming in. King George had also lowered his sail and taken to his oars, but just as he would have been alongside, the postmaster caught up his own oars, and pulled smartly toward the landing. This proceeding stimulated his pursuer to a stern-chase, and presently the boats were together, but Pennell pushed straight on through the low waves to the strand, and his pursuer lingered just outside, took in his oars, and dropped his killock[5] over the bow. He knew perfectly well that the representative of the government would go ashore and take all the time he could to sort the contents of the mail-bag in his place of business. It would even be good luck if he did not go home to supper first, and keep everybody waiting all the while. Sometimes his constituents had hailed him from their fishing-boats on the high seas, and taken their weekly newspaper over the boat's side, but it was only in moments of great amiability or forgetfulness that the King of Folly Island was so kindly served. This was tyranny pure and simple. But what could be done? So was winter cold, and so did the dog-fish spoil the trawls. Even the John's-Islanders needed a fearless patriot to lead them to liberty.

The three men on the strand and King George from the harbor were all watching with curious eyes the stranger who had crossed in Jabez Pennell's boat. He was deeply interested in them also; but at that moment such a dazzling glow of sunlight broke from the cloud in the west that Frankfort turned away to look at the strange, remote landscape that surrounded him. He felt as if he had taken a step backward into an earlier age – these men had the look of pioneers or of colonists – yet the little country-side showed marks of long occupancy. He had really got to the outer boundary of civilization.

'Now it's too bad o' you, Jabez, to keep George Quint a-waitin',' deprecated the peace-maker. 'He's got a good ways to go 'way over to Folly Island, an' like's not he means to underrun his trawl too. We all expected ye sooner with this fair wind.' At which the postmaster gave an unintelligible growl.

'This 'ere passenger was comin' over, calc'latin' to stop a spell, an' wants to be accommodated,' he announced presently.

But one of the group on the strand interrupted him. He was considered the wag of that neighborhood. 'Ever b'en to Folly Island, stranger?' he asked, with great civility. 'There's the King of it, layin' off in his boat. George!' he called lustily, 'I want to know ef you can't put up a trav'ler that wants to view these parts o' the airth?'

Frankfort somehow caught the spirit of the occasion, and understood that there was a joke underlying this request. Folly Island had an enticing sound, and he listened eagerly for the answer. It was well known by everybody except himself that Jabez Pennell monopolized the entertainment of the traveling public, and King George roared back, delightedly, that he would do the best he could on short notice, and pulled his boat farther in. Frankfort made ready to transfer his luggage, and laughed again with the men on the shore. He was not sorry to have a longer voyage in that lovely sunset light and the hospitality of John's Island, already represented by these specimens of householders, was not especially alluring. Jabez Pennell was grumbling to himself, and turned to go to the store. King George reminded him innocently of some groceries which he had promised to have ready, and always fearful of losing one of his few customers, he nodded and went his way. It seemed to be a strange combination of dependence and animosity between the men. The King followed his purveyor with a blasting glance of hatred, and turned his boat, and held it so that Frankfort could step in and reach back afterward for his possessions.

In a few minutes Mr Pennell returned with some packages and a handful of newspapers.

'Have ye put in the cough drops?' asked the fisherman, gruffly, and was answered by a nod of the merchant's head.

'Bring them haddick before Thu'sday,' he commanded the island potentate, who was already setting his small sail.

The wind had freshened. They slid out of the bay, and presently the figures on the shore grew indistinct, and Frankfort found himself outward bound on a new tack toward a low island several miles away. It seemed to be at considerable distance from any other land; the light of the sun was full upon it. Now he certainly was as far away as he could get from city life and the busy haunts of men. He wondered at the curious chain of circumstances that he had followed that day. This man looked like a hermit, and really lived in the outermost island of all.

Frankfort grew more and more amused with the novel experiences of the day. He had wished for a long time to see these Maine islands for himself. A week at Mount Desert had served to make him very impatient of the imported society of that renowned watering-place, so incongruous with the native simplicity and quiet. There was a serious look to the dark forests and bleak rocks that seemed to have been broken into fragments by some convulsion of nature, and scattered in islands and reefs along the coast. A strange population clung to these isolated bits of the world, and it was rewarding to Frankfort's sincere interest in such individualized existence that he should now be brought face to face with it.

The boat sailed steadily. A colder air, like the very breath of the great sea, met the voyagers presently. Two or three lighthouse lamps flashed out their first pale rays like stars, and evening had begun. Yet there was still a soft glow of color over the low seaboard. The western sky was slow to fade, and the islands looked soft and mirage-like in the growing gloom. Frankfort found himself drifting away into dreams as if he were listening to music; there was something lulling in the motion of the boat. As for the King, he took no notice of his passenger, but steered with an oar and tended the sheet and hummed a few notes occasionally of some quaint minor tune, which must have been singing itself more plainly to his own consciousness. The stranger waked from his reverie before very long, and observed with delight that the man before him had a most interesting face, a nobly moulded forehead, and brave, commanding eyes. There was truly an air of distinction and dignity about this King of Folly Island, an uncommon directness and independence. He was the son and heir of the old Vikings[6] who had sailed that stormy coast and discovered its harborage and its vines five hundred years before Columbus was born in Italy, or was beggar to the surly lords and gentlemen of Spain.

The silence was growing strange, and provoking curiosity between the new-made host and guest, and Frankfort asked civilly some question about the distance. The King turned to look at him with surprise, as if he had forgotten his companionship. The discovery seemed to give him pleasure, and he answered, in a good clear voice, with a true fisherman's twang and brogue: 'We're more'n half there. Be you cold?' And Frankfort confessed to a stray shiver now and then, which seemed to inspire a more friendly relationship in the boat's crew. Quick as thought, the King pulled off his own rough coat and wrapped it about the shoulders of the paler city man. Then he stepped forward along the boat, after handing the oar to his companion, and busied himself ostentatiously with a rope, with the packages that he had bought from Pennell. One would have thought he had freed himself from his coat merely as a matter of convenience; and Frankfort, who was not a little touched by the kindness, paid his new sovereign[7] complete deference. George Quint was evidently a man whom one must be very careful about thanking, however, and there was another time of silence.

'I hope my coming will not make any trouble in your family,' ventured the stranger, after a while.

'Bless ye, no!' replied the host. 'There's only Phebe, my daughter, and nothing would please her better than somebody extra to do for. She's dreadful folksy[8] for a girl that's hed to live alone on a far island, Phebe is. 'Tain't every one I'd pick to carry home, though,' said the King, magnificently. ''T has been my plan to keep clear o' humans much as could be. I had my fill o' the John's-Islanders a good while ago.'

'Hard to get on with?' asked the listener, humoring the new tone which his ears had caught.

'I could get on with 'em ef 'twas anyways wuth while,' responded the island chieftain. 'I didn't see why there was any need o' being badgered and nagged all my days by a pack o' curs like them John's-Islanders. They'd hunt ye to death if ye was anyways their master; and I got me a piece o' land as far off from 'em as I could buy, and here I be. I ain't stepped foot on any man's land but my own these twenty-six years. Ef anybody wants to deal with me, he must come to the water's edge.'

The speaker's voice trembled with excitement, and Frankfort was conscious of a strange sympathy and exhilaration.

'But why didn't you go ashore and live on the main-land, out of the way of such neighbors altogether?' he asked, and was met by a wondering look.

'I didn't belong there,' replied the King, as if the idea had never occurred to him before. 'I had my living to get. It took me more than twelve years to finish paying for my island, besides what hard money I laid down. Some years the fish is mighty shy. I always had an eye to the island sence I was a boy; and we've been better off here, as I view it. I was some sorry my woman should be so fur from her folks when she was down with her last sickness.'

The sail was lowered suddenly, and the boat rose and fell on the long waves near the floats of a trawl, which Quint pulled over the bows, slipping the long line by with its empty hooks until he came to a small haddock, which he threw behind him to flop and beat itself about at Frankfort's feet as if imploring him not to eat it for his supper. Then the sprit-sail was hoisted again, and they voyaged toward Folly Island slowly with a failing breeze. The King stamped his feet, and even struck his arms together as if they were chilled, but took no notice of the coat which his guest had taken off again a few minutes before. To Frankfort the evening was growing mild, and his blood rushed through his veins with a delicious thrill. The island loomed high and black, as if it were covered with thick woods; but there was a light ashore in the window of a small house, and presently the pilgrim found himself safe on land, quite stiff in his legs, but very serene in temper. A brisk little dog leaped about him with clamorous barks, a large gray cat also appeared belligerent and curious; then a voice came from the doorway: 'Late, ain't you, father?'

Without a word of reply, the King of that isle led the way to his castle, haddock in hand. Frankfort and the dog and cat followed after. Before they reached the open door, the light shone out upon a little wilderness of bright flowers, yellow and red and white. The King stepped carefully up the narrow pathway, and waited on the step for his already loyal subject to enter.

'Phebe, he said, jokingly, 'I've brought ye some company – a gentleman from Lord knows where, who couldn't seem to content himself without seeing Folly Island.'

Phebe stepped forward with great shyness, but perfect appreciation of the right thing to be done. 'I give you welcome,' she said, quietly, and offered a thin affectionate hand. She was very plain in her looks, with a hard-worked, New England plainness, but as Frankfort stood in the little kitchen he was immediately conscious of a peculiar delicacy and refinement in his surroundings. There was an atmosphere in this out-of-the-way corner of civilization that he missed in all but a few of the best houses he had ever known.

The ways of the Folly Island housekeeping were too well established to be thrown out of their course by even so uncommon an event as the coming of a stranger. The simple supper was eaten, and Frankfort was ready for his share of it. He was touched at the eagerness of his hostess to serve him, at her wistful questioning of her father to learn whom he had seen and what he had heard that day. There was no actual exile in the fisherman's lot after all; he met his old acquaintances almost daily on the fishing grounds, and it was upon the women of the household that an unmistakable burden of isolation had fallen. Sometimes a man lived with them for a time to help cultivate the small farm, but Phebe was skilled in out-door handicrafts. She could use tools better than her father, the guest was told proudly, and that day she had been digging potatoes – a great pleasure evidently, as anything would have been that kept one out-of-doors in the sunshiny field.

When the supper was over, the father helped his daughter to clear away the table as simply and fondly as could be, and as if it were as much his duty as hers. It was very evident that the cough drops were for actual need; the poor girl coughed now and then with a sad insistence and hollowness. She looked ill already, so narrow-chested and bent-shouldered, while a bright spot of color flickered in her thin cheeks. She had seemed even elderly to Frankfort when he first saw her, but he discovered from something that was said that her age was much less than his own. What a dreary lifetime! he thought, and then reproached himself, for he had never seen a happier smile than poor Phebe gave her father at that moment. The father was evidently very anxious about the cough; he started uneasily at every repetition of it, with a glance at his guest's face to see if he also were alarmed by the foreboding. The wind had risen again, and whined in the chimney. The pine-trees near the house and the wind and sea united in a solemn, deep sound which affected the new-comer strangely. Above this undertone was the lesser, sharper noise of waves striking the pebbly beach and retreating. There was a loneliness, a remoteness, a feeling of being an infinitesimal point in such a great expanse of sea and stormy sky, that was almost too heavy to be borne. Phebe knitted steadily, with an occasional smile at her own thoughts. The tea-kettle sang and whistled away; its cover clicked now and then as if with hardly suppressed cheerfulness, and the King of Folly Island read his newspaper diligently, and doled out bits of information to his companions. Frankfort was surprised at the tenor of these. The reader was evidently a man of uncommon depth of thought and unusual common sense. It was both less and more surprising that he should have chosen to live alone; one would imagine that his instinct would have led him among people of his own sort. It was no wonder that he had grown impatient of such society as the postmaster's; but at this point of his meditation the traveler's eyes began to feel strangely heavy, and he fell asleep in his high-backed rocking-chair. What peacefulness had circled him in! the rush and clamor of his business life had fallen away as if he had begun another existence, without the fretful troubles of this present world.

'He's a pretty man,'[9] whispered Phebe to her father, and the old fisherman nodded a grave assent, and folded his hand upon the county newspaper while he took a long honest look at the stranger within his gates.

The next morning Frankfort made his appearance in the kitchen at a nobly early hour, to find that the master of the house had been out in his boat since four o'clock, and would not be in for some time yet. Phebe was waiting to give him his breakfast, and soon after he saw her going to the potato field, and joined her. The sun was bright, and the island was gay with color; the asters were in their best pale lavender and royal purple tints; the bay was flecked with sails of fishing-boats, because the mackerel had again struck in; and outside the island, at no great distance, was the highway of the coasting vessels to and from the eastern part of the state and the more distant provinces. There were near two hundred craft in sight, great and small, and John Frankfort dug his potatoes with intermittent industry as he looked off east and west at such a lovely scene. They might have been an *abbé galant* and a dignified *marquise*,[10] he and Phebe – it did not matter what work they toyed with. They were each filled with a charming devotion to the other, a grave reverence and humoring of the mutual desire for quiet and meditation. Toward noon the fishing-boat which Phebe had known constantly and watched with affectionate interest was seen returning deep laden, and she hastened to the little landing. Frankfort had already expressed his disdain of a noonday meal, and throwing down his hoe, betook himself to the highest point of the island. Here was a small company of hemlocks, twisted and bent by the northeast winds, and on the soft brown carpet of their short pins, our pilgrim to the outer boundaries spent the middle of the day. A strange drowsiness, such as he had often felt before in such bracing air, seemed to take possession of him, and to a man who had been perplexing himself with hard business problems and erratic ventures in financiering, potato-digging on a warm September day was not exciting.

The hemlocks stood alone on the summit of the island, and must have been a landmark for the King to steer home by. Before Frankfort stretched a half-cleared pasture, where now and then, as he lazily opened his eyes, he could see a moving sheep's back among the small birches and fern and juniper. Behind him were the cleared fields and the house, and a fringe of forest trees stood all round the rocky shore of the domain. From the water one could not see that there was such a well-arranged farm on Folly Island behind this barrier of cedars, but the inhabitants of that region thriftily counted upon the natural stockade to keep the winter winds away.

The sun had changed its direction altogether when he finally waked, and shone broadly down upon him from a point much nearer the western horizon. At that moment the owner of the island made his appearance, looking somewhat solicitous.

'We didn't know what had become of ye, young man,' he said, in a fatherly way. ''Tain't nateral for ye to go without your dinner, as I view it. We'll soon hearten ye up, Phebe an' me; though she don't eat no more than a chippin'-sparrer, Phebe don't,' and his face returned to its sadder lines.

'No,' said Frankfort; 'she looks very delicate. Don't you think it might be better to take her inland, or to some more sheltered place, this winter?'

The question was asked with hesitation, but the speaker's kind-heartedness was in all his words. The father turned away and snapped a dry hemlock twig with impatient fingers.

'She wouldn't go withouten me,' he answered, in a choked voice, 'an' my vow is my vow. I shall never set foot on another man's land while I'm alive.'

The day had been so uneventful, and Folly Island had appeared to be such a calm, not to say prosaic place, that its visitor was already forgetting the thrill of interest with which he had first heard its name. Here again, however, was the unmistakable tragic element in the life of the inhabitants; this man, who should be armed and defended by his common-sense, was yet made weak by some prejudice or superstition. What could have warped him in this strange way? for, indeed, the people of most unenlightened communities were prone to herd together, to follow each other's lead, to need a dictator, no matter how much they might rebel at his example or demands. This city gentleman was moved by a deep curiosity to know for himself the laws and charts of his new-found acquaintance's existence; he had never felt a keener interest in a first day's acquaintance with any human being.

'Society would be at a stand-still,' he said, with apparent lightness, 'if each of us who found his neighbors unsatisfactory should strike out for himself as you have done.'

The King of Folly Island gave a long shrewd look at his companion, who was still watching the mackerel fleet; then he blushed like a girl through all the sea-changed color of his cheeks.

'Look out for number one, or else number two's got to look out for you,' he said, with some uncertainty in the tone of his voice.

'Yes,' answered Frankfort, smiling. 'I have repeated that to myself a great many times. The truth is, I don't belong to my neighbors any more than you do.'

'I expect that you have got a better chance nor me; ef I had only been started amon'st Christians, now!' exclaimed Quint, with gathering fury at the thought of his John's-Islanders.

'Human nature is the same the world over,' said the guest, quietly, as if more to himself than his listener. 'I dare say that the fault is apt to be our own;' but there was no response to this audacious opinion.

Frankfort had risen from the couch of hemlock pins, and the two men walked toward the house together. The cares of modern life could not weigh too heavily on such a day. The shining sea, the white sails, gleaming or gray-shadowed, and the dark green of the nearer islands made a brilliant picture, and the younger man was impatient with himself for thinking the armada of small craft a parallel to the financial ventures which were made day after day in city life. What a question of chance it was, after all, for either herring or dollars – some of these boats were sure to go home disappointed, or worse, at night; but at this point he shrugged his shoulders angrily because he could not forget some still undecided ventures of his own. How degraded a man became who chose to be only a money-maker! The zest of the chase for wealth and the power of it suddenly seemed a very trivial and foolish thing to Frankfort, who confessed anew that he had no purpose in making his gains.

'You ain't a married man; live a bachelor life, don't ye?' asked the King, as if in recognition of these thoughts, and Frankfort, a little startled, nodded assent.

'Makes it a sight easier,' was the unexpected response. 'You don't feel as if you might be wronging other folks when you do what suits you best. Now my woman was wuth her weight in gold, an' she lays there in the little yard over in the corner of the field – she never fought me, nor argued the p'int again after she found I was sot, but it aged her, fetchin' of her away from all her folks, an' out of where she was wonted. I didn't foresee it at the time.'

There was something martyr-like and heroic in the exile's appearance as he spoke, and his listener had almost an admiration for such heroism, until he reminded himself that this withdrawal from society had been willful, and, so far as he knew, quite selfish. It could not be said that Quint had stood in his lot and place as a brave man should, unless he had left John's Island as the Pilgrim Fathers left England, for conscientious scruples and a necessary freedom. How many pilgrims since those have falsely made the same plea for undeserved liberty!

'What was your object in coming here?' the stranger asked, quietly, as if he had heard no reason yet that satisfied him.

'I wanted to be by myself;' and the King rallied his powers of eloquence to make excuses. 'I wa'n't one that could stand them folks that overlooked an' harried me, an' was too mean to live. They could go their way, an' I mine. I wouldn't harm 'em, but I wanted none of 'em. Here, you see, I get my own livin'. I raise my own hog, an' the women-folks have more hens than they want, an' I keep a few sheep a-runnin' over the other side o' the place. The fish o' the sea is had for the catchin', an' I owe no man anything. I should ha' b'en beholden if I'd stopped where we come from;' and he turned with an air of triumph to look at Frankfort, who glanced at him in return with an air of interest.

'I see that you depend upon the larger islands for some supplies – cough drops, for instance?' said the stranger, with needless clearness. 'I cannot help feeling that you would have done better to choose a less exposed island – one nearer the main-land, you know, in a place better sheltered from the winds.'

'They do cut us 'most in two,' said the King, meekly, and his face fell. Frankfort felt quite ashamed of himself, but he was conscious already of an antagonistic feeling. Indeed, this was an island of folly; this man who felt himself to be better than his neighbors, was the sacrificer of his family's comfort; he was heaping up riches, and who would gather them? Not the poor pale daughter, that was certain. In this moment they passed the corner of the house, and discovered Phebe herself standing on the door-step, watching some distant point of the sea or sky with a heavy, much battered spy-glass.

She looked pleased as she lowered the glass for a moment, and greeted Frankfort with a silent welcome.

'Oh, so 'tis; now I forgot 'twas this afternoon,' said Quint. 'She's a-watching' the funeral; ain't you, daughter? Old Mis' Danforth, over onto Wall Island, that has been layin' sick all summer – a cousin o' my mother's,' he confessed, in a lower tone, and turned away with feigned unconcern as Frankfort took the spy-glass which Phebe offered. He was sure that his hostess had been wishing that she could share in the family gathering. Was it possible that Quint was a tyrant, and had never let this grown woman leave his chosen isle? Freedom, indeed!

He forgot the affairs of Folly Island the next moment, as he caught sight of the strange procession. He could see the coffin with its black pall in a boat rowed by four men, who had pushed out a little way from shore, and other boats near it. From the low gray house near the water came a little group of women stepping down across the rough beach and getting into their boats; then all fell into a rude sort or orderliness, the hearse-boat going first, and the procession went away across the wide bay toward the main-land. He lowered the glass for an instant, and Phebe reached for it eagerly.

'They were just bringing out the coffin before you came,' she said, with a little sigh; and Frankfort, who had seen many pageants and ceremonials, rebuked himself for having stolen so much of this rare pleasure from his hostess. He could still see the floating funeral. Though it was only a far-away line of boats, there was a strange awe and fascination in watching them follow their single, steady course.

'Danforth's folks bury over to the Foreside,' explained the King of Folly Island; but his guest had taken a little book from his pocket, and seated himself on a rock that made one boundary of the gay, disorderly garden. It was very shady and pleasant at this side of the house, and he was too warm after his walk across the unshaded pastures. It was very hot sunshine for that time of the year, and his holiday began to grow dull. Was he, after all, good for nothing but money-making? The thought fairly haunted him; he had lost his power of enjoyment, and there might be no remedy.

The fisherman had disappeared; the funeral was a dim speck off there where the sun glittered on the water, yet he saw it still, and his book closed over his listless fingers. Phebe sat on the door-step knitting now, with the old glass laid by her side ready for use. Frankfort looked at her presently with a smile.

'Will you let me see your book?' she asked, with a child's eagerness; and he gave it to her.

'It is an old copy of Wordsworth's shorter poems,' he said. 'It belonged to my mother. Her name was the same as yours.'

'She spelled it with the *o*,' said Phebe radiant with interest in this discovery, and closely examining the flyleaf. 'What a pretty hand she wrote! Is it a book you like?'

'I like it best because it was hers, I am afraid,' replied Frankfort, honestly. 'Yes, it does one good to read such poems; but I find it hard to read anything in these days; my business fills my mind. You know so little, here on your island, of the way the great world beyond pushes and fights and wrangles.'

'I suppose there are some pleasant folks,' said Phebe, simply. 'I used to like to read, but I found it made me lonesome. I used to wish I could go ashore and do all the things that folks in books did. But I don't care now; I wouldn't go away from the island for anything.'

'No,' said Frankfort, kindly; 'I wouldn't if I were you. Go on dreaming about the world; that is better. And it does people good to come here and see you so comfortable and contented,' he added, with a tenderness in his voice that was quite foreign to it of late years. But Phebe gave one quick look at the far horizon, her thin cheeks grew very rosy, and she looked down again at her knitting.

Presently she went into the house. At tea-time that evening the guest was surprised to find the little table decked out for a festival, with some flowered china, and a straight-backed old mahogany chair from the best room in his own place of honor. Phebe looked gay and excited, and Frankfort wondered at the feast, as well as the master of the house, when they came to take their places.

'You see, you found me unawares last night, coming so unexpected,' said the poor pale mistress. 'I didn't want you to think that we had forgotten how to treat folks.'

And somehow the man whose face was usually so cold and unchanging could hardly keep back his tears while, after the supper was cleared away, he was shown a little model of a meeting-house steeple and all, which Phebe had made from card-board and covered with small shells a winter or two before. She brought it to him with a splendid sense of its art, and Frankfort said everything that could be said except that it was beautiful. He even begged to be told exactly how it was done, and they sat by the light together and discussed the poor toy, while the King of Folly Island dozed and waked again with renewed pleasure as he contemplated his daughter's enjoyment. But she coughed very often, poor Phebe, and the guest wondered if the postmaster's supply of drugs were equal to this pitiful illness. Poor Phebe! and winter would be here soon!

Day after day, in the bright weather, Frankfort lingered with his new friends, spending a morning now and then in fishing with his host, and coming into closer contact with the inhabitants of that part of the world.

Before the short visit was over, the guest was aware that he had been very tired and out of sorts when he had yielded to the desire to hide away from civilization, and had drifted, under some pilotage that was beyond himself, into this quiet haven. He felt stronger and in much better spirits, and remembered afterward that he had been as merry as a boy on Folly Island in the long evenings when Phebe was busy with her knitting-work, and her father told long and spirited stories of his early experiences along the coast and among the fisherman. But business cares began to fret this holiday-maker, and as suddenly as he had come he went away again on a misty morning that promised rain. He was very sorry when he said goodbye to Phebe; she was crying as he left the house, and a great wave of compassion poured itself over Frankfort's heart. He never should see her again, that was certain; he wished that he could spirit her away to some gentler climate, and half spoke his thought as he stood hesitating that last minute on the little beach. The next moment he was fairly in the boat and pushing out from shore. George Quint looked as hardy and ruddy and weather-beaten as his daughter was pale and faded, like some frost-bitten flower that tries to lift itself when morning comes and it feels the warmth of the sun. The tough fisherman, with his pet doctrines and angry aversions, could have no idea of the loneliness of his wife and daughter all these unvarying years on his Folly Island. And yet how much they had been saved of useless rivalries and jealousies, of petty tyranny from narrow souls! Frankfort had a bitter sense of all that, as he leaned back against the side of the boat, and sailed slowly out into the bay, while Folly Island seemed to retreat into the gathering fog and slowly disappear. His thoughts flew before him to his office, to his clerks and accounts; he thought of his wealth which was buying him nothing, of his friends who were no friends at all, for he had pushed away some who might have been near, strangely impatient of familiarity, and on the defense against either mockery or rivalry. He was the true King of Folly Island, not this work-worn fisherman; he had been a lonelier and a more selfish man these many years.

George Quint was watching Frankfort eagerly, as if he had been waiting for this chance to speak to him alone.

'You seem to be a kind of solitary creatur',' he suggested, with his customary frankness. 'I expect it never crossed your thought that 'twould be nateral to git married?'

'Yes, I thought about it once, some years ago,' answered Frankfort seriously.

'Disapp'inted, was you? Well, 'twas better soon nor late, if it had to be,' said the sage. 'My mind has been dwellin' on Phebe's case. She was a master pooty gal 'arlier on, an' I was dreadful set against lettin' her go, though I call to mind there was a likely chap as found her out, an' made bold to land, an' try to court her. I drove him, I tell you, an' ducked him under when I caught him afterward out a-fishin', an' he took the hint. Phebe didn't know what was to pay, though I dare say she liked to have him follerin' about.'

Frankfort made no answer, – he was very apt to be silent when you expected him to speak, – and presently the King resumed his suggestions.

'I've been thinking that Phebe ought to have some sort o' brightenin' up. She pines for her mother: they was a sight o' company for each other. Now I s'pose you couldn't take no sort o' fancy for her in course o' time? I've got more hard cash stowed away than folks expects, an' you should have everything your own way. I could git a cousin o' mine, a widow woman, to keep the house winters, an' you an' the gal needn't only summer here. I take it you've got some means?'

Frankfort found himself smiling at this pathetic appeal, and was ashamed of himself directly, and turned to look seaward. 'I'm afraid I couldn't think of it,' he answered. 'You don't suppose' –

'Lor' no,' said George Quint, sadly, shifting his sail. '*She* ain't give no sign, except that I never see her take to no stranger as she has to you. I thought you might kind of have a feelin' for her, an' I knowed you thought the island was a sightly place; 'twould do no harm to speak, leastways.'

They were on their way to John's Island, where Frankfort was to take the postmaster's boat to the main-land. Quint found his fog-bound way by some mysterious instinct, and at their journey's ends the friends parted with little show of sentiment or emotion. Yet there was much expression in Quint's grasp of his hand, Frankfort thought, and both men turned more than once as the boats separated, to give a kindly glance backward. People are not brought together in this world for nothing, and poor Quint had no idea of the confusion that his theories and his manner of life had brought into the well-regulated affairs of John Frankfort. Jabez Pennell was brimful of curiosity about the visit, but he received little satisfaction. 'Phebe Quint was the pootiest gal on these islands some ten years ago,' he proclaimed, 'an' a born lady. Her mother's folks was ministers over to Castine.'

The winter was nearly gone when Frankfort received a letter in a yellow envelope, unbusiness-like in its appearance. The King of Folly Island wrote to say that Phebe had been hoping to get strength enough to thank him for the generous Christmas-box which Frankfort had sent. He had taxed both his imagination and memory to supply the minor wants and fancies of the islanders.

But Phebe was steadily failing in health, and the elderly cousin had already been summoned to take care of her and to manage the house-keeping. The King wrote a crabbed hand, as if he had used a fish-hook instead of a pen, and he told the truth about his sad affairs with simple, unlamenting bravery. Phebe only sent a message of thanks, and an assurance that she liked to think of Frankfort's being there in the fall. She would soon send him a small keepsake.

One morning Frankfort opened a much-crushed bundle which lay upon his desk, and found this keepsake, the shell meeting-house, which looked sadly trivial and astray. He was entirely confused by its unexpected appear-ance; he did not dare to meet the eyes of an office-boy who stood near; there was an uncomfortable feeling in his throat, but he bravely unfastened a letter from the battered steeple, and read it slowly, without a very clear understand-ing of the words:–

'DEAR FRIEND' (said poor Phebe), – 'I was very thankful for all that you sent in the box – I take such pleasure in the things. I find it hard to write, but I think about you every day. Father sends his best respects. We have had rough weather, and he stays right here with me. You must keep your promise and come back to the island; he will be lonesome, and you are one that takes father just right. It seems as if I hadn't been any use in the world, but it rests me, laying here, to think what a sight of use you must be. And so goodbye.'

A sudden vision of the poor girl came before his eyes as he saw her stand on the door-step the day they watched the boat funeral. She had worn a dress with a quaint pattern, like gray and yellowish willow leaves as one sees them fallen by the country roadsides. A vision of her thin, stooping shoulders and her simple, pleasant look touched him with real sorrow. 'Much use in the world!' Alas! alas! how had her affection made her fancy such a thing!

The day was stormy, and Frankfort turned anxiously to look out of the window beside him as he thought how the wind must blow across the distant bay. He felt a strange desire to sweep away everything that might vex poor Phebe or make her less comfortable. Yet she must die, at any rate, before the summer came. The King of Folly Island would reign only over his sheep pastures and the hemlock-trees and pines. Much use in the world! The words stung him more and more.

The office-boy still stood waiting, and now Frankfort became unhappily conscious of his presence. 'I used to see one o' them shell-works where I come from, up in the country,' the boy said, with unexpected forbearance and sympathy; but Frankfort dismissed him, with a needless question about the price of certain railroad bonds, and dropped the embarrassing gift, the poor little meeting-house, into a deep lower drawer of his desk. He had hardly thought of the lad before except as a willing, half mechanical errand-runner; now he was suddenly conscious of the hopeful, bright young face. At that moment a whole new future of human interests spread out before his eyes, from which a veil had suddenly been withdrawn, and Frankfort felt like another man, or as if there had been a revivifying of his old, uninterested, self-occupied nature. Was there really such a thing as taking part in the heavenly warfare against ignorance and selfishness? Had Phebe given him in some mysterious way a legacy of all her unsatisfied hopes and dreams?

THE COURTING OF SISTER WISBY

All the morning there had been an increasing temptation to take an out-door holiday, and early in the afternoon the temptation outgrew my power of resistance. A far-away pasture on the long southwestern slope of a high hill was persistently present to my mind, yet there seemed to be no particular reason why I should think of it. I was not sure that I wanted anything from the pasture, and there was no sign, except the temptation, that the pasture wanted anything of me. But I was on the farther side of as many as three fences before I stopped to think again where I was going, and why.

There is no use in trying to tell another person about that afternoon unless he distinctly remembers weather exactly like it. No number of details concerning an Arctic ice-blockade will give a single shiver to a child of the tropics. This was one of those perfect New England days in late summer, when the spirit of autumn takes a first stealthy flight, like a spy, through the ripening country-side, and, with feigned sympathy for those who droop with August heat, puts her cool cloak of bracing air about leaf and flower and human shoulders. Every living thing grows suddenly cheerful and strong; it is only when you catch sight of a horror-stricken little maple in swampy soil, – a little maple that has second sight and foreknowledge of coming disaster to her race, – only then does a distrust of autumn's friendliness dim your joyful satisfaction.

In midwinter there is always a day when one has the first foretaste of spring; in late August there is a morning when the air is for the first time autumn like. Perhaps it is a hint to the squirrels to get in their first supplies for the winter hoards, or a reminder that summer will soon end, and everybody had better make the most of it. We are always looking forward to the passing and ending of winter, but when summer is here it seems as if summer must always last. As I went across the fields that day, I found myself half lamenting that the world must fade again, even that the best of her budding and bloom was only a preparation for another spring-time, for an awakening beyond the coming winter's sleep.

The sun was slightly veiled; there was a chattering group of birds, which had gathered for a conference about their early migration. Yet, oddly enough, I heard the voice of a belated bobolink,[1] and presently saw him rise from the grass and hover leisurely, while he sang a brief tune. He was much behind time if he were still a housekeeper; but as for the other birds, who listened, they cared only for their own notes. An old crow went sagging by, and gave a croak at his despised neighbor, just as a black reviewer croaked at Keats: so hard it is to be just to one's contemporaries. The bobolink was indeed singing out of season, and it was impossible to say whether he really belonged most to this summer or to the next. He might have been delayed on his northward journey: at any rate, he had a light heart now, to judge from his song, and I wished that I could ask him a few questions, – how he liked being the last man among the bobolinks, and where he had taken singing lessons in the South.

Presently I left the lower fields, and took a path that led higher, where I could look beyond the village to the northern country mountainward. Here the sweet fern grew, thick and fragrant, and I also found myself heedlessly treading on pennyroyal. Near by, in a field corner, I long ago made a most comfortable seat by putting a stray piece of board and bit of rail across the angle of the fences. I have spent many a delightful hour there, in the shade and shelter of a young pitch-pine and a wild-cherry tree, with a lovely outlook toward the village, just far enough away beyond the green slopes and tall elms of the lower meadows. But that day I still had the feeling of being outward bound, and did not turn aside nor linger. The high pasture land grew more and more enticing.

I stopped to pick some blackberries that twinkled at me like beads among their dry vines, and two or three yellow-birds[2] fluttered up from the leaves of a thistle, and then came back again, as if they had complacently discovered that I was only an overgrown yellow-bird, in strange disguise but perfectly harmless. They made me feel as if I were an intruder, though they did not offer to peck at me, and we parted company very soon. It was good to stand at last on the great shoulder of the hill. The wind was coming in from the sea, there was a fine fragrance from the pines, and the air grew sweeter every moment. I took new pleasure in the thought that in a piece of wild pasture land like this one may get closest to Nature, and subsist upon what she gives of her own free will. There have been no drudging, heavy-shod ploughmen to overturn the soil, and vex it into yielding artificial crops. Here one has to take just what Nature is pleased to give, whether one is a yellow-bird or a human being. It is very good entertainment for a summer wayfarer, and I am asking my reader now to share the winter provision which I harvested that day. Let us hope that the small birds are also faring well after their fashion, but I give them an anxious thought while the snow goes hurrying in long waves across the buried fields, this windy winter night.

I next went farther down the hill, and got a drink of fresh cool water from the brook, and pulled a tender sheaf of sweet flag³ beside it. The mossy old fence just beyond was the last barrier between me and the pasture which had sent an invisible messenger earlier in the day, but I saw that somebody else had come first to the rendezvous: there was a brown gingham cape-bonnet and a sprigged shoulder-shawl bobbing up and down, a little way off among the junipers. I had taken such uncommon pleasure in being alone that I instantly felt a sense of disappointment; then a warm glow of pleasant satisfaction rebuked my selfishness. This could be no one but dear old Mrs Goodsoe, the friend of my childhood and fond dependence of my maturer years. I had not seen her for many weeks, but here she was, out on one of her famous campaigns for herbs, or perhaps just returning from a blueberrying expedition. I approached with care, so as not to startle the gingham bonnet; but she heard the rustle of the bushes against my dress, and looked up quickly, as she knelt, bending over the turf. In that position she was hardly taller than the luxuriant junipers themselves.

'I'm a-gittin' in my mulleins,' she said briskly, 'an' I've been thinking o' you these twenty times since I come out o' the house. I begun to believe you must ha' forgot me at last.'

'I have, been away from home,' I explained. 'Why don't you get in your pennyroyal too? There's a great plantation of it beyond the next fence but one.'

'Pennr'yal!' repeated the dear little old woman, with an air of compassion for inferior knowledge; ''tain't the right time, darlin'. Pennyr'yal's too rank now. But for mulleins this day is prime. I've got a dreadful graspin' fit for 'em this year; seems if I must be goin' to need 'em extry. I feel like the squirrels must when they know a hard winter's comin'.' And Mrs Goodsoe bent over her work again, while I stood by and watched her carefully cut the best full-grown leaves with a clumsy pair of scissors, which might have served through at least half a century of herb-gathering. They were fastened to her apron-strings by a long piece of list.

'I'm going to take my jack-knife and help you,' I suggested, with some fear of refusal. 'I just passed a flourishing family of six or seven heads that must have been growing on purpose for you.'

'Now be keerful, dear heart,' was the anxious response; 'choose 'em well. There's odds in mulleins same's there is in angels. Take a plant that's all run up to stalk, and there ain't but little goodness in the leaves. This one I'm at now must ha' been stepped on by some creatur' and blighted of its bloom, and the leaves is han'some! When I was small I used to have a notion that Adam an' Eve must a took mulleins fer their winter wear. Ain't they just like flannel, for all the world? I've had experience, and I know there's plenty of sickness might be saved to folks if they'd quit horse-radish and such fiery, exasperating things, and use mullein drarves[4] in proper season. Now I shall spread these an' dry 'em nice on my spare floor in the garrit, an' come to steam 'em for use along in the winter there'll be the valley of the whole summer's goodness in 'em, sartin.' And she snipped away with the dull scissors, while I listened respectfully, and took great pains to have my part of the harvest present a good appearance.

'This is most too dry a head,' she added presently, a little out of breath. 'There! I can tell you there's win'rows[5] o' young doctors, bilin' over with book-larnin', that is truly ignorant of what to do for the sick, or how to p'int out those paths that well people foller toward sickness. Book-fools I call 'em, them young men, an' some of 'em never'll live to know much better; if they git to be Methuselahs. In my time every middle-aged woman, who had brought up a family, had some proper ideas o' dealin' with complaints. I won't say but there was some fools amongst *them*, but I'd rather take my chances, unless they'd forsook herbs and gone to dealin' with patent stuff. Now my mother really did sense the use of herbs and roots. I never see anybody that come up to her. She was a meek-looking woman, but very understandin', mother was.'

'Then that's where you learned so much yourself, Mrs Goodsoe,' I ventured to say.

'Bless your heart, I don't hold a candle to her; 'tis but little I can recall of what she used to say. No, her l'arnin' died with her,' said my friend, in a self-depreciating tone. 'Why, there was as many as twenty kinds of roots alone that she used to keep by her, that I forget the use of; an' I'm sure I shouldn't know where to find the most of 'em, any. There was an herb' – *airb*, she called it – 'an herb called masterwort, that she used to get away from Pennsylvany; and she used to think everything of noble-liverwort,[6] but I never could seem to get the right effects from it as she could. Though I don't know as she ever really did use masterwort where somethin' else wouldn't a served. She had a cousin married out in Pennsylvany that used to take pains to get it to her every year or two, and so she felt 'twas important to have it. Some set more by such things as come from a distance, but I rec'lect mother always used to maintain that folks was meant to be doctored with the stuff that grew right about 'em; 'twas sufficient, an' so ordered. That was before the whole population took to livin' on wheels, the way they do now. 'Twas never my idea that we was meant to know what's goin' on all over the world to once. There's goin' to be some sort of a set-back one o' these days, with these telegraphs an' things, an' letters comin' every hand's turn, and folks leavin' their proper work to answer 'em. I may not live to see it. 'Twas allowed to be difficult for folks to git about in old times, or to git word across the country, and they stood in their lot an' place, and weren't all just alike, either, same as pine-spills.'

We were kneeling side by side now, as if in penitence for the march of progress, but we laughed, as we turned to look at each other.

'Do you think it did much good when everybody brewed a cracked quart mug of herb-tea?' I asked, walking away on my knees to a new mullein.

'I've always lifted my voice against the practice, far 's I could,' declared Mrs Goodsoe; 'an' I won't deal out none o' the herbs I save for no such nonsense. There was three houses along our road, – I call no names, – where you couldn't go into the livin' room without findin' a mess o' herb-tea drorin'[7] on the stove or side o' the fireplace, winter or summer, sick or well. One was thoroughwut, one would be camomile, and the other, like as not, yellow dock; but they all used to put in a little new rum to git out the goodness, or keep it from spilin'.' (Mrs Goodsoe favored me with a knowing smile.) 'Land, how mother used to laugh! But, poor creaturs, they had to work hard, and I guess it never done 'em a mite o' harm; they was all good herbs. I wish you could bear the quawkin' there used to be when they was indulged with a real case o' sickness. Everybody would collect from far an' near; you'd see 'em coming along the road and across the pastures then; everybody clamorin' that nothin' wouldn't do no kind o' good but her choice o' teas or drarves to the feet. I wonder there was a babe lived to grow up in the whole lower part o' the town; an' if nothin' else 'peared to ail 'em, word was passed about that 'twas likely Mis' So-and So's last young one was goin' to be foolish. Land, how they'd gather! I know one day the doctor come to Widder Peck's and the house was crammed so 't he could scarcely git inside the door; and he says, just as polite, "Do send for some of the neighbors!" as if there wa'n't a soul to turn to, right or left. You'd ought to seen 'em begin to scatter.'

'But don't you think the cars[8] and telegraphs have given people more to interest them, Mrs Goodsoe? Don't you believe people's lives were narrower then, and more taken up with little things?' I asked, unwisely, being a product of modern times.

'Not one mite, dear,' said my companion stoutly. 'There was as big thoughts then as there is now; these times was born o' them. The difference in folks themselves; but now, instead o' doin' their own house-keepin' and watchin' their own neighbors, – though that was carried to excess, – they git word that a niece's child is ailin' the other side o' Massachusetts, and they drop everything and git on their best clothes, and off they jiggit⁹ in the cars. 'Tis a bad sign when folks wears out their best clothes faster 'n they do their everyday ones. The other side o' Massachusetts has got to look after itself by rights. An' besides that, Sunday-keepin's all gone out o' fashion. Some lays it to one thing an' some another, but some o' them old ministers that folks are all a-sighin' for did preach a lot o' stuff that wa'n't nothin' but chaff; twa'n't the word o' God out o' either Old Testament or New. But everybody went to meetin' and heard it, and come home, and was set to fightin' with their next door neighbor over it. Now I'm a believer, and I try to live a Christian life, but I'd as soon hear a surveyor's book read out, figgers an' all, as try to get any simple truth out o' most sermons. It's them as is most to blame.'

'What was the matter that day at Widow Peck's?' I hastened to ask, for I knew by experience that the good, clear-minded soul beside me was apt to grow unduly vexed and distressed when she contemplated the state of religious teaching.

'Why, there wa'n't nothin' the matter, only a gal o' Miss Peck's had met with a dis'pintment and had gone into screechin' fits. 'Twas a rovin' creatur' that had come along hayin' time, and he'd gone off an forsook her betwixt two days; nobody ever knew what become of him. Them Pecks was "Good Lord, anybody!" kind o' gals, and took up with whoever they could get. One of 'em married Heron, the Irishman; they lived in that little house that was burnt this summer, over on the edge o' the plains. He was a good-hearted creatur', with a laughin' eye and a clever word for everybody. He was the first Irishman that ever came this way, and we was all for gettin' a look at him, when he first used to go by. Mother's folks was what they call Scotch-Irish, though; there was an old race of 'em settled about here. They could foretell events, some on 'em, and had the second sight. I know folks used to say mother's grandmother had them gifts, but mother was never free to speak about it to us. She remembered her well, too.'

'I suppose that you mean old Jim Heron, who was such a famous fiddler?' I asked with great interest, for I am always delighted to know more about that rustic hero, parochial Orpheus that he must have been!

'Now, dear heart, I suppose you don't remember him, do you?' replied

Mrs Goodsoe, earnestly. 'Fiddle! He'd about break your heart with them tunes of his, or else set your heels flying up the floor in a jig, though you was minister o' the First Parish and all wound up for a funeral prayer. I tell ye there ain't no tunes sounds like them used to. It used to seem to me summer nights when I was comin' along the plains road, and he set by the window playin', as if there was a bewitched human creatur' in that old red fiddle o' his. He could make it sound just like a woman's voice tellin' somethin' over and over, as if folks could help her out o' her sorrows if she could only make 'em understand. I've set by the stone-wall and cried as if my heart was broke, and dear knows it wa'n't in them days. How he would twirl off them jigs and dance tunes! He used to make somethin' han'some out of 'em in fall an' winter, playin' at huskins and dancin' parties; but he was unstiddy by spells, as he got along in years, and never knew what it was to be forehanded. Everybody felt bad when he died; you couldn't help likin' the creatur'. He'd got the gift – that's all you could say about it.

'There was a Mis' Jerry Foss, that lived over by the brook bridge, on the plains road, that had lost her husband early, and was left with three child'n. She set the world by 'em, and was a real pleasant, ambitious little woman, and was workin' on as best she could with that little farm, when there come a rage o' scarlet fever, and her boy and two girls was swept off and laid dead within the same week. Every one o' the neighbors did what they could, but she'd had no sleep since they was taken sick, and after the funeral she set there just like a piece o' marble, and would only shake her head when you spoke to her. They all thought her reason would go; and 'twould certain, if she couldn't have shed tears. An one o' the neighbors – 'twas like mother's sense, but it might have been somebody else – spoke o' Jim Heron. Mother an' one or two o' the women that knew her best was in the house with her. 'Twas right in the edge o' the woods and some of us younger ones was over by the wall on the other side of the road where there was a couple of old willows, – I remember just how the brook damp felt; and we kept quiet's we could, and some other folks come along down the road, and stood waitin' on the little bridge, hopin' somebody'd come out, I suppose, and they'd git news. Everybody was wrought up, and felt a good deal for her, you know. By an' by Jim Heron come stealin' right out o' the shadows an' set down on the doorstep, an' 'twas a good while before we heard a sound; then, oh, dear me! 'twas what the whole neighborhood felt for that mother all spoke in the notes, an' they told me afterwards that Mis' Foss's face changed in a minute, and she come right over an' got into my mother's lap, – she was a little woman, – an' laid her head down, and there she cried herself into a blessed sleep. After awhile one o' the other women stole out an' told the folks, and we all went home. He only played that one tune.

'But there!' resumed Mrs Goodsoe, after a silence, during which my eyes were filled with tears. 'His wife always complained that the fiddle made her nervous. She never 'peared to think nothin' o' poor Heron after she'd once got him.'

'That's often the way,' said I, with harsh cynicism, though I had no guilty person in my mind at the moment; and we went straying off, not very far apart, up through the pasture. Mrs Goodsoe cautioned me that we must not get so far off that we could not get back the same day. The sunshine began to feel very hot on our backs, and we both turned toward the shade. We had already collected a large bundle of mullein leaves, which were carefully laid into a clean, calico apron, held together by the four corners, and proudly carried by me, though my companion regarded them with anxious eyes. We sat down together at the edge of the pine woods, and Mrs Goodsoe proceeded to fan herself with her limp cape-bonnet.

'I declare, how hot it is! The east wind's all gone again,' she said. 'It felt so cool this forenoon that I overburdened myself with as thick a petticoat as any I've got. I'm despri't afeared of having a chill, now that I ain't so young as once. I hate to be housed up.'

'It's only August, after all,' I assured her unnecessarily, confirming my statement by taking two peaches out of my pocket, and laying them side by side on the brown pine needles between us.

'Dear sakes alive!' exclaimed the old lady, with evident pleasure. 'Where did you get them, now? Doesn't anything taste twice better out-o'-doors? I ain't had such a peach for years. Do le's keep the stones, an' I'll plant 'em; it only takes four year for a peach pit to come to bearing, an' I guess I'm good for four year, 'thout I meet with some accident.'

I could not help agreeing, or taking a fond look at the thin little figure, and her wrinkled brown face and kind, twinkling eyes. She looked as if she had properly dried herself, by mistake, with some of her mullein leaves, and was likely to keep her goodness, and to last the longer in consequence. There never was a truer, simple-hearted soul made out of the old-fashioned country dust than Mrs Goodsoe. I thought, as I looked away from her across the wide country, that nobody was left in any of the farm-houses so original, so full of rural wisdom and reminiscence, so really able and dependable, as she. And nobody had made better use of her time in a world foolish enough to sometimes undervalue medicinal herbs.

When we had eaten our peaches we still sat under the pines, and I was not without pride when I had poked about in the ground with a little twig, and displayed to my crony a long fine root, bright yellow to the eye, and a wholesome bitter to the taste.

'Yis, dear, goldthread,' she assented indulgently. 'Seems to me there's more of it than anything except grass an' hardhack.[10] Good for canker, but no better than two or three other things I can call to mind; but I always lay in a good wisp of it, for old times' sake. Now, I want to know why you should a bit it, and took away all the taste o' your nice peach? I was just thinkin' what a han'some entertainment we've had. I've got so I 'sociate certain things with certain folks, and goldthread was somethin' Lizy Wisby couldn't keep house without, no ways whatever. I believe she took so much it kind o' puckered her disposition.

'Lizy Wisby?' I repeated inquiringly.

'You know her, if ever, by the name of Mis' Deacon Brimblecom,' answered my friend, as if this were only a brief preface to further information, so I waited with respectful expectation. Mrs Goodsoe had grown tired out in the sun, and a good story would be an excuse for sufficient rest. It was a most lovely place where we sat, halfway up the long hillside; for my part, I was perfectly contented and happy. 'You've often heard of Deacon Brimblecom?' she asked, as if a great deal depended upon his being properly introduced.

'I remember him,' said I. 'They called him Deacon Brimfull, you know, and he used to go about with a witch-hazel branch to show people where to dig wells.'

'That's the one,' said Mrs Goodsoe, laughing. 'I didn't know's you could go so far back. I'm always divided between whether you can remember everything I can, or are only a babe in arms.'

'I have a dim recollection of there being something strange about their marriage,' I suggested, after a pause, which began to appear dangerous. I was so much afraid the subject would be changed.

'I can tell you all about it,' I was quickly answered. 'Deacon Brimblecom was very pious accordin' to his lights in his early years. He lived way back in the country then, and there come a rovin' preacher along, and set everybody up that way all by the ears. I've heard the old folks talk it over, but I forget most of his doctrine, except some of his followers was persuaded they could dwell among the angels while yet on airth, and this Deacon Brimfull, as you call him, felt sure he was called by the voice of a spirit bride. So he left a good, deservin' wife he had, an' four children, and built him a new house over to the other side of the land he'd had from his father. They didn't take

157

much pains with the buildin', because they expected to be translated before long, and then the spirit brides and them folks was goin' to appear and divide up the airth amongst 'em, and the world's folks and on-believers was goin' to serve 'em or be sent to torments. They had meetins about in the school-houses, an' all sorts o' goins on; some of 'em went crazy, but the deacon held on to what wits he had, an' by an' by the spirit bride didn't turn out to be much of a housekeeper, an' he had always been used to good livin', so he sneaked home ag'in. One o' mother's sisters married up to Ash Hill, where it all took place; that's how I come to have the particulars.'

'Then how did he come to find his Eliza Wisby?' I inquired. 'Do tell me the whole story; you've got mullein leaves enough.'

'There's all yesterday's at home, if I haven't,' replied Mrs Goodsoe. 'The way he come a-courtin' o' Sister Wisby was this: she went a-courtin' o' him.

'There was a spell he lived to home, and then his poor wife died, and he had a spirit bride in good earnest, an' the child'n was placed about with his folks and hers, for they was both out o' good families; and I don't know what come over him, but he had another pious fit that looked for all the world like the real thing. He hadn't no family cares, and he lived with his brother's folks, and turned his land in with theirs. He used to travel to every meetin' an' conference[11] that was within reach of his old sorrel hoss's feeble legs; he j'ined the Christian Baptists that was just in their early prime, and he was a great exhorter,[12] and got to be called deacon,[13] though I guess he wa'n't deacon, 'less it was for a spare hand when deacon timber was scercer 'n usual. An' one time there was a four days' protracted meetin' to the church in the lower part of the town. 'Twas a real solemn time; something more 'n usual was goin' forward, an' they collected from the whole country round. Women folks like it, an' the men too; it give 'em a change, an' they was quartered round free, same as conference folks now. Some on 'em, for a joke, sent Silas Brimblecom up to Lizy Wisby's, though she'd give out she couldn't accommodate nobody, because of expectin' her cousin's folks. Everybody knew 'twas a lie; she was amazin' close considerin' she had plenty to do with. There was a streak that wa'n't just right somewhere in Lizy's wits, I always thought. She was very kind in case o' sickness, I'll say that for her.

'You know where the house is over there on what they call Windy Hill? There the deacon went, all unsuspectin', and 'stead o' Lizy's resentin' of him she put in her own hoss, and they come back together to evenin' meetin'. She was prominent among the sect herself, an' he bawled and talked, and she bawled and talked, an' took up more 'n the time allotted in the exercises, just as if they was showin' off to each other what they was able to do at expoundin'. Everybody was laughin' at 'em after the meetin' broke up, and that next day an' the next, an' all through, they was constant, and seemed to be havin' a beautiful occasion. Lizy had always give out she scorned the men, but when she got a chance at a particular one 'twas altogether different, and the deacon seemed to please her somehow or 'nother, and – There! you don't want to listen to this old stuff that's past an' gone?'

'Oh yes, I do,' said I.

'I run on like a clock that's onset her striking hand,' said Mrs Goodsoe mildly. 'Sometimes my kitchen timepiece goes on half the forenoon, and I says to myself the day before yesterday I would let it be a warnin', and keep it in mind for a check on my own speech. The next news that was heard was that the deacon an' Lizy – well, opinions differed which of 'em had spoke first, but them fools settled it before the protracted meetin' was over, and give away their hearts before he started for home. They considered 'twould be wise, though, considerin' their short acquaintance, to take one another on trial a spell; 'twas Lizy's notion, and she asked him why he wouldn't come over and stop with her till spring, and then, if they both continued to like, they could git married any time 'twas convenient. Lizy, she come and talked it over with mother, and mother disliked to offend her, but she spoke pretty plain; and Lizy felt hurt, an' thought they was showin' excellent judgment, so much harm come from hasty unions and folks comin' to a realizin' sense of each other's failin's when 'twas too late.

'So one day our folks saw Deacon Brimfull a-ridin' by with a gre't coopful of hens in the back o' his wagon, and bundles o' stuff tied on top and hitched to the exes[14] underneath; and he riz a hymn just as he passed the house, and was speedin' the old sorrel with a willer switch. 'Twas most Thanksgivin' time, an' sooner 'n she expected him. New Year's was the time she set; but he thought he'd better come while the roads was fit for wheels. They was out to meetin' together Thanksgivin' Day, an' that used to be a gre't season for marryin'; so the young folks nudged each other, and some on' 'em ventured to speak to the couple as they come down the aisle. Lizy carried it off real well; she wa'n't afraid o' what nobody said or thought, and so home they went. They'd got out her yaller sleigh and her hoss; she never would ride after the deacon's poor old creatur', and I believe it died long o' the winter from stiffening up.

'Yes,' said Mrs Goodsoe emphatically, after we had silently considered the situation for a short space of time, – 'yes, there was considerable talk, now I tell you! The raskil boys pestered 'em just about to death for a while. They used to collect up there an' rap on the winders, and they'd turn out all the deacon's hens 'long at nine o'clock o'night, and chase 'em all over the dingle; an' one night they even lugged the pig right out o' the sty, and shoved it into the back entry, an' run for their lives. They'd stuffed its mouth full o' somethin', so it couldn't squeal till it got there. There wa'n't a sign o' nobody to be seen when Lizy hasted out with a light, and she an' the deacon had to persuade the creatur' back as best they could; 'twas a cold night, and they said it took 'em till towards mornin'. You see the deacon was just the kind of a man that a hog wouldn't budge for; it takes a masterful man to deal with a hog. Well, there was no end to the works nor the talk, but Lizy left 'em pretty much alone. She did 'pear kind of dignified about it, I must say!'

'And then, were they married in the spring?'

'I was tryin' to remember whether it was just before Fast Day or just after,' responded my friend, with a careful look at the sun, which was nearer the west than either of us had noticed. 'I think likely 'twas along in the last o' April, any way some of us looked out o' the window one Monday morning' early, and says, "For goodness' sake! Lizy's sent the deacon home again!" His old sorrel havin' passed away, he was ridin' in Ezry Welsh's hoss-cart, with his hen-coop and more bundles than he had when he come, and he looked as meechin' as ever you see. Ezry was drivin', and he let a glance fly swiftly round to see if any of us was lookin' out; an' then I declare if he didn't have the malice to turn right in towards the barn, where he see my oldest brother, Joshuay, an' says he real natural, "Joshuay, just step out with your wrench. I believe I hear my kingbolt rattlin' kind o' loose." Brother, he went out an' took in the sitooation, an' the deacon bowed kind of stiff. Joshuay was so full o' laugh, and Ezry Welsh, that they couldn't look one another in the face. There wa'n't nothing ailed the kingbolt, you know, an' when Josh riz up he says, "Goin' up country for a spell, Mr Brimblecom?"

'"I be," says the deacon, lookin' dreadful mortified and cast down.

'"Ain't things turned out well with you an' Sister Wisby?" says Joshuay. "You had ought to remember that the woman is the weaker vessel."

'"Hang her, let her carry less sail; then!" the deacon bu'st out, and he stood right up an' shook his fist there by the hen-coop, he was so mad; an' Ezry's hoss was a young creatur', an' started up an set the deacon right over backwards into the chips. We didn't know but he'd broke his neck; but when he see the women folks runnin' out, he jumped up quick as a cat, an' clim' into the cart, an' off they went. Ezry said he told him that he couldn't git along with Lizy, she was so fractious in thundery weather; if there was a rumble in the day-time she must go right to bed an' screech and if 'twas night she must git right up an' go an' call him out of a sound sleep. But everybody knew he'd never a gone home unless she'd sent him.

'Somehow they made it up agin right away, him an' Lizy, and she had him back. She'd been countin' all along on not havin' to hire nobody to work about the gardin an' so on, an' she said she wa'n't going' to let him have a whole winter's board for nothin'. So the old hens was moved back, and they was married right off fair an' square, an' I don't know but they got along well as most folks. He brought his youngest girl down to live with 'em after a while, an' she was a real treasure to Lizy; everybody spoke well o' Phebe Brimblecom. The deacon got over his pious fit, and there was consider'ble work in him if you kept right after him. He was an amazin' cider-drinker, and he airnt the name you know him by in his latter days. Lizy never trusted him with nothin', but she kep' him well. She left everything she owned to Phebe, when she died, 'cept somethin' to satisfy the law. There, they're all gone now: seems to me sometimes, when I get thinkin', as if I'd lived a thousand years!'

I laughed, but I found that Mrs Goodsoe's thoughts had taken a serious turn.

'There, I come by some old graves down here in the lower edge of the pasture,' she said as we rose to go. 'I couldn't help thinking how I should like to be laid right out in the pasture ground, when my time comes; it looked sort o' comfortable, and I have ranged these slopes so many summers. Seems as if I could see right up through the turf and tell when the weather was pleasant, and get the goodness o' the sweet fern. Now, dear, just hand me my apernful o' mulleins out o' the shade. I hope you won't come to need none this winter, but I'll dry some special for you.'

'I'm going home by the road,' said I, 'or else by the path across the meadows, so I will walk as far as the house with you. Aren't you pleased with my company?' for she demurred at my going the least bit out of the way.

So we strolled toward the little gray house, with our plunder of mullein leaves slung on a stick which we carried between us. Of course I went in to make a call, as if I had not seen my hostess before; she is the last maker of muster-gingerbread, and before I came away I was kindly measured for a pair of mittens.

'You'll be sure to come an' see them two peach-trees after I get 'em well growin'?' Mrs Goodsoe called after me when I had said good-by, and was almost out of hearing down the road.

MISS PECK'S PROMOTION

Miss Peck had spent a lonely day in her old farm-house, high on a long Vermont hillside that sloped toward the west. She was able for an hour at noon to overlook the fog in the valley below, and pitied the people in the village whose location she could distinguish only by means of the church steeple which pricked through the gray mist, like a buoy set over a dangerous reef. During this brief time, when the sun was apparently shining for her benefit alone, she reflected proudly upon the advantage of living on high land, but in the early afternoon, when the fog began to rise slowly, and at last shut her in, as well as the rest of the world, she was conscious of uncommon depression of spirits.

'I might as well face it now as any time,' she said aloud, as she lighted her clean kerosene lamp and put it on the table. 'Eliza Peck! just set down and make it blazing clear how things stand with you, and what you're going to do in regard to 'em! 'Tain't no use matching your feelin's to the weather, without you've got reason for it.' And she twitched the short curtains across the windows so that their brass rings squeaked on the wires, opened the door for the impatient cat that was mewing outside, and then seated herself in the old rocking-chair at the table end.

It is quite a mistake to believe that people who live by themselves find every day a lonely one. Miss Peck and many other solitary persons could assure us that it is very seldom that they feel their lack of companionship. As the habit of living alone grows more fixed, it becomes confusing to have other people about, and seems more or less bewildering to be interfered with by other people's plans and suggestions. Only once in a while does the feeling of solitariness become burdensome, or a creeping dread and sense of defenselessness assail one's comfort. But when Miss Peck was aware of the approach of such a mood she feared it, and was prepared to fight it with her best weapon of common-sense.

She was much given to talking aloud, as many solitary persons are; not merely talking to herself in the usual half-conscious way, but making her weaker self listen to severe comment and pointed instruction. Miss Peck the less was frequently brought to trial in this way by Miss Peck the greater, and when it was once announced that justice must be done, no amount of quailing or excuse averted the process of definite conviction.

This evening she turned the light up to its full brightness, reached for her knitting-work, lifted it high above her lap, for a moment, as her favorite cat jumped up to its evening quarters; then she began to rock to and fro with regularity and decision. "'tis all nonsense,' she said, as if she were addressing some one greatly her inferior – "'Tis all nonsense for you to go on this way, Elizy Peck! you're better off than you've been this six year, if you only had sense to feel so.'

There was no audible reply, and the speaker evidently mistook the silence for unconvinced stubbornness.

'If ever there was a woman who was determined to live by other folks' wits, and to eat other folks' dinners, 'twas and is your lamented brother's widder, Harri't Peck – Harri't White that was. She's claimed the town's compassion till it's good as run dry, and she's thought that you, Elizy Peck, a hard-workin' and self-supportin' woman, was made for nothin' but her use and comfort. Ever since your father died and you've been left alone you've had her for a clog to your upward way. Six years you've been at her beck an' call, and now that a respectable man, able an' willing to do for her, has been an' fell in love with her, and shouldered her and all her whims, and promised to do for the children as if they was his own, you've been grumpin' all day, an' *I'd* like to know what there is to grump about!'

There was a lack of response even to this appeal to reason, and the knitting-needles clicked in dangerous nearness to the old cat's ears, so that they twitched now and then, and one soft paw unexpectedly revealed its white curving claws.

'Yes,' said Miss Peck, presently, in a more lenient tone, 'I s'pose 'tis the children you're thinking most. I declare I should like to see that Tom's little red head, and feel it warm with my two hands this minute! There's always somethin' hopeful in havin' to do with children, 'less they come of *too* bad a stock. Grown folks – well, you can make out to grin an' bear 'em if you must; but like 's not young ones'll turn out to be somebody, and what you do for 'em may count towards it. There's that Tom, he looks just as his father used to, and there ain't a day he won't say somethin' real pleasant, and never sees the difference betwixt you an' somebody handsome. I expect they'll spile him – you don't know what kind o' young ones they'll let him play with, nor how they'll let him murder the king's English, and never think o' boxin' his ears. Them big factory towns is all for eatin' and clothes. I'm glad you was raised in a good old academy town,[1] if 'twas the Lord's will to plant you in the far outskirts. Land, how Harri't did smirk at that man! I will say she looked pretty – 'tis hard work and worry makes folks plain like me – I believe she's fared better to be left a widder with three child'n, and everybody saying how hard it was, an' takin' holt, than she would if brother had lived and she'd had to stir herself to keep house and do for him. You've been the real widder that Tom left – you've mourned him, and had your way to go alone – not she! The colonel's lady,' repeated Miss Peck, scornfully – 'that's what sp'ilt her. She never could come down to common things, Mis' Colonel Peck! Well, she may have noble means now, but she's got to be spoke of as Mis' Noah Pigley all the rest of her days. Not that I'm goin' to fling at any man's accident of name,' said the just Eliza, in an apologetic tone. 'I did want to adopt little Tom, but 'twas to be expected he'd object – a boy's goin' to be useful in his business, and poor Tommy's the likeliest. I would have 'dopted him out an' out, and he shall have the old farm anyway. But oh dear me, he's all spoilt for farming now, is little Tom, unless I can make sure of him now and then for a good long visit in summer time.

'Summer an' winter; I s'pose, you're likely to live a great many years, Elizy,' sighed the good woman. 'All sole alone, too! There, I've landed right at the startin' point,' – and the kitchen was very still while some dropped stitches in a belated stocking for the favorite nephew were obscured by a mist of tears like the fog outside. There was no more talking aloud, for Miss Peck fell into a revery about old days and the only brother who had left his little household in her care and marched to the war whence for him there was to be no return. She had remembered very often, with a great sense of comfort, a message in one of his very last letters. 'Tell Eliza that she's more likely to be promoted than I am,' he said (when he had just got his step of Major); 'she's my superior officer, however high I get, and now I've heard what luck she's had with the haying, I appoint her Brigadier-General for gallantry in the field.' How poor Tom's jokes had kept their courage up even when they were most anxious! Yes, she had made many sacrifices of personal gain, as every good soldier must. She had meant to be a school-teacher. She had the gift for it, and had studied hard in her girlhood. One thing after another had kept her at home, and now she must stay here – her ambitions were at an end. She would do what good she could among her neighbors, and stand in her lot and place. It was the first time she had found to think soberly about her life, for her sister-in-law and the children had gone to their new home within a few days, and since then she had stifled all power of proper reflection by hard work at setting the house in order and getting in her winter supplies. 'Thank Heaven the house and place belong to me,' she said in a decisive tone. ''Twas wise o' father to leave it so – and let her have the money. She'd left me no peace till I moved off if I'd only been half-owner; she's always meant to get to a larger place – but what I want is real promotion.'

The Peck farm-house was not only on a by-road that wandered among the slopes of the hills, but it was at the end of a long lane of its own. There was rarely any sound at night except from the winds of heaven or the soughing of the neighboring pine-trees. By day, there was a beautiful inspiriting outlook over the wide country from the farm-house windows, but on such a night as this the darkness made an impenetrable wall. Miss Peck was not afraid of it; on the contrary, she had a sense of security in being shut safe into the very heart of the night. By day she might be vexed by intruders, by night they could scarcely find her – her bright light could not be seen from the road. If she were to wither away in the old gray house like an unplanted kernel in its shell, she would at least wither undisturbed. Her sorrow of loneliness was not the fear of molestation. She was fearless enough at the thought of physical dangers.

The evening did not seem so long as she expected – a glance at her reliable time-keeper told her at last that it was already past eight o'clock, and her eyes began to feel heavy. The fire was low, the fog was making its presence felt even in the house, for the autumn night was chilly, and Miss Peck decided that when she came to the end of the stitches on a certain needle she would go to bed. Tomorrow, she meant to cut her apples for drying, a duty too long delayed. She had sent away some of her best fruit that day to make the annual barrel of cider with which she provided herself, more from habit than from real need of either the wholesome beverage or its resultant vinegar. 'If this fog lasts, I've got to dry my apples by the stove,' she thought, doubtfully, and was conscious of a desire to survey the weather from the outer doorway before she slept. How she missed Harriet and the children! – though they had been living with her only for a short time before the wedding, and since the half-house they had occupied in the village had been let. The thought of bright-eyed, red-headed little Tom still brought the warm tears very near to falling. He had cried bitterly when he went away. So had his mother – at least, she held up her pocket-handkerchief. Miss Peck never had believed in Harriet's tears.

Out of the silence of the great hillslope came the dull sound of a voice, and as Miss Peck sprang from her chair to the window, dropping the sleeping cat in a solid mass on the floor, she recognized the noise of a carriage. Her heart was beating provokingly; she was tired by the excitement of the last few days. She did not remember this, but was conscious of being startled in an unusual way. It must be some strange crisis in her life; she turned and looked about the familiar kitchen as if it were going to be altogether swept away. 'Now, you needn't be afraid that Pigley's comin' to bring her back, Elizy Peck!' she assured herself with grim humor in that minute's apprehension of disaster.

A man outside spoke sternly to his horse. Eliza stepped quickly to the door and opened it wide. She was not afraid of the messenger, only of the message.

'Hold the light so's I can see to tie this colt,' said a familiar voice; 'it's as dark as a pocket, 'Liza. I'll be right in. You must put on a good warm shawl; 'tis as bad as rain, this fog is. The minister wants you to come down to his house; he's at his wits' end, and there was nobody we could think of that's free an' able except you. His wife's gone, died at quarter to six, and left a mis'able baby; but the doctor expects 't will live. The nurse they bargained with 's failed 'em, and 'tis an awful state o' things as you ever see. Half the women in town are there, and the minister's overcome; he is sort of fainted away two or three times, and they don't know who else to get, till the doctor said your name, and he groaned right out you was the one. 'Tain't right to refuse, as I view it. Mis' Spence and Mis' Corbell is going to watch with the dead, but there needs a head.'

Eliza Peck felt for once as if she lacked that useful possession herself, and sat down, with amazing appearance of calmness, in one of her splint-bottomed chairs to collect her thoughts. The messenger was a good deal excited; so was she; but in a few moments she rose, cutting short his inconsequent description of affairs at the parsonage.

'You just put out the fire as best you can,' she said. 'We'll talk as we go along. There's plenty o' ashes there, I'm sure; I let the stove cool off considerable, for I was meanin' to go to bed in another five minutes. The cat'll do well enough. I'll leave her plenty for tomorrow, and she's got a place where she can crep in an' out of the wood-shed. I'll just slip on another dress and put the nails over the windows, an' we'll be right off.' She was quite herself again now; and, true to her promise, it was not many minutes before the door was locked, the house left in darkness, and Ezra Weston and Miss Peck were driving comfortably down the lane. The fog had all blown away, suddenly the stars were out, and the air was sweet with the smell of the wet bark of black birches and cherry and apple-trees that grew by the fences. The leaves had fallen fast through the day, weighted by the dampness until their feeble stems could keep them in place no longer; for the bright colors of the foliage there had come at night sweet odors and a richness of fragrance in the soft air.

"'Tis an unwholesome streak o' weather, ain't it?' asked Ezra Weston. 'Feels like a dog-day evenin',[2] don't it? Come this time o' year we want bracin' up.'

Miss Peck did not respond; her sympathetic heart was dwelling on the thought that she was going, not only to a house of mourning, but to a bereft parsonage. She would not have felt so unequal to soothing the sorrows of her everyday acquaintances, but she could hardly face the duty of consoling the new minister. But she never once wished that she had not consented so easily to respond to his piteous summons.

There was a strangely festive look in the village, for the exciting news of Mrs Elbury's death had flown from house to house – lights were bright everywhere, and in the parsonage brightest of all. It looked as if the hostess were receiving her friends, and helping them to make merry, instead of being white and still, and done with this world, while the busy women of the parish were pulling open her closets and bureau drawers in search of household possessions. Nobody stopped to sentimentalize over the poor soul's delicate orderliness, or the simple, loving preparations she had made for the coming of the baby which fretfully wailed in the next room.

'Here's a nice black silk that never was touched with the scissors!' said one good dame, as if a kind Providence ought to have arranged for the use of such a treasure in setting the bounds of the dead woman's life.

'Does seem too bad, don't it? I always heard her folks was well off,' replied somebody in a loud whisper; 'she had everything to live for.' There was great eagerness to be of service to the stricken pastor, and the kind neighbors did their best to prove the extent of their sympathy. One after another went to the room where he was, armed with various excuses, and the story of his sad looks and distress was repeated again and again to a grieved audience.

When Miss Peck came in she had to listen to a full description of the day's events, and was decorously slow in assuming her authority; but at last the house was nearly empty again, and only the watchers and one patient little mother of many children, who held this motherless child in loving arms, were left with Miss Peck in the parsonage. It seemed a year since she had sat in her quiet kitchen, a solitary woman whose occupations seemed too few and too trivial for her eager capacities and ambitions.

The autumn days went by, winter set in early, and Miss Peck was still mistress of the parsonage housekeeping. Her own cider was brought to the parsonage, and so were the potatoes and the apples; even the cat was transferred to a dull village existence, far removed in every way from her happy hunting-grounds among the snow-birds[3] and plump squirrels. The minister's pale little baby loved Miss Peck and submitted to her rule already. She clung fast to the good woman with her little arms, and Miss Peck, who had always imagined that she did not care for infants, found herself watching the growth of this spark of human intelligence and affection with intense interest. After all, it was good to be spared the long winter at the farm; it had never occurred to her to dread it, but she saw now that it was a season to be dreaded, and one by one forgot the duties which at first beckoned her homeward and seemed so unavoidable. The farm-house seemed cold and empty when she paid it an occasional visit. She would not have believed that she could content herself so well away from the dear old home. If she could have had her favorite little Tom within reach, life would have been perfectly happy.

The minister proved at first very disappointing to her imaginary estimate and knowledge of him. If it had not been for her sturdy loyalty to him as pastor and employer, she could sometimes have joined more or less heartily in the expressions of the disaffected faction which forms a difficult element in every parish. Her sense of humor was deeply gratified when the leader of the opposition remarked that the minister was beginning to take notice a little, and was wearing his best hat every day, like every other widower since the world was made. Miss Peck's shrewd mind had already made sure that Mr Elbury's loss was not so great as she had at first sympathetically believed; she knew that his romantic, ease-loving, self-absorbed, and self-admiring nature had been curbed and held in check by the literal, prosaic, faithful-in-little-things disposition of his dead wife. She was self-denying, he was self-indulgent; she was dutiful, while he was given to indolence – and the unfounded plea of ill-health made his only excuse. Miss Peck soon fell into the way of putting her shoulder to the wheel, and unobtrusively, even secretly, led the affairs of the parish. She never was deaf to the explanation of the wearing effect of brain-work, but accepted the weakness as well as the power of the ministerial character; and nobody listened more respectfully to his somewhat flowery and inconsequent discourses on Sunday than Miss

Peck. The first Sunday they went to church together Eliza slipped into her own pew, halfway up the side aisle, and thought well of herself for her prompt decision afterward, though she regretted the act for a moment as she saw the minister stop to let her into the empty pew of the parsonage. He had been sure she was just behind him, and gained much sympathy from the congregation as he sighed and went his lonely way up the pulpit-stairs. Even Mrs Corbell, who had been averse to settling the Rev. Mr Elbury was moved by this incident, but directly afterward whispered to her next neighbor that 'Lizy Peck would be sitting there before the year was out if she had the business-head they had all given her credit for.'

It gives rise to melancholy reflections when one sees how quickly those who have suffered most cruel and disturbing bereavements learn to go their way alone. The great plan of our lives is never really broken nor suffers accidents. However stunning the shock, one can almost always understand gratefully that it was best for the vanished friend to vanish just when he did; that this world held no more duties or satisfactions for him; that his earthly life was in fact done and ended. Our relations with him must be lifted to a new plane. Miss Peck thought often of the minister's loss, and always with tender sympathy, yet she could not help seeing that he was far from being unresigned or miserable in his grief. She was ready to overlook the fact that he depended upon his calling rather than upon his own character and efforts. The only way in which she made herself uncongenial to the minister was by persistent suggestions that he should take more exercise and 'stir about outdoors a little.' Once, when she had gone so far as to briskly inform him that he was getting logy,[4] Mr Elbury showed entire displeasure; and a little later, in the privacy of the kitchen, she voiced the opinion that Elizy Peck knew very well that she never did think ministers were angels – only human beings, like herself, in great danger of being made fools of. But the two good friends made up their little quarrel at supper-time.

'I have been looking up the derivation of that severe word you applied to me this noon,' said the Reverend Mr Elbury, pleasantly. 'It is a localism; but it comes from the Dutch word *log*, which means heavy or unwieldy.'

These words were pronounced plaintively, with evident consciousness that they hardly applied to his somewhat lank figure; and Miss Peck felt confused and rebuked, and went on pouring tea until both cup and saucer were full, and she scalded the end of her thumb. She was very weak in the hands of such a scholar as this, but later she had a reassuring sense of not having applied the epithet unjustly. With a feminine reverence for his profession, and for his attainment, she had a keen sense of his human fallibility; and neither his grief, nor his ecclesiastical halo, nor his considerate idea of his own value, could blind her sharp eyes to certain shortcomings. She forgave them readily, but she knew them all by sight and name.

If there were any gift of Mr Elbury's which could be sincerely called perfectly delightful by many people, it was his voice. When he was in a hurry, and gave hasty directions to his housekeeper about some mislaid possession, or called her down-stairs to stop the baby's vexatious crying, the tones were entirely different from those best known to the parish. Nature had gifted him with a power of carrying his voice into the depths of his sympathetic being and recovering it again gallantly. He had been considered the superior, in some respects, of that teacher of elocution who led the students of the theological seminary toward the glorious paths of oratory. There was a mellow middle-tone, most suggestive of tender feeling; but though it sounded sweet to other feminine ears, Miss Peck was always annoyed by it and impatient of a certain artificial quality in its cadences. To hear Mr Elbury talk to his child in this tone, and address her as 'my motherless babe', however affecting to other ears, was always unpleasant to Miss Peck. But she thought very well of his preaching; and the more he let all the decisions and responsibilities of everyday life fall to her share, the more she enjoyed life and told her friends that Mr Elbury was a most amiable man to live with. And when spring was come the hillside farm was let on shares to one of Miss Peck's neighbors whom she could entirely trust. It was not the best of bargains for its owner, who had the reputation of being an excellent farmer, and the agreement cost her many sighs and not a little wakefulness. She felt too much shut in by this village life; but the minister pleaded his hapless lot, the little child was even more appealing in her babyhood, and so the long visit from little Tom and his sisters, the familiar garden, the three beehives, and the glory of the sunsets in the great, unbroken, western sky were all given up together for that year.

It was not so hard as it might have been. There was one most rewarding condition of life – the feast of books, which was new and bewilderingly delightful to the minister's housekeeper. She had made the most of the few well-chosen volumes of the farmhouse, but she never had known the joy of having more books than she could read, or their exquisite power of temptation, the delight of their friendly company. She was oftenest the student, the brain-wearied member, of the parsonage-family, but she never made it an excuse, or really recognized the new stimulus either. Life had never seemed so full to her; she was working with both hands earnestly, and no half-heartedness. She was filled with reverence in the presence of the minister's books; to her his calling, his character, and his influence were all made positive and respectable by this foundation of learning on his library-shelves. He was to her a man of letters, a critic, and a philosopher, besides being an experienced theologian from the very nature of his profession. Indeed, he had an honest liking for books, and was fond of reading aloud or being read to; and many an evening went joyfully by in the presence of the great English writers, whose best thoughts were rolled out in Mr Elbury's best tones, and Miss Peck listened with delight, and cast many an affectionate glance at the sleeping child in the cradle at her feet, filled with gratitude as she was for all her privileges.

Mr Elbury was most generous in his appreciation of Miss Peck's devotion, and never hesitated to give expression to sincere praise of her uncommon power of mind. He was led into paths of literature, otherwise untrod, by her delight; and sometimes, to rest his brain and make him ready for a good night's sleep, he asked his companion to read him a clever story. It was all a new world to the good woman whose schooling and reading had been sound, but restricted; and if ever a mind waked up with joy to its possession of the world of books, it was hers. She became ambitious for the increase of her own little library; and it was in reply to her outspoken plan for larger crops and more money from the farm another year, for the sake of bookbuying, that Mr Elbury once said, earnestly, that his books were hers now. This careless expression was the spark which lit a new light for Miss Peck's imagination. For the first time a thrill of personal interest in the man made itself felt, through her devoted capacity for service and appreciation. He had ceased to be simply himself; he stood now for a widened life, a suggestion of added good and growth, a larger circle of human interests; in fact, his existence had made all the difference between her limited rural home and that connection with the great world which even the most contracted parsonage is sure to hold.

And that very night, while Mr Elbury had gone, somewhat ruefully and ill-prepared, to his Bible class, Miss Peck's conscience set her womanly weakness before it for a famous arraigning. It was so far successful that words failed the defendant completely, and the session was dissolved in tears. For some days Miss Peck was not only stern with herself, but even with the minister, and was entirely devoted to her domestic affairs.

The very next Sunday it happened that Mr Elbury exchanged pulpits with a brother-clergyman in the next large town, a thriving manufacturing centre, and he came home afterward in the best of spirits. He never had seemed so appreciative of his comfortable home, or Miss Peck's motherly desire to shield his weak nature from these practical cares of life to which he was entirely inadequate. He was unusually gay and amusing, and described, not with the best taste, the efforts of two of his unmarried lady-parishioners to make themselves agreeable. He had met them on the short journey, and did not hesitate to speak of himself lightly as a widower; in fact, he recognized his own popularity and attractions in a way that was not pleasing to Miss Peck, yet she was used to his way of speaking and unaffectedly glad to have him home again. She had been much disturbed and grieved by her own thoughts in his absence. She could not be sure whether she was wise in drifting toward a nearer relation to the minister. She was not exactly shocked at finding herself interested in him, but with her usual sense of propriety and justice, she insisted upon taking everybody's view of the question before the weaker Miss Peck was accorded a hearing. She was enraged with herself of feeling abashed and liking to avoid the direct scrutiny of her fellow-parishioners. Mrs Corbell and she had always been the best of friends, but for the first time Miss Peck was annoyed by such freedom of comment and opinion. And Sister Corbell had never been so forward about spending the afternoon at the parsonage, or running in for half-hours of gossip in the morning, as in these latter days. At last she began to ask the coy Eliza about her plans for the wedding, in a half-joking, half-serious tone which was hard to bear.

'You're a sight too good for him,' was the usual conclusion, 'and so I tell everybody. The whole parish has got it settled for you; and there's as many as six think hard of you, because you've given 'em no chance, bein' right here on the spot.'

It seemed as if a resistless torrent of fate were sweeping our independent friend toward the brink of a great change. She insisted to the quailing side of her nature that she did not care for the minister himself, that she was likely to age much sooner than he, with his round, boyish face and plump cheeks. 'They'll be takin' you for his mother, Lizy, when you go amongst strangers, little and dried up as you're gettin' to be a'ready; you're three years older anyway, and look as if 'twas nine.' Yet the capable, clear-headed woman was greatly enticed by the high position and requirements of mistress of the parsonage. She liked the new excitement and authority, and grew more and more happy in the exercise of powers which a solitary life at the farm would hardly arouse or engage. There was a vigorous growth of independence and determination in Miss Peck's character, and she had not lived alone so many years for nothing. But there was no outward sign yet of capitulation. She was firmly convinced that the minister could not get on without her, and that she would rather not get on without him and the pleasure of her new activities. If possible, she grew a little more self-contained and reserved in manner and speech, while carefully anticipating his wants and putting better and better dinners on the parochial table.

As for Mr Elbury himself, he became more cheeful every day, and was almost demonstrative in his affectionate gratitude. He spoke always as if they were one in their desire to interest and benefit the parish; he had fallen into a pleasant, home-like habit of saying 'we' whenever household or parish affairs were under discussion. Once, when somebody had been remarking the too-evident efforts of one of her sister-parishioners to gain Mr Elbury's affection, he had laughed leniently; but when this gossiping caller had gone away the minister said, gently, 'We know better, don't we Miss Peck?' and Eliza could not help feeling that his tone meant a great deal. Yet she took no special notice of him, and grew much more taciturn than was natural. Her heart beat warmly under her prim alpacca-dress; she already looked younger and a great deal happier than when she first came to live at the parsonage. Her executive ability was made glad by the many duties that fell upon her, and those who knew her and Mr Elbury best thought nothing could be wiser than their impending marriage. Did not the little child need Miss Peck's motherly care? did not the helpless minister need the assistance of a clear-sighted business-woman and good housekeeper? did not Eliza herself need and deserve a husband? But even with increasing certainty she still gave no outward sign of their secret understanding. It was likely that Mr Elbury thought best to wait a year after his wife's death, and when he spoke right out was the time to show what her answer would be. But somehow the thought of the dear old threadbare farm in the autumn weather was always a sorrowful thought; and on the days when Mr Elbury hired a horse and wagon, and invited her and the baby to accompany him on a series of parochial visitations, she could not bear to look at the home-fields and the pasture-slopes. She was thankful that the house itself was not in sight from the main road. The crops that summer had been unusually good; something called her thoughts back continually to the old home, and accused her of disloyalty. Yet she consoled herself by thinking it was very natural to have such regrets, and to consider the importance of such a step at her sensible time of life. So it drew near winter again, and she grew more and more unrelenting and scornful whenever her acquaintances suggested the idea that her wedding ought to be drawing near.

Mr Elbury seemed to have taken a new lease of youthful hope and ardor. He was busy in the parish and very popular, particularly among his women-parishioners. Miss Peck urged him on with his good works, and it seemed as if they expressed their interest in each other by their friendliness to the parish in general. Mr Elbury had joined a ministers' club in the large town already spoken of, and spent a day there now and then, besides his regular Monday-night attendance on the club-meeting. He was preparing a series of sermons on the history of the Jews, and was glad to avail himself of a good free-library, the lack of which he frequently lamented in his own village. Once he said, eagerly, that he had no idea of ending his days here, and this gave Miss Peck a sharp pang. She could not bear to think of leaving her old home, and the tears filled her eyes. When she had reached the shelter of the kitchen, she retorted to the too-easily ruffled element of her character that there was no need of crossing that bridge till she came to it; and, after an appealing glance at the academy-steeple above the maple-trees, she returned to the study to finish dusting. She saw, without apprehension, that the minister quickly pushed something under the leaves of his blotting-paper and frowned a little. It was not his usual time for writing – she had a new proof of her admiring certainty that Mr Elbury wrote for the papers at times under an assumed name.

One Monday evening he had not returned from the ministers' meeting until later than usual, and she began to be slightly anxious. The baby had not been very well all day, and she particularly wished to have an errand done before night, but did not dare to leave the child alone, while, for a wonder, nobody had been in. Mr Elbury had shown a great deal of feeling before he went away in the morning, and as she was admiringly looking at his well-fitting clothes and neat clerical attire, a thrill of pride and affection had made her eyes shine unwontedly. She was really beginning to like him very much. For the first and last time in his life the minister stepped quickly forward and kissed her on the forehead. 'My good, kind friend!' he exclaimed, in that deep tone which the whole parish loved; then he hurried away. Miss Peck felt a strange dismay, and stood by the breakfast-table like a statue. She even touched her forehead with trembling fingers. Somehow she inwardly rebelled, but kissing meant more to her than to some people. She never had been used to it, except with little Tom – though the last brotherly kiss his father gave her, before he went to the war had been one of the treasures of her memory. All that day she was often reminded of the responsible and darker side, the inspected and criticized side, of the high position of minister's wife. It was clearly time for proper rebuke when evening came; and as she sat by the light, mending Mr Elbury's stockings, she said over and over again that she had walked into this with her eyes wide open, and if the experience of forty years hadn't put any sense into her it was too late to help it now.

Suddenly she heard the noise of wheels in the side yard. Could anything have happened to Mr Elbury? were they bringing him home hurt, or dead even? He never drove up from the station unless it were bad weather. She rushed to the door with a flaring light, and was bewildered at the sight of trunks and, most of all, at the approach of Mr Elbury, for he wore a most sentimental expression, and led a young person by the hand.

'Dear friend,' he said, in that mellow tone of his, 'I hope you, too, will love my little wife.'

Almost any other woman would have dropped the kerosene lamp on the doorstep, but not Miss Eliza Peck. Luckily a gust of autumn wind blew it out, and the bride had to fumble her way into her new home. Miss Peck quickly procured one of her own crinkly lamplighters, and bent toward the open fire to kindle a new light.

'You've taken me by surprise,' she managed to say, in her usual tone of voice, though she felt herself shaking with excitement.

At that moment the ailing step-daughter gave a forlorn little wail from the wide sofa, where she had been put to sleep with difficulty. Miss Peck's kind heart felt the pathos of the situation; she lifted the little child and stilled it, then she held out a kindly hand to the minister's new wife, while Mr Elbury stood beaming by.

'I wish you may be very happy here, as I have been,' said the good woman, earnestly. 'But Mr Elbury, you ought to have let me know. I could have kept a secret.' – and satisfaction filled Eliza Peck's heart that she never, to use her own expression, had made a fool of herself before the First Parish. She had kept her own secret, and in this earthquake of a moment was clearly conscious that she was hero enough to behave as if there had never been any secret to keep. And indignation with the Reverend Mr Elbury, who had so imprudently kept his own counsel, threw down the sham temple of Cupid which a faithless god called Propinquity had succeeded in rearing.

Miss Peck made a feast, and for the last time played the part of hostess at the minister's table. She had remorselessly inspected the conspicuous bad taste of the new Mrs Elbury's dress, the waving, cheap-looking feather of her hat, the make-believe richness of her clothes, and saw, with dire compassion, how unused she was to young children. The brave Eliza tried to make the best of things – but one moment she found herself thinking how uncomfortable Mr Elbury's home would be henceforth with this poor reed to lean upon, a townish, empty-faced, tiresomely pretty girl; the next moment she pitied the girl herself, who would have the hard task before her of being the wife of an indolent preacher in a country town. Miss Peck had generously allowed her farm to supplement the limited salary of the First Parish; in fact, she had been a silent partner in the parsonage establishment rather than a dependent. Would the First Parish laugh at her now? It was a stinging thought; but she honestly believed that the minister himself would be most commiserated when the parish opinion had found time to simmer down.

The next day our heroine, whose face was singularly free from disappointment, told the minister that she would like to leave at once, for she was belated about many things, not having had notice in season of his change of plan.

'I've been telling your wife all about the house and parish interests the best I can, and it's likely she wants to take everything into her own hands right away,' added the uncommon housekeeper, with a spice of malice; but Mr Elbury flushed, and looked down at the short, capable Eliza appealingly. He knew her virtues so well that this announcement gave him a crushing blow.

'Why, I thought of course you would continue here as usual,' he said, in a strange, harsh voice that would have been perfectly surprising in the pulpit. 'Mrs Elbury has never known any care. We count upon your remaining.'

Whereupon Miss Peck looked him disdainfully in the face, and, for a moment, mistook him for that self so often reproved and now sunk into depths of ignominy.

'If you thought that, you ought to have known better,' she said. 'You can't expect a woman who has property and relations of her own to give up her interests for yours altogether. I got a letter this morning from my brother's boy, little Tom, and he's got leave from his mother and her husband to come and stop with me a good while – he says all winter. He's been sick, and they've had to take him out o' school. I never supposed that such stived-up[5] air would agree with him,' concluded Miss Peck, triumphantly. She was full of joy and hope at this new turn of affairs, and the minister was correspondingly hopeless. 'I'll take the baby home for a while, if 'twould be a convenience for you,' she added, more leniently. 'That is, after I get my house well warmed, and there's something in it to eat. I wish you could have spoken to me a fortnight ago; but I saw Joe Farley today – that boy that lived with me quite a while – he's glad to come back. He only engaged to stop till after cider time where he's been this summer, and he's promised to look about for a good cow for me. I always thought well of Joe.'

The minister turned away ruefully, and Miss Peck went about her work. She meant to leave the house in the best of order; but the whole congregation came trooping in that day and the next, and she hardly had time to build a fire in her own kitchen before Joe Farley followed her from the station with the beloved little Tom. He looked tall and thin and pale, and largely freckled under his topknot of red hair. Bless his heart! how his lonely aunt hugged him and kissed him, and how thankful he was to get back to her, though she never would have suspected it if she had not known him so well. A shy boy-fashion of reserve and stolidity had replaced his early demonstrations, but he promptly went to the shelf of books to find the familiar old *Robinson Crusoe*. Miss Peck's heart leaped for joy as she remembered how much more she could teach the child about books. She felt a great wave of gratitude fill her cheerful soul as she remembered the pleasure and gain of those evenings when she and Mr Elbury had read together.

There was a great deal of eager discussion in the village and much amused scrutiny of Eliza's countenance, as she walked up the side aisle that first Sunday after the minister was married. She led little Tom by the hand, but he opened the pew-door and ushered her in handsomely, and she looked smilingly at her neighbors and nodded her head sideways at the boy in a way that made them suspect that she was much more in love with him, freckles and all, than she had ever been with Mr Elbury. A few minutes later she frowned at Tom sternly for greeting his old acquaintances over the pew-rail in a way that did not fit the day or place. There was no chance to laugh at her disappointment; for nobody could help understanding that her experience at the parsonage had been merely incidental in her life, and that she had returned willingly to her old associations. The dream of being a minister's wife had been only a dream, and she was surprised to find herself waking from it with such resignation to her lot.

'I'd just like to know what sort of a breakfast they had,' she said to herself, as the bride's topknot went waving and bobbing up to the parsonage pew. 'If ever there was a man who was fussy about his cup o' coffee, 'tis Reverend Wilbur Elbury! There now, Elizy Peck, don't you wish 'twas you a-setting there up front and feeling the eyes of the whole parish sticking in your back? You could have had him, you know, if you'd set right about it. I never did think you had proper ideas of what gettin' promoted is; but if you ain't discovered a new world for yourself like C'lumbus, I miss my guess. If you'd stayed on the farm all alone last year you'd had no thoughts but hens and rutabagys,[6] and as 'tis you've been livin' amon'st books. There's nothin' to regret if you did just miss makin' a fool o' yourself.'

At this moment Mr Elbury's voice gently sounded from the pulpit, and Miss Peck sprang to her feet with the agility of a jack-in-the-box – she had forgotten her surroundings in the vividness of her revery. She hardly knew what the minister said in that first prayer; for many reasons this was an exciting day.

A little later our heroine accepted the invitation of her second cousin, Mrs Corbell, to spend the hour or two between morning and afternoon services. They had agreed that it seemed like old times, and took pleasure in renewing this custom of the Sunday visit. Little Tom was commented upon as to health and growth and freckles and family resemblance; and when he strayed out-of-doors, after such an early dinner as only a growing boy can make vanish with the enchanter's wand of his appetite, the two women indulged in a good talk.

'I don't know how you viewed it, this morning,' began Cousin Corbell; 'but, to my eyes, the minister looked as if he felt cheap as a broom. There, I never was one o' his worshipers, you well know. To speak plain, Elizy, I was really concerned at one time for fear you would be over-persuaded. I never said one word to warp your judgment, but I did feel as if 'twould be a shame. I' –

But Miss Peck was not ready yet to join the opposition, and she interrupted at once in an amiable but decided tone. 'We'll let by-gones be by-gones; it's just as well, and a good deal better. Mr Elbury always treated me the best he knew how; and I knew he wa'n't perfect, but 'twas full as much his misfortune as his fault. I declare I don't know what else there was he could ha' done if he hadn't taken to preaching; and he has very kind feelings, specially if any one's in trouble. Talk of "leading about captive silly women,"[7] there are some cases where we've got to turn around and say it right the other way – 'tis the silly women that do the leadin' themselves. And I tell you,' concluded Miss Peck, with apparent irrelevancy, 'I was glad last night to have a good honest look at a yellow sunset. If ever I do go and set my mind on a minister, I'm going to hunt for one that's well-settled in a hill parish. I used to feel as if I was shut right in, there at the parsonage; it's a good house enough, if it only stood where you could see anything out of the windows. I can't carry out my plans o' life in any such situation.'

'I expect to hear that you've blown right off the top o' your hill some o' these windy days,' said Mrs Corbell, without resentment, though she was very dependent, herself, upon seeing the passing.

The church bell began to ring, and our friends rose to put on their bonnets and answer its summons. Miss Peck's practical mind revolved the possibility of there having been a decent noonday meal at the parsonage. 'Maria Corbell!' she said, with dramatic intensity, 'mark what I'm goin' to say – it ain't I that's goin' to reap the whirlwind;[8] it's your pastor, the Reverend Mr Elbury, of the First Parish!'

THE GUESTS OF MRS TIMMS

I

Mrs Persis Flagg stood in her front doorway taking leave of Miss Cynthia Pickett, who had been making a long call. They were not intimate friends. Miss Pickett always came formally to the front door and rang when she paid her visits, but, the week before, they had met at the county conference, and happened to be sent to the same house for entertainment, and so had deepened and renewed the pleasures of acquaintance.

It was an afternoon in early June; the syringa-bushes[1] were tall and green on each side of the stone doorsteps, and were covered with their lovely white and golden flowers. Miss Pickett broke off the nearest twig, and held it before her prim face as she talked. She had a pretty childlike smile that came and went suddenly, but her face was not one that bore the marks of many pleasures. Mrs Flagg was a tall, commanding sort of person, with an air of satisfaction and authority.

'Oh, yes, gather all you want,' she said stiffly, as Miss Pickett took the syringa without having asked beforehand; but she had an amiable expression, and just now her large countenance was lighted up by pleasant anticipation.

'We can tell early what sort of a day it's goin' to be,' she said eagerly. 'There ain't a cloud in the sky now. I'll stop for you as I come along, or if there should be anything unforeseen to detain me, I'll send you word. I don't expect you'd want to go if it wa'n't so that I could?'

'Oh my sakes, no!' answered Miss Pickett discreetly, with a timid flush. 'You feel certain that Mis' Timms won't be put out? I shouldn't feel free to go unless I went 'long o' you.'

'Why, nothin' could be plainer than her words,' said Mrs Flagg in a tone of reproval. 'You saw how she urged me, an' had over all that talk about how we used to see each other often when we both lived to Longport, and told how she'd been thinkin' of writin', and askin' if it wa'nt so I should be able to come over and stop three or four days as soon as settled weather come, because she couldn't make no fire in her best chamber on account of the chimbley smokin' if the wind wa'n't just right. You see how she felt toward me, kissin' of me comin' and goin'? Why, she even asked me who I employed to do over my bonnet, Miss Pickett, just as interested as if she was a sister; an' she remarked she should look for us any pleasant day after we all got home, an' were settled after the conference.'

Miss Pickett smiled, but did not speak, as if she expected more arguments still.

'An' she seemed just about as much gratified to meet with you again. She seemed to desire to meet you again very particular,' continued Mrs Flagg. 'She really urged us to come together an' have a real good day talkin' over old times – there, don't le' 's go all over it again! I've always heard she'd made that old house of her aunt Bascoms' where she lives look real handsome. I once heard her best parlor carpet described as being an elegant carpet, different from any there was round here. Why, nobody couldn't be more cordial, Miss Pickett; you ain't goin' to give out just at the last?'

'Oh, no!' answered the visitor hastily; 'no, 'm! I want to go full as much as you do, Mis' Flagg, but you see I never was so well acquainted with Mis' Cap'n Timms, an' I always seem to dread putting myself for'ard. She certain was very urgent, an' she said plain enough to come any day next week, an' here 'tis Wednesday, though of course she wouldn't look for us either Monday or Tuesday. 'Twill be a real pleasant occasion, an' now we've been to the conference it don't seem near so much effort to start.'

'Why, I don't think nothin' of it,' said Mrs Flagg proudly. 'We shall have a grand good time, goin' together an' all, I feel sure.'

Miss Pickett still played with her syringa flower, tapping her thin cheek, and twirling the stem with her fingers. She looked as if she were going to say something more, but after a moment's hesitation she turned away.

'Good-afternoon, Mis' Flagg,' she said formally, looking up with a quick little smile; 'I enjoyed my call; I hope I ain't kep' you too late; I don't know but what it's 'most tea-time. Well, I shall look for you in the mornin'.'

'Good-afternoon, Miss Pickett; I'm glad I was in when you came. Call again, won't you?' said Mrs Flagg. 'Yes; you may expect me in good season,' and so they parted. Miss Pickett went out at the neat clicking gate in the white fence, and Mrs Flagg a moment later looked out of her sitting-room window to see if the gate were latched, and felt the least bit disappointed to find that it was. She sometimes went out after the departure of a guest, and fastened the gate herself with a loud, rebuking sound. Both of these Woodville women lived alone, and were very precise in their way of doing things.

II

The next morning dawned clear and bright, and Miss Pickett rose even earlier than usual. She found it most difficult to decide which of her dresses would be best to wear. Summer was still so young that the day had all the freshness of spring, but when the two friends walked away together along the shady street, with a chorus of golden robins singing high overhead in the elms, Miss Pickett decided that she had made a wise choice of her second-best black silk gown, which she had just turned again and freshened. It was neither too warm for the season nor too cool, nor did it look overdressed. She wore her large cameo pin, and this, with a long watch-chain, gave an air of proper mural decoration. She was a straight, flat little person, as if, when not in use, she kept herself, silk dress and all, between the leaves of a book. She carried a noticeable parasol with a fringe, and a small shawl, with a pretty border, neatly folded over her left arm. Mrs Flagg always dressed in black cashmere, and looked, to hasty observers, much the same one day as another; but her companion recognized the fact that this was the best black cashmere of all, and for a moment quailed at the thought that Mrs Flagg was paying such extreme deference to their prospective hostess. The visit turned for a moment into an unexpectedly solemn formality, and pleasure seemed to wane before Cynthia Pickett's eyes, yet with great courage she never slackened a single step. Mrs Flagg carried a somewhat worn black leather handbag, which Miss Pickett regretted; it did not give the visit that casual and unpremeditated air which she felt to be more elegant.

'Shan't I carry your bag for you?' she asked timidly. Mrs Flagg was the older and more important person.

'Oh, dear me, no,' answered Mrs Flagg. 'My pocket's so remote, in case I should desire to sneeze or anything, that I thought 'twould be convenient for carrying my handkerchief and pocket-book; an' then I just tucked in a couple o' glasses o' my crab-apple jelly for Mis' Timms. She used to be a great hand for preserves of every sort, an' I thought 'twould be a kind of an attention, an' give rise to conversation. I know she used to make excellent drop-cakes[2] when we was both residin' to Longport; folks used to say she never would give the right receipt, but if I get a real good chance, I mean to ask her. Or why can't you, if I start talkin' about receipts – why can't you say, sort of innocent, that I have always spoken frequently of her drop-cakes, an' ask for the rule?[3] She would be very sensible to the compliment, and could pass it off if she didn't feel to indulge us. There, I do so wish you would!'

'Yes, 'm,' said Miss Pickett doubtfully; 'I'll try to make the opportunity. I'm very partial to drop-cakes. Was they flour or rye, Mis' Flagg?'

'They was flour, dear,' replied Mrs Flagg approvingly; 'crisp an' light as any you ever see.'

'I wish I had thought to carry somethin' to make pleasant,' said Miss Pickett, after they had walked a little farther; 'but there, I don't know's 'twould look just right, this first visit, to offer anything to such a person as Mis' Timms. In case I ever go over to Baxter again I won't forget to make her some little present, as nice as I've got. 'Twas certain very polite of her to urge me to come with you. I did feel very doubtful at first. I didn't know but she thought it behooved her, because I was in your company at the conference, and she wanted to save my feelin's, and yet expected I would decline. I never was well acquainted with her; our folks wasn't well off when I first knew her; 'twas before uncle Cap'n Dyer passed away an' remembered mother an' me in his will. We couldn't make no han'some companies in them days, so we didn't go to none, an' kep' to ourselves; but in my grandmother's time, mother always said, the families was very friendly. I shouldn't feel like goin' over to pass the day with Mis' Timms if I didn't mean to ask her to return the visit. Some don't think o' these things, but mother was very set about not bein' done for when she couldn't make no return.'

'"When it rains porridge hold up your dish,"' said Mrs Flagg; but Miss Pickett made no response beyond a feeble 'Yes, 'm,' which somehow got caught in her pale-green bonnet-strings.

'There, 'tain't no use to fuss too much over all them things,' proclaimed Mrs Flagg, walking along at a good pace with a fine sway of her skirts, and carrying her head high. 'Folks walks right by an' forgits all about you; folks can't always be going through with just so much. You'd had a good deal better time, you an' your ma, if you'd been freer in your ways; now don't you s'pose you would? 'Tain't what you give folks to eat so much as 'tis makin' 'em feel welcome. Now, there's Mis' Timms; when we was to Longport she was dreadful methodical. She wouldn't let Cap'n Timms fetch nobody home to dinner without lettin' of her know, same's other cap'ns' wives had to submit to. I was thinkin'; when she was so cordial over to Danby, how she'd softened with time. Years do learn folks somethin'! She did seem very pleasant an' desirous. There, I am so glad we got started; if she'd gone an' got up a real good dinner today, an' then not had us come till tomorrow, 'twould have been real too bad. Where anybody lives alone such a thing is very tryin'.'

'Oh, so 'tis!' said Miss Pickett. 'There, I'd like to tell you what I went through with year before last. They come an' asked me one Saturday night to entertain the minister, that time we was having candidates' –

'I guess we'd better step along faster,' said Mrs Flagg suddenly. 'Why, Miss Pickett, there's the stage comin' now! It's dreadful prompt, seems to me. Quick! there's folks awaitin', an' I sha'nt get to Baxter in no state to visit Mis' Cap'n Timms if I have to ride all the way there backward!'

III

The stage was not full inside. The group before the store proved to be made up of spectators, except one man, who climbed at once to a vacant seat by the driver. Inside there was only one person, after two passengers got out, and she preferred to sit with her back to the horses, so that Mrs Flagg and Miss Pickett settled themselves comfortably in the coveted corners of the back seat. At first they took no notice of their companion, and spoke to each other in low tones, but presently something attracted the attention of all three and engaged them in conversation.

'I never was over this road before,' said the stranger. 'I s'pose you ladies are well acquainted all along.'

'We have often traveled it in past years. We was over this part of it last week goin' and comin' from the county conference,' said Mrs Flagg in a dignified manner.

'What persuasion?' inquired the fellow-traveler, with interest.

'Orthodox,' said Miss Pickett quickly, before Mrs Flagg could speak. 'It was a very interestin' occasion; this other lady an' me stayed through all the meetin's.'

'I ain't Orthodox,' announced the stranger, waiving any interest in personalities. 'I was brought up amongst the Freewill Baptists.'

'We're well acquainted with several of that denomination in our place,' said Mrs Flagg, not without an air of patronage. 'They've never built 'em no church; there ain't but a scattered few.'

'They prevail where I come from,' said the traveler. 'I'm goin' now to visit with a Freewill lady. We was to a conference together once, same's you an' your friend, but 'twas a state conference. She asked me to come some time an' make her a good visit, and I'm on my way now. I didn't seem to have nothin' to keep me to home.'

'We're all goin' visitin' today, ain't we?' said Mrs Flagg sociably; but no one carried on the conversation.

The day was growing very warm; there was dust in the sandy road, but the fields of grass and young growing crops looked fresh and fair. There was a light haze over the hills, and birds were thick in the air. When the stage-horses stopped to walk, you could hear the crows caw, and the bobolinks singing, in the meadows. All the farmers were busy in their fields.

'It don't seem but little ways to Baxter, does it?' said Miss Pickett, after a while. 'I felt we should pass a good deal o' time on the road, but we must be pretty near halfway there a'ready.'

'Why, more'n half!' exclaimed Mrs Flagg. 'Yes; there's Beckett's Corner right ahead, an' the old Beckett house. I haven't been on this part of the road for so long that I feel kind of strange. I used to visit over here when I was a girl. There's a nephew's widow owns the place now. Old Miss Susan Beckett willed it to him, an' he died; but she resides there an' carries on the farm, an unusual smart woman, everybody says. Ain't it pleasant here, right out among the farms!'

'Mis' Beckett's place, did you observe?' said the stranger, leaning forward to listen to what her companions said. 'I expect that's where I'm goin' – Mis' Ezra Beckett's?'

'That's the one,' said Miss Pickett and Mrs Flagg together, and they both looked out eagerly as the coach drew up to the front door of a large old yellow house that stood close upon the green turf of the roadside.

The passenger looked pleased and eager, and made haste to leave the stage with her many bundles and bags. While she stood impatiently tapping at the brass knocker, the stage-driver landed a large trunk, and dragged it toward the door across the grass. Just then a busy-looking middle-aged woman made her appearance, with floury hands and a look as if she were prepared to be somewhat on the defensive.

'Why, how do you do, Mis' Beckett?' exclaimed the guest. 'Well, here I be at last. I didn't know's you thought I was ever comin'. Why, I do declare, I believe you don't recognize me, Mis' Beckett.'

'I believe I don't,' said the self-possessed hostess. 'Ain't you made some mistake ma'am?'

'Why, don't you recollect we was together that time to the state conference, an' you said you should be pleased to have me come an' make you a visit sometime, an' I said I would certain. There, I expect I look more natural[4] to you now.'

Mrs Beckett appeared to be making the best possible effort, and gave a bewildered glance, first at her unexpected visitor, and then at the trunk. The stage-driver, who watched this encounter with evident delight, turned away with reluctance. 'I can't wait all day to see how they settle it,' he said, and mounted briskly to the box, and the stage rolled on.

'He might have waited just a minute to see,' said Miss Pickett indignantly, but Mrs Flagg's head and shoulders were already far out of the stage window – the house was on her side. 'She ain't got in yet,' she told Miss Pickett triumphantly. 'I could see 'em quite a spell. With that trunk, too! I do declare, how inconsiderate some folks is!'

''Twas pushin' an acquaintance most too far, wa'n't it?' agreed Miss Pickett. 'There, 'twill be somethin' laughable to tell Mis' Timms. I never see anything more divertin'. I shall kind of pity that woman if we have to stop an' git her as we go back this afternoon.'

'Oh, don't let's forgit to watch for her,' exclaimed Mrs Flagg, beginning to brush off the dust of travel. 'There, I feel an excellent appetite, don't you? And we ain't got more'n three or four miles to go, if we have that. I wonder what Mis' Timms is likely to give us for dinner; she spoke of makin' a good many chicken-pies, an' I happened to remark how partial I was to 'em. She felt above most of the things we had provided for us over to the conference. I know she was always counted the best o' cooks when I knew her so well to Longport. Now, don't forget, if there's a suitable opportunity, to inquire about the drop-cakes;' and Miss Pickett, a little less doubtful than before, renewed her promise.

IV

'My gracious, won't Mis' Timms be pleased to see us! It's just exactly the day to have company. And ain't Baxter a sweet pretty place?' said Mrs Flagg, as they walked up the main street. 'Cynthy Pickett, now ain't you proper glad you come? I felt sort o' calm about it part o' the time yesterday, but I ain't felt so like a girl for a good while. I do believe I'm goin' to have a splendid time.'

Miss Pickett glowed with equal pleasure as she paced along. She was less expansive and enthusiastic than her companion, but now that they were fairly in Baxter, she lent herself generously to the occasion. The social distinction of going away to spend a day in company with Mrs Flagg was by no means small. She arranged the folds of her shawl more carefully over her arm so as to show the pretty palm-leaf border, and then looked up with great approval to the row of great maples that shaded the broad sidewalk. 'I wonder if we can't contrive to make time to go an' see old Miss Nancy Fell?' she ventured to ask Mrs Flagg. 'There ain't a great deal o' time before the stage goes at four o'clock; 'twill pass quickly, but I should hate to have her feel hurt. If she was one we had visited often at home, I shouldn't care so much, but such folks feel any little slight. She was a member of our church; I think a good deal of that.'

'Well, I hardly know what to say,' faltered Mrs Flagg coldly. 'We might just look in a minute; I shouldn't want her to feel hurt.'

'She was one that always did her part, too,' said Miss Pickett, more boldly. 'Mr Cronin used to say that she was more generous with her little than many was with their much. If she hadn't lived in a poor part of the town, and so been occupied with a different kind of people from us, 'twould have made a difference. They say she's got a comfortable little home over here, an' keeps house for a nephew. You know she was to our meeting one Sunday last winter, and 'peared dreadful glad to get back; folks seemed glad to see her, too. I don't know as you were out.'

'She always wore a friendly look,' said Mrs Flagg indulgently. 'There, now, there's Mis' Timms's residence; it's handsome, ain't it, with them big spruce-trees? I expect she may be at the window now, an' see us as we come along. Is my bonnet on straight, an' everything? The blind looks open in the room this way; I guess she's to home fast enough.'

The friends quickened their steps, and with shining eyes and beating hearts hastened forward. The slightest mists of uncertainty were now cleared away; they gazed at the house with deepest pleasure; the visit was about to begin.

They opened the front gate and went up the short walk, noticing the pretty herringbone pattern of the bricks, and as they stood on the high steps Cynthia Pickett wondered whether she ought not to have worn her best dress, even though there was lace at the neck and sleeves, and she usually kept it for the most formal of tea-parties and exceptional parish festivals. In her heart she commended Mrs Flagg for that familiarity with the ways of a wider social world which had led her to wear the very best among her black cashmeres.

'She's a good while coming to the door,' whispered Mrs Flagg presently. 'Either she didn't see us, or else she's slipped upstairs to make some change, an' is just goin' to let us ring again. I've done it myself sometimes. I'm glad we come right over after her urgin' us to; it seems more cordial than to keep her expectin' us. I expect she'll urge us terribly to remain with her over-night.'

'Oh, I ain't prepared,' began Miss Pickett, but she looked pleased. At that moment there was a slow withdrawal of the bolt inside, and a key was turned, the front door opened, and Mrs Timms stood before them with a smile. Nobody stopped to think at that moment what kind of smile it was.

'Why, if it ain't Mis' Flagg,' she exclaimed politely, 'an' Miss Pickett too! I am surprised!'

The front door entry behind her looked well furnished, but not exactly hospitable; the stairs with their brass rods looked so clean and bright that it did not seem as if anybody had ever gone up or come down. A cat came purring out, but Mrs Timms pushed her back with a determined foot, and hastily closed the sitting-room door. Then Miss Pickett let Mrs Flagg precede her, as was becoming, and they went into a darkened parlor, and found their way to some chairs, and seated themselves solemnly.

''Tis a beautiful day, ain't it?' said Mrs Flagg, speaking first. 'I don't know's I ever enjoyed the ride more. We've been having a good deal of rain since we saw you at the conference, and the country looks beautiful.'

'Did you leave Woodville this morning? I thought I hadn't heard you was in town,' replied Mrs Timms formally. She was seated just a little too far away to make things seem exactly pleasant. The darkness of the best room seemed to retreat somewhat, and Miss Pickett looked over by the door, where there was a pale gleam from the side-lights in the hall, to try to see the pattern of the carpet; but her effort failed.

'Yes, 'm,' replied Mrs Flagg to the question. 'We left Woodville about half past eight, but it is quite a ways from where we live to where you take the stage. The stage does come slow, but you don't seem to mind it such a beautiful day.'

'Why, you must have come right to see me first!' said Mrs Timms, warming a little as the visit went on. 'I hope you're going to make some stop in town. I'm sure it was very polite of you to come right an' see me; well, it's very pleasant, I declare. I wish you'd been in Baxter last Sabbath; our minister did give us an elegant sermon on faith an' works. He spoke of the conference, and gave his views on some o' the questions that came up, at Friday evenin' meetin'; but I felt tired after getting home, an' so I wasn't out. We feel very much favored to have such a man amon'st us. He's building up the parish very considerable. I understand the pew-rents come to thirty-six dollars more this quarter than they did last.'

'We also feel grateful in Woodville for our pastor's efforts,' said Miss Pickett; but Mrs Timms turned her head away sharply, as if the speech had been untimely, and trembling Miss Pickett had interrupted.

'They're thinking here of raisin' Mr Barlow's salary another year,' the hostess added; 'a good many of the old parishioners have died off, but every one feels to do what they can. Is there much interest among the young people in Woodville, Mis' Flagg?'

'Considerable at this time, ma'am,' answered Mrs Flagg, without enthusiasm, and she listened with unusual silence to the subsequent fluent remarks of Mrs Timms.

The parlor seemed to be undergoing the slow processes of a winter dawn. After a while the three women could begin to see one another's faces, which aided them somewhat in carrying on a serious and impersonal conversation. There were a good many subjects to be touched upon, and Mrs Timms said everything that she should have said, except to invite her visitors to walk upstairs and take off their bonnets. Mrs Flagg sat her parlor-chair as if it were a throne, and carried her banner of self-possession as high as she knew how, but toward the end of the call even she began to feel hurried.

'Won't you ladies take a glass of wine an' a piece of cake after your ride?' inquired Mrs Timms, with an air of hospitality that almost concealed the fact that neither cake nor wine was anywhere to be seen; but the ladies bowed and declined with particular elegance. Altogether it was a visit of extreme propriety on both sides, and Mrs Timms was very pressing in her invitation that her guests should stay longer.

'Thank you, but we ought to be going,' answered Mrs Flagg, with a little show of ostentation, and looking over her shoulder to be sure that Miss Pickett had risen too. 'We've got some little ways to go,' she added with dignity. 'We should be pleased to have you call an' see us in case you have occasion to come to Woodville,' and Miss Pickett faintly seconded the invitation. It was in her heart to add, 'Come any day next week,' but her courage did not rise so high as to make the words audible. She looked as if she were ready to cry; her usual smile had burnt itself out into gray ashes; there was a white, appealing look about her mouth. As they emerged from the dim parlor and stood at the open front door, the bright June day, the golden-green trees, almost blinded their eyes. Mrs Timms was more smiling and cordial than ever.

'There, I ought to have thought to offer you fans; I am afraid you was warm after walking,' she exclaimed, as if to leave no stone of courtesy unturned. 'I have so enjoyed meeting you again, I wish it was so you could stop longer. Why, Mis' Flagg, we haven't said one word about old times when we lived to Longport. I've had news from there, too, since I saw you; my brother's daughter-in-law was here to pass the Sabbath after I returned.'

Mrs Flagg did not turn back to ask any questions as she stepped stiffly away down the brick walk. Miss Pickett followed her, raising the fringed parasol; they both made ceremonious little bows as they shut the high white gate behind them. 'Goodbye,' said Mrs Timms finally, as she stood in the door with her set smile; and as they departed she came out and began to fasten up a rose-bush that climbed a narrow white ladder by the steps.

'Oh, my goodness alive!' exclaimed Mrs Flagg, after they had gone some distance in aggrieved silence, 'if I haven't gone and forgotten my bag! I ain't goin' back, whatever happens. I expect she'll trip over it in that dark room and break her neck!'

'I brought it; I noticed you'd forgotten it,' said Miss Pickett timidly, as if she hated to deprive her companion of even that slight consolation.

'There, I'll tell you what we'd better do,' said Mrs Flagg gallantly; 'we'll go right over an' see poor old Miss Nancy Fell; 'twill please her about to death. We can say we felt like goin' somewhere today, an' 'twas a good many years since either one of us had seen Baxter, so we come just for the ride, an' to make a few calls. She'll like to hear all about the conference; Miss Fell was always one that took a real interest in religious matters.'

Miss Pickett brightened, and they quickened their step. It was nearly twelve o'clock, they had breakfasted early, and now felt as if they had eaten nothing since they were grown up. An awful feeling of tiredness and uncertainty settled down upon their once buoyant spirits.

'I can forgive a person,' said Mrs Flagg, once, as if she were speaking to herself; 'I can forgive a person, but when I'm done with 'em, I'm done.'

V

'I do declare, 'twas like a scene in Scriptur' to see that poor good-hearted Nancy Fell run down her walk to open the gate for us!' said Mrs Persis Flagg later that afternoon, when she and Miss Pickett were going home in the stage. Miss Pickett nodded her head approvingly.

'I had a good sight better time with her than I should have had at the other place,' she said with fearless honesty. 'If I'd been Mis' Cap'n Timms, I'd made some apology or just passed us the compliment. If it wa'n't convenient, why couldn't she just tell us so after all her urgin' and sayin' how she should expect us?'

'I thought then she'd altered from what she used to be,' said Mrs Flagg. 'She seemed real sincere an' open away from home. If she wa'n't prepared today, 'twas easy enough to say so; we was reasonable folks, an' should have gone away with none but friendly feelin's. We did have a grand good time with Nancy. She was as happy to see us as if we'd been queens.'

''Twas a real nice little dinner,' said Miss Pickett gratefully. 'I thought I was goin' to faint away just before we got to the house, and I didn't know how I should hold out if she undertook to do anything extra, and keep us a-waitin'; but there, she just made us welcome, simple-hearted, to what she had. I never tasted such dandelion greens; an' that nice little piece o' pork and new biscuit, why, they was just splendid. She must have an excellent good cellar, if 'tis such a small house. Her potatoes was truly remarkable for this time o' year. I myself don't deem it necessary to cook potatoes when I'm goin' to have dandelion greens. Now, didn't it put you in mind of that verse in the Bible that says, "Better is a dinner of herbs where love is"?[5] An' how desirous she'd been to see somebody that could tell her some particulars about the conference!'

'She'll enjoy tellin' folks about our comin' over to see her. Yes, I'm glad we went; 'twill be of advantage every way, an' our bein' of the same church an' all, to Woodville. If Mis' Timms hears of our bein' there, she'll see we had reason, an' knew of a place to go. Well, I needn't have brought this old bag!'

Miss Pickett gave her companion a quick resentful glance, which was followed by one of triumph directed at the dust that was collecting on the shoulders of the best black cashmere; then she looked at the bag on the front seat, and suddenly felt illuminated with the suspicion that Mrs Flagg had secretly made preparations to pass the night in Baxter. The bag looked plump, as if it held much more than the pocket-book and the jelly.

Mrs Flagg looked up with unusual humility. 'I did think about that jelly,' she said, as if Miss Pickett had openly reproached her. 'I was afraid it might look as if I was tryin' to pay Nancy for her kindness.'

'Well, I don't know,' said Cynthia; 'I guess she'd been pleased. She'd thought you just brought her over a little present: but I do' know as 'twould been any good to her after all; she'd thought so much of it, comin' from you, that she'd kep' it till 'twas all candied.' But Mrs Flagg didn't look exactly pleased by this unexpected compliment, and her fellow-traveler colored with confusion and a sudden feeling that she had shown undue forwardness.

Presently they remembered the Beckett house, to their great relief, and, as they approached, Mrs Flagg reached over and moved her hand-bag from the front seat to make room for another passenger. But nobody came out to stop the stage, and they saw the unexpected guest sitting by one of the front windows comfortably swaying a palm-leaf fan, and rocking to and fro in calm content. They shrank back into their corners, and tried not to be seen. Mrs Flagg's face grew very red.

'She got in, didn't she?' said Miss Pickett, snipping her words angrily, as if her lips were scissors. Then she heard a call, and bent forward to see Mrs Beckett herself appear in the front doorway, very smiling and eager to stop the stage.

The driver was only too ready to stop his horses. 'Got a passenger for me to carry back, ain't ye?' said he facetiously. 'Them's the kind I like; carry both ways, make somethin' on a double trip,' and he gave Mrs Flagg and Miss Pickett a friendly wink as he stepped down over the wheel. Then he hurried toward the house, evidently in a hurry to put the baggage on; but the expected passenger still sat rocking and fanning at the window.

'No, sir; I ain't got any passengers,' exclaimed Mrs Beckett, advancing a step or two to meet him, and speaking very loud in her pleasant excitement. 'This lady that come this morning wants her large trunk with her summer things that she left to the depot in Woodville. She's very desirous to git into it, so don't you go an' forgit; ain't you got a book or somethin', Mr Ma'sh? Don't you forget to make a note of it; here's her check, an' we've kep' the number in case you should mislay it or anything. There's things in the trunk she needs; you know how you overlooked stoppin' to the milliner's for my bunnit last week.'

'Other folks disremembers things as well's me,' grumbled Mr Marsh. He turned to give the passengers another wink more familiar than the first, but they wore an offended air, and were looking the other way. The horses had backed a few steps, and the guest at the front window had ceased the steady motion of her fan to make them a handsome bow, and been puzzled at the lofty manner of their acknowledgment.

'Go 'long with your foolish jokes, John Ma'sh!' Mrs Beckett said cheerfully, as she turned away. She was a comfortable, hearty person, whose appearance adjusted the beauties of hospitality. The driver climbed to his seat, chuckling, and drove away with the dust flying after the wheels.

'Now, she's a friendly sort of a woman, that Mis' Beckett,' said Mrs Flagg unexpectedly, after a few moments of silence, when she and her friend had been unable to look at each other. 'I really ought to call over an' see her some o' these days, knowing her husband's folks as well as I used to, an' visitin' of 'em when I was a girl.' But Miss Pickett made no answer.

'I expect it was all for the best, that woman's comin',' suggested Mrs Flagg again hopefully. 'She looked like a willing person who would take right hold. I guess Mis' Beckett knows what she's about, and must have had her reasons. Perhaps she thought she'd chance it for a couple o' weeks anyway, after the lady'd come so fur, an' bein' one o' her own denomination. Hayin'-time'll be here before we know it. I think myself, gen'rally speakin', 'tis just as well to let anybody know you're comin'.'

'Them seemed to be Mis' Cap'n Timms's views,' said Miss Pickett in a low tone; but the stage rattled a good deal, and Mrs Flagg looked up inquiringly, as if she had not heard.

THE QUEEN'S TWIN

I

The coast of Maine was in former years brought so near to foreign shores by its busy fleet of ships that among the older men and women one still finds a surprising proportion of travelers. Each seaward-stretching headland with its high-set houses, each island of a single farm, has sent its spies to view many a Land of Eshcol;[1] one may see plain, contented old faces at the windows, whose eyes have looked at far-away ports and known the splendors of the Eastern world. They shame the easy voyager of the North Atlantic and the Mediterranean; they have rounded the Cape of Good Hope and braved the angry seas of Cape Horn in small wooden ships; they have brought up their hardy boys and girls on narrow decks; they were among the last of the Northmen's children to go adventuring to unknown shores. More than this one cannot give to a young State for its enlightenment; the sea captains and the captains' wives of Maine knew something of the wide world, and never mistook their native parishes for the whole instead of a part thereof; they knew not only Thomaston and Castine and Portland,[2] but London and Bristol and Bordeaux, and the strange-mannered harbors of the China Sea.

One September day, when I was nearly at the end of a summer spent in a village called Dunnet Landing, on the Maine coast, my friend Mrs Todd, in whose house I lived, came home from a long, solitary stroll in the wild pastures, with an eager look as if she were just starting on a hopeful quest instead of returning. She brought a little basket with blackberries enough for supper, and held it towards me so that I could see that there were also some late and surprising raspberries sprinkled on top, but she made no comment upon her wayfaring. I could tell plainly that she had something very important to say.

'You haven't brought home a leaf of anything,' I ventured to this practiced herb-gatherer. 'You were saying yesterday that the witch-hazel[3] might be in bloom.'

'I dare say, dear,' she answered in a lofty manner; 'I ain't goin' to say it wasn't; I ain't much concerned either way 'bout the facts o' witch-hazel. Truth is, I've been off visitin'; there's an old Indian footpath leadin' over towards the Back Shore through the great heron swamp that anybody can't travel over all summer. You have to seize your time some day just now, while the low ground's summer-dried as it is today, and before the fall rains set in. I never thought of it till I was out o' sight o' home, and I says to myself, "Today's the day, certain!" and stepped along smart as I could. Yes, I've been visitin'. I did get into one spot that was wet underfoot before I noticed; you wait till I get me a pair o' dry woolen stockings, in case of cold, and I'll come an' tell ye.'

Mrs Todd disappeared. I could see that something had deeply interested her. She might have fallen in with either the sea-serpent or the lost tribes of Israel,[4] such was her air of mystery and satisfaction. She had been away since just before mid-morning, and as I sat waiting by my window I saw the last red glow of autumn sunshine flare along the gray rocks of the shore and leave them cold again, and touch the far sails of some coast-wise schooners so that they stood like golden houses on the sea.

I was left to wonder longer than I liked. Mrs Todd was making an evening fire and putting things in train for supper; presently she returned, still looking warm and cheerful after her long walk.

'There's a beautiful view from a hill over where I've been,' she told me; 'yes, there's a beautiful prospect of land and sea. You wouldn't discern the hill from any distance, but 'tis the pretty situation of it that counts. I sat there a long spell, and I did wish for you. No, I didn't know a word about goin' when I set out this morning' (as if I had openly reproached her!); 'I only felt one o' them travelin' fits comin' on, an' I ketched up my little basket; I didn't know but I might turn and come back time for dinner. I thought it wise to set out your luncheon for you in case I didn't. Hope you had all you wanted; yes, I hope you had enough.'

'Oh, yes, indeed,' said I. My landlady was always peculiarly bountiful in her supplies when she left me to fare for myself, as if she made a sort of peace-offering or affectionate apology.

'You know that hill with the old house right on top, over beyond the heron swamp? You'll excuse me for explainin',' Mrs Todd began, 'but you ain't so apt to strike inland as you be to go right along shore. You know that hill; there's a path leadin' right over to it that you have to look sharp to find nowadays; it belonged to the up-country Indians[5] when they had to make a carry to the landing here to get to the out' islands. I've heard the old folks say that there used to be a place across a ledge where they'd worn a deep track with their moccasin feet, but I never could find it. 'Tis so overgrown in some places that you keep losin' the path in the bushes and findin' it as you can; but it runs pretty straight considerin' the lay o' the land, and I keep my eye on the sun and the moss that grows one side o' the tree trunks. Some brook's been choked up and the swamp's bigger than it used to be. Yes; I did get in deep enough, one place!'

I showed the solicitude that I felt. Mrs Todd was no longer young, and in spite of her strong, great frame and spirited behavior, I knew that certain ills were apt to seize upon her, and would end some day by leaving her lame and ailing.

'Don't you go to worryin' about me,' she insisted, 'settin' still's the only way the Evil One'll ever get the upper hand o' me. Keep me movin' enough, an' I'm twenty year old summer an' winter both. I don't know why 'tis, but I've never happened to mention the one I've been to see. I don't know why I never happened to speak the name of Abby Martin, for I often give her a thought, but 'tis a dreadful out-o'-the-way place where she lives, and I haven't seen her myself for three or four years. She's a real good interesting woman, and we're well acquainted; she's nigher mother's age than mine, but she's very young feeling. She made me a nice cup o' tea, and I don't know but I should have stopped all night if I could have got word to you not to worry.'

Then there was a serious silence before Mrs Todd spoke again to make a formal announcement.

'She is the Queen's Twin,' and Mrs Todd looked steadily to see how I might bear the great surprise.

'The Queen's Twin?' I repeated.

'Yes, she's come to feel a real interest in the Queen,[6] and anybody can see how natural 'tis. They were born the very same day, and you would be astonished to see what a number o' things have corresponded. She was speaking o' some o' the facts to me today, an' you'd think she'd never done nothing but read history. I see how earnest she was about it as I never did before. I've often and often heard her allude to the facts, but now she's got to be old and the hurry's over with her work, she's come to live a good deal in her thoughts, as folks often do, and I tell you 'tis a sight o' company for her. If you want to hear about Queen Victoria, why Mis' Abby Martin'll tell you everything. And the prospect from that hill I spoke of is as beautiful as anything in this world; 'tis worth while your goin' over to see her just for that.'

'When can you go again?' I demanded eagerly.

'I should say tomorrow,' answered Mrs Todd; 'yes, I should say tomorrow; but I expect 'twould be better to take one day to rest, in between. I considered that question as I was comin' home, but I hurried so that there wa'n't much time to think. It's a dreadful long way to go with a horse; you have to go 'most as far as the old Bowden place an' turn off to the left, a master long, rough road, and then you have to turn right round as soon as you get there if you mean to get home before nine o'clock at night. But to strike across country from here, there's plenty o' time in the shortest day, and you can have a good hour or two's visit beside; 'tain't but a very few miles, and it's pretty all the way along. There used to be a few good families over there, but they've died and scattered, so now she's far from neighbors. There, she really cried, she was so glad to see anybody comin'. You'll be amused to hear her talk about the Queen, but I thought twice or three times as I set there 'twas about all the company she'd got.'

'Could we go day after tomorrow?' I asked eagerly.

''Twould suit me exactly,' said Mrs Todd.

II

One can never be so certain of good New England weather as in the days when a long easterly storm has blown away the warm late-summer mists, and cooled the air so that however bright the sunshine is by day, the nights come nearer and nearer to frostiness. There was a cold freshness in the morning air when Mrs Todd and I locked the house-door behind us; we took the key of the fields into our own hands that day, and put out across country as one puts out to sea. When we reached the top of the ridge behind the town it seemed as if we had anxiously passed the harbor bar and were comfortably in open sea at last.

'There, now!' proclaimed Mrs Todd, taking a long breath, 'now I do feel safe. It's just the weather that's liable to bring somebody to spend the day; I've had a feeling of Mis' Elder Caplin from North Point bein' close upon me ever since I waked up this mornin', an' I didn't want to be hampered with our present plans. She's a great hand to visit; she'll be spendin' the day somewhere from now till Thanksgivin', but there's plenty o' places at the Landin' where she goes, an' if I ain't there she'll just select another. I thought mother might be in, too, 'tis so pleasant; but I run up the road to look off this mornin' before you was awake, and there was no sign o' the boat. If they hadn't started by that time they wouldn't start, just as the tide is now;

besides, I see a lot o' mackerel-men headin' Green Island way, and they'll detain William. No, we're safe now, an' if mother should be comin' in tomorrow we'll have all this to tell her. She an' Mis' Abby Martin's very old friends.'

We were walking down the long pasture slopes towards the dark woods and thickets of the low ground. They stretched away northward like an unbroken wilderness; the early mists still dulled much of the color and made the uplands beyond look like a very far-off country.

'It ain't so far as it looks from here,' said my companion reassuringly, 'but we've got no time to spare either,' and she hurried on, leading the way with a fine sort of spirit in her step; and presently we struck into the old Indian footpath, which could be plainly seen across the long-unploughed turf of the pastures, and followed it among the thick, low-growing spruces. There the ground was smooth and brown under foot, and the thin-stemmed trees held a dark and shadowy roof overhead. We walked a long way without speaking; sometimes we had to push aside the branches, and sometimes we walked in a broad aisle where the trees were larger. It was a solitary wood, birdless and beastless; there was not even a rabbit to be seen, or a crow high in air to break the silence.

'I don't believe the Queen ever saw such a lonesome trail as this,' said Mrs Todd, as if she followed the thoughts that were in my mind. Our visit to Mrs Abby Martin seemed in some strange way to concern the high affairs of royalty. I had just been thinking of English landscapes, and of the solemn hills of Scotland with their lonely cottages and stone-walled sheepfolds, and the wandering flocks on high cloudy pastures. I had often been struck by the quick interest and familiar allusion to certain members of the royal house which one found in distant neighborhoods of New England; whether some old instincts of personal loyalty have survived all changes of time and national vicissitudes, or whether it is only that the Queen's own character and disposition have won friends for her so far away, it is impossible to tell. But to hear of a twin sister was the most surprising proof of intimacy of all, and I must confess that there was something remarkably exciting to the imagination in my morning walk. To think of being presented at Court in the usual way was for the moment quite commonplace.

III

Mrs Todd was swinging her basket to and fro like a schoolgirl as she walked, and at this moment it slipped from her hand and rolled lightly along the ground as if there were nothing in it. I picked it up and gave it to her, whereupon she lifted the cover and looked in with anxiety.

"Tis only a few little things, but I don't want to lose 'em,' she explained humbly. "Twas lucky you took the other basket if I was goin' to roll it round. Mis' Abby Martin complained o' lacking some pretty pink silk to finish one o' her little frames, an' I thought I'd carry her some, and I had a bunch o' gold thread that had been in a box o' mine this twenty year. I never was one to do much fancy work, but we're all liable to be swept away by fashion. And then there's a small packet o' very choice herbs that I gave a good deal of attention to; they'll smarten her up[7] and give her the best of appetites, come spring. She was tellin' me that spring weather is very wiltin' an' trying' to her, and she was beginnin' to dread it already. Mother's just the same way; if I could prevail on mother to take some o' these remedies in good season 'twould make a world o' difference, but she gets all down hill before I have a chance to hear of it, and then William comes in to tell me, sighin' and bewailin', how feeble mother is. "Why can't you remember 'bout them good herbs that I never let her be without?" I say to him – he does provoke me so; and then off he goes, sulky enough, down to his boat. Next thing I know, she comes in to go to meetin', wantin' to speak to everybody and feelin' like a girl. Mis' Martin's case is very much the same; but she'd nobody to watch her. William's kind o' slow-moulded; but there, any William's better than none when you get to be Mis' Martin's age.'

'Hadn't she any children?' I asked.

'Quite a number,' replied Mrs Todd grandly, 'but some are gone and the rest are married and settled. She never was a great hand to go about visitin'. I don't know but Mis' Martin might be called a little peculiar. Even her own folks has to make company of her;[8] she never slips in and lives right along with the rest as if 'twas at home, even in her own children's houses. I heard one o' her sons' wives say once she'd much rather have the Queen to spend the day if she could choose between the two, but I never thought Abby was so difficult as that. I used to love to have her come; she may have been sort o' ceremonious, but very pleasant and sprightly if you had sense enough to treat her her own way. I always think she'd know just how to live with great folks, and feel easier 'long of them an' their ways. Her son's wife's a great driver with farm-work, boards a great tableful o' men in hayin' time, an' feels right in her element. I don't say but she's a good woman an' smart, but sort o' rough. Anybody that's gentle-mannered an' precise like Mis' Martin would be a sort o' restraint.

'There's all sorts o' folks in the country, same's there is in the city,' concluded Mrs Todd gravely, and I as gravely agreed. The thick woods were behind us now, and the sun was shining clear overhead, the morning mists were gone, and a faint blue haze softened the distance; as we climbed the hill where we were to see the view, it seemed like a summer day. There was an old house on the height, facing southward, – a mere forsaken shell of an old house, with empty windows that looked like blind eyes. The frost-bitten grass grew close about it like brown fur, and there was a single crooked bough of lilac holding its green leaves close by the door.

'We'll just have a good piece of bread-an'-butter now,' said the commander of the expedition, 'and then we'll hang up the basket on some peg inside the house out o' the way o' the sheep, and have a han'some entertainment as we're comin' back. She'll be all through her little dinner when we get there, Mis' Martin will; but she'll want to make us some tea, an' we must have our visit an' be startin' back pretty soon after two. I don't want to cross all that low ground again after it's begun to grow chilly. An' it looks to me as if the clouds might begin to gather late in the afternoon.'

Before us lay a splendid world of sea and shore. The autumn colors already brightened the landscape; and here and there at the edge of a dark tract of pointed firs stood a row of bright swamp-maples like scarlet flowers. The blue sea and the great tide inlets were untroubled by the lightest winds.

'Poor land, this is!' sighed Mrs Todd as we sat down to rest on the worn doorstep. 'I've known three good hard-workin' families that come here full o' hope an' pride and tried to make something o' this farm, but it beat 'em all. There's one small field that's excellent for potatoes if you let half of it rest every year; but the land's always hungry. Now, you see them little peaked-topped spruces an' fir balsams comin' up over the hill all green an' hearty; they've got it all their own way! Seems sometimes as if wild Natur' got jealous over a certain spot, and wanted to do just as she'd a mind to. You'll see here; she'll do her own ploughin' an' harrowin' with frost an' wet, an' plant just what she wants and wait for her own crops. Man can't do nothin' with it, try as he may. I tell you those little trees mean business!'

I looked down the slope, and felt as if we ourselves were likely to be surrounded and overcome if we lingered too long. There was a vigor of growth, a persistence and savagery about the sturdy little trees that put weak human nature at complete defiance. One felt a sudden pity for the men and women who had been worsted after a long fight in that lonely place; one felt a sudden fear of the unconquerable, immediate forces of Nature, as in the irresistible moment of a thunderstorm.

'I can recollect the time when folks were shy o' these woods we just come through,' said Mrs Todd seriously. 'The men-folks themselves never'd venture into 'em alone; if their cattle got strayed they'd collect whoever they could get, and start off all together. They said a person was liable to get bewildered in there alone, and in old times folks had been lost. I expect there was considerable fear left over from the old Indian times, and the poor days o' witchcraft; anyway, I've seen bold men act kind o' timid. Some women o' the Asa Bowden family went out one afternoon berryin' when I was a girl, and got lost and was out all night; they found 'em middle o' the mornin' next day, not half a mile from home, scared most to death, an' sayin' they'd heard wolves and other beasts sufficient for a caravan. Poor creatur's! they'd strayed at last into a kind of low place amongst some alders, an' one of 'em was so overset she never got over it, an' went off in a sort o' slow decline. 'Twas like them victims that drowns in a foot o' water; but their minds did suffer dreadful. Some folks is born afraid of the woods and all wild places, but I must say they've always been like home to me.'

I glanced at the resolute, confident face of my companion. Life was very strong in her, as if some force of Nature were personified in this simple-hearted woman and gave her cousinship to the ancient deities. She might have walked the primeval fields of Sicily;[9] her strong gingham skirts might at that very moment bend the slender stalks of asphodel[10] and be fragrant with trodden thyme, instead of the brown wind-brushed grass of New England and frost-bitten goldenrod. She was a great soul, was Mrs Todd, and I her humble follower, as we went our way to visit the Queen's Twin, leaving the bright view of the sea behind us, and descending to a lower country-side through the dry pastures and fields.

The farms all wore a look of gathering age, though the settlement was, after all, so young. The fences were already fragile, and it seemed as if the first impulse of agriculture had soon spent itself without hope of renewal. The better houses were always those that had some hold upon the riches of the sea; a house that could not harbor a fishing-boat in some neighboring inlet was far from being sure of everyday comforts. The land alone was not enough to live upon in that stony region; it belonged by right to the forest, and to the forest it fast returned. From the top of the hill where we had been sitting we had seen prosperity in the dim distance, where the land was good and the sun shone upon fat barns, and where warm-looking houses with three or four chimneys apiece stood high on their solid ridge above the bay.

As we drew nearer to Mrs Martin's it was sad to see what poor bushy fields, what thin and empty dwelling-places had been left by those who had chosen this disappointing part of the northern country for their home. We crossed the last field and came into a narrow rain-washed road, and Mrs Todd looked eager and expectant and said that we were almost at our journey's end. 'I do hope Mis' Martin'll ask you into her best room where she keeps all the Queen's pictures. Yes, I think likely she will ask you; but 'tain't everybody she deems worthy to visit 'em, I can tell you!' said Mrs Todd warningly. 'She's been collectin' 'em an' cuttin' 'em out o' newspapers an' magazines time out o' mind, and if she heard of anybody sailin' for an English port she'd contrive to get a little money to 'em and ask to have the last likeness there was. She's most covered her best-room wall now; she keeps that room shut up sacred as a meetin'-house! "I won't say but I have my favorites amongst 'em," she told me t'other day, "but they're all beautiful to me as they can be!" And she's made some kind o' pretty little frames for 'em all – you know there's always a new fashion o' frames comin' round; first 'twas shell-work, and then 'twas pine-cones, and bead-work's had its day, and now she's much concerned with perforated cardboard worked with silk. I tell you that best room's a sight to see! But you mustn't look for anything elegant,' continued Mrs Todd, after a moment's reflection. 'Mis' Martin's always been in very poor, strugglin' circumstances. She had ambition for her children, though they took right after their father an' had little for themselves; she wa'n't over an' above well married, however kind she may see fit to speak. She's been patient an' hard-workin' all her life, and always high above makin' mean complaints of other folks. I expect all this business about the Queen has buoyed her over many a shoal place in life. Yes, you might say that Abby'd been a slave, but there ain't any slave but has some freedom.'

IV

Presently I saw a low gray house standing on a grassy bank close to the road. The door was at the side, facing us, and a tangle of snowberry bushes and cinnamon roses[11] grew to the level of the window-sills. On the door-step stood a bent-shouldered, little old woman; there was an air of welcome and of unmistakable dignity about her.

'She sees us coming,' exclaimed Mrs Todd in an excited whisper. 'There, I told her I might be over this way again if the weather held good, and if I came I'd bring you. She said right off she'd take great pleasure in havin' a visit from you; I was surprised, she's usually so retirin'.'

Even this reassurance did not quell a faint apprehension on our part; there was something distinctly formal in the occasion, and one felt that consciousness of inadequacy which is never easy for the humblest pride to bear. On the way I had torn my dress in an unexpected encounter with a little thornbush, and I could now imagine how it felt to be going to Court and forgetting one's feathers or her Court train.

The Queen's Twin was oblivious of such trifles; she stood waiting with a calm look until we came near enough to take her kind hand. She was a beautiful old woman, with clear eyes and a lovely quietness and genuineness of manner; there was not a trace of anything pretentious about her, or high-flown, as Mrs Todd would say comprehensively. Beauty in age is rare enough in women who have spent their lives in the hard work of a farmhouse; but autumn-like and withered as this woman may have looked, her features had kept, or rather gained, a great refinement. She led us into her old kitchen and gave us seats, and took one of the little straight-backed chairs herself and sat a short distance away, as if she were giving audience to an ambassador. It seemed as if we should all be standing; you could not help feeling that the habits of her life were more ceremonious, but that for the moment she assumed the simplicities of the occasion.

Mrs Todd was always Mrs Todd, too great and self-possessed a soul for any occasion to ruffle. I admired her calmness, and presently the slow current of neighborhood talk carried one easily along; we spoke of the weather and the small adventures of the way, and then, as if I were after all not a stranger, our hostess turned almost affectionately to speak to me.

'The weather will be growing dark in London now. I expect that you've been in London, dear?' she said.

'Oh, yes,' I answered. 'Only last year.'

'It is a great many years since I was there, along in the forties,' said Mrs Martin. ''Twas the only voyage I ever made; most of my neighbors have been great travelers. My brother was master of a vessel, and his wife usually sailed with him; but that year she had a young child more frail than the others, and she dreaded the care of it at sea. It happened that my brother got a chance for my husband to go as super-cargo,[12] being a good accountant, and came one day to urge him to take it; he was very ill-disposed to the sea, but he had met with losses, and I saw my own opportunity and persuaded them both to let me go too. In those days they didn't object to a woman's being aboard to wash and mend, the voyages were sometimes very long. And that was the way I come to see the Queen.'

Mrs Martin was looking straight in my eyes to see if I showed any genuine interest in the most interesting person in the world.

'Oh, I am very glad you saw the Queen,' I hastened to say. 'Mrs Todd has told me that you and she were born the very same day.'

'We were indeed, dear!' said Mrs Martin, and she leaned back comfortably and smiled as she had not smiled before. Mrs Todd gave a satisfied nod and glance, as if to say that things were going on as well as possible in this anxious moment.

'Yes,' said Mrs Martin again, drawing her chair a little nearer, ''twas a very remarkable thing; we were born the same day, and at exactly the same hour, after you allowed for all the difference in time. My father figured it out sea-fashion. Her Royal Majesty and I opened our eyes upon this world together; say what you may, 'tis a bond between us.'

Mrs Todd assented with an air of triumph, and untied her hat-strings and threw them back over her shoulders with a gallant air.

'And I married a man by the name of Albert, just the same as she did, and all by chance, for I didn't get the news that she had an Albert too till a fortnight afterward; news was slower coming then than it is now. My first baby was a girl, and I called her Victoria after my mate; but the next one was a boy, and my husband wanted the right to name him, and took his own name and his brother Edward's, and pretty soon I saw in the paper that the little Prince o' Wales had been christened just the same. After that I made excuse to wait till I knew what she'd named her children. I didn't want to break the chain, so I had an Alfred, and my darling Alice that I lost long before she lost hers, and there I stopped. If I'd only had a dear daughter to stay at home with me, same's her youngest one, I should have been so thankful! But if only one of us could have a little Beatrice, I'm glad 'twas the Queen; we've both seen trouble, but she's had the most care.'

I asked Mrs Martin if she lived alone all the year, and was told that she did except for a visit now and then from one of her grandchildren, 'the only one that really likes to come an' stay quiet 'long o' grandma. She always says quick as she's through her schoolin' she's goin' to live with me all the time, but she's very pretty an' has taking ways,' said Mrs Martin, looking both proud and wistful, 'so I can tell nothing at all about it! Yes, I've been alone most o' the time since my Albert was taken away, and that's a great many years; he had a long time o' failing and sickness first.' (Mrs Todd's foot gave an impatient scuff on the floor.) 'An' I've always lived right here. I ain't like the Queen's Majesty, for this is the only palace I've got,' said the dear old thing, smiling again. 'I'm glad of it too, I don't like changing about, an' our stations in life are set very different. I don't require what the Queen does, but sometimes I've thought 'twas left to me to do the plain things she don't have time for. I expect she's a beautiful house-keeper, nobody couldn't have done better in her high place, and she's been as good a mother as she's been a queen.'

'I guess she has, Abby,' agreed Mrs Todd instantly. 'How was it you happened to get such a good look at her? I meant to ask you again when I was here t'other day.'

'Our ship was layin' in the Thames, right there above Wapping.[13] We was dischargin' cargo, and under orders to clear as quick as we could for Bordeaux to take on an excellent freight o' French goods,' explained Mrs Martin eagerly. 'I heard that the Queen was goin' to a great review of her army, and would drive out o' her Buckin'ham Palace about ten o'clock in the mornin', and I run aft to Albert, my husband, and brother Horace where they was standin' together by the hatchway, and told 'em they must one of 'em take me. They laughed, I was in such a hurry, and said they couldn't go; and I found they meant it and got sort of impatient when I began to talk, and I was 'most broken-hearted; 'twas all the reason I had for makin' that hard voyage. Albert couldn't help often reproachin' me, for he did so resent the sea, an' I'd known how 'twould be before we sailed; but I'd minded nothing all the way till then, and I just crep' back to my cabin an' begun to cry. They was disappointed about their ship's cook, an' I'd cooked for fo'c's'le an' cabin[14] myself all the way over; 'twas dreadful hard work, specially in rough weather; we'd had head winds an' a six weeks' voyage. They'd acted sort of ashamed o' me when I pled so to go ashore, an' that hurt my feelin's most of all. But Albert come below pretty soon; I've never given way so in my life, an' he begun to act frightened, and treated me gentle just as he did when we was goin' to be married, an' when I got over sobbin' he went on deck and saw Horace an' talked it over what they could do; they really had their duty to the vessel, and couldn't be spared that day. Horace was real good when he understood everything, and he come an' told me I'd more than worked my passage an' was goin' to do just as I liked now we was in port. He'd engaged a cook, too, that was comin' aboard that mornin', and he was goin' to send the ship's carpenter with me – a nice fellow from up Thomaston way; he'd gone to put on his ashore clothes as quick's he could. So then I got ready, and we started off in the small boat and rowed up river. I was afraid we were too late, but the tide was setting up very strong, and we landed an' left the boat to a keeper, and I run all the way up those great streets and across a park. 'Twas a great day, with sights

205

o' folks everywhere, but 'twas just as if they was nothin' but wax images to me. I kep' askin' my way an' runnin' on, with the carpenter comin' after as best he could, and just as I worked to the front o' the crowd by the palace, the gates was flung open and out she came; all prancin' horses and shinin' gold, and in a beautiful carriage there she sat; 'twas a moment o' heaven to me. I saw her plain, and she looked right at me so pleasant and happy, just as if she knew there was somethin' different between us from other folks.'

There was a moment when the Queen's Twin could not go on and neither of her listeners could ask a question.

'Prince Albert was sitting right beside her in the carriage,' she continued. 'Oh, he was a beautiful man! Yes, dear, I saw 'em both together just as I see you now, and then she was gone out o' sight in another minute, and the common crowd was all spread over the place pushin' an' cheerin'. 'Twas some kind o' holiday, an' the carpenter and I got separated, an' then I found him again after I didn't think I should, an' he was all for makin' a day of it, and goin' to show me all the sights; he'd been in London before, but I didn't want nothin' else, an' we went back through the streets down to the waterside an' took the boat. I remember I mended an old coat o' my Albert's as good as I could, sittin' on the quarter-deck in the sun all that afternoon, and 'twas all as if I was livin' in a lovely dream. I don't know how to explain it, but there hasn't been no friend I've felt so near to me ever since.'

One could not say much – only listen. Mrs Todd put in a discerning question now and then, and Mrs Martin's eyes shone brighter and brighter as she talked. What a lovely gift of imagination and true affection was in this fond old heart! I looked about the plain New England kitchen, with its wood-smoked walls and homely braided rugs on the worn floor, and all its simple furnishings. The loud-ticking clock seemed to encourage us to speak; at the other side of the room was an early newspaper portrait of Her Majesty the Queen of Great Britain and Ireland. On a shelf below were some flowers in a little glass dish, as if they were put before a shrine.

'If I could have had more to read, I should have known 'most everything about her,' said Mrs Martin wistfully. 'I've made the most of what I did have, and thought it over and over till it came clear. I sometimes seem to have her all my own, as if we'd lived right together. I've often walked out into the woods alone and told her what my troubles was, and it always seemed as if she told me 'twas all right, an' we must have patience. I've got her beautiful book about the Highlands;[15] 'twas dear Mis' Todd here that found out about her printing it and got a copy for me, and it's been a treasure to my heart, just as if 'twas written right to me. I always read it Sundays now, for my Sunday treat. Before that I used to have to imagine a good deal, but when I come to read her book, I knew what I expected was all true. We do think alike about so many things,' said the Queen's Twin with affectionate certainty. 'You see, there is something between us, being born just at the some time; 'tis what they call a birthright. She's had great tasks put upon her, being the Queen, an' mine has been the humble lot; but she's done the best she could, nobody can say to the contrary, and there's something between us; she's been the great lesson I've had to live by. She's been everything to me. An' when she had her Jubilee,[16] oh, how my heart was with her!'

'There, 'twouldn't play the part in her life it has in mine,' said Mrs Martin generously, in answer to something one of her listeners had said. 'Sometimes I think, now she's older, she might like to know about us. When I think how few old friends anybody has left at our age, I suppose it may be just the same with her as it is with me; perhaps she would like to know how we came into life together. But I've had a great advantage in seeing her, an' I can always fancy her goin' on, while she don't know nothin' yet about me, except she may feel my love stayin' her heart sometimes an' not know just where it comes from. An' I dream about our being together out in some pretty fields, young as ever we was, and holdin' hands as we walk along. I'd like to know if she ever has that dream too. I used to have days when I made believe she did know, an' was comin' to see me,' confessed the speaker shyly, with a little flush on her cheeks; 'and I'd plan what I could have nice for supper, and I wasn't goin' to let anybody know she was here havin' a good rest, except I'd wish you, Almira Todd, or dear Mis' Blackett would happen in, for you'd know just how to talk with her. You see, she likes to be up in Scotland, right out in the wild country, better than she does anywhere else.'

'I'd really love to take her out to see mother at Green Island,' said Mrs Todd with a sudden impulse.

'Oh, yes! I should love to have you,' exclaimed Mrs Martin, and then she began to speak in a lower tone. 'One day I got thinkin' so about my dear Queen,' she said, 'an' livin' so in my thoughts, that I went to work an' got all ready for her, just as if she was really comin'. I never told this to a livin' soul before, but I feel you'll understand. I put my best fine sheets and blankets I spun an' wove myself on the bed, and I picked some pretty flowers and put 'em all round the house, an' I worked as hard an' happy as I could all day, and had as nice a supper ready as I could get, sort of telling myself a story all the time. She was comin' an' I was goin' to see her again, an' I kep' it up until nightfall; an' when I see the dark an' it come to me I was all alone, the dream left me, an' I sat down on the doorstep an' felt all foolish an' tired. An', if you'll believe it, I heard steps comin', an' an old cousin o' mine come wanderin' along, one I was apt to be shy of. She wasn't all there, as folks used to say, but harmless enough and a kind of poor old talking body. And I went right to meet her when I first heard her call, 'stead o' hidin' as I sometimes did, an' she come in dreadful willin', an' we sat down to supper together; 'twas a supper I should have had no heart to eat alone.'

'I don't believe she ever had such a splendid time in her life as she did then. I heard her tell all about it afterwards,' exclaimed Mrs Todd compassionately. 'There, now I hear all this it seems just as if the Queen might have known and couldn't come herself, so she sent that poor old creatur' that was always in need!'

Mrs Martin looked timidly at Mrs Todd and then at me. ''Twas childish o' me to go an' get supper,' she confessed.

'I guess you wa'n't the first one to do that,' said Mrs Todd. 'No, I guess you wa'n't the first one who's got supper that way, Abby,' and then for a moment she could say no more.

Mrs Todd and Mrs Martin had moved their chairs a little so that they faced each other, and I, at one side, could see them both.

'No, you never told me o' that before, Abby,' said Mrs Todd gently. 'Don't it show that for folks that have any fancy in 'em, such beautiful dreams is the real part o' life? But to most folks the common things that happens outside 'em is all in all.'

Mrs Martin did not appear to understand at first, strange to say, when the secret of her heart was put into words; then a glow of pleasure and comprehension shone upon her face. 'Why, I believe you're right, Almira!' she said, and turned to me.

'Wouldn't you like to look at my pictures of the Queen?' she asked, and we rose and went into the best room.

V

The mid-day visit seemed very short; September hours are brief to match the shortening days. The great subject was dismissed for a while after our visit to the Queen's pictures, and my companions spoke much of lesser persons until we drank the cup of tea which Mrs Todd had foreseen. I happily remembered that the Queen herself is said to like a proper cup of tea, and this at once seemed to make her Majesty kindly join so remote and reverent a company. Mrs Martin's thin cheeks took on a pretty color like a girl's. 'Somehow I always have thought of her when I made it extra good,' she said. 'I've got a real china cup that belonged to my grandmother, and I believe I shall call it hers now.'

'Why don't you?' responded Mrs Todd warmly, with a delightful smile.

Later they spoke of a promised visit which was to be made in the Indian summer to the Landing and Green Island, but I observed that Mrs Todd presented the little parcel of dried herbs, with full directions, for a cure-all in the spring, as if there were no real chance of their meeting again first. As we looked back from the turn of the road the Queen's Twin was still standing on the door-step watching us away, and Mrs Todd stopped, and stood still for a moment before she waved her hand again.

'There's one thing certain, dear,' she said to me with great discernment; 'it ain't as if we left her all alone!'

Then we set out upon our long way home over the hill, where we lingered in the afternoon sunshine, and through the dark woods across the heron-swamp.

MARTHA'S LADY

I

One day, many years ago, the old Judge Pyne house wore an unwonted look of gayety and youthfulness. The high-fenced green garden was bright with June flowers. Under the elms in the large shady front yard you might see some chairs placed near together, as they often used to be when the family were all at home and life was going on gayly with eager talk and pleasure-making; when the elder judge, the grandfather, used to quote that great author, Dr Johnson, and say to his girls, 'Be brisk, be splendid, and be public.'

One of the chairs had a crimson silk shawl thrown carelessly over its straight back, and a passer-by, who looked in through the latticed gate between the tall gate-posts with their white urns, might think that this piece of shining East Indian color was a huge red lily that had suddenly bloomed against the syringa bush. There were certain windows thrown wide open that were usually shut, and their curtains were blowing free in the light wind of a summer afternoon; it looked as if a large household had returned to the old house to fill the prim best rooms and find them full of cheer.

It was evident to every one in town that Miss Harriet Pyne, to use the village phrase, had company. She was the last of her family, and was by no means old; but being the last, and wonted to live with people much older than herself, she had formed all the habits of a serious elderly person. Ladies of her age, something past thirty, often wore discreet caps in those days, especially if they were married, but being single, Miss Harriet clung to youth in this respect, making the one concession of keeping her waving chestnut hair as smooth and stiffly arranged as possible. She had been the dutiful companion of her father and mother in their latest years, all her elder brothers and sisters having married and gone, or died and gone, out of the old house. Now that she was left alone it seemed quite the best thing frankly to accept the fact of age, and to turn more resolutely than ever to the companionship of duty and serious books. She was more serious and given to routine than her elders themselves, as sometimes happened when the daughters of New England gentlefolks were brought up wholly in the society of their elders. At thirty-five she had more reluctance than her mother to face an unforeseen occasion, certainly more than her grandmother, who had preserved some cheerful inheritance of gayety and worldliness from colonial times.

There was something about the look of the crimson silk shawl in the front yard to make one suspect that the sober customs of the best house in a quiet New England village were all being set at defiance, and once when the mistress of the house came to stand in her own doorway, she wore the pleased but somewhat apprehensive look of a guest. In these days New England life held the necessity of much dignity and discretion of behavior; there was the truest hospitality and good cheer in all occasional festivities, but it was sometimes a self-conscious hospitality, followed by an inexorable return to asceticism both of diet and of behavior. Miss Harriet Pyne belonged to the very dullest days of New England, those which perhaps held the most priggishness for the learned professions, the most limited interpretation of the word 'evangelical,' and the pettiest indifference to large things. The outbreak of a desire for larger religious freedom caused at first a most determined reaction toward formalism, especially in small and quiet villages like Ashford, intently busy with their own concerns. It was high time for a little leaven to begin its work in this moment when the great impulses of the war for liberty had died away and those of the coming war for patriotism and a new freedom[1] had hardly yet begun.

The dull interior, the changed life of the old house, whose former activities seemed to have fallen sound asleep, really typified these larger conditions, and a little leaven had made its easily recognized appearance in the shape of a light-hearted girl. She was Miss Harriet's young Boston cousin, Helena Vernon, who, half-amused and half-impatient at the unnecessary sober-mindedness of her hostess and of Ashford in general, had set herself to the difficult task of gayety. Cousin Harriet looked on at a succession of ingenious and, on the whole, innocent attempts at pleasure, as she might have looked on at the frolics of a kitten who easily substitutes a ball of yarn for the uncertainties of a bird or a wind-blown leaf, and who may at any moment ravel the fringe of a sacred curtain-tassel in preference to either.

Helena, with her mischievous appealing eyes, with her enchanting old songs and her guitar, seemed the more delightful and even reasonable because she was so kind to everybody, and because she was a beauty. She had the gift of most charming manners. There was all the unconscious lovely ease and grace that had come with the good breeding of her city home, where many pleasant people came and went; she had no fear, one had almost said no respect, of the individual, and she did not need to think of herself. Cousin Harriet turned cold with apprehension when she saw the minister coming in at the front gate, and wondered in agony if Martha were properly attired to go to the door, and would by any chance hear the knocker; it was Helena who, delighted to have anything happen, ran to the door to welcome the Reverend Mr Crofton as if he were a congenial friend of her own age. She could behave with more or less propriety during the stately first visit, and even contrive to lighten it with modest mirth, and to extort the confession that the guest had a tenor voice, though sadly out of practice; but when the minister departed a little flattered, and hoping that he had not expressed himself too strongly for a pastor upon the poems of Emerson,[2] and feeling the unusual stir of gallantry in his proper heart, it was Helena who caught the honored hat of the late Judge Pyne from its last resting-place in the hall, and holding it securely in both hands, mimicked the minister's self-conscious entrance. She copied his pompous and anxious expression in the dim parlor in such delicious fashion that Miss Harriet, who could not always extinguish a ready spark of the original sin of humor, laughed aloud.

'My dear!' she exclaimed severely the next moment, 'I am ashamed of your being so disrespectful!' and then laughed again, and took the affecting old hat and carried it back to its place.

'I would not have had anyone else see you for the world,' she said sorrowfully as she returned, feeling quite self-possessed again, to the parlor doorway; but Helena still sat in the minister's chair, with her small feet placed as his stiff boots had been, and a copy of his solemn expression before they came to speaking of Emerson and of the guitar. 'I wish I had asked him if he would be so kind as to climb the cherry-tree,' said Helena, unbending a little at the discovery that her cousin would consent to laugh no more. 'There are all those ripe cherries on the top branches. I can climb as high as he, but I can't reach far enough from the last branch that will bear me. The minister is so long and thin' –

'I don't know what Mr Crofton would have thought of you; he is a very serious young man,' said cousin Harriet, still ashamed of her laughter. 'Martha will get the cherries for you, or one of the men. I should not like to have Mr Crofton think you were frivolous, a young lady of your opportunities' – but Helena had escaped through the hall and out at the garden door at the mention of Martha's name. Miss Harriet Pyne sighed anxiously, and then smiled, in spite of her deep convictions, as she shut the blinds and tried to make the house look solemn again.

The front door might be shut, but the garden door at the other end of the broad hall was wide open upon the large sunshiny garden, where the last of the red and white peonies and the golden lilies, and the first of the tall blue larkspurs lent their colors in generous fashion. The straight box borders were all in fresh and shining green of their new leaves, and there was a fragrance of the old garden's inmost life and soul blowing from the honeysuckle blossoms on a long trellis. It was now late in the afternoon, and the sun was low behind great apple-trees at the garden's end, which threw their shadows over the short turf of the bleaching-green. The cherry-trees stood at one side in full sunshine, and Miss Harriet, who presently came to the garden steps to watch like a hen at the water's edge, saw her cousin's pretty figure in its white dress of India muslin hurrying across the grass. She was accompanied by the tall, ungainly shape of Martha the new maid, who, dull and indifferent to everyone else, showed a surprising willingness and allegiance to the young guest.

'Martha ought to be in the dining-room, already, slow as she is; it wants but half an hour of tea-time,' said Miss Harriet, as she turned and went into the shaded house. It was Martha's duty to wait at table, and there had been many trying scenes and defeated efforts toward her education. Martha was certainly very clumsy, and she seemed the clumsier because she had replaced her aunt, a most skillful person, who had but lately married a thriving farm and its prosperous owner. It must be confessed that Miss Harriet was a most bewildering instructor, and that her pupil's brain was easily confused and prone to blunders. The coming of Helena had been somewhat dreaded by reason of this incompetent service, but the guest took no notice of frowns or futile gestures at the first tea-table, except to establish friendly relations with Martha on her own account by a reassuring smile. They were about the same age, and next morning, before cousin Harriet came down, Helena showed by a word and a quick touch the right way to do something that had gone wrong and been impossible to understand the night before. A moment later the anxious mistress came in without suspicion, but Martha's eyes were as affectionate as a dog's, and there was a new look of hopefulness on her face; this dreaded guest was a friend after all, and not a foe come from proud Boston to confound her ignorance and patient efforts.

The two young creatures, mistress and maid, were hurrying across the bleaching-green.

'I can't reach the ripest cherries,' explained Helena politely, 'and I think that Miss Pyne ought to send some to the minister. He has just made us a call. Why Martha, you haven't been crying again!'

'Yes'm,' said Martha sadly. 'Miss Pyne always loves to send something to the minister,' she acknowledged with interest, as if she did not wish to be asked to explain these latest tears.

'We'll arrange some of the best cherries in a pretty dish. I'll show you how, and you shall carry them over to the parsonage after tea,' said Helena cheerfully, and Martha accepted the embassy with pleasure. Life was beginning to hold moments of something like delight in the last few days.

'You'll spoil your pretty dress, Miss Helena,' Martha gave shy warning, and Miss Helena stood back and held up her skirts with unusual care while the country girl, in her heavy blue checked gingham, began to climb the cherry-tree like a boy.

Down came the scarlet fruit like bright rain into the green grass.

'Break some nice twigs with the cherries and leaves together; oh, you're a duck, Martha!' and Martha, flushed with delight, and looking far more like a thin and solemn blue heron, came rustling down to earth again, and gathered the spoils into her clean apron.

That night at tea, during her handmaiden's temporary absence, Miss Harriet announced, as if by way of apology, that she thought Martha was beginning to understand something about her work. 'Her aunt was a treasure, she never had to be told anything twice; but Martha has been as clumsy as a calf,' said the precise mistress of the house. 'I have been afraid sometimes that I never could teach her anything. I was quite ashamed to have you come just now, and find me so unprepared to entertain a visitor.'

'Oh, Martha will learn fast enough because she cares so much,' said the visitor eagerly. 'I think she is a dear good girl. I do hope that she will never go away. I think she does things better every day, cousin Harriet,' added Helena pleadingly, with all her kind young heart. The china-closet door was open a little way, and Martha heard every word. From that moment, she not only knew what love was like, but she knew love's dear ambitions. To have come from a stony hill-farm and a bare small wooden house, was like a cave-dweller's coming to make a permanent home in an art museum, such had seemed the elaborateness and elegance of Miss Pyne's fashion of life; and Martha's simple brain was slow enough in its processes and recognitions. But with this sympathetic ally and defender, this exquisite Miss Helena who believed in her, all difficulties appeared to vanish.

Later that evening, no longer homesick or hopeless, Martha returned from her polite errand to the minister, and stood with a sort of triumph before the two ladies, who were sitting in the front doorway, as if they were waiting for visitors. Helena still in her white muslin and red ribbons, and Miss Harriet in a thin black silk. Being happily self-forgetful in the greatness of the moment, Martha's manners were perfect, and she looked for once almost pretty and quite as young as she was.

'The minister came to the door himself, and returned his thanks. He said that cherries were always his favorite fruit, and he was much obliged to both Miss Pyne and Miss Vernon. He kept me waiting a few minutes, while he got this book ready to send to you, Miss Helena.'

'What are you saying, Martha? I have sent him nothing!' exclaimed Miss Pyne, much astonished. 'What does this mean, Helena?'

'Only a few cherries,' explained Helena. 'I thought Mr Crofton would like them after his afternoon of parish calls. Martha and I arranged them before tea, and I sent them with our compliments.'

'Oh, I am very glad you did,' said Miss Harriet, wondering, but much relieved. 'I was afraid' –

'No, it was none of my mischief,' answered Helena daringly. 'I did not think that Martha would be ready to go so soon. I should have shown you how pretty they looked among their green leaves. We put them in one of your best white dishes with the openwork edge. Martha shall show you tomorrow; mamma always likes to have them so.' Helena's fingers were busy with the hard knot of a parcel.

'See this, cousin Harriet!' she announced proudly, as Martha disappeared round the corner of the house, beaming with the pleasures of adventure and success. 'Look! the minister has sent me a book: Sermons on *what*? Sermons – it is so dark that I can't quite see.'

'It must be his "Sermons on the Seriousness of Life;" they are the only ones he has printed, I believe,' said Miss Harriet, with much pleasure. 'They are considered very fine discourses. He pays you a great compliment, my dear. I feared that he noticed your girlish levity.'

'I behaved beautifully while he stayed,' insisted Helena. 'Ministers are only men,' but she blushed with pleasure. It was certainly something to receive a book from its author, and such a tribute made her of more value to the whole reverent household. The minister was not only a man, but a bachelor, and Helena was at the age that best loves conquest; it was at any rate comfortable to be reinstated in cousin Harriet's good graces.

'Do ask the kind gentleman to tea! He needs a little cheering up,' begged the siren in India muslin, as she laid the shiny black volume of sermons on the stone door-step with an air of approval, but as if they had quite finished their mission.

'Perhaps I shall, if Martha improves as much as she has within the last day or two,' Miss Harriet promised hopefully. 'It is something I always dread a little when I am all alone, but I think Mr Crofton likes to come. He converses so elegantly.'

II

These were the days of long visits, before affectionate friends thought it quite worth while to take a hundred miles' journey merely to dine or to pass a night in one another's houses. Helena lingered through the pleasant weeks of early summer, and departed unwillingly at last to join her family at the White Hills, where they had gone, like other households of high social station, to pass the month of August out of town. The happy-hearted young guest left many lamenting friends behind her, and promised each that she would come back again next year. She left the minister a rejected lover, as well as the preceptor of the academy, but with their pride unwounded, and it may have been with wider outlooks upon the world and a less narrow sympathy both for their own work in life and for their neighbors' work and hindrances. Even Miss Harriet Pyne herself had lost some of the unnecessary provincialism and prejudice which had begun to harden a naturally good and open mind and affectionate heart. She was conscious of feeling younger and more free, and not so lonely. Nobody had ever been so gay, so fascinating, or so kind as Helena, so full of social resource, so simple and undemanding in her friendliness. The light of her young life cast no shadow on either young or old companions, her pretty clothes never seemed to make other girls look dull or out of fashion. When she went away up the street in Miss Harriet's carriage to take the slow train toward Boston and the gayeties of the new Profile House, where her mother waited impatiently with a group of Southern friends, it seemed as if there would never be any more picnics or parties in Ashford, and as if society had nothing left to do but to grow old and get ready for winter.

Martha came into Miss Helena's bedroom that last morning, and it was easy to see that she had been crying; she looked just as she did in that first sad week of homesickness and despair. All for love's sake she had been learning to do many things, and to do them exactly right; her eyes had grown quick to see the smallest chance for personal service. Nobody could be more humble and devoted; she looked years older than Helena, and wore already a touching air of caretaking.

'You spoil me, you dear Martha!' said Helena from the bed. 'I don't know what they will say at home, I am so spoiled.'

Martha went on opening the blinds to let in the brightness of the summer morning, but she did not speak.

'You are getting on splendidly, aren't you?' continued the little mistress. 'You have tried so hard that you make me ashamed of myself. At first you crammed all the flowers together, and now you make them look beautiful. Last night cousin Harriet was so pleased when the table was so charming, and I told her that you did everything yourself, every bit. Won't you keep the flowers fresh and pretty in the house until I come back? It's so much pleasanter for Miss Pyne, and you'll feed my little sparrows, won't you? They're growing so tame.'

'Oh, yes, Miss Helena!' and Martha looked almost angry for a moment, then she burst into tears and covered her face with her apron. 'I couldn't understand a single thing when I first came. I never had been anywhere to see anything, and Miss Pyne frightened me when she talked. It was you made me think I could ever learn. I wanted to keep the place, 'count of mother and the little boys; we're dreadful hard pushed. Hepsy has been good in the kitchen; she said she ought to have patience with me, for she was awkward herself when she first came.'

Helena laughed; she looked so pretty under the tasseled white curtains.

'I dare say Hepsy tells the truth,' she said. 'I wish you had told me about your mother. When I come again, some day we'll drive up country, as you call it, to see her. Martha! I wish you would think of me sometimes after I go away. Won't you promise?' and the bright young face suddenly grew grave. 'I have hard times myself; I don't always learn things that I ought to learn, I don't always put things straight. I wish you wouldn't forget me ever, and would just believe in me. I think it does help more than anything.'

'I won't forget,' said Martha slowly. 'I shall think of you every day.' She spoke almost with indifference, as if she had been asked to dust a room, but she turned aside quickly and pulled the little mat under the hot water jug quite out of its former straightness; then she hastened away down the long white entry,[3] weeping as she went.

III

To lose out of sight the friend whom one has loved and lived to please is to lose joy out of life. But if love is true, there comes presently a higher joy of pleasing the ideal, that is to say, the perfect friend. The same old happiness is lifted to a higher level. As for Martha, the girl who stayed behind in Ashford, nobody's life could seem duller to those who could not understand; she was slow of step, and her eyes were almost always downcast as if intent upon incessant toil; but they startled you when she looked up with their shining light. She was capable of the happiness of holding fast to a great sentiment, the ineffable satisfaction of trying to please one whom she truly loved. She never thought of trying to make other people pleased with herself; all she lived for was to do the best she could for others, and to conform to an ideal, which grew at last to be like a saint's vision, a heavenly figure painted upon the sky.

On Sunday afternoons in summer, Martha sat by the window of her chamber, a low-storied little room, which looked into the side yard and the great branches of an elm-tree. She never sat in the old wooden rocking-chair except on Sundays like this; it belonged to the day of rest and to happy meditation. She wore her plain black dress and a clean white apron, and held in her lap a little wooden box, with a brass ring on top for a handle. She was past sixty years of age and looked even older, but there was the same look on her face that it had sometimes worn in girlhood. She was the same Martha; her hands were old-looking and work-worn, but her face still shone. It seemed like yesterday that Helena Vernon had gone away, and it was more than forty years.

War and peace had brought their changes and great anxieties, the face of the earth was furrowed by floods and fire, the faces of mistress and maid were furrowed by smiles and tears, and in the sky the stars shone on as if nothing had happened. The village of Ashford added a few pages to its unexciting history, the minister preached, the people listened; now and then a funeral crept along the street, and now and then the bright face of a little child rose above the horizon of a family pew. Miss Harriet Pyne lived on in the large white house, which gained more and more distinction because it suffered no changes, save successive repaintings and a new railing about its stately roof. Miss Harriet herself had moved far beyond the uncertainties of an anxious youth. She had long ago made all her decisions, and settled all necessary questions; her scheme of life was as faultless as the miniature landscape of a Japanese garden, and as easily kept in order. The only important change she would ever be capable of making was the final change to another and a better world; and for that nature itself would gently provide, and her own innocent life.

Hardly any great social event had ruffled the easy current of life since Helena Vernon's marriage. To this Miss Pyne had gone, stately in appearance and carrying gifts of some old family silver which bore the Vernon crest, but not without some protest in her heart against the uncertainties of married life. Helena was so equal to a happy independence and even to the assistance of other lives grown strangely dependent upon her quick sympathies and instinctive decisions, that it was hard to let her sink her personality in the affairs of another. Yet a brilliant English match was not without its attractions to an old-fashioned gentlewoman like Miss Pyne, and Helena herself was amazingly happy; one day there had come a letter to Ashford, in which her very heart seemed to beat with love and self-forgetfulness, to tell cousin Harriet of such new happiness and high hope. 'Tell Martha all that I say about my dear Jack,' wrote the eager girl; 'please show my letter to Martha, and tell her that I shall come home next summer and bring the handsomest and best man in the world to Ashford. I have told him all about the dear house and the dear garden; there never was such a lad to reach for cherries with his six-foot-two.' Miss Pyne, wondering a little, gave the letter to Martha, who took it deliberately and as if she wondered too, and went away to read it slowly by herself. Martha cried over it, and felt a strange sense of loss and pain; it hurt her heart a little to read about the cherry-picking. Her idol seemed to be less her own since she had become the idol of a stranger. She never had taken such a letter in her hands before, but love at last prevailed, since Miss Helena was happy, and she kissed the last page where her name was written, feeling overbold, and laid the envelope on Miss Pyne's secretary[4] without a word.

The most generous love cannot but long for reassurance, and Martha had the joy of being remembered. She was not forgotten when the day of the wedding drew near, but she never knew that Miss Helena had asked if cousin Harriet would not bring Martha to town; she should like to have Martha there to see her married. 'She would help about the flowers,' wrote the happy girl; 'I know she will like to come, and I'll ask mamma to plan to have some one take her all about Boston and make her have a pleasant time after the hurry of the great day is over.'

Cousin Harriet thought it was very kind and exactly like Helena, but

Martha would be out of her element; it was most imprudent and girlish to have thought of such a thing. Helena's mother would be far from wishing for any unnecessary guest just then, in the busiest part of her household, and it was best not to speak of the invitation. Some day Martha should go to Boston if she did well, but not now. Helena did not forget to ask if Martha had come, and was astonished by the indifference of the answer. It was the first thing which reminded her that she was not a fairy princess having everything her own way in that last day before the wedding. She knew that Martha would have loved to be near, for she could not help understanding in that moment of her own happiness the love that was hidden in another heart. Next day this happy young princess, the bride, cut a piece of a great cake and put it into a pretty box that had held one of her wedding presents. With eager voices calling her, and all her friends about her, and her mother's face growing more and more wistful at the thought of parting, she still lingered and ran to take one or two trifles from her dressing-table, a little mirror and some tiny scissors that Martha would remember, and one of the pretty handkerchiefs marked with her maiden name. These she put in the box too; it was half a girlish freak and fancy, but she could not help trying to share her happiness, and Martha's life was so plain and dull. She whispered a message, and put the little package into cousin Harriet's hand for Martha as she said goodbye. She was very fond of cousin Harriet. She smiled with a gleam of her old fun; Martha's puzzled look and tall awkward figure seemed to stand suddenly before her eyes, as she promised to come again to Ashford. Impatient voices called to Helena, her lover was at the door, and she hurried away, leaving her old home and her girlhood gladly. If she had only known it, as she kissed cousin Harriet goodbye, they were never going to see each other again until they were old women. The first step that she took out of her father's house that day, married, and full of hope and joy, was a step that led her away from the green elms of Boston Common and away from her own country and those she loved best, to a brilliant, much-varied foreign life, and to nearly all the sorrows and nearly all the joys that the heart of one woman could hold or know.

On Sunday afternoons Martha used to sit by the window in Ashford and hold the wooden box which a favorite young brother, who afterward died at sea, had made for her, and she used to take out of it the pretty little box with a gilded cover that had held the piece of wedding-cake, and the small scissors, and the blurred bit of a mirror in its silver case; as for the handkerchief with the narrow lace edge, once in two or three years she sprinkled it as if it were a flower, and spread it out in the sun on the old bleaching-green, and sat near by in the shrubbery to watch lest some bold robin or cherry-bird[5] should seize it and fly away.

IV

Miss Harriet Pyne was often congratulated on the good fortune of having such a helper and friend as Martha. As time went on this tall, gaunt woman, always thin, always slow, gained a dignity of behavior and simple affectionateness of look which suited the charm and dignity of the ancient house. She was unconsciously beautiful like a saint, like the picturesqueness of a lonely tree which lives to shelter unnumbered lives and to stand quietly in its place. There was such rustic homeliness and constancy belonging to her, such beautiful powers of apprehension, such reticence, such gentleness for those who were troubled or sick; all these gifts and graces Martha hid in her heart. She never joined the church[6] because she thought she was not good enough, but life was such a passion and happiness of service that it was impossible not to be devout, and she was always in her humble place on Sundays, in the back pew next the door. She had been educated by a remembrance; Helena's young eyes forever looked at her reassuringly from a gay girlish face. Helena's sweet patience in teaching her own awkwardness could never be forgotten.

'I owe everything to Miss Helena,' said Martha, half aloud, as she sat alone by the window; she had said it to herself a thousand times. When she looked in the little keepsake mirror she always hoped to see some faint reflection of Helena Vernon, but there was only her own brown old New England face to look back at her wonderingly.

Miss Pyne went less and less often to pay visits to her friends in Boston; there were very few friends left to come to Ashford and make long visits in the summer, and life grew more and more monotonous. Now and then there came news from across the sea and messages of remembrance, letters that were closely written on thin sheets of paper, and that spoke of lords and ladies, of great journeys, of the death of little children and the proud successes of boys at school, of the wedding of Helena Dysart's only daughter; but even that had happened years ago. These things seemed far away and vague, as if they belonged to a story and not to life itself; the true links with the past were quite different. There was the unvarying flock of ground-sparrows that Helena had begun to feed; every morning Martha scattered crumbs for them from the side door-steps while Miss Pyne watched from the dining-room window, and they were counted and cherished year by year.

Miss Pyne herself had many fixed habits, but little ideality or imagination, and so at last it was Martha who took thought for her mistress, and gave freedom to her own good taste. After a while, without anyone's observing the change, the everyday ways of doing things in the house came to be the stately ways that had once belonged only to the entertainment of guests. Happily both mistress and maid seized all possible chances for hospitality, yet Miss Harriet nearly always sat alone at her exquisitely served table with its fresh flowers, and the beautiful old china which Martha handled so lovingly that there was no good excuse for keeping it hidden on closet shelves. Every year when the old cherry-trees were in fruit, Martha carried the round white old English dish with a fretwork edge, full of pointed green leaves and scarlet cherries, to the minister, and his wife never quite understood why every year he blushed and looked so conscious of the pleasure, and thanked Martha as if he had received a very particular attention. There was no pretty suggestion toward the pursuit of the fine art of housekeeping in Martha's limited acquaintance with newspapers that she did not adopt; there was no refined old custom of the Pyne housekeeping that she consented to let go. And every day, as she had promised, she thought of Miss Helena, – oh, many times in every day: whether this thing would please her, or that be likely to fall in with her fancy or ideas of fitness. As far as was possible the rare news that reached Ashford through an occasional letter or the talk of guests was made part of Martha's own life, the history of her own heart. A worn old geography often stood open at the map of Europe on the light-stand in her room, and a little old-fashioned gilt button, set with a bit of glass like a ruby, that had broken and fallen from the trimming of one of Helena's dresses, was used to mark the city of her dwelling-place. In the changes of a diplomatic life Martha followed her lady all about the map. Sometimes the button was at Paris, and sometimes at Madrid; once, to her great anxiety, it remained long at St Petersburg. For such a slow scholar Martha was not unlearned at last, since everything about life in these foreign towns was of interest to her faithful heart. She satisfied her own mind as she threw crumbs to the tame sparrows; it was all part of the same thing and for the same affectionate reasons.

V

One Sunday afternoon in early summer Miss Harriet Pyne came hurrying along the entry that led to Martha's room and called two or three times before its inhabitant could reach the door. Miss Harriet looked unusually cheerful and excited, and she held something in her hand. 'Where are you, Martha?' she called again. 'Come quick, I have something to tell you!'

'Here I am, Miss Pyne,' said Martha, who had only stopped to put her precious box in the drawer, and to shut the geography.

'Who do you think is coming this very night at half-past six? We must have everything as nice as we can; I must see Hannah at once. Do you remember my cousin Helena who has lived abroad so long? Miss Helena Vernon, – the Honorable Mrs Dysart, she is now.'

'Yes, I remember her,' answered Martha, turning a little pale.

'I knew that she was in this country, and I had written to ask her to come for a long visit,' continued Miss Harriet, who did not often explain things, even to Martha, though she was always conscientious about the kind messages that were sent back by grateful guests. 'She telegraphs that she means to anticipate her visit by a few days and come to me at once. The heat is beginning in town, I suppose. I daresay, having been a foreigner so long, she does not mind traveling on Sunday. Do you think Hannah will be prepared? We must have tea a little later.'

'Yes, Miss Harriet,' said Martha. She wondered that she could speak as usual, there was such a ringing in her ears. 'I shall have time to pick some fresh strawberries; Miss Helena is so fond of our strawberries.'

'Why, I had forgotten,' said Miss Pyne, a little puzzled by something quite unusual in Martha's face. 'We must expect to find Mrs Dysart a good deal changed, Martha; it is a great many years since she was here; I have not seen her since her wedding, and she has had a great deal of trouble, poor girl. You had better open the parlor chamber, and make it ready before you go down.'

'It is all ready,' said Martha. 'I can carry some of those little sweet-brier roses upstairs before she comes.'

'Yes, you are always thoughtful,' said Miss Pyne, with unwonted feeling.

Martha did not answer. She glanced at the telegram wistfully. She had never really suspected before that Miss Pyne knew nothing of the love that had been in her heart all these years; it was half a pain and half a golden joy to keep such a secret; she could hardly bear this moment of surprise.

Presently the news gave wings to her willing feet. When Hannah, the cook, who never had known Miss Helena, went to the parlor an hour later on some errand to her old mistress, she discovered that this stranger guest must be a very important person. She had never seen the tea-table look exactly as it did that night, and in the parlor itself there were fresh blossoming boughs in the old East India jars, and lilies in the paneled hall, and flowers everywhere, as if there were some high festivity.

Miss Pyne sat by the window watching, in her best dress, looking stately and calm; she seldom went out now, and it was almost time for the carriage. Martha was just coming in from the garden with the strawberries, and with more flowers in her apron. It was a bright cool evening in June, the golden robins sang in the elms, and the sun was going down behind the apple-trees at the foot of the garden. The beautiful old house stood wide open to the long-expected guest.

'I think that I shall go down to the gate,' said Miss Pyne, looking at Martha for approval, and Martha nodded and they went together slowly down the broad front walk.

There was a sound of horses and wheels on the roadside turf: Martha could not see at first; she stood back inside the gate behind the white lilac-bushes as the carriage came. Miss Pyne was there; she was holding out both arms and taking a tired, bent little figure in black to her heart. 'Oh, my Miss Helena is an old woman like me!' and Martha gave a pitiful sob; she had never dreamed it would be like this; this was the one thing she could not bear.

'Where are you, Martha?' called Miss Pyne. 'Martha will bring these in; you have not forgotten my good Martha, Helena?' Then Mrs Dysart looked up and smiled just as she used to smile in the old days. The young eyes were there still in the changed face, and Miss Helena had come.

That night Martha waited in her lady's room just as she used, humble and silent, and went through with the old unforgotten loving services. The long years seemed like days. At last she lingered a moment trying to think of something else that might be done, then she was going silently away, but Helena called her back. She suddenly knew the whole story and could hardly speak.

'Oh, my dear Martha!' she cried, 'won't you kiss me goodnight? Oh, Martha, have you remembered like this, all these long years!'

THE FOREIGNER

I

One evening, at the end of August, in Dunnet Landing, I heard Mrs Todd's firm footstep crossing the small front entry outside my door, and her conventional cough which served as a herald's trumpet, or a plain New England knock, in the harmony of our fellowship.

'Oh, please come in!' I cried, for it had been so still in the house that I supposed my friend and hostess had gone to see one of her neighbors. The first cold northeasterly storm of the season was blowing hard outside. Now and then there was a dash of great raindrops and a flick of wet lilac leaves against the window, but I could hear that the sea was already stirred to its dark depths, and the great rollers were coming in heavily against the shore. One might well believe that Summer was coming to a sad end that night, in the darkness and rain and sudden access of autumnal cold. It seemed as if there must be danger offshore among the outer islands.

'Oh, there!' exclaimed Mrs Todd, as she entered. 'I know nothing ain't ever happened out to Green Island since the world began, but I always do worry about mother in these great gales. You know those tidal waves occur sometimes down to the West Indies, and I get dwellin' on em' so I can't set still in my chair, nor knit a common row to a stocking. William might get mooning, out in his small bo't, and not observe how the sea was making, an' meet with some accident. Yes, I thought I'd come in and set with you if you wa'n't busy. No, I never feel any concern about 'em in winter 'cause then they're prepared, and all ashore and everything snug. William ought to keep help, as I tell him; yes, he ought to keep help.'

I hastened to reassure my anxious guest by saying that Elijah Tilley had told me in the afternoon, when I came along the shore past the fish houses, that Johnny Bowden and the Captain were out at Green Island; he had seen them beating up the bay, and thought they must have put into Burnt Island cove, but one of the lobstermen brought word later that he saw them hauling out at Green Island as he came by, and Captain Bowden pointed ashore and shook his head to say that he did not mean to try to get in. 'The old *Miranda* just managed it, but she will have to stay at home a day or two and put new patches in her sail,' I ended, not without pride in so much circumstantial evidence.

Mrs Todd was alert in a moment. 'Then they'll have a very pleasant evening,' she assured me, apparently dismissing all fears of tidal waves and other sea-going disasters. 'I was urging Alick Bowden to go ashore some days and see mother before cold weather. He's her own nephew; she sets a great deal by him. And Johnny's a great chum o' William's; don't you know the first day we had Johnny out 'long of us, he took an' give Williams his money to keep for him that he'd been a-savin', and William showed it to me an' was so affected I thought he was goin' to shed tears? 'Twas a dollar an' eighty cents; yes, they'll have a beautiful evenin' all together, and like's not the sea'll be flat as a doorstep come morning.'

I had drawn a large wooden rocking-chair before the fire, and Mrs Todd was sitting there jogging herself a little, knitting fast, and wonderfully placid of countenance. There came a fresh gust of wind and rain, and we could feel the small wooden house rock and hear it creak as if it were a ship at sea.

'Lord, hear the great breakers!' exclaimed Mrs Todd. 'How they pound! – there, there! I always run of an idea that the sea knows anger these nights and gets full o' fight. I can hear the rote o' them old black ledges way down the thoroughfare. Calls up all those stormy verses in the Book o' Psalms; David he knew how old sea-goin' folks have to quake at the heart.'

I thought as I had never thought before of such anxieties. The families of sailors and coastwise adventurers by sea must always be worrying about somebody, this side of the world or the other. There was hardly one of Mrs Todd's elder acquaintances, men or women, who had not at some time or other made a sea voyage, and there was often no news until the voyagers themselves came back to bring it.

'There's a roaring high overhead, and a roaring in the deep sea,' said Mrs Todd solemnly, 'and they battle together nights like this. No, I couldn't sleep; some women folks always goes right to bed an' to sleep, so's to forget, but 'tain't my way. Well, it's a blessin' we don't all feel alike; there's hardly any of our folks at sea to worry about, nowadays, but I can't help my feelin's, an' I got thinking of mother all alone, if William had happened to be out lobsterin' and couldn't make the cove gettin' back.'

'They will have a pleasant evening,' I repeated. 'Captain Bowden is the best of good company.'

'Mother'll make him some pancakes for his supper, like's not,' said Mrs

Todd, clicking her knitting needles and giving a pull at her yarn. Just then the old cat pushed open the unlatched door and came straight toward her mistress's lap. She was regarded severely as she stepped about and turned on the broad expanse, and then made herself into a round cushion of fur, but was not openly admonished. There was another great blast of wind overhead, and a puff of smoke came down the chimney.

'This makes me think o' the night Mis' Cap'n Tolland died,' said Mrs Todd, half to herself. 'Folks used to say these gales only blew when somebody's a-dyin', or the devil was a-comin' for his own, but the worst man I ever knew died a real pretty mornin' in June.'

'You have never told me any ghost stories,' said I; and such was the gloomy weather and the influences of the night that I was instantly filled with reluctance to have this suggestion followed. I had not chosen the best of moments; just before I spoke we had begun to feel as cheerful as possible. Mrs Todd glanced doubtfully at the cat and then at me, with a strange absent look, and I was really afraid that she was going to tell me something that would haunt my thoughts on every dark stormy night as long as I lived.

'Never mind now; tell me to-morrow by daylight, Mrs Todd,' I hastened to say, but she still looked at me full of doubt and deliberation.

'Ghost stories!' she answered. 'Yes, I don't know but I've heard a plenty of 'em first an' last. I was just sayin' to myself that this is like the night Mis' Cap'n Tolland died. 'Twas the great line storm[1] in September all of thirty, or maybe forty, year ago. I ain't one that keeps much account o' time.'

'Tolland? That's a name I have never heard in Dunnet,' I said.

'Then you haven't looked well about the old part o' the buryin' ground, no'theast corner,' replied Mrs Todd. 'All their women folks lies there; the sea's got most o' the men. They were a known family o' shipmasters in the early times. Mother had a mate, Ellen Tolland, that she mourns to this day; died right in her bloom with quick consumption, but the rest o' that family was all boys but one, and older than she, an' they lived hard seafarin' lives an' all died hard. They were called very smart seamen. I've heard that when the youngest went into one o' the old shippin' houses in Boston, the head o' the firm called out to him: "Did you say Tolland from Dunnet? That's recommendation enough for any vessel!" There was some o' them old shipmasters as tough as iron, an' they had the name o' usin' their crews very severe, but there wa'n't a man that wouldn't rather sign with 'em an' take his chances, than with the slack ones that didn't know how to meet accidents.'

II

There was so long a pause, and Mrs Todd still looked so absent-minded, that I was afraid she and the cat were growing drowsy together before the fire, and I should have no reminiscences at all. The wind struck the house again, so that we both started in out chairs and Mrs Todd gave a curious, startled look at me. The cat lifted her head and listened too, in the silence that followed, while after the wind sank we were more conscious than ever of the awful roar of the sea. The house jarred now and then, in a strange, disturbing way.

'Yes, they'll have a beautiful evening out to the island,' said Mrs Todd again; but she did not say it gayly. I had not seen her before in her weaker moments.

'Who was Mrs Captain Tolland?' I asked eagerly, to change the current of our thoughts.

'I never knew her maiden name; if I ever heard it, I've gone an' forgot; 'twould mean nothing to me,' answered Mrs Todd.

'She was a foreigner, an' he met with her out in the Island o' Jamaica. They said she'd been left a widow with property. Land knows what become of it; she was French born, an' her first husband was a Portugee, or somethin'.'

I kept silence now, a poor and insufficient question being worse than none.

'Cap'n John Tolland was the least smartest of any of 'em, but he was full smart enough, an' commanded a good brig at the time, in the sugar trade; he'd taken out a cargo o' pine lumber to the islands from somewheres up the river, an' had been loadin' for home in the port o' Kingston, an' had gone ashore that afternoon for his papers, an' remained afterwards 'long of three friends o' his, all shipmasters. They was havin' their suppers together in a tavern; 'twas late in the evenin' an' they was more lively than usual, an' felt boyish; and over opposite was another house full o' company, real bright and pleasant lookin', with a lot o' lights, an' they heard somebody singin' very pretty to a guitar. They wa'n't in no go-to-meetin' condition, an' one of 'em, he slapped the table an' said, "Le' 's go over an' hear that lady sing!" an' over they all went, good honest sailors, but three sheets in the wind,[2] and stepped in as if they was invited, an' made their bows inside the door, an' asked if they could hear the music; they were all respectable well-dressed men. They saw the woman that had the guitar, an' there was a company a-listenin', regular highbinders[3] all of 'em; an' there was a long table all spread out with big candlesticks like little trees o' light, and a sight o' glass an' silver ware; an' part o' the men was young officers in uniform, an' the colored folks was steppin' round servin' 'em an' they had the lady singin'. 'Twas a wasteful scene, an' a loud talkin' company, an' though they was three sheets in the wind themselves there wa'n't one o' them cap'ns but had sense to perceive it. The others had pushed back their chairs, an' their decanters an' glasses was standin' thick about, an' they was teasin' the one that was singin' as if they'd just got her in to amuse 'em. But they quieted down; one o' the young officers had beautiful manners, an' invited the four cap'ns to join 'em, very polite; 'twas a kind of pubic house, and after they'd all heard another song, he come to consult with 'em whether they wouldn't git up and dance a hornpipe or somethin' to the lady's music.

'They was all elderly men an' shipmasters, and owned property; two of 'em was church members in good standin',' continued Mrs Todd loftily, 'an' they wouldn't lend theirselves to no such kick-shows as that, an' spite o' bein' three sheets in the wind, as I have once observed; they waved aside the tumblers of wine the young officer was pourin' out for 'em so freehanded, and said they should rather be excused. An' when they all rose, still very dignified, as I've been well informed, and made their partin' bows and was goin' out, them young sports got round 'em an' tried to prevent 'em, and they had to push an' strive considerable, but out they come. There was this Cap'n Tolland and two Cap'n Bowdens, and the fourth was my own father.' (Mrs Todd spoke slowly, as if to impress the value of her authority.) 'Two of them was very religious, upright men, but they would have their night off sometimes, all o' them old-fashioned cap'ns, when they was free of business and ready to leave port.

'An' they went back to their tavern an' got their bills paid, an' set down kind o' mad with everybody by the front windows, mistrusting some o' their tavern charges, like's not, by that time, an' when they got tempered down, they watched the house over across, where the party was.

'There was a kind of grove o' trees between the house an' the road, an' they heard the guitar a-goin' an' a stoppin' short by turns, and pretty soon somebody began to screech, an' they saw a white dress come runnin' out through the bushes, an' tumbled over each other in their haste to offer help; an' out she come, with the guitar, cryin' into the street, and they just walked off four square with her amongst 'em, down toward the wharves where they felt more to home. They couldn't make out at first what 'twas she spoke, – Cap'n Lorenzo Bowden was well acquainted in Havre an' Bordeaux, an' spoke a poor quality o' French, an' she knew a little mite o' English, but not much; and they come somehow or other to discern that she was in real distress. Her husband and her children had died o' yellow fever; they'd all come up to Kingston from one o' the far Wind'ard Islands to get passage on a steamer to France, an' a negro had stole their money off her husband while he lay sick o' the fever, an' she had been befriended some, but the folks that knew about her had died too; it had been a dreadful run o' the fever that season, an' she fell at last to playin' an' singin' for hire, and for what money they'd throw to her round them harbor houses.

'' 'Twas a real hard case, an' when them cap'ns made out about it, there wa'n't one that meant to take leave without helpin' of her. They was pretty mellow, an' whatever they might lack o' prudence they more'n made up with charity: they didn't want to see nobody abused, an' she was sort of a pretty woman, an' they stopped in the street then an' there an' drew lots who should take her aboard, bein' all bound home. An' the lot fell to Cap'n Jonathan Bowden who did act discouraged; his vessel had but small accommodations, though he could stow a big freight, an' she was a dreadful slow sailer through bein' square as a box, an' his first wife, that was livin' then, was a dreadful jealous woman. He threw himself right onto the mercy o' Cap'n Tolland.'

Mrs Todd indulged herself for a short time in a session of calm reflection.

'I always thought they'd have done better, and more reasonable, to give her some money to pay her passage home to France, or wherever she may have wanted to go,' she continued.

I nodded and looked for the rest of the story.

'Father told mother,' said Mrs Todd confidently, 'that Cap'n Jonathan Bowden an' Cap'n John Tolland had both taken a little more than usual; I wouldn't have you think, either, that they both wasn't the best o' men, an' they was solemn as owls, and argued the matter between 'em, an' waved aside the other two when they tried to put their oars in. An' spite o' Cap'n Tolland's bein' a settled old bachelor they fixed it that he was to take the prize on his brig; she was a fast sailer, and there was a good spare cabin or two where he'd sometimes carried passengers, but he'd filled 'em with bags o' sugar on his own account an' was loaded very heavy beside. He said he'd shift the sugar an' get along somehow, an' the last the other three cap'ns saw of the party was Cap'n John handing the lady into his bo't, guitar and all, an' off they set tow'ds their ships with their men rowin' 'em in the bright moonlight down to Port Royal where the anchorage was, an' where they all lay, goin' out with the tide an' mornin' wind at break o' day. An' the others thought they heard music of the guitar, two o' the bo'ts kept well together, but it may have come from another source.'

'Well; and then?' I asked eagerly after a pause. Mrs Todd was almost laughing aloud over her knitting and nodding emphatically. We had forgotten about the noise of the wind and sea.

'Lord bless you! He comes sailing into Portland with his sugar, all in good time, an' they stepped right afore a justice o' the peace, and Cap'n John Tolland come paradin' home to Dunnet Landin' a married man. He owned one o' them thin, narrow-lookin' houses with one room each side o' the front door, and two slim black spruces spindlin' up against the front windows to make it gloomy inside. There was no horse nor cattle of course, though he owned pasture land, an' you could see rifts o' light right through the barn as you drove by. And there was a good excellent kitchen, but his sister reigned over that; she had a right to two rooms, and took the kitchen an' a bedroom that led out of it; an' bein' given no rights in the kitchen had angered the cap'n so they weren't on no kind o' speakin' terms. He preferred his old brig for comfort, but now and then, between voyages, he'd come home for a few days, just to show he was master over his part o' the house, and show Eliza she couldn't commit no trespass.

'They stayed a little while; 'twas pretty spring weather, an' I used to see Cap'n John rollin' by with his arms full o' bundles from the store, lookin' as pleased and important as a boy; an' then they went right off to sea again, an' was gone a good many months. Next time he left her to live there alone, after they'd stopped at home together some weeks, an' they said she suffered from bein' at sea, but some said that the owners wouldn't have a woman aboard. 'Twas before father was lost on that last voyage of his, an' he and mother went up once or twice to see them. Father said there wa'n't a mite o' harm in her, but somehow or other a sight o' prejudice arose; it may have been caused by the remarks of Eliza an' her feelin's tow'ds her brother. Even my mother had no regard for Eliza Tolland. But mother asked the cap'n's wife to come with her one evenin' to a social circle that was down to the meetin'-house vestry, so she'd get acquainted a little, an' she appeared very pretty until they started to have some singin' to the melodeon. Mari' Harris an' one o' the younger Caplin girls undertook to sing a duet, an' they sort o' flatted, an' she put her hands right up to her ears, and give a little squeal, an' went quick as could be an' give 'em the right notes, for she could read music like plain print, an' made 'em try it over again. She was real willin' an' pleasant, but that didn't suit, an' she made faces when they got it wrong. An' then there fell a dead calm, an' we was all settin' round prim as dishes, an' my mother that never expects ill feelin', asked her if she wouldn't sing somethin', an' up she got, – poor creatur', it all seems so different to me now, – an' sung a lovely little song standin' in the floor; it seemed to have something gay about it that kept a-repeatin', an' nobody could help keepin' time, an' all of a sudden she looked round at the tables and caught up a tin plate that somebody'd fetched a Washin'ton pie[4] in, an' she begun to drum it with her fingers like one o' them tambourines, an' went right on singin' faster an' faster, and next minute she begun to dance a little pretty dance between the verses, just as light and pleasant as a child. You couldn't help seein' how pretty 'twas; we all got to trottin' a foot, an' some o' the men clapped their hands quite loud, a-keepin' time, 'twas so catchin', an' seemed so natural to her. There wa'n't one of 'em but enjoyed it; she just tried to do her part, an' some urged her on, till she stopped with a little twirl of her skirts an' went to her place again by mother. And I can see mother now, reachin' over an' smilin' an' pattin' her hand.

'But next day there was an awful scandal goin' in the parish, an' Mari' Harris reproached my mother to her face, an' I never wanted to see her since, but I've had to a good many times. I said Mis' Tolland didn't intend no impropriety, – I reminded her of David's dancin' before the Lord;[5] but she said such a man as David never would have thought o' dancin' right there in the Orthodox vestry, and she felt I spoke with irreverence.

'And next Sunday Mis' Tolland come walkin' into our meeting, but I must say she acted like a cat in a strange garret, and went right out down the aisle with her head in air, from the pew Deacon Caplin had showed her into. 'Twas just in the beginning of the long prayer. I wish she'd stayed through, whatever her reasons were. Whether she'd expected somethin' different, or misunderstood some o' the pastor's remarks, or what 'twas, I don't really feel able to explain, but she kind o' declared war, at least folks thought so, an' war 'twas from that time. I see she was cryin', or had been, as she passed me by; perhaps bein' in meetin' was what had power to make her feel homesick and strange.

'Cap'n John Tolland was away fittin' out; that next week he come home to see her and say farewell. He was lost with his ship in the Straits of Malacca, and she lived there alone in the old house a few months longer till she died. He left her well off; 'twas said he hid his money about the house and she knew where 'twas. Oh, I expect you've heard that story told over an' over twenty times, since you've been here at the Landin'?'

'Never one word,' I insisted.

'It was a good while ago,' explained Mrs Todd, with reassurance. 'Yes, it all happened a great while ago.'

III

At this moment, with a sudden flaw of the wind, some wet twigs outside blew against the window panes and made a noise like a distressed creature trying to get in. I started with sudden fear, and so did the cat, but Mrs Todd knitted away and did not even look over her shoulder.

'She was a good-looking woman; yes, I always thought Mis' Tolland was good-looking, though she had, as was reasonable, a sort of foreign cast, and she spoke very broken English, no better than a child. She was always at work about her house, or settin' at a front window with her sewing; she was a beautiful hand to embroider. Sometimes, summer evenings, when the windows was open, she'd set an' drum on her guitar, but I don't know as I ever heard her sing but once after the cap'n went away. She appeared very happy about havin' him, and took on dreadful at partin' when he was down here on the wharf, going back to Portland by boat to take ship for that last v'y'ge. He acted kind of ashamed, Cap'n John did; folks about here ain't so much accustomed to show their feelings. The whistle had blown an' they was waitin' for him to get aboard, an' he was put to it to know what to do and treated her very affectionate in spite of all impatience; but mother happened to be there and she went an' spoke, and I remember what a comfort she seemed to be. Mis' Tolland clung to her then, and she wouldn't give a glance after the boat when it had started, though the captain was very eager a-wavin' to her. She wanted mother to come home, and mother had just come in to stop all night with me an' had plenty o' time ashore, which didn't always happen, so they walked off together, an' 'twas some considerable time before she got back.

'"I want you to neighbor with that poor lonesome creatur'," says mother to me, lookin' reproachful. "She's a stranger in a strange land,"[6] says mother. "I want you to make her have a sense that somebody feels kind to her."

'"Why, since that time she flaunted out o' meetin', folks have felt she liked other ways better'n our'n," says I. I was provoked, because I'd had a nice supper ready, and mother'd let it wait so long 'twas spoiled. "I hope you'll like your supper!" I told her. I was dreadful ashamed afterward of speakin' so to mother.

'"What consequence is my supper?" says she to me; mother can be very stern, – "or your comfort or mine, beside letting a foreign person an' stranger feel so desolate; she's done the best a woman could do in her lonesome place, and she asks nothing of anybody except a little common kindness. Think if 'twas you in a foreign land!"

'And mother set down to drink her tea, an' I set down humbled enough over by the wall to wait till she finished. An' I did think it all over, an' next day I never said nothin', but I put on my bonnet, and went to see Mis' Cap'n Tolland, if 'twas only for mother's sake. 'Twas about three quarters of a mile up the road here, beyond the schoolhouse. I forgot to tell you that the cap'n had bought out his sister's right at three or four times what 'twas worth, to save trouble, so they'd got clear o' her, an' I went round into the side yard sort o' friendly an' sociable, rather than stop an' deal with the knocker an' the front door. It looked so pleasant an' pretty I was glad I come; she had set a little table for supper, though 'twas still early, with a white cloth on it, right out under an old apple tree close by the house. I noticed 'twas same as with me at home, there was only one plate. She was just coming out with a dish; you couldn't see the door nor the table from the road.

'In the few weeks she'd been there she'd got some bloomin' pinks an' other flowers next the doorstep. Somehow it looked as if she'd known how to make it homelike for the cap'n. She asked me to set down; she was very polite, but she looked very mournful, and I spoke of mother, an' she put down her dish and caught holt o' me with both hands an' said my mother was an angel. When I see the tears in her eyes 'twas all right between us, and we were always friendly after that, and mother had us come out and make a little visit that summer; but she come a foreigner and she went a foreigner, and never was anything but a stranger among our folks. She taught me a sight o' things about herbs I never knew before nor since; she was well acquainted with the virtues o' plants. She'd act awful secret about some things too, an' used to work charms for herself sometimes, an' some o' the neighbors told to an' fro after she died that they knew enough not to provoke her, but 'twas all nonsense; 'tis the believin' in such things that causes 'em to be any harm, an' so I told 'em,' confided Mrs Todd contemptuously. 'That first night I stopped to tea with her, she'd cooked some eggs with some herb or other sprinkled all through, and 'twas she that first led me to discern mushrooms; an' she went right down on her knees in my garden here when she saw I had my different officious herbs.[7] Yes, 'twas she that learned me the proper use o' parsley too; she was a beautiful cook.'

Mrs Todd stopped talking, and rose, putting the cat gently in the chair, while she went away to get another stick of apple-tree wood. It was not an evening when one wished to let the fire go down, and we had a splendid bank of bright coals. I had always wondered where Mrs Todd had got such an unusual knowledge of cookery, of the varieties of mushrooms, and the use of sorrel as a vegetable, and other blessings of that sort. I had long ago learned that she could vary her omelettes like a child of France, which was indeed a surprise in Dunnet Landing.

IV

All these revelations were of the deepest interest, and I was ready with a question as soon as Mrs Todd came in and had well settled the fire and herself and the cat again.

'I wonder why she never went back to France, after she was left alone?'

'She come here from the French islands,' explained Mrs Todd. 'I asked her once about her folks, an' she said they were all dead; 'twas the fever took 'em. She made this her home, lonesome as 'twas; she told me she hadn't been in France since she was "so small," and measured me off a child o' six. She'd lived right out in the country before, so that part wa'n't unusual to her. Oh yes, there was something very strange about her, and she hadn't been brought up in high circles nor nothing o' that kind. I think she'd been really pleased to have the cap'n marry her an' give her a good home, after all she'd passed through, and leave her free with his money an' all that. An' she got over bein' so strange-looking to me after a while, but 'twas a very singular expression: she wore a fixed smile that wa'n't a smile; there wa'n't no light behind it, same's a lamp can't shine if it ain't lit. I don't know just how to express it, 'twas a sort of made countenance.'

One could not help thinking of Sir Philip Sidney's phrase, 'A made countenance, between simpering and smiling.'[8]

'She took it hard, havin' the captain go off on that last voyage,' Mrs Todd went on. 'She said somethin' told her when they was partin' that he would never come back. He was lucky to speak a home-bound ship this side o' the Cape o' Good Hope, an' got a chance to send her a letter, an' that cheered her up. You often felt as if you was dealin' with a child's mind, for all she had so much information that other folks hadn't. I was a sight younger than I be now, and she made me imagine new things, and I got interested watchin' her an' findin' out what she had to say, but you couldn't get to no affectionateness with her. I used to blame me sometimes; we used to be real good comrades goin' off for an afternoon, but I never give her a kiss till the day she laid in her coffin and it come to my heart there wa'n't no one else to do it.'

'And Captain Tolland died,' I suggested after a while.

'Yes, the cap'n was lost,' said Mrs Todd, 'and of course word didn't come for a good while after it happened. The letter come from the owners to my uncle, Cap'n Lorenzo Bowden, who was in charge of Cap'n Tolland's affairs at home, and he come right up for me an' said I must go with him to the house. I had known what it was to be a widow, myself, for near a year, an' there was plenty o' widow women along this coast that the sea had made desolate, but I never saw a heart broke as I did then.

''Twas this way: we walked together along the road, me an' uncle Lorenzo. You know how it leads straight from just above the schoolhouse to the brook bridge, and their house was just this side o' the brook bridge on the left hand; the cellar's there now and a couple or three good-sized gray birches growin' in it. And when we come near enough I saw that the best room, this way, where she most never set, was all lighted up, and the curtains up so that the light shone bright down the road, and as we walked those lights would dazzle and dazzle in my eyes, and I could hear the guitar a goin', an' she was singin'. She heard our steps with her quick ears and come running to the door with her eyes a-shinin', an' all that set look gone out of her face, an' begun to talk French, gay as a bird, an' shook hands and behaved very pretty an' girlish, sayin' 'twas her fête day.⁹ I didn't know what she meant then. And she had gone an' put a wreath o' flowers on her hair an' wore a handsome gold chain that the cap'n had given her; an' there she was, poor creatur', makin' believe have a party all alone in her best room; 'twas prim enough to discourage a person, with too many chairs set close to the walls, just as the cap'n's mother had left it, but she had put sort o' long garlands on the walls, droopin' very graceful, and a sight of green boughs in the corners, till it looked lovely, and all lit up with a lot o' candles.'

'Oh dear!' I sighed. 'Oh, Mrs Todd, what did you do?'

'She beheld our countenances,' answered Mrs Todd solemnly. 'I expect they was telling everything plain enough, but Cap'n Lorenzo spoke the sad words to her as if he had been her father; and she wavered a minute and then over she went on the floor before we could catch hold of her, and then we tried to bring her to herself and failed, and at last we carried her upstairs, an' I told uncle to run down and put out the lights, and then go fast as he could for Mrs Begg, being very experienced in sickness, an' he so did. I got off her clothes and her poor wreath, and I cried as I done it. We both stayed there that night, and the doctor said 'twas a shock when he come in the morning; he'd been over to Black Island an' had to stay all night with a very sick child.'

'You said that she lived alone some time after the news came,' I reminded Mrs Todd then.

'Oh yes, dear,' answered my friend sadly, 'but it wa'n't what you'd call livin'; no, it was only dyin', though at a snail's pace. She never went out again those few months, but for a while she could manage to get about the house a little, and do what was needed, an' I never let two days go by without seein' her or hearin' from her. She never took much notice as I came an' went except to answer if I asked her anything. Mother was the one who gave her the only comfort.'

'What was that?' I asked softly.

'She said that anybody in such trouble ought to see their minister, mother did, and one day she spoke to Mis' Tolland, and found that the poor soul had been believin' all the time that there weren't any priests here. We'd come to know she was a Catholic by her beads and all, and that had set some narrow minds against her. And mother explained it just as she would to a child; and uncle Lorenzo sent word right off somewheres up river by a packet that was bound up the bay, and the first o' the week a priest come by the boat, an' uncle Lorenzo was on the wharf 'tendin' to some business; so they just come up for me, and I walked with him to show him the house. He was a kindhearted old man; he looked so benevolent an' fatherly I could ha' stopped an' told him my own trouble; yes, I was satisfied when I first saw his face, an' when poor Mis' Tolland beheld him enter the room, she went right down on her knees and clasped her hands together to him as if he'd come to save her life, and he lifted her up and blessed her, an' I left 'em together, and slipped out into the open field and walked there in sight so if they needed to call me, and I had my own thoughts. At last I saw him at the door; he had to catch the return boat. I meant to walk back with him and offer him some supper, but he said no, and said he was comin' again if needed, and signed me to go into the house to her, and shook his head in a way that meant he understood everything. I can see him now; he walked with a cane, rather tired and feeble; I wished somebody would come along, so's to carry him down the shore.

'Mis' Tolland looked up at me with a new look when I went in, an' she even took hold o' my hand and kept it. He had put some oil on her forehead, but nothing anybody could do would keep her alive very long; 'twas his medicine for the soul rather'n the body. I helped her to bed, and next morning she couldn't get up to dress her, and that was Monday, and she began to fail, and 'twas Friday night she died.' (Mrs Todd spoke with unusual haste and lack of detail.) 'Mrs Begg and I watched with her, and made everything nice and proper, and after all the ill will there was a good number gathered to the funeral. 'Twas in Reverend Mr Bascom's day, and he done very well in his prayer, considering he couldn't fill in with mentioning all the near connections by name as was his habit. He spoke very feeling about her being a stranger and twice widowed, and all he said about her being reared among the heathen was to observe that there might be roads leadin' up to the New Jerusalem from various points. I says to myself that I guessed quite a number must ha' reached there that wa'n't able to set out from Dunnet Landin'!'

Mrs Todd gave an odd little laugh as she bent toward the firelight to pick up a dropped stitch in her knitting, and then I heard a heartfelt sigh.

' 'Twas most forty years ago,' she said; 'most everybody's gone a'ready that was there that day.'

V

Suddenly Mrs Todd gave an energetic shrug of her shoulders, and a quick look at me, and I saw that the sails of her narrative were filled with a fresh breeze.

'Uncle Lorenzo, Cap'n Bowden that I have referred to' –

'Certainly!' I agreed with eager expectation.

'He was the one that had been left in charge of Cap'n John Tolland's affairs, and had now come to be of unforeseen importance.

'Mrs Begg an' I had stayed in the house both before an' after Mis' Tolland's decease, and she was now in haste to be gone, having affairs to call her home; but uncle come to me as the exercises was beginning, and said he thought I'd better remain at the house while they went to the buryin' ground. I couldn't understand his reasons, an' I felt disappointed, bein' as near to her as most anybody; 'twas rough weather, so mother couldn't get in, and didn't even hear Mis' Tolland was gone till next day. I just nodded to satisfy him, 'twa'n't no time to discuss anything. Uncle seemed flustered; he'd gone out deep-sea fishin' the day she died, and the storm I told you of rose very sudden, so they got blown off way down the coast beyond Monhegan, and he'd just got back in time to dress himself and come.

'I set there in the house after I'd watched her away down the straight road far's I could see from the door; 'twas a little short walkin' funeral an' a cloudy sky, so everything looked dull an' gray, an' it crawled along all in one piece, same's walking funerals do, an' I wondered how it ever come to the Lord's mind to let her begin down among them gay islands all heat and sun, and end up here among the rocks with a north wind blowin'. 'Twas a gale that begun the afternoon before she died, and had kept blowin' off an' on ever since. I'd thought more than once how glad I should be to get home an' out o' sound o' them black spruces a-beatin' an' a scratchin' at the front windows.

'I set to work pretty soon to put the chairs back, an' set outdoors some that was borrowed, an' I went out in the kitchen, an' I made up a good fire in case somebody come an' wanted a cup o' tea; but I didn't expect any one to travel way back to the house unless 'twas uncle Lorenzo. 'Twas growin' so chilly that I fetched some kindlin' wood and made fires in both the fore rooms. Then I set down an' begun to feel as usual, and I got my knittin' out of a drawer. You can't be sorry for a poor creatur' that's come to the end o' all her troubles; my only discomfort was I thought I'd ought to feel worse at losin' her than I did; I was younger then than I be now. And as I set there, I begun to hear some long notes o' dronin' music from upstairs that chilled me to the bone.'

Mrs Todd gave a hasty glance at me.

'Quick's I could gather me, I went right upstairs to see what 'twas,' she added eagerly, 'an' 'twas just what I might ha' known. She'd always kept her guitar hangin' right against the wall in her room; 'twas tied by a blue ribbon, and there was a window left wide open; the wind was veerin' a good deal, an' it slanted in and searched the room. The strings was jarrin' yet.

' 'Twas growin' pretty late in the afternoon, an' I begun to feel lonesome as I shouldn't now, and I was disappointed at having to stay there, the more I thought it over, but after a while I saw Cap'n Lorenzo polin' back up the road all alone, and when he come nearer I could see he had a bundle under his arm and had shifted his best black clothes for his everyday ones. I run out and put some tea into the teapot and set it back on the stove to draw, an' when he come in I reached down a little jug o' spirits, – Cap'n Tolland had left his house well provisioned as if his wife was goin' to put to sea same's himself, an' there she'd gone an' left it. There was some cake that Mis' Begg an' I had made the day before. I thought that uncle an' me had a good right to the funeral supper, even if there wa'n't anyone to join us. I was lookin' forward to my cup o' tea; 'twas beautiful tea out of a green lacquered chest that I've got now.'

'You must have felt very tired,' said I, eagerly listening.

'I was 'most beat out, with watchin' an' tendin' and all,' answered Mrs Todd, with as much sympathy in her voice as if she were speaking of another person. 'But I called out to uncle as he came in, "Well, I expect it's all over now, an' we've all done what we could. I thought we'd better have some tea or somethin' before we go home. Come right out in the kitchen, sir," says I, never thinking but we only had to let the fires out and lock up everything safe an' eat our refreshment, an' go home.

'"I want both of us to stop here tonight," says uncle, looking at me very important.

'"Oh, what for?" says I, kind o' fretful.

'"I've got my proper reasons," says uncle. "I'll see you well satisfied, Almira. Your tongue ain't so easy-goin' as some o' the women folks, an' there's property here to take charge of that you don't know nothin' about."

'"What do you mean?" says I.

'"Cap'n Tolland acquainted me with his affairs; he hadn't no sort o' confidence in nobody but me an' his wife, after he was tricked into signin' that Portland note,[10] an' lost money. An' she didn't know nothin' about business; but what he didn't take to sea to be sunk with him he's hid somewhere in this house. I expect Mis' Tolland may have told you where she kept things?" said uncle.

'I see he was dependin' a good deal on my answer,' said Mrs Todd, 'but I had to disappoint him; no, she had never said nothin' to me.

'"Well, then, we've got to make a search," says he, with considerable relish; but he was all tired and worked up, and we set down to the table, an' he had somethin', an' I took my desired cup o' tea, and then I begun to feel more interested.

'"Where you goin' to look first?" says I, but he give me a short look an' made no answer, and begun to mix me very small portion out of the jug, in another glass. I took it to please him; he said I looked tired, speakin' real fatherly, and I did feel better for it, and we set talkin' a few minutes, an' then he started for the cellar, carrying an old ship's lantern he fetched out o' the stairway an' lit.

'"What are you lookin' for, some kind of a chist?" I inquired, and he said yes. All of a sudden it come to me to ask who was the heirs; Eliza Tolland, Cap'n John's own sister, had never demeaned herself to come near the funeral, and uncle Lorenzo faced right about and begun to laugh, sort o' pleased. I thought queer of it; 'twa'n't what he'd taken, which would be nothin' to an old weathered sailor like him.

' "Who's the heir?" says I the second time.

' "Why, it's *you*, Almiry," says he; and I was so took aback I set right down on the turn o' the cellar stairs.

' "Yes 'tis," said uncle Lorenzo. "I'm glad of it too. Some thought she didn't have no sense but foreign sense, an' a poor stock o' that, but she said you was friendly to her, an' one day after she got news of Tolland's death, an' I had fetched up his will that left everything to her, she said she was goin' to make a writin', so's you could have things after she was gone, an' she give five hundred to me for bein' executor. Square Pease fixed up the paper, an' she signed it; it's all accordin' to the law." There, I begun to cry,' said Mrs Todd; 'I couldn't help it. I wished I had her back again to do somethin' for, an' to make her know I felt sisterly to her more'n I'd ever showed, an' it come over me 'twas all too late, an' I cried the more, till uncle showed impatience, an' I got up an' stumbled along down cellar with my apern to my eyes the greater part of the time.

' "I'm goin' to have a clean search," says he; "you hold the light." An' I held it, and he rummaged in the arches an' under the stairs, an' over in some old closet where he reached out bottles an' stone jugs an' canted some kags an' one or two casks, an' chuckled well when he heard there was somethin' inside, – but there wa'n't nothin' to find but things usual in a cellar, an' then the old lantern was givin' out an' we come away.

' "He spoke to me of a chist, Cap'n Tolland did," says uncle in a whisper. "He said a good sound chist was as safe a bank there was, an' I beat him out of such nonsense, 'count o' fire an' other risks." "There's no chist in the rooms above," says I; "no, uncle, there ain't no sea-chist, for I've been here long enough to see what there was to be seen." Yet he wouldn't feel contented till he'd mounted up into the toploft; 'twas one o' them single, hip-roofed[11] houses that don't give proper accommodation for a real garret, like Cap'n Littlepage's down here at the Landin'. There was broken furniture and rubbish, an' he let down a terrible sight o' dust into the front entry, but sure enough there wasn't no chist. I had it all to sweep up next day.

' "He must have took it away to sea," says I to the cap'n, an' even then he didn't want to agree, but we was both beat out. I told him where I'd always seen Mis' Tolland get her money from and we found much as a hundred dollars there in an old red morocco wallet. Cap'n John had been gone a good while a'ready, and she had spent what she needed. 'Twas in an old desk o' his in the settin' room that we found the wallet.'

'At the last minute he may have taken his money to sea,' I suggested.

'Oh yes,' agreed Mrs Todd. 'He did take considerable to make his venture to bring home, as was customary, an' that was drowned with him as uncle agreed; but he had other property in shipping, and a thousand dollars invested in Portland in a cordage shop, but 'twas about the time shipping begun to decay, and the cordage shop failed, and in the end I wa'n't so rich as I thought I was goin' to be for those few minutes on the cellar stairs. There was an auction that accumulated something. Old Mis' Tolland, the cap'n's mother, had heired some good furniture from a sister: there was above thirty chairs in all, and they're apt to sell well. I got over a thousand dollars when we come to settle up, and I made uncle take his five hundred; he was getting along in years and had met with losses in navigation, and he left it back to me when he died, so I had a real good lift. It all lays in the bank over to Rockland, and I draw my interest fall an' spring, with the little Mr Todd was able to leave me; but that's kind o' sacred money; 'twas earnt and saved with the hope o' youth, an' I'm very particular what I spend it for. Oh yes, what with ownin' my house, I've been enabled to get along very well, with prudence!' said Mrs Todd contentedly.

'But there was the house and land,' I asked, – 'What became of that part of the property?'

Mrs Todd looked into the fire, and a shadow of disapproval flitted over her face.

'Poor old uncle!' she said, 'he got childish about the matter. I was hoping to sell at first, and I had an offer, but he always run an idea that there was more money hid away, and kept wanting me to delay; an' he used to go up there all alone and search, and dig in the cellar, empty an' bleak as 'twas in winter weather or any time. An' he'd come and tell me he'd dreamed he found gold behind a stone in the cellar wall, or somethin'. And one night we all see the light o' fire up that way, an' the whole Landin' took the road, and run to look, and the Tolland property was all in a light blaze. I expect the old gentleman had dropped fire about; he said he'd been up there to see if everything was safe in the afternoon. As for the land, 'twas so poor that everybody used to have a joke that the Tolland boys preferred to farm the sea instead. It's 'most all grown up to bushes now, where it ain't poor water grass in the low places. There's some upland that has a pretty view, after you cross the brook bridge. Years an' years after she died, there was some o' her flowers used to come up an' bloom in the door garden. I brought two or three that was unusual down here; they always come up and remind me of her, constant as the spring. But I never did want to fetch home that guitar, some way or 'nother; I wouldn't let it go at the auction, either. It was hangin' right there in the house when the fire took place. I've got some o' her other little things scattered about the house: that picture on the mantelpiece belonged to her.'

I had often wondered where such a picture had come from, and why Mrs Todd had chosen it; it was a French print of the statue of the Empress Josephine[12] in the Savane at old Fort Royal , Martinique.

VI

Mrs Todd drew her chair closer to mine; she held the cat and her knitting with one hand as she moved, but the cat was so warm and so sound asleep that she only stretched a lazy paw in spite of what must have felt like a slight earthquake. Mrs Todd began to speak almost in a whisper.

'I ain't told you all,' she continued; 'no, I haven't spoken of all to but very few. The way it came was this,' she said solemnly, and then stopped to listen to the wind, and sat for a moment in deferential silence, as if she waited for the wind to speak first. The cat suddenly lifted her head with quick excitement and gleaming eyes, and her mistress was leaning forward toward the fire with an arm laid on either knee, as if they were consulting the glowing coals for some augury. Mrs Todd looked like an old prophetess as she sat there with the firelight shining on her strong face; she was posed for some great painter. The woman with the cat was as unconscious and as mysterious as any sibyl of the Sistine Chapel.[13]

'There, that's the last struggle o' the gale,' said Mrs Todd, nodding her head with impressive certainty and still looking into the bright embers of the fire. 'You'll see!' She gave me another quick glance, and spoke in a low tone as if we might be overheard.

' 'Twas such a gale as this the night Mis' Tolland died. She appeared more comfortable the first o' the evenin'; and Mrs Begg was more spent than I, bein' older, and a beautiful nurse that was the first to see and think of everything, but perfectly quiet an' never asked a useless question. You remember her funeral when you first come to the Landing? And she consented to goin' an' havin' a good sleep while she could, and left me one o' those good little pewter lamps that burnt whale oil an' made plenty o' light in the room, but not too bright to be disturbin'.

'Poor Mis' Tolland had been distressed the night before, an' all that day, but as night come on she grew more and more easy, an' was layin' there asleep; 'twas like settin' by any sleepin' person, and I had none but usual thoughts. When the wind lulled and the rain, I could hear the seas, though more distant than this, and I don' know's I observed any other sound than what the weather made; 'twas a very solemn feelin' night. I set close by the bed; there was times she looked to find somebody when she was awake. The light was on her face, so I could see her plain; there was always times when she wore a look that made her seem a stranger you'd never set eyes on before. I did think what a world it was that her an' me should have come together so, and she have nobody but Dunnet Landin' folks about her in her extremity. "You're one o' the stray ones, poor creatur'," I said. I remember those very words passin' through my mind, but I saw reason to be glad she had some comforts, and didn't lack friends at the last, though she'd seen misery an' pain. I was glad she was quiet; all day she'd been restless, and we couldn't understand what she wanted from her French speech. We had the window open to give her air, an' now an' then a gust would strike that guitar that was on the wall and set it swinging by the blue ribbon, and soundin' as if somebody begun to play it. I come near takin' it down, but you never know what'll fret a sick person an' put 'em on the rack, an' that guitar was one o' the few things she'd brought with her.'

I nodded assent, and Mrs Todd spoke still lower.

'I set there close by the bed; I'd been through a good deal for some days back, and I thought I might's well be droppin' asleep too, bein' a quick person to wake. She looked to me as if she might last a day longer, certain, now she'd got more comfortable, but I was real tired, an' sort o' cramped as watchers will get, an' a fretful feeling begun to creep over me such as they often do have. If you give way, there ain't no support for the sick person; they can't count on no composure o' their own. Mis' Tolland moved then, a little restless, an' I forgot me quick enough, an' begun to hum out a little part of a hymn tune just to make her feel everything was as usual an' not wake up into a poor uncertainty. All of a sudden she set right up in bed with her eyes wide open, an' I stood an' put my arm behind her; she hadn't moved like that for days. And she reached out both her arms toward the door, an' I looked the way she was lookin', an' I see some one was standin' there against the dark. No, 'twa'n't Mis' Begg; 'twas somebody a good deal shorter than Mis' Begg. The lamplight struck across the room between us. I couldn't tell the shape, but 'twas a woman's dark face lookin' right as us; 'twa'n't but an instant I could see. I felt dreadful cold, and my head began to swim; I thought the light went out; 'twa'n't but an instant, as I say, an' when my sight come back I couldn't see nothing there. I was one that didn't know what it was to faint away, no matter what happened; time was I felt above it in others, but 'twas somethin' that made poor human natur' quail. I saw very plain while I could see: 'twas a pleasant enough face, shaped somethin' like Mis' Tolland's, and a kind of expectin' look.

'No, I don't expect I was asleep.' Mrs Todd assured me quietly, after a moment's pause, though I had not spoken. She gave a heavy sigh before she went on. I could see that the recollection moved her in the deepest way.

'I suppose if I hadn't been so spent an' quavery with long watchin', I might have kept my head an' observed much better,' she added humbly; 'but I see all I could bear. I did try to act calm, an' I laid Mis' Tolland down on her pillow, an' I was a-shakin' as I done it. All she did was to look up to me so satisfied and sort o' questioning, an' I looked back to her.

'"You saw her, didn't you?" she says to me, speakin' perfectly reasonable. "'Tis my mother," she says again, very feeble, but lookin' straight up at me, kind of surprised with the pleasure, and smiling as if she saw I was overcome, an' would have said more if she could, but we had hold of hands. I see then her change was comin', but I didn't call Mis' Begg, nor make no uproar. I felt calm then, an' lifted to somethin' different as I never was since. She opened her eyes just as she was goin' –

'"You saw her, didn't you?" she said the second time, an' I says, "Yes, dear, I did; you ain't never goin' to feel strange an' lonesome no more." An' then in a few minutes 'twas all over. I felt they'd gone away together. No, I wa'n't alarmed afterward; 'twas just that one moment I couldn't live under, but I never called it beyond reason I should see the other watcher. I saw plain enough there was somebody there with me in the room.

VII

''Twas just such a night as this Mis' Tolland died,' repeated Mrs Todd, returning to her usual tone and leaning back comfortably in her chair as she took up her knitting. ''Twas just such a night as this. I've told the circumstances to but very few; but I don't call it beyond reason. When folks is goin' 'tis all natural, and only common things can jar upon the mind. You know plain enough there's somethin' beyond this world; the doors stand wide open. "There's somethin' of us that must still live on; we've got to join both worlds together an' live in one but for the other." The doctor said that to me one day, an' I never could forget it; he said 'twas in one o' his old doctor's books.'

We sat together in silence in the warm little room; the rain dropped heavily from the eaves, and the sea still roared, but the high wind had done blowing. We heard the far complaining fog horn of a steamer up the Bay.

'There goes the Boston boat out, pretty near on time,' said Mrs Todd with satisfaction. 'Sometimes these late August storms'll sound a good deal worse than they really be. I do hate to hear the poor steamers callin' when they're bewildered in thick nights in winter, comin' on the coast. Yes, there goes the boat; they'll find it rough at sea, but the storm's all over.'

WILLIAM'S WEDDING

I

The hurry of life in a large town, the constant putting aside of preference to yield to a most unsatisfactory activity, began to vex me, and one day I took the train, and only left it for the eastward-bound boat. Carlyle says somewhere that the only happiness a man ought to ask for is happiness enough to get his work done;[1] and against this the complexity and futile ingenuity of social life seems a conspiracy. But the first salt wind from the east, the first sight of a lighthouse set boldly on its outer rock, the flash of a gull, the waiting procession of seaward-bound firs on an island, made me feel solid and definite again, instead of a poor, incoherent being. Life was resumed, and anxious living blew away as if it had not been. I could not breathe deep enough or long enough. It was a return to happiness.

The coast had still a wintry look; it was far on in May, but all the shore looked cold and sterile. One was conscious of going north as well as east, and as the day went on the sea grew colder, and all the warmer air and bracing strength and stimulus of the autumn weather, and storage of the heat of summer, were quite gone. I was very cold and very tired when I came at evening up the lower bay, and saw the white houses of Dunnet Landing climbing the hill. They had a friendly look, these little houses, not as if they were climbing up the shore, but as if they were rather all coming down to meet a fond and weary traveler, and I could hardly wait with patience to step off the boat. It was not the usual eager company on the wharf. The coming-in of the mailboat was the one large public event of a summer day, and I was disappointed at seeing none of my intimate friends but Johnny Bowden, who had evidently done nothing all winter but grow, so that his short sea-smitten clothes gave him a look of poverty.

Johnny's expression did not change as we greeted each other, but I suddenly felt that I had shown indifference and inconvenient delay by not coming sooner; before I could make an apology he took my small portmanteau, and walking before me in his old fashion he made straight up the hilly road toward Mrs Todd's. Yes, he was much grown – it had never occurred to me the summer before that Johnny was likely, with the help of time and other forces, to grow into a young man; he was such a well-framed and well-settled chunk of a boy that nature seemed to have set him aside as something finished, quite satisfactory, and entirely completed.

The wonderful little green garden had been enchanted away by winter. There were a few frost-bitten twigs and some thin shrubbery against the fence, but it was a most unpromising small piece of ground. My heart was beating like a lover's as I passed it on the way to the door of Mrs Todd's house, which seemed to have become much smaller under the influence of winter weather.

'She hasn't gone away?' I asked Johnny Bowden with a sudden anxiety just as we reached the doorstep.

'Gone away!' he faced me with blank astonishment, – 'I see her settin' by Mis' Caplin's window, the one nighest the road, about four o'clock!' And eager with suppressed news of my coming he made his entrance as if the house were a burrow.

Then on my homesick heart fell the voice of Mrs Todd. She stopped, through what I knew to be excess of feeling, to rebuke Johnny for bringing in so much mud, and I dallied without for one moment during the ceremony; then we met again face to face.

II

'I dare say you can advise me what shapes they are goin' to wear. My meetin'-bunnit ain't goin' to do me again this year; no! I can't expect 'twould do me forever,' said Mrs Todd, as soon as she could say anything. 'There! do set down and tell me how you have been! We've got a weddin' in the family, I s'pose you know?'

'A wedding!' said I, still full of excitement.

'Yes; I expect if the tide serves and the line storm don't overtake him they'll come in and appear out on Sunday. I shouldn't have concerned me about the bunnit for a month yet, nobody would notice, but havin' an occasion like this I shall show consider'ble. 'Twill be an ordeal for William!'

'For *William!*' I exclaimed. 'What do you mean, Mrs Todd?'

She gave a comfortable little laugh. 'Well, the Lord's seen reason at last an' removed Mis' Cap'n Hight up to the farm, an' I don't know but the weddin's goin' to be this week. Esther's had a great deal of business disposin' of her flock, but she's done extra well – the folks that owns the next place goin' up country are well off. 'Tis elegant land north side o' that bleak ridge, an' one o' the boys has been Esther's right-hand man of late. She instructed him in all matters, and after she markets the early lambs he's goin' to take the farm on halves, an' she's give the refusal to him to buy her out within two years. She's reserved the buryin'-lot, an' the right o' way in, an' –'

I couldn't stop for detail. I demanded reassurance of the central fact.

'William going to be married?' I repeated; whereat Mrs Todd gave me a searching look that was not without scorn.

'Old Mis' Hight's funeral was a week ago Wednesday, and 'twas very well attended,' she assured me after a moment's pause.

'Poor thing!' said I, with a sudden vision of her helpless and angry battle against the fate of illness; 'it was very hard for her.'

'I thought it was hard for Esther!' said Mrs Todd without sentiment.

III

I had an odd feeling of strangeness: I missed the garden, and the little rooms, to which I had added a few things of my own the summer before, seemed oddly unfamiliar. It was like the hermit crab in a cold new shell, – and with the windows shut against the raw May air, and a strange silence and grayness of the sea all that first night and day of my visit, I felt as if I had after all lost my hold of that quiet life.

Mrs Todd made the apt suggestion that city persons were prone to run themselves to death, and advised me to stay and get properly rested now that I had taken the trouble to come. She did not know how long I had been home-sick for the conditions of life at the Landing the autumn before – it was natural enough to feel a little unsupported by compelling incidents on my return.

Some one has said that one never leaves a place, or arrives at one, until the next day! But on the second morning I woke with the familiar feeling of interest and ease, and the bright May sun was streaming in, while I could hear Mrs Todd's heavy footsteps pounding about in the other part of the house as if something were going to happen. There was the first golden robin singing somewhere close to the house, and a lovely aspect of spring now, and I looked at the garden to see that in the warm night some of its treasures had grown a hand's breadth; the determined spikes of yellow daffies stood tall against the doorsteps, and the bloodroot was unfolding leaf and flower. The belated spring which I had left behind farther south had overtaken me on this northern coast. I even saw a presumptuous dandelion in the garden border.

It is difficult to report the great events of New England; expression is so slight, and those few words which escape us in moments of deep feeling look but meagre on the printed page. One has to assume too much of the dramatic fervor as one reads; but as I came out of my room at breakfast-time I met Mrs Todd face to face, and when she said to me, 'This weather'll bring William in after her; 'tis their happy day!' I felt something take possession of me which ought to communicate itself to the least sympathetic reader of this cold page. It is written for those who have a Dunnet Landing of their own: who either kindly share this with the writer, or possess another.

'I ain't seen his comin' sail yet; he'll be likely to dodge round among the islands so he'll be the less observed,' continued Mrs Todd. 'You can get a dory up the bay, even a clean new painted one, if you know as how, keepin' it against the high land.' She stepped to the door and looked off to sea as she spoke. I could see her eye follow the gray shores to and fro, and then a bright light spread over her calm face. 'There he comes, and he's strikin' right across the open bay like a man!' she said with splendid approval. 'See, there he comes! Yes, there's William, and he's bent his new sail.'[2]

I looked too, and saw the fleck of white no larger than a gull's wing yet, but present to her eager vision.

I was going to France for the whole long summer that year, and the more I thought of such an absence from these simple scenes the more dear and delightful they became. Santa Teresa says that the true proficiency of the soul is not in much thinking, but in much loving, and sometimes I believed that I had never found love in its simplicity as I had found at Dunnet Landing in the various hearts of Mrs Blackett and Mrs Todd and William. It is only because one came to know them, these three, loving and wise and true, in their own habitations. Their counterparts are in every village in the world, thank heaven, and the gift to one's life is only in its discernment. I had only lived in Dunnet until the usual distractions and artifices of the world were no longer in control, and I saw these simple natures clear. 'The happiness of life is in its recognitions. It seems that we are not ignorant of these truths, and even that we believe them; but we are so little accustomed to think of them, they are so strange to us —'[3]

★

'Well now, deary me!' said Mrs Todd, breaking into exclamation; 'I've got to fly round – I thought he'd have to beat; he can't sail far on that tack, and he won't be in for a good hour yet – I expect he's made every arrangement, but he said he shouldn't go up after Esther unless the weather was good, and I declare it did look doubtful this morning.'

I remembered Esther's weather-worn face. She was like a Frenchwoman who had spent her life in the fields.[4] I remembered her pleasant look, her childlike eyes, and thought of the astonishment of joy she would feel now in being taken care of and tenderly sheltered from the wind and weather after all these years. They were going to be young again now, she and William, to forget work and care in the spring weather. I could hardly wait for the boat to come to land, I was so eager to see his happy face.

'Cake an' wine I'm goin' to set 'em out!' said Mrs Todd. 'They won't stop to set down for an ordered meal, they'll want to get right out home quick's they can. Yes, I'll give 'em some cake an' wine – I've got a rare plum-cake from my best receipt, and a bottle o' wine that old Cap'n Denton of all give me, one of two, the day I was married, one we had and one we saved, and I've never touched it till now. He said there wa'n't none like it in the State o' Maine.'

It was a day of waiting, that day of spring; the May weather was as expectant as our fond hearts, and one could see the grass grow green hour by hour. The warm air was full of birds, there was a glow of light on the sea instead of the cold shining of chilly weather which had lingered late. There was a look on Mrs Todd's face which I saw once and could not meet again. She was in her highest mood. Then I went out early for a walk, and when I came back we sat in different rooms for the most part. There was such a thrill in the air that our only conversation was in her most abrupt and incisive manner. She was knitting, I believe, and as for me I dallied with a book. I heard her walking to and fro, and, the door being wide open now, she went out and paced the front walk to the gate as if she walked a quarter-deck.

It is very solemn to sit waiting for the great events of life – most of us have done it again and again – to be expectant of life or expectant of death gives one the same feeling.

But at the last Mrs Todd came quickly back from the gate, and standing in the sunshine at the door, she beckoned me as if she were a sibyl.

'I thought you comprehended everything the day you was up there,' she added with a little more patience in her tone, but I felt that she thought I had lost instead of gained since we parted the autumn before.

'William's made this pretext o' goin' fishin' for the last time. 'Twouldn't done to take notice, 'twould 'a scared him to death! but there never was nobody took less comfort out o' forty years courtin'. No, he won't have to make no further pretexts,' said Mrs Todd, with an air of triumph.

'Did you know where he was going that day?' I asked, with a sudden burst of admiration at such discernment.

'I did!' replied Mrs Todd grandly.

'Oh! but that pennyroyal lotion,' I indignantly protested, remembering that under pretext of mosquitoes she had besmeared the poor lover in an awful way – why, it was outrageous! Medea[5] could not have been more conscious of high ultimate purposes.

'Darlin',' said Mrs Todd, in the excitement of my arrival and the great concerns of marriage, 'he's got a beautiful shaped face, and they pison him very unusual – you wouldn't have had him present himself to his lady all lop-sided with a mosquito-bite? Once when he was young I rode up with him, and they set upon him in concert the minute we entered the woods.' She stood before me reproachfully, and I was conscious of deserved rebuke. 'Yes, you've come just in the nick of time to advise me about a bunnit. They say large bows on top is liable to be worn.'

IV

The period of waiting was one of direct contrast to these high moments of recognition. The very slowness of the morning hours wasted that sense of excitement with which we had begun the day. Mrs Todd came down from the mount where her face had shone so bright,[6] to the cares of common life, and some acquaintances from Black Island for whom she had little natural preference or liking came, bringing a poor, sickly child to get medical advice. They were noisy women, with harsh, clamorous voices, and they stayed a long time. I heard the clink of teacups, however, and could detect no impatience in the tones of Mrs Todd's voice; but when they were at last going away, she did not linger unduly over her leave-taking, and returned to me to explain that they were people she had never liked, and they had made an excuse of a friendly visit to save their doctor's bill; but she pitied the poor little child, and knew beside that the doctor was away.

'I had to give 'em the remedies right out,' she told me; 'they wouldn't have bought a cent's worth o' drugs down to the store for that dwindlin' thing. She needed feedin' up, and I don't expect she gets milk enough; they're great butter-makers down to Black Island, 'tis excellent pasturage, but they use no milk themselves, and their butter is laden with salt to make weight, so that you'd think all their ideas come down from Sodom.'

She was very indignant and very wistful about the pale little girl. 'I wish they'd let me kept her,' she said. 'I kind of advised it, and her eyes was so wishful in that pinched face when she heard me, so that I could see what was the matter with her, but they said she wa'n't prepared. Prepared!' And Mrs Todd snuffed like an offended war-horse, and departed; but I could hear her still grumbling and talking to herself in high dudgeon an hour afterward.

At the end of that time her arch enemy, Mari' Harris, appeared at the side-door with a gingham handkerchief over her head. She was always on hand for the news, and made some formal excuses for her presence, – she wished to borrow the weekly paper. Captain Littlepage, whose housekeeper she was, had taken it from the post-office in the morning, but had forgotten, being of failing memory, what he had done with it.

'How is the poor old gentleman?' asked Mrs Todd with solicitude, ignoring the present errand of Maria and all her concerns.

I had spoken the evening before of intended visits to Captain Littlepage and Elijah Tilley, and I now heard Mrs Todd repeating my inquiries and intentions, and fending off with unusual volubility of her own the curious questions that were sure to come. But at last Maria Harris secured an opportunity and boldly inquired if she had not seen William ashore early that morning.

'I don't say he wasn't,' replied Mrs Todd; 'Thu'sday's a very usual day with him to come ashore.'

'He was all dressed up,' insisted Maria – she really had no sense of propriety. 'I didn't know but they was going to be married?'

Mrs Todd did not reply. I recognized from the sounds that reached me that she had retired to the fastnesses of the kitchen-closet and was clattering the tins.

'I expect they'll marry soon anyway,' continued the visitor.

'I expect they will if they want to,' answered Mrs Todd. 'I don't know nothin' 't all about it; that's what folks say.' And presently the gingham handkerchief retreated past my window.

'I routed her, horse and foot,'[7] said Mrs Todd proudly, coming at once to stand at my door. 'Who's comin' now?' as two figures passed inward bound to the kitchen.

They were Mrs Begg and Johnny Bowden's mother, who were favorites, and were received with Mrs Todd's usual civilities. Then one of the Mrs Caplins came with a cup in hand to borrow yeast. On one pretext or another nearly all our acquaintances came to satisfy themselves of the facts, and see what Mrs Todd would impart about the wedding. But she firmly avoided the subject through the length of every call and errand, and answered the final leading question of each curious guest with her noncommittal phrase, 'I don't know nothin' 'tall about it; that's what folks say!'

She had just repeated this for the fourth or fifth time and shut the door upon the last comers, when we met in the little front entry. Mrs Todd was not in a bad temper, but highly amused. 'I've been havin' all sorts o' social privileges, you may have observed. They didn't seem to consider that if they could only hold out till afternoon they'd know as much as I did. There wa'n't but one o' the whole sixteen that showed real interest, the rest demeaned themselves to ask out o' cheap curiosity; no, there wa'n't but one showed any real feelin'.'

'Miss Maria Harris, you mean?' and Mrs Todd laughed.

'Certain, dear,' she agreed, 'how you do understand poor human natur'!'

A short distance down the hilly street stood a narrow house that was newly painted white. It blinded one's eyes to catch the reflection of the sun. It was the house of the minister, and a wagon had just stopped before it; a man was helping a woman to alight, and they stood side by side for a moment, while Johnny Bowden appeared as if by magic, and climbed to the wagon-seat. Then they went into the house and shut the door. Mrs Todd and I stood close together and watched; the tears running down her cheeks. I watched Johnny Bowden, who made light of so great a moment by so handling the whip that the old white Caplin horse started up from time to time and was inexorably stopped as if he had some idea of running away. There was something in the back of the wagon which now and then claimed the boy's attention; he leaned over as if there were something very precious left in his charge; perhaps it was only Esther's little trunk going to its new home.

At last the door of the parsonage opened, and two figures came out. The minister followed them and stood in the doorway, delaying them with parting words; he could not have thought it was a time for admonition.

'He's all alone; his wife's up to Portland to her sister's,' said Mrs Todd aloud, in a matter-of-fact voice. 'She's a nice woman, but she might ha' talked too much. There! see, they're comin' here. I didn't know how 'twould be. Yes, they're comin' up to see us before they go home. I declare, if William ain't lookin' just like a king!'

Mrs Todd took one step forward, and we stood and waited. The happy pair came walking up the street, Johnny Bowden driving ahead. I heard a plaintive little cry from time to time to which in the excitement of the moment I had stopped not to listen; but when William and Esther had come and shaken hands with Mrs Todd and then with me, all in silence, Esther stepped quickly to the back of the wagon, and unfastening some cords returned to us carrying a little white lamb. She gave a shy glance at William as she fondled it and held it to her heart, and then, still silent, we went into the house together. The lamb had stopped bleating. It was lovely to see Esther carry it in her arms.

When we got into the house, all the repression of Mrs Todd's usual manner was swept away by her flood of feeling. She took Esther's thin figure, lamb and all, to her heart and held her there, kissing her as she might have kissed a child, and then held out her hand to William and they gave each other the kiss of peace. This was so moving, so tender, so free from their usual fetters of self-consciousness, that Esther and I could not help giving each other a happy glance of comprehension. I never saw a young bride half so touching in her happiness as Esther was that day of her wedding. We took the cake and wine of the marriage feast together, always in silence, like a true sacrament, and then to my astonishment I found that sympathy and public interest in so great an occasion were going to have their way. I shrank from the thought of William's possible sufferings, but he welcomed both the first group of neighbors and the last with heartiness; and when at last they had gone, for there were thoughtless loiterers in Dunnet Landing, I made ready with eager zeal and walked with William and Esther to the water-side. It was only a little way, and kind faces nodded reassuringly from the windows, while kind voices spoke from the doors. Esther carried the lamb on one arm; she found time to tell me that its mother had died that morning and she could not bring herself to the thought of leaving it behind. She kept the other hand on William's arm until we reached the landing. Then he shook hands with me, and looked me full in the face to be sure I understood how happy he was, and stepping into the boat held out his arms to Esther – at last she was his own.

I watched him make a nest for the lamb out of an old sea-cloak at Esther's feet, and then he wrapped her own shawl round her shoulders and finding a pin in the lapel of his Sunday coat he pinned it for her. She looked at him fondly while he did this, and then glanced up at us, a pretty, girlish color brightening her cheeks.

We stood there together and watched them go far out into the bay. The sunshine of the May day was low now, but there was a steady breeze, and the boat moved well.

'Mother'll be watching for them,' said Mrs Todd. 'Yes, mother'll be watching all day, and waiting. She'll be so happy to have Esther come.'

We went home together up the hill, and Mrs Todd said nothing more; but we held each other's hands all the way.

NOTES

THE COUNTRY OF THE POINTED FIRS

1 *The Return*

1. *spruces and balsam firs*: Until the advent of steamships, this part of Maine had supplied timber for ship-building (see the later image of the trees waiting to embark), so the novel's title links sea and land, past and present, wild nature and human manufacture. Though quite distinct botanically from the medicinal balsam, these firs take on its associations of healing and the preservation of health.

2 *Mrs Todd*

1. *hollyhocks . . . not only sweet-brier* [eglantine rose] *and sweet-mary* [costmary/balsam herb], *but balm* [lemon balm/*Melissa officinalis*] *and sage and borage and mint, wormwood and southernwood* [appleringie/*Artemisia abrotanum*] *. . . thyme . . . Indian remedy* [ipecac] *. . . thoroughwort* [boneset/*Eupatorium perfoliatum*]: Generally speaking, Mrs Todd is treating her neighbours for a range of common ailments, some of them potentially serious – childhood infections, respiratory and digestive problems, rheumatism, wounds and fractures, women's health problems, headaches, toothache, sore throat, kidney and liver disorders. These notes will single out those herbs (also called 'simples') that carry a significance beyond the purely medical. Other less meaning-laden herbs mentioned later are hyssop, elecampane (*Inula helenium*), tansy, the rare lobelia (*Lobelia inflata*, an Indian remedy), bloodroot (*Sanguinaria candensis*), catnip, spearmint, yarrow (*Achillea millefolium*). It is not known if Jewett's knowledge of herbs was practical, anecdotal or based on herbals such as Culpeper's and other later compilations.

Thoroughwort elixir was used to promote the healing of fractures and relieve bone pain; too much would cause vomiting.

2. *spruce beer*: An agreeable, slightly fermented summer beverage made with the green tops of black spruce, with spices, treacle and yeast.

3. *cunner*: Northern wrasse (abundant small shore fish, found over rocks and around pilings).

4. *herb of the night*: This remains a puzzle, since the narrator would be familiar with nicotiana and mignonette.

5. *sibyl*: A woman consulted for her powers of prophecy or divination; there was a sybil at Delphi, a key healing place in the ancient world. This is one of several classical references in the novel (see Introduction on nineteenth-century attitudes to herbalists, and Chapter 10 on how healing with 'primeval herbs' links Mrs Todd with ancient Greece).

3 The Schoolhouse

1. *white windflower*: Wood anemone, a delicate spring wild flower sometimes flushed pink.

2. *cottonless ears*: The classical Greek example of trying to have both it ways – Odysseus listened to the seductive female voices of the sirens, while his crew, with cotton stuffed in their ears, rowed him away to continue his quest.

3. *bayberry*: An American form of myrtle (aromatic bush, also used medicinally).

4. *selectmen*: Elected members of the board carrying out a town meeting's decisions and with minor powers of appointment.

5. *pennyroyal*: See Introduction for significance of Mrs Todd's favourite herb. It has many uses. Culpeper notes that 'it is of subtle, warm, and penetrating parts'.

4 At the Schoolhouse Window

1. *West Indian curiosities . . . lumber-laden ships*: Sea-trade and whaling were central to Maine's economy, originally to the Caribbean (hence later references to Tobago) and then to China, until after the Civil War.

2. *cant to leeward*: Leaning away from the prevailing wind.

3. *bergamot*: Bee balm (*monarda*), as its common name implies, attracts bees; medicinally it induces relaxation and sleep, so not a good perfume for ink.

5 Captain Littlepage

1. *A happy, rural seat of various views*: *Paradise Lost*, IV, 247. Milton's utopian vision of the unfallen Eden is initially presented through the eyes of Satan, who is for ever excluded from bliss; the poem also stresses at this point that Eden is *not* the site of the Persephone myth (the story of the daughter's separation from the mother).

2. *Countess of Carberry*: Jewett has Littlepage nearly quoting from the 1650 funeral sermon by the English divine and religious writer, Jeremy Taylor (1613–67), for the Countess of Carbery (the correct spelling). Taylor's remark is itself a quotation from the classical author Cicero.

3. *Darwin*: See the Introduction for how Darwin's ideas strongly affected American thought in the closing thirty years of the nineteenth century. I have not been able to trace this remark to either Darwin's *Autobiography* or *The Voyage of the 'Beagle'*.

4. *kingbird*: Eastern kingbird, notoriously aggressive to other birds within its nesting territory.

5. *full-rigged ship, called the* Minerva: One of the largest sailing ships, square-rigged on all three masts. Naming the ship after the Roman goddess of wisdom ironically picks up on the theme, already hinted at in the *Paradise Lost* quotation, of the pursuit of knowledge and the suffering that this search entails.

6. *caught astern o' the lighter*: Nautical phrase implying getting into difficulties because of poor seamanship, literally getting dangerously close to shore behind the barge you're supposed to be towing.

7. *with a light pair o' heels*: Riding high in the water without ballast.

8. *like a chip in a bucket*: The chip was the small piece of wood, loaded to keep it upright in the water, at the end of a logline for measuring the ship's speed.

9. *that class o' men who never get beyond the fo'cas'le*: Sailors who never became ship's officers continued to live in the forward part of the merchant ship under the deck.

10. *cheap, unprincipled newspaper*: The Captain may be referring to the takeover of many small newspapers by big corporations in the closing years of the century.

11. *Solomon's Temple*: This building's description (with detailed measurements, see I Kings 6) had attracted much debate and speculation among biblical scholars.

12. *late golden robin*: Not the British red-breast, but a member of the thrush family, with a fine song like the European blackbird; migratory, it spends only the spring and summer months in the north of the USA.

6 The Waiting Place

1. *Parry's Discoveries*: Littlepage refers to early nineteenth-century Arctic expeditions on the northern Canadian seaboard and islands, rather than to more recent discoveries (see below).

2. *Moravians*: A Christian sect of Czech origins, noted for its missionary enterprise, lack of a creed, and belief in the fundamental unity of all Christians (a relevant backdrop to Littlepage's tale of belief, disbelief and desire to transmit a vision to others).

3. *English exploring parties*: Sir John Franklin died in 1845 within a few miles of having discovered the North West Passage; relief expeditions searched for him 1847–57 (giving us a rough date for Littlepage's story).

4. *Man cannot live by fish alone*: A sardonic reference to Jesus' admonition to the devil when tempted in the wilderness, that 'Man shall not live by bread alone, but by every word that proceedeth out of the mouth of God' (Matthew 4:4).

5. *Fox Channel*: Foxe Channel between Baffin Island and mainland Canada.

6. *like the ridges of grim war; no thought o' flight, none of retreat. Sometimes a standing fight, then soaring on main wing tormented all the air*: Littlepage is quoting almost verbatim from *Paradise Lost*, VI, 236–7, 242–4. This is Milton's account of the War in Heaven between Satan's rebel army (thus described) and God's angels.

7. *Ge'graphical Society . . . a map of North America*: Geographical Societies in Europe and the Americas were gathering material for scientific research throughout the nineteenth century. However, the point at issue here is that Littlepage is out of touch with some of the most important geographical discoveries of his day. Although the North Pole was not reached until 1909, expeditions throughout the latter decades of the nineteenth century gathered enough data to map a great deal more of that region than was known mid century. Jewett is playing with the great interest in the Arctic in the nineteenth century, an interest which was linked by some women with dreams of an alternative universe – Jewett resists this in placing her utopia in an actual Maine.

7 The Outer Island

1. *sleevin'*: Taking the Captain's arm.
2. *caryatide*: Statue of a woman used in Greek architecture as a supporting column; note too that caryatids were priestesses of Artemis, the goddess who protected the young and those giving birth.
3. *camomile*: This is German, not common, camomile (*Matricaria chamomilla*), which soothes aches and pain, and deals with general disability.

8 Green Island

1. *dory*: A small flat-bottomed boat, carried stacked inside each other on decks of the Grand Banks fishing schooners and launched daily for line fishing. Note how Asa's elaborate instructions about how to keep the boat *trimmed* (balanced) and sailing with the wind behind her (the *sheet* is the rope controlling the main sail) are nicely set against the women's earlier command both of a working boat and of nautical terms. The sail, *furled* (rolled) so that it will hoist easily, is placed along the boat's *gunwale* (top) edge.
2. *underrun a trawl*: Pull in from a boat a buoyed fishing line in order to clear it of catch.
3. *the war*: The American Civil War (1861–5).
4. *herrin' weirs*: Enclosure for taking fish.
5. *schooners*: Sea-going ships with two or more masts, but smaller than the full-rigged ship of Chapter 5 and without its square sails.
6. *took a firmer grasp of the sheet, and gave an impatient look up at the gaff and the leech of the little sail, and twitched the sheet*: Again, command of the boat (Mrs Todd's ability to adjust the sail properly for the wind) is expressed through Jewett's accurate command of the special language of sailing unfamiliar to the general reader. The leech is the edge of the sail furthest from the mast, and the gaff the spar at top of the sail.
7. *likely*: Strong, capable-looking.
8. *portulacas*: Low growing garden flower (a purslane) with showy flowers.
9. *mallows*: Wild flower, probably a prostrate version with pink flowers.

10. *Victory*: Ancient Greek statue of a winged female figure. This nicely suggests both Mrs Todd's mood and her large body, as well as confirming her archaic powers.

9 William

1. *linnæa*: Possibly *Linnaea borealis*, though this short evergreen grows in shade, not open ground. The echo of Linneaus is apposite, since his great botanical schema was upset by Darwin, and this novel resists some Darwinian notions.

10 Where Pennyroyal Grew

1. *snap*: Vigour.

2. *daguerreotypes*: First introduced into America in 1839, this early form of photography on glass spread fast. Mrs Blackett with a sixty-year-old daughter could not in fact have had her likeness taken in this way 'soon after her marriage' – a minor slip on Jewett's part.

3. *loom of the land*: Dim coastal outline (a nautical term, referring to magnification caused by fog or reflected light).

4. *the right pattern of the plant, and all the rest I ever see is but an imitation*: Pattern in the sense of a design from which copies are manufactured (a hint of resisting the mass production of industrial America), or in the cognate sense of an ideal model (thus hinting at Platonic forms, though, unlike Plato's ideas, this 'pattern' actually exists on earth).

5. *Antigone alone on the Theban plain*: This reference to Sophocles' tragedy picks up more on the young girl Antigone's solitary faithful grief for her unburied dead brother than her defiance of the state and entombment alive (though it is true that Mrs Todd's first love, still grieved for after many years, was unsanctioned by upper-class authority). Antigone calls her tomb her bridal bower.

11 The Old Singers

1. *Sweet Home . . . Cupid an' the Bee*: 'Home Sweet Home', most celebrated parlour song of the century (music by Henry Bishop): 'Be it ever so humble, there's no place like home / A charm from the skies seems to hallow us there, / Which, seek through the world, is ne'er met with elsewhere.' 'Cupid and the Bee' has not been identified.

12 A Strange Sail

1. *Lottin'*: Very much wanting.

2. *Oolong*: A dark variety of cured China tea. Mrs Fosdick is a reminder of America's global mercantile power.

3. *like the child who stood at the gate in Hans Andersen's story*: None of Andersen's forty-five *Danish Fairy Tales and Legends* (1846 and 1852) has this exact image, but Jewett is probably thinking of his Little Match-girl standing in a corner formed by two houses and having a vision of food on the dining table in the room beyond the wall.

4. *idyl of Theocritus*: These third century BC Greek pastoral poems, including love poems, laments and images of country life, continued to influence literature into the nineteenth century.

13 Poor Joanna

1. *Franklin stove*: Cast-iron heating stove resembling an open fireplace when its doors are opened.

2. *thoroughfares*: Main sea-channels.

3. *bangeing-place*: Bangeing is a New England word for lounging about and loafing (an early European reaction to native Americans in this area was that they were lazy because they lived as hunter-gatherers). Mrs Todd's remarks seem to reflect some residual memories of the semi-nomadic Abenaki (part of the Algonquian-speaking peoples), who had traditionally depended heavily on the sea and summered on the Maine coast until the eighteenth century. Early European responses saw these tribes as 'gentle' and civilized, though genuine attempts through the seventeenth and eighteenth centuries to create alliances between Native American and European in Maine failed. They also believed in mythic giants, non-persons ostracized from the tribe for cannibalism. Mrs Fosdick's remark about 'savages' finds its parallel in Darwin's sense of superiority over native inhabitants in *The Voyage of the 'Beagle'*.

4. *sloop*: Small single-masted sailing vessel.

5. *Mullein . . . wormwood . . . catnip*: Mullein deals with winter complaints like coughs and catarrhs, but Culpeper also notes its power over colic 'arising from sharp humours'; its efficacy in dealing with throat complaints picks up on Joanna's unspoken feelings. Catnip provides a 'female' medicine, 'good against hysteric complaints, vapours and fits' (Culpeper). Wormwood is noted for its intense bitterness, though its power to cure those whom Culpeper calls 'hysterics' (i.e. women emotionally and physically ill) is also relevant.

6. *piece-bag*: Bag containing scraps of cloth kept for making patchwork quilts or rag-rugs.

7. *lemon balm*: Culpeper notes that balm should 'be kept in every gentlewoman's house to relieve the weak stomachs and sick bodies of their poor and sickly neighbours', and that it 'causeth the mind and heart to become merry . . . [and] driveth away all troublesome cares and thoughts out of the mind, arising from melancholy and black choler'. *Gerard's Herball* reports that in classical times it was believed that bees which have strayed found their way home by it (see later image of the family reunion as bees swarming at lilac bushes).

8. *fasten the sheet*: Tie the mainsail rope to save his hands from chafing – a piece of bad workmanship, because, when the *flaw* (gust of wind) came, the sail was too tight and the boat in danger of capsizing.

14 The Hermitage

1. *the unpardonable sin*: This is usually taken theologically to mean a despair of God's power to save.

2. *sparrows*: Unlike the British sparrow, some of the American species have very musical songs.

15 On Shell-heap Island

1. *let the reef out of his mainsail*: Increase the area of a sail.

2. *tag-boat*: Small row boat which would cause drag.

3. *fetch*: Arrive.

4. *running the great boat in*: Sailing with the wind behind you.

5. *hold fast for'ard*: Wait in forward part of boat.

6. *shyin' by*: Almost, but not quite, touching the bottom.

16 The Great Expedition

1. *chaise*: Small light open carriage.

2. *hearts and rounds*: Small sponge cakes in these traditional shapes.

3. *beat . . . fetch . . . tack*: The previous evening's winds being directly against them, they would have had a long, tiring journey constantly having to alter the direction of sail, but the next morning they were able to row to a point from which they could complete the passage with only one change of sail to turn the ship into the wind.

17 A Country Road

1. *check-rein*: Rein designed to keep horse's head high in a grand style.

2. *fetch up 'long o' the tide and land near the flood*: Come up with the rising tide and arrive at high water.

3. *flakes*: Frames for drying fish.

18 The Bowden Reunion

1. *bound girl*: Servant under contract

2. *stim'lates*: Drinks alcohol to excess.

3. *Waterloo . . . Bunker Hill*: Napolean's final defeat by the European allies (1815), and one of the key battles of the American Revolution (1775).

4. *Decoration Day*: Northern States' precursor of Memorial Day – the annual remembrance day (30 May) for the Civil War dead.

5. *laurel*: Probably the bay tree (though it always has inconspicuous flowers). Jewett may have wanted the laurel's classical associations with crowns for victors (see the earlier image of the reunion like a company of ancient Greeks).

6. *holler square*: Hollow square, an infantry formation in battle.

7. *the great hall of some old French house*: See Jewett's juvenile history, *The Story of the Normans* (1886), for the source of this idea. This book credits the Normans with the origins of Western civilization in Europe (an idea current at the time) and traces the influence of this 'national character' on government and social life even in America, thus blending an aristocratic past with the 'young republic' of the United States (see earlier in the chapter the narrator's remarks about Huguenot/French Protestant settlers in New England). Jewett praises the Normans for qualities also validated in this novel – what she identifies as energy, intellect, courtliness, tact, grace, nobility, vision and enthusiasm. Jewett gives her contemporary utopia a myth of origins which might seem to have similarities to nativism (a form of racism at the turn of the century directed against non-Anglo-Saxon immigrants). But her position on race is not identical with nativism, does not share its Darwinian justifications, and is in itself contradictory and multifaceted. Two of her other tales about the aftermath of slavery are unconsciously but disturbingly racist, but she also wrote tales about the Irish immigrants which, though deeply stereotyped, seek to valorize a maligned group in nineteenth-century America, and Mrs Todd's attacks in this chapter on those who are not Bowdens are somewhat questioned.

19 The Feast's End

1. *fragrance of wet ferns*: Not a fern but an aromatic shrub, *Comptonia asplendifolia*.

20 Along Shore

1. *smack*: Small fishing craft.

2. *sliver porgies*: Cut up various kinds of local fish to bait the trawl lines.

3. *way-wise*: Directionally stable.

4. *landmark pine*: Pines were used for navigational signs, see Jewett's story, 'A Neighbor's Landmark'.

5. *mackerel kits*: Tubs or barrels of fish.

6. *fish*: Cod.

7. *dog-fish*: Small New England sharks (*squalus acanthias*).

8. *japanned waiter*: Small lacquered tea-tray.

21 The Backward View

1. *southernwood and a sprig of bay*: Bay was traditionally considered a cure for almost any illness. Southernwood, traditionally used for its long-lasting, lemony smell, was kept among clothes and linen. There are references, for instance in Scottish literature of this period, to southernwood (appleringie) being given as a pledge of love or worn on one's gown; another of its common names is old maid's comfort.

2. *old sea running*: Waves left over by the wind that has since decreased.

A White Heron

1. *the little white heron*: Snowy egret (*Egretta thula*). By the beginning of the twentieth century, it had been hunted virtually to extinction for its feathers, which were used by the millinery trade.

2. *old pine*: A reference to Maine's ship-building economy superseded by industrialization (represented by the 'crowded manufacturing town' Sylvia had lived in). Note the later description of Sylvia's tree as 'a great main-mast' from which she can see the sea.

3. *whippoorwills*: A species of nightjar, a nocturnal woodland bird.

4. *hemlocks*: Tree related to spruce and fir.

5. *cat-birds*: A species of mockingbird.

Marsh Rosemary

1. *ghostly flying Dutchmen:* Omen of ill-luck. From the legend, used in Wagner's opera and here with complicated ironies, of a sea-captain doomed to sail the seas in perpetuity and to put to port once in seven years only, until redeemed by a woman's lifelong fidelity.

2. *pussy-clover*: Haresfoot clover (*Trifolium arvense*).

3. *dimity*: Stout cotton with woven patterns.

4. *whatever she had to give, good measure, pressed down and running over*: A biblical quotation with certain subsequent ironies: 'give, and it shall be given unto you; good measure, pressed down, and shaken together, and running over, shall men give into your bosom' (Luke 6: 38).

5. *splint-bottomed*: With basketwork seat.

6. *keep him in good trim*: Nautical metaphor, adjusting sails for wind and direction of course.

7. *opodeldoc*: Soft ointment made with camphor and rosemary, a popular remedy.

8. *I'll spudge up*: Actively exert myself, get to work fast.

9. *meechin'*: Skulking, shirking, truanting, cheating.

10. *Shediac*: Port in New Brunswick, Canada.

11. *the piece*: Fenced-in land round the house.

12. *meeting*: Church service or assembly.

13. *Marsh Rosemary*: Andromeda polifolia, low shrub with small, pink, drooping flowers, used herbally for its restringent (drying and binding) properties.

14. *lotus . . . rose*: Flowers associated with luxurious ease and romantic love.

The King of Folly Island

1. *dory . . . cat-boat*: A flat-bottomed boat suitable for carrying freight for his store, contrasted with a faster craft with a single large sail and light draft.

2. *the Banks*: Fishing grounds in north-west Canada.

3. *punky*: 'Punk' is partially decayed wood used as tinder, so here metaphorically punky means either easily provoked to anger or mentally deficient.

4. *scattery*: In a distracted state.

5. *killock*: Small anchor, often a heavy stone.

6. *Vikings*: Jewett had published *The Story of the Normans* two years previous to this story (see note to *The Country of the Pointed Firs*, Chapter 18) – so a laudatory ascription. She speculates about what might have happened if the Vikings had settled in America: 'What a change that would have made in the world's history!'

7. *King George . . . tyranny . . . patriot . . . pioneers . . . colonists . . . customer . . . independence . . . sovereign*: Jewett is half-humorously playing with the traditional oppositions and values of the American War of Independence, thereby questioning the nature of individualism and authority. Her last novel, *The Tory Lover*, set during that war, is a more sentimental attempt to suggest complexities behind the standard histories of that period.

8. *folksy*: Sociable, fond of company.

9. *He's a pretty man*: General expression of appreciation.

10. *an* abbé gallant *and a dignified* marquise: Aristocratic pre-Revolutionary French courtiers.

The Courting of Sister Wisby

1. *belated bobolink*: Migratory songbird, member of oriole family, summering in New England.

2. *yellow-birds*: American goldfinch.

3. *sweet flag*: *Acorus calamus*, aromatic marsh plant, herbally a powerful tonic.

4. *drarves*: Probably poultices.

5. *win'rows*: Mown hay raked into rows to dry, so a sardonic metaphor.

6. *masterwort . . . noble-liverwort*: *Imperatoria ostruthium* for chest diseases and fever, and *Anemone (hepatica) triloba* (liverleaf) for liver diseases.

7. *drorin'*: Infusing.

8. *cars*: Railways.

9. *jiggit*: Hop, fidget.

10. *goldthread . . . hardhack*: *Coptis trifolia* (for ulcers and gangrene) and *Spiraea tomentosa*, a low shrub.

11. *conference*: Religious assembly.

12. *exhorter*: Person appointed by pastor to give religious talks.

13. *deacon*: Church elder taking care of the secular affairs of the congregation.

14. *exes*: Axles.

Miss Peck's Promotion

1. *academy town*: Township with a high school (the word 'academy' had a certain snob value in the eighteenth and nineteenth centuries).

2. *dog-day evenin'*: July to early August, traditionally seen as the unhealthiest time of the year.

3. *snow-birds*: Snow bunting.

4. *logy*: Dull and sluggish.

5. *stived-up*: Suffocating.

6. *rutabagys*: Turnips.

7. *leading about captive silly women*: Biblical description (2 Timothy 3: 6–7) of men who are 'lovers of self' and 'never able to come to the knowledge of the truth'.

8. *reap the whirlwind*: another biblical condemnation (Hosea 8: 7) of moral decay and a warning of dire consequences: 'to sow the wind and reap the whirlwind'.

The Guests of Mrs Timms

1. *syringa-bushes*: Mock-orange (*Philadelphus*).

2. *drop-cakes*: Small flat cakes.

3. *rule*: Recipe.

4. *more natural*: Not dressed up for a formal occasion (unlike the two protagonists).

5. *Better is a dinner of herbs where love is*: Proverbs 15: 17: 'Better is a dinner of herbs where love is, than a stalled ox and hatred therewith'.

The Queen's Twin

1. *Land of Eshcol*: The biblical Promised Land (Numbers 12): men sent out by the children of Israel in the desert came back with bunches of grapes. This tale, therefore, suggests that for some of its inhabitants, Dunnet Landing is not a place of spiritual plenty, and the self's true place is located elsewhere.

2. *Thomaston and Castine and Portland*: Towns in Maine.

3. *witch hazel*: *Hamamelis virginiana*, the American species, blooms in autumn; used medicinally to soothe.

4. *lost tribes of Israel*: Ten ancient Hebrew tribes, subject to much later speculation and legend (some placing them in the Americas).

5. *up-country Indians*: See note on *The Country of the Pointed Firs*, Chapter 13.

6. *the Queen*: Victoria, Queen of Great Britain and Ireland (born 24 May 1819, died 1901, so alive at time of this story).

7. *smarten her up*: Make her feel more lively.

8. *make company of her*: Treat her ceremoniously like a visitor.

9. *primeval fields of Sicily*: Continuing the references found in the *The Country of the Pointed Firs* to Theocrites' pastoral poems.

10. *asphodel*: The immortal flower growing in the Elysian fields of the classical afterlife.

11. *snowberry bushes and cinnamon roses*: *Symphoricarpos* is a rampant shrub which will flourish anywhere; *rosa majalis* dates back to the seventeenth century or earlier.

12. *super-cargo*: The ship's owners' representative on a merchant ship.

13. *Wapping*: Part of London docks.

14. *cooked for fo'c's'le an' cabin*: Cooked for the seamen as well the ship's officers.

15. *her beautiful book about the Highlands*: *Leaves from the Journal of Our Life in the Highlands* (1868).

16. *Jubilee*: Fiftieth anniversary of Victoria's succession, 1887.

Martha's Lady

1. *the outbreak for larger religious freedom . . . reaction toward formalism . . . the war for liberty . . . coming war for patriotism and a new freedom*: Jewett carefully sets her story of private figures in relation to major social events – the War of Independence, the evangelical movement called the Second Great Awakening (1800) and subsequent conservative religious retrenchment, the Civil War of 1861–5 and the Emancipation of the slaves – thus suggesting a connection between this encounter of a young upper-class woman and her maid, and wider movements for change. Helena's values, however, keep their roots in her cousin's traditional, pre-industrial, pre-bourgeois America – a culture of deference which was steadily eroded throughout the nineteenth century by middle-class self-reliant democracy.

2. *the poems of Emerson*: American Transcendentalist philosopher/writer (1803–82) who, though in later years a highly respected figure, was a figure of some notoriety in church circles with his well-publicized break with the Church in the 1830s. Poems published in 1846.

3. *entry* Passageway.

4. *secretary*: Writing-desk.

5. *cherry-bird*: Waxwing.

6. *She never joined the church*: Church membership was a major commitment taken only at a mature age and by some but not all people.

The Foreigner

1. *line storm*: Equinoctial storm.

2. *three sheets in the wind*: Very drunk.

3. *highbinders*: Rowdies, rogues.

4. *Washin'ton pie*: Layer cake; there is possibly an ironic allusion to the American Revolution.

5. *David's dancin' before the Lord*: See 2 Samuel 6: 14. Michal, daughter of Saul, who despises David for dancing during the journey of the ark of the Lord to the city of David, is reproved.

6. *a stranger in a strange land*: Another quite appropriate biblical reference (Exodus 2: 22). Moses, having fled from Egypt to the Land of Michah, is given a wife by a priest there.

7. *officious herbs*: Medicinal herbs.

8. *A made countenance, between simpering and smiling*: Sir Philip Sidney (1554–86), possibly from the romantic pastoral *Arcadia*.

9. *fête day*: Festival of the saint after whom a person is named, celebrated as a birthday.

10. *signin' that Portland note*: Underwriting a loan, which presumably (it is a detail we are told nothing further about) was called in.

11. *hip-roofed*: Roof with sloping ends and sides.

12. *Empress Josephine*: First wife of Napoleon, born 1763 in Martinique.

13. *sibyl of the Sistine Chapel*: Five of these classical figures of prophecy and healing (all powerful seated figures, both old and young, with books or scrolls) encircle Michelangelo's ceiling depicting Creation and the Fall.

William's Wedding

1. *Carlyle says somewhere that the only happiness a man ought to ask for is happiness enough to get his work done*: Thomas Carlyle (1795–1881), historian and social critic. See possibly *Past and Present* (1843): 'to learn, or to be taught, what work he actually was able for ... That is the true blessedness, honour, "liberty" and maximum of well-being.'

2. *bent his new sail*: Fastened on the sail.

3. *Santa Teresa says that the true proficiency of the soul is not in much thinking, but in much loving ... 'The happiness of life is in its recognitions. It seems that we are not ignorant of these truths, and even that we believe them; but we are so little accustomed to think of them, they are so strange to us –'*: Teresa of Avila (1515–82), Christian mystic and author of *The Book of Her Life* and other spiritual teachings.

4. *like a Frenchwoman who had spent her life in the fields*: In the tale of Esther and William's courtship, 'A Dunnet Shepherdess', Esther is described as being 'like a figure of Millet' (the nineteenth-century French realist painter, noted for his pictures of peasant life).

5. *Medea*: Classical legend in which Medea, abandoned by her lover Jason, sent a poisoned shirt to his bride.

6. *Mrs Todd came down from the mount where her face had shone so bright*: Reference to the scene of Jesus' Transfiguration, where his 'face did shine as the sun' (Matthew 17: 2). See also Jewett's comment in a letter in 1897: 'One remembers the story of the transfiguration in the New Testament, and sees over and over in life what the great

shining hours can do, and how one goes down from the mountain where they are, into the fret of everyday life again, but strong in remembrance.'

7. *routed her, horse and foot*: A military metaphor – defeating the whole opposing army.